Violet Stone

Of the Ravens of Berengar

Robin John Morgan

www.heirstothekingdom.com

First published in the UK in 2024 by Violet Circle Publishing.

Manchester, England, UK.

Print ISBN: 978-1-910299-44-9
Digital ISBN: 978-1-910299-45-6

British Library Cataloguing in Publication Data.
A catalogue record for this book is available from the British Library.

All papers used in the production of this book are sourced only from wood grown in sustainable forests.

www.violetcirclepublishing.co.uk

There are two truths

The actual facts.
The blind belief of those who manipulate the facts.

Embrace the actual facts, no matter how unpleasant.

"She is the one that will favour you most, and
she will be the centre of the next circle when
I leave here. Iona will have the biggest power
ever known, for she will hold her mother's
power of two lines, but she will also contain
the power of her father. Pure love makes
magic more powerful my darling, and she has
such a lot of it."

(Runestone to Robbie, *The Lost Sword of Carnac*)

Truth.

The truth is there, but you are blinded to it.

A young blue eyed naked girl, lived her life running through the forest, and was considered wild by most standards. She understood stealth, and being one with everything, and through her ability to walk silently on the earth, she gained great wisdom, as she encountered conversations, never meant for the ears of others.

She was young, and did not completely understand everything she heard, but she was also gifted, and within that she was wise enough to know, that not all that was said was truth. When she encountered a knight, as he wept at the banks of the river, and asked why he looked to the mists and wept, she learned of the death of Arthur, and yet, she was not saddened. The young Opal already knew more than she was supposed to, and within that, she had hope for a future renewed, and she offered the knight some advice, to ease his distress and give him hope.

"Know, there is one who can see what will become in times ahead. This I tell you today as truth, another will come, for his line has not been broken."

Opal knew of the visit of Tidguyde, and her meeting with the wounded Gwendolyn. From that day on, she learned more, advising the knight that he should look to the Bowman, for he would herald the start of new days, and she was right. It was the blood in his veins that would bring times of peace and truth, and the final injustices of the past, would be corrected.

Opal had told the knight, without revealing the full truth of a new queen who would come to rule. She would be called truth seeker, peace bringer, and as she took the throne, the age of dreams would end, and a new age would begin. She is my sister, I know her as Iona, but to the rest of the realms, she is Violet Stone, Queen of Fae of Earth, and her age, is the Age of Light.

Queen Violet Stone was destined to do one thing, look to the past, and learn the truth for the future. It was her task, to illuminate the past, and bring to light the lies, misdeeds, and misrepresentations, and in doing so, bring hope for the future of all.

'Halbert Thorn, Bright Stone, Lord of Loxley'

Chapter One.

Coming to terms.

Runestone smiled, and pulled Ariel close.

"I am sad to see you leave, you have done wonders for the recovering men. I am sure Alice will miss you at her side, but I know how important it is that you return home to Florae." Ariel gave a smile, her grey eyes shining with tears, as she took a deep breath.

"I am afraid to return, it has been an age since I walked in my homeland, but I feel now is the time to face the life I was meant to have. I have things I must do for the safety of my people, and I need time to readjust to the new life that awaits me." Rune understood.

"I feel your apprehension, but go with a glad heart in the knowledge that you return to the land of your people, and know in your heart, that Bridget Violet surrounds the realm in protection. I am sure with your keen senses you will feel her. All is not lost Ariel, you have much to offer your people, and I know that there are a few familiar faces left there to guide you as they once did." Ariel took a deep breath and smiled, she turned to Sapphire.

"I am ready." Sapphire nodded, as Tila gave Rune a regal bow.

"My Lady of Life, I am thankful for the home you opened to share with me, and for being allowed to hold my queen. Your realm is safe, and I will return with my people to help you rebuild the house that is the heart of all the realms, it will be my honour." Rune smiled as Crystal rolled her eyes.

"Tila, you have no need for such formality with me, you are considered one of us, and you will always be welcome in my realm. It is a realm I may add you defended with great valour." Tila smiled.

"It is right, as I represent my people of Fae, it would be wrong for me not to address you with respect." She gave a giggle.

"I am coming back soon, oh on Ninians toes, I am so excited to get to return, honestly, it has been as Jade says, Awesome!"

Rune giggled as Tila picked up her bag, Crystal shook her head, and walked towards Sapphire and Ariel, as a bright blue window opened behind them. Together, the group walked through, and Rune turned to look at the blackened remains of her home. Furry Face gave a deep whine and pushed his head onto her leg, and her hand softly scratched at his ear.

"I know baby boy, but we will rebuild it, and it will be a home of great love once again."

*T*he sun shone over Florae, it was Gleefall, and behind the House of Scribes, on the hill that rose up to the base of Mount Kivi, the trees had started to turn, and paint the valley in hues of red, yellow, and orange. The day was warming as the two large doors swung open, and the tall grey haired figure of Bade, assisted the elderly figure of Elgin, as he leaned on his stick, and shuffled forward towards the top of the steps. He breathed in the Gleefall air and gave a contented sigh, as he looked out on the large circle of space that surrounded the opening where the rivers met, and fell into the Whispering Falls.

"This will not be an easy thing for her Bade, she has been gone a long time, things have changed. Go easy on her, and handle her with great care, she will be fragile."

Bade stared out, his stomach in knots, he had believed her dead for so long, and had lost all hope, yet today, he would see her for the first time in what had felt like a life time. He swallowed hard and felt the tension grow inside him, as the bright blue orb exploded into view at the base of the steps.

Sapphire stepped out, followed by Tila and Crystal, and came forward, Bade stared at the orb as she came through, and he drew in a great breath, as his eyes filled with tears, she had hardly aged a day. Tila came up the steps with a huge smile, and bowed to Lord Elgin.

"I have returned Master Elgin, and as you can see, I lived." He gave a chuckle, and his eyes twinkled.

"It is a great relief, I am too old to train another to your standard, I am also very pleased to see you in your prime condition, Scribe Tila."

His old eyes moved up as he saw Ariel walk onto the steps, and he broke into a smile, her grey eyes held her tears, as he nodded at her. Ariel stood on the top step, and gave a bow, and her voice trembled slightly.

"My Lords, I request your consent to enter the realm of my

people."

Bade shook, and then suddenly fell to his knees, as if momentarily he had lost the use of his legs, and his tears fell to the floor. Ariel looked at Master Elgin and he gave a slight nod, Ariel understood and knelt down, and rested her hand on his shoulder.

"Hello my old friend, please, this is hard for me too. Stand tall and greet me as my friend, and my companion in the house we built together." He lifted his head, as his tears ran down his face.

Bade suddenly lurched forward and pulled her into him, and held her tight, as he wept. Tila had never seen him so emotional, and felt tears form in her own eyes. Ariel put her arms around him and held him tight, as he mumbled.

"I am so sorry, I lost all hope, I tried, I really did, but I gave up on you when I know I should not have." Ariel pulled him tighter.

"Bade, that is done, it is over, it is time to leave what was done behind us, and try to move forward together. Now come, stand by my side as you always have, for I will need guidance, much has changed here, and we will have much to do, for we need to prepare for the coming of our new queen."

He gave a sniffle and released her, and looked to the floor as he dried his eyes. Ariel wiped hers and then lifted him up, and faced him, she gave a smile.

"It is good to see you, I feared I may have lost you too." He took a deep breath, and swallowed hard.

"I am not as fast as I was, but there again, my body is just the means to carry my mind, which I assure you, has not faltered as yet with age." He lifted his hand to her shoulder.

"It is good to have you home again, the house has felt empty without you." She gave a smile.

"It will ring soon to the sound of our whispered voices as it has in the past, we have much to catch up." He gave a smile and nodded. Ariel turned to Elgin.

"Master Elgin, I am pleased to see you are still in the service of this house, and I am very pleased to see you well." His smile was soft as he lifted his hand to her face, and cupped her cheek.

"Your appearance is a rich reward to my old eyes, although, I see some of the weariness of the life you lived has etched onto you. I am very happy indeed to see you safe, you have always been the most valuable asset of this house. You will need time Ariel, there will be much to adjust to, the house is still here, there is no rush. I would request you join me tomorrow and we will talk of many things then. It is good to see you my dear, my heart rests knowing you have returned to us as was the wish of our beloved queen."

Ariel could not speak, as the emotion rose up within her, she stood for a second with tears in her eyes, as she summoned the composure to speak.

"I would dearly love to visit her and pay my respects to her; I owe her that." He gave a gentle nod.

"She would like that, she never gave up hope that you would return, her belief in you was total." Ariel lifted a lace edged hankie out of her pocket, and wiped her eyes as she sniffled.

"I did not desert her, my thoughts were with her at the end, as I performed the ritual on her behalf." He smiled.

"She knew, she felt it. Ariel, she left things for you, there are papers in your room from her. I feel that due to the circumstances, you should take a few days to settle back in and come to terms with the turmoil that resides within you, before attending the house."

Ariel gave a nod, and took a deep breath, as she tried to clear the emotions surging around inside her.

"I was not sure I still had rooms here, I am relieved to know they are still there." Bade moved closer, and lifted a key.

"All is as you left it, those rooms were given you by our queen, you are the owner of them, and they have been locked since the day you left."

He placed the key in her hand as she looked up at him, he smiled his old familiar smile, although his eyes bore the lines beneath them of his great age, and his hair hung like grey ash twine to his shoulders. Ariel turned to Master Elgin, and gave a bow.

"With your grace my Lord Elgin, I shall retire to my rooms, and unpack my things?" He gave a nod.

"Go, settle in, I believe I have a tea appointment with our teacher, ambassador, and Scribe Tila." Tila blinked.

"You do?" He gave a chuckle.

"I do indeed, I have questions about your conduct in Loxley." Tila swallowed hard, and suddenly looked worried.

*B*ade lifted Ariel's bags, and she linked his arm, and suddenly it felt like no time had passed at all, as together they walked down the wooden walkway towards the small door, that she knew was the entrance to her rooms. The span of time since she had left was vast, and yet even though the timbers of the house had aged to a subtle grey colour, and the planks of the deck showed the signs of many feet over many lifetimes, it felt very much like old times, as memories of those days of struggle came to her mind, as she evaded Rhiannon and Luminaria.

They reached the door, and Ariel stood motionless for a second as she stared at the lock, Bade understood.

"It has not changed; it is still filled with her images. If you wish, I shall enter first and remove them?" Ariel shook her head, her voice soft and low.

"No… They will stay as I placed them." She turned and faced Bade.

"I know you do not understand, I knew back then you did not. Bade, she is the love of my life, and I know that probably makes no sense to you, but the fact remains I went to her, and I lived with her, and I loved her. I will never regret going to her, because it was the happiest time of my life, and even though the truth will make no sense to you, Bran was not the evil villain she has been painted. I saw the real Bran, I am Enaria's daughter, I have some of her gifts, and if she was truly as dark as they all have said, I could never have loved her. Do you understand that Bade, because you need to, because that is who I am, it is who I always was?" He gave a nod, as he stared into her eyes.

"I have had many years alone to think, and yes, I do understand. I did not know or meet this Bran, and so as to who she was, I cannot say. What I can say, is that over the years there has been a great deal of discussion in private, and I have always defended you and explained that if you loved her that deeply, then she could not be truly evil, for the blood of your mother would never have allowed it." Ariel gave a nod, and took a deep breath.

"This is something I must do alone Bade, please leave me here, as I confront my life, and I will see you tomorrow." He gave a nod of understanding, and handed over her bag, then turned to leave her.

"You know where I will be if you need me?" Ariel turned and slipped the key in the door, for a second, she looked back.

"Bade?" He turned back to look at her.

"Thank you for being here to meet me, thank you for walking with me. I am happy to find you still here, I needed a friend today, and as always you did not let me down." He smiled.

"I hope I never have, and never will. I am glad you are home; I have missed you deeply. See you tomorrow."

Ariel watched as he walked away, he had not changed much, but he did look much older than he had been. It was strange that she had not aged much in her time within the crystal box, the charm Branna had done had been good, and had preserved and protected her. Ariel smiled at the thought, all those years alone and yet she had kept her word, and kept her safe at her side. She turned the key, and the door creaked slightly, and then holding her bag, she stepped in.

*T*he room had not changed at all, she dropped her bag on the floor, and stood frozen in the centre of the room. As she turned slowly, she was confronted with all her pictures and every memory of her life here all those years ago, and her mind and heart flooded with the pictures and the pain she had been holding in for over six weeks of being free. Her mind flashed with precious images, and memories of moments from her time alone with Branna.

Branna sat quietly watching him go, and then turned to the horse and flicked the reigns.

"Come on then, let's get away from this awful place, and find some peace and quiet. I am Branna by the way, and you are Ariel of Florae I am told?" She nodded.

"I am, it's nice to meet you, Branna." She smiled.

"You don't know me yet; you may regret saying that."

Ariel gave a gasp and clutched her chest, as Branna's voice echoed in her mind.

"Who exactly is going to hear me Ariel? Look where we live, we are high up on the valley side with the advantage of seeing every road for miles, no one can get close to this place without us knowing, it is why I picked it." Branna gave a wide smile, as she gestured out across the valley, almost spilling her freshly filled glass of wine.

"Why you picked it, you mean, you deliberately chose this place to ensure you could have a clear view of what… Enemies?" Branna nodded.

"We are a lower class of citizen within the ranks of the Fae Ofmoon, our purpose is to serve and work, we can be replaced or killed at will. I made sure when I chose this spot that if anyone wants to turf me out, I will see them long before they arrive, and make sure

I am ready for the fight. I hate to say it, but having you stay with me is a little bit of added insurance." Ariel gave a violent sob, as she stood in the centre of her room, and the pictures flowed through her brain.

Branna jumped up on the bed and giggled, she slapped Ariel on the buttock.

"Come on, let's go for a quick swim before we eat." She bounced off the bed, and ran out of the door. Ariel jumped up and shouted after her.

"BRAN, YOU FORGOT YOUR CLOTHES!"

*H*er mind swirled, as all the memories and pain she had been holding inside her since she had been released from the box flooded her, as finally, Ariel faced the truth of her life, a life she knew would be spent alone without her beloved Branna. She felt dizzy, as pictures flashed through her thoughts, and she staggered through into her bedroom, where her bed had been freshly made, and she sat with a thump, holding her hands to her face.

Branna gave a mighty sob and shook her head, tears streamed from her eyes. Her voice was soft and showed her heartbreak.

"Please Ariel, I am begging you, do not leave me, do not give up on me, you are the only part of me that is still living, and I want it to keep on living. I will protect you, Ariel please, I need you." Ariel wept and the tears dripped from her face onto the dry hard soil.

"You cannot protect me, I know you want to, but you are fooling yourself, the darkness has taken them all, and it will get worse. Bran, please. if you truly love me, let me go, and live for the memories we have made. It is the only way left now, please my love, let me go." Branna fell to her knees, and cradled her face in her hands, as her tears dripped down through her fingers.

"Ariel, I cannot endure my life alone without you, with all of the powers I have gained, I am not strong enough to let you go. Without you, there will be no life, and no light, and I will be lost to the darkness forever. Please Ariel, I beg you, do not leave me alone here to endure eternity without you." Ariel gave a mighty sob, sat alone in her old apartment in Florae, and shook her head.

"Branna, I love you too, how can I endure my life without you?"

Her pain wailed out of her, she bent forward holding her hands to her face as they dripped with her tears on to the old rug, more pictures flashed into her thoughts.

"Some would call me foolish, but my dreams tell me my words reach you, I know you wear the veil of your mother, but I am stronger now. Ariel, I am darker than I wish to be, but my feelings of loss, and the way I miss you, has increased the process. I am sorry my love, but I am losing you slowly, I am fighting so hard against the darkness for you, I want to keep you inside, but I fear now the darkness will completely take me. I know I have lost you, I hate it so much, but I have accepted it, and soon I will come here no longer." She gave a sob, and tried to hold back, she looked up and her tears filled her eyes.

"You were right to leave, Otto and Maud have grown strong, they think I do not know, but I hear all the evil things they say about you, and one day I fear, they will hunt you down and kill you, for that is their wish. I do not blame you Ariel, you need to know I understand. I want only good for you, and you should walk in the light, but sadly for me that is no longer possible, so this is goodbye forever. I am leaving my bag, for I have brought your books, remember, one day you said if you got back to Florae, you would write about me, and tell the truth of my story? Ariel, I have read what you wrote and you wrote the truth, so here they are, take them from this land, for if I fall the veil will lift, it will not be for long, so use it well, take your books and finish them."

Ariel wailed into her hands. "I will… I will, I will write it all Bran, I will tell them the truth, I promise, I promise… I love you, and I will tell all of them your story." The pictures began to flash in her mind, and Branna's voice rang out in her ears.

"This is not right, it is not fair Ariel, what is the point of being a queen of these people if I cannot be happy? I do not want to do this, you are the love of my life, I do not want to seal you up in a glass box. I want to walk in the woodland with you, curl around you at night and laugh at your side, as we always have. I want what we had in Avalon; it is the reason I have done all this. Ariel, I just want to be free and share every moment with you. If you are here sealed in a box, there is no point to anything I have done."

The tears streamed down her face, as she stepped back, and fell to her knees and wept deep painful sorrowful sobs.

"I will have no life without you, I already know what that is like Ariel, I got swallowed up by the darkness. I was not living; I may as well just have been dead." Ariel felt her own tears, watching Branna break like this was painful, she dropped to her knees and lifted Branna's face to hers.

"Bran, listen to me, this is not as before." She held her face in her hands, and softly kissed her.

"Last time I was hidden from you, I was not around to remind you, but here I will always be on view, and at your side. Bran you are so clever, I know you can find a way, I have seen your notes and diagrams, I mean, they are coded, but I can see how you are working to find a balance like Merlin's. Don't you see, with me here at your side as you work, you will see your reason to fight every day, and you will find a way through to a balance. When the time is right, I will be waiting for you to awaken me." Branna took a deep breath and swallowed back her tears, as she looked into her soft loving grey eyes.

"Ariel it is not the same, I was so alone without you, I just want us to be together always as we promised each other in Avalon." Ariel leaned forward and kissed her again.

"But we will be Bran, I will always be there in your heart and in your thoughts, can you not see, we can never really be parted, our love is too strong. Bran, we have eaten a wonderful meal together, we made love, and then bathed together, it was a perfect day together for us. Remember today, hold it in your heart for me, for it was perfect and filled with love, but now I am tired, hold me until I fall asleep to dream of you. Let me fall asleep in your arms, and then do the spell, and let me rest a while. When it is done, then control the darkness, find the balance, and rule this family as an equal to Rhiannon."

*A*riel wailed louder. "I am so sorry, but it was the only way I could save you, Bran you must know I was right? I am sorry to make you endure that, but it was the only way. We had a perfect day, a moment I will always cherish, and I hope you cherished it to?"

She threw herself sideways and flopped onto the bed, and buried her face in the blankets, as she let out a howling wail of pain, and her mind filled with an image she had never seen before. Branna lay on the floor between the two trees where they had made love so many times in the past, her top was torn, and her stomach oozed blood. It soaked into her clothes and ran down, pooling on the hard earth. Her tatty hair was splayed out across the flattened grass and weeds, and Branna stared up into the sky and smiled at her, as her dark eyes twinkled. Her voice was soft as she winced in pain.

"Ariel, I am free, it is finally over. Remember me always, you are the love of my life, and my spirit will never leave you. I love you my beautiful Ariel." She lay with her face in the blankets sobbing softer as the pictures flowed through her mind.

"I love you too Bran, I could never forget you, you were my life, my reason to live."

She lay still on the bed, and for a moment she felt like someone stroked her long brown hair, and then she felt the softest of kisses on the top of her head.

"Live for me Ariel, honour our life together." Ariel sat bolt upright, and looked around, breathing hard and swallowed.

"Bran?"

*T*here was no one there, the room was empty and as still as it had always been, and yet all around her she felt the strong sense of her, almost as if she had just left the room. Ariel sat and stared at the basin on the small unit, trying to understand what had just happened, not completely sure of whether Bran had been there or not, she felt disorientated and sick to the stomach, and had a strange feeling building up inside her.

She did not know why, but as she stared at the basin, she slid forward on the bed, and without thinking, she stood up and walked to the basin and lifted it up. Underneath was the key to her chest. She picked it up, even though she still had the other around her neck, and turned back to the bed and knelt down.

Ariel slid the old chest out from under the bed and slipped the key into the lock, it gave a soft click, and the top came up as Ariel gave a gasp. There on the top of the pile of parchments and drawings were her books, and also the book she had made and left in Avalon for Branna. She lifted it up and looked at it, her voice was low, and filled with surprise.

"How is this even possible?"

Ariel opened the book, and there was a new piece of parchment, she placed the book down and opened it up, it was written in the neat hand of Branna.

'Ariel, my love,

I have watched over you as you have watched over me, and so I return to you the book you left me, it has been a great comfort and help to me in my loneliness. I have fought so hard to keep the darkness at bay, but there are things I have done I am not proud of, for in my pain, I had moments of weakness.

Forgive me my love, I wanted so badly to honour my promise, but things went ill from the day I sealed you away, and I have had times of great struggle to overcome the power of the Merle within me. I wanted you to know, I wanted to tell you face to face, that I never stopped loving you, and having you near helped to save most of me. It has been hard without you, and I wish with all my heart it could have been different, for all I ever truly wanted was to live at your side in our cottage at Avalon.

I have carried the blame always for the mistakes I made out of ignorance, and yet I have gained a greater wisdom because of it, and so I have lived with the choices I have made, but know this, at the end, for I fear that time is close, it was you who ultimately saved me.

I need you to live for both of us, I need you to honour our dreams, for sadly, I will no longer be able to be a part of it. Live for me Ariel, breathe the air, swim in the water, be freer than any Fae ever could be, and celebrate the love we held. My spirit will always walk at your side.

I love you.

Goodbye my love.

Bran.'

Ariel flopped back against the bed staring at the letter as her tears ran down her cheeks, and yet she did not cry out loud. It was almost as if she had finally accepted her fate, her life from now on, would match that of Branna's, as she endured her years of loneliness alone in Florae.

She placed the letter on her bedside table, and locked up the chest and pushed it back under the bed, and then she washed her face and returned to her living room for her bag, to unpack the few clothes that Rune and Alice had given her. She smiled as she lifted out a long black shawl, and pulled it round her shoulders, it was her most precious possession, as it had been inside the bag, Branna had brought to the woodland that day with her books. Ena had kept it and returned it to her in Loxley, and it meant everything to Ariel to hold it again.

All her memories of Branna during their evening walks brought the pictures to her mind, as she wore the shawl that she had made her. It no longer carried her scent, but it was all she had left of her, and it was very precious to her. She hung her things up and sat at her window, as she ate a meagre meal from what had been placed in her small kitchen area for her, and thought about all that happened and where she was.

In truth this was no longer her home, not in her heart, that would always reside in Avalon with her memories of Branna, but for now, and until she knew what she was going to do with her life now, this was a home of sorts. The day drifted slowly by, and she wrote in her journal, and as the sun fell, she locked the door, and wandered into her small room and stripped. Ariel lay back in her bed, the letter of Branna left folded neatly at her side, she rolled over and touched it.

"Goodnight my love, sleep well wherever you are."

She closed her eyes, and drifted into sleep as her mind wandered through her life with Branna, and her dreams were filled with the happy giggling white face, with bright dark eyes, and long tatty scruffy black hair.

*S*he slept late into the morning, and when she surfaced in her living room, she found a small note pushed under the door, requesting a meeting with Master Elgin. Ariel ate little, as she sat by her window, and as the hour approached, she pulled on her shawl, and left her rooms to walk the long front deck of the royal apartments, and the House of Scribes.

The word was out she had returned, and many she passed gave a courteous nod towards her, and treated her with great respect. At the doors of the house, she smiled as she saw Bade waiting patiently for her, it was almost like old times. She linked his arm, and for the first time in what was now a whole era gone by, she walked into the house she designed, and marvelled at the building.

As she entered the long room of scribes and saw her old familiar desk with a red rope around it, she smiled, and then gave a slight gasp, as every scribe in the room stood up at their desks and bowed to her, with a chorus of.

"Welcome home, Mistress Ariel!"

It took her completely by surprise, as Tila gave a wink and smiled from her desk, Bade patted her hand.

"You will have to get used to that, to all of these you are a legend, and the person who designed this, to them, you are the Mistress to the House of Scribes, and I actually think it has been a long time coming, you earned it."

It was a strange moment for her, she had given up her life as a scribe when she had returned from Avalon, and been held prisoner in her rooms. In many ways, living with Bran had broken the bond with the house, and yet here she was with a title that was equal to Master Elgin, it would take a lot of getting used to.

Ariel walked around the house, as Bade explained the many things that had changed. The archive had grown vast since she had last been there, and the archive of the other races was equally as large. It was nice to talk as they walked round, and he talked of his life and his work, and how much he had missed her. She had always understood his feelings for her, but she knew, she would never be able to love another, but kept quiet and just smiled politely. They made their way down from the archive, and eventually they arrived at the door of Master Elgin's study.

*B*ade gave a tap and walked in, as she had seen him do a thousand times before, and a moment later, the door opened and he waved her in, bowed, and then left them alone. Elgin remained seated as she sat opposite, he poured tea and offered her cakes, and they sat back as she lifted her cup to sip.

"I admire you greatly Ariel, you have endured much, and yet handled it with dignity. You would make a very positive addition to the council, and you should consider applying, the new queen would benefit greatly from your wisdom." Ariel smiled.

"I am sorry, but it is not for me, I will always serve a queen with great loyalty, but I have no need of a seat on the council to talk to a queen should she require it." He gave a chuckle and understood.

"You learned much of diplomacy from Bridget, she would be very proud of you if she were here, and if I may say so, you have grown very likened to your mother, she was good at hiding her feelings also." Ariel sat back as she looked at the wise old man, who all those years ago had been kind to her. She had never forgotten him, and had thought of him many times after leaving Florae.

"I have always wanted to thank you for what you did for me. I know it was not easy for you at that time, Rhiannon made things harder than they needed to be, and yet you supported me. You should know, I was always grateful for that, there were times when the only person I felt truly believed me, was you." He gave an appreciative nod.

"I never doubted your innocence, I will not deny Ariel, I was unsure about your friend." She understood that.

"Bran was wild and carefree, and very intelligent, but she was blinded by her feelings of injustice towards the way her and her friends were treated. The sad thing was she was brilliant in her work, she just made one foolish error, and it turned her life upside down forever. Not many will believe this, but I feel you may, although I am not sure Master Elgin. The truth is, she was not the dark and terrible person she has been portrayed to be in recent days, she tried to control her family and prevent them from many of their evil doings, but she lost control. Bran understood the Merle better than any, and she was fighting what had taken over her, and for a long time she suppressed it and controlled it. I was a part of helping her do that. It may surprise you to know, she was researching a way to cleanse her and her family of it, it was a foolish error made at a time when the Merle took advantage of her weakness, and she realised that, and she never stopped fighting it."

"I can actually believe that, because knowing who you are, then you must have been protecting her, just your presence would have helped her. Sadly, few will ever understand that, I am quite sure Bade has tried to, but I fear it will be a long time before his understanding is complete." She smiled.

"Bade is a good person, but he is blinded by his feelings for me. It pains me to know they have not changed, I had hoped before I returned, I would find him settled with a family. He will never understand, I cannot give him what he wants, I will never love another in the way I loved Bran, and he would want me to." Elgin finally started to understand the bigger picture, as he sat back and considered his next words, he gave a long sigh.

"I feared this would happen, it saddens me to know you will leave again." She gave a chuckle as she lifted her cup.

"I see you too learned much from Bridget." He laughed.

"I think I already knew, but I fear I must ask, where will you go?" Ariel sat back in the plush seat.

"I have been free for almost six weeks, I have such a lot on my mind, and I need to sort things out. I have given it great thought, as a Queen will come to replace Gwendolyn, and I will offer my loyal service to her. I wish to maintain a connection to the house, but I aim to petition Queen Amethyst to have my home in Avalon returned to me. It is isolated and quiet, and filled with happy memories, and so I will wish to spend time between there and here." Elgin understood.

"I would assume the majority of your time will be there, I suspected this and have requested the Queen of Avalon consider it on your behalf, it is the least I can do to aid you. I am feeling old and tired, and I want to tie up as many loose ends as possible before I step down completely from the council, I have already passed on the role as head of the council. The loss of my granddaughter has served a heavy blow to my family, and I wish to spend more time with them."

"Did you name a successor, or did you allow them to fight it out?" He smiled.

"I would wish Bade to continue to be a member, but he is not ready to head the council up. Alder has served as my second for a long time, and he has been filling in for me on certain days. Alder, I feel has more wisdom, and understands the role better, he will be a dedicated and loyal servant when I retire, and it is my hope lead well." Ariel smirked.

"He was one of those who wanted to hand me over to Rhiannon. I worked with him many times, he was good at his job, although as for wisdom, I feel at times he clouds his judgement with his personal feelings." Elgin gave a nod.

"He has learned much in his time at my side, I still feel, he will do the job better than Bade can at this time." Ariel gave a shrug.

"I cannot comment, I have been away for a very long time, and ultimately wish to leave again. I am a simple Scribe, and wish only to be given the peace to write what I know is truth."

"You will be, it pleases me that you will be a regular visitor, for I would indeed enjoy your opinion on many matters of this realm at times. I would also consider it a privilege if you would allow me to visit you there from time to time, you did paint quite a lovely picture of it many years ago if I can recall our previous conversations." She gave a giggle.

"You talk as if the queen has already granted me access to the house, let us see what she says first, I may never be able to return, I simply do not know." Elgin smiled.

"As I said, I have already made the request, and Queen Amethyst has granted it. The papers are over there on the table, you will find the royal pardon from her father Rayne of Moon, and the full titles to the house, you are a co owner with Branna of Fae. It was a formality to include Branna, as you cannot own property alone, so on the advice of her father, she granted it to both of you." He smiled.

"I hope that is within your acceptance?" Ariel felt the surge of emotion within her, as she turned to look across the room to the neatly rolled parchments, tied with a royal blue ribbon.

"I can go back?" Her eyes filled with tears, he leaned forward and patted her hand.

"Ariel, go and live whatever life you choose, honour her by living in that house, your time of suffering needs to end. Go and be happy, but be a regular visitor, this is the house you designed and we built, and whether you believe it or not, your vision is still required here. I would suggest, you visit your queen first, and then, I believe there is some unfinished business in the Whispering Falls, after that, go to the house, which let's be honest, you consider your true home, and live well."

The old master of the house, pushed his walking stick into the floor and stood up, he walked over to the table and lifted the papers, and turned as Ariel rose up and approached him. He placed the papers into her hand.

"I fear there will be more tears, save them until you are alone. Ariel, it has been yet another pleasure to have sat and spoken with you. Organise your affairs here, and then go and live the life you promised her all those years ago, and please, find some happiness for yourself. Now, if you will excuse me, my other granddaughter is fully healed and will leave for Loxley tomorrow to continue her duty to our future queen, and I promised her last evening, I would be with her. The Lady of Loxley has requested no other as she feels Filomena was an asset that cannot be replaced, so I wish to talk with Isolde before she goes."

Ariel smiled and gave him a nod, as she looked down at the papers in her hand.

"My Lord and Master Elgin, I cannot thank you enough for this, you are a very kind man, and I have no idea how, but I shall repay your kindness one day." She looked up, and he smiled at her.

"Live for her Ariel, live a full life, and find happiness in familiar settings. You know, that is the best way to honour the person you knew, no matter what others might say." She gave a nod, and turned for the door, as she approached it, she turned and gave a regal bow.

"Master Elgin, it has been an honour to serve you as house master." He smiled, and she slipped through the door, and headed back down the long corridor and out into the fresh air.

Chapter two.

Queen and Mother.

Many tears were shed that night as Ariel looked at the royal papers, and understood that she could at least have half of her dream. Branna was gone forever, but being able to return to her home gave her hope, as she could live out her life in the one place, she thought she would never walk in again.

She sorted through her things, and divided them between what she would take, and what she would leave, then packed what she could in a large bag, and left it at the bottom of her bed. She slipped into bed and was soon asleep, as she dreamt of her return, and her life with Bran in the only place she really considered home now.

*T*he following morning, Bade came to visit, and they sat for a long time talking of the house and his future plans for it, and as the morning wore on, Ariel plucked up the courage to tell him of her own plans. It was not an easy thing for her, he had waited all these years and it had aged him, but she had never lied to him, and he sensed something was coming. His voice dropped as he looked at her.

"You may as well say it Ariel, you have spent all morning trying to, and ducked many of my questions. We have always been honest with each other, so just say it, you are leaving again, aren't you?"

Ariel gave a sigh and sat back in her seat, she hated how he did this to her, and had hoped the time apart has lessened his ability, she took a deep breath.

"It is not so much leaving, as sharing my time here. Queen Amethyst has granted me the rights to ownership of the house in Avalon, so I aim to live there and share my time here in the house." She saw his look of sadness, and she leaned forward and took his hands in hers.

"Bade, she is the love of my life. I am sorry, because I know you do not want to hear that. Bade, you are the only real friend I have, but you must accept, that the Ariel you fell in love with does not exist anymore. I have changed, so much has happened and I have witnessed so much pain, Bade, I lost her, she has gone forever, and I miss her so much, I need to grieve her loss, and I cannot do that here. I will be here a lot of the time, but on those days, and there will be many, where I will suffer her loss, I will stay close to the place where we shared our love. I know this is hard for you, but you must let me go, you cannot carry a hope in your heart forever, I will always love you, you are so dear to me, but I could never love another the way I love Bran, do you understand that?" She could see the hurt in his eyes, he let go of her hands, and moved back.

"Don't you mean loved, she is gone forever Ariel, she cannot return from where she was taken?" His voice held the sting of his pain, and Ariel shook her head.

"No, I meant love, I do love her still and I always will. I know she is gone and I will be alone, I have no need of reminders, there is not a minute in my life, and has not been since I awoke in that box to see Runestone and not Bran, that I have not felt the pain of her loss. It is why I must leave; I need to return to the place we made a home, and alone, I need to face the truth of my life and grieve for her loss and the shattered dreams I have in my heart. I understand your bitterness, I do, but this is something I have to do, because this is the only way I can ever live again. I plan to visit my queen and repeat the farewells I said lost in a forest many years ago, and then I shall go to the waters as instructed to do, and when all that is done, I am leaving for Avalon. I will return here to the house when I have done what is needed." He stood up, and his manner was cooler than normal, he gave a nod and turned for the door.

"I am grateful for your frankness, and I am sorry if I have distressed you. I am glad you shall return, you have always been an asset to the house, so go, and do what you need to. I shall await your return; we have much to prepare for the new queen's arrival." Ariel gave a long sigh.

"Bade, please wait." The door shut, and he was gone. Ariel gave a longer sigh.

"Why does no one understand, how can anyone think I can simply return to an old life, when I have lived a life that was worth living, even if only for a short time?"

*T*wo hours later, with a small posy of Edelweiss in her hand, Ariel entered the entrance to the long cave, that held the remains of her adopted family. She entered the chamber where there was a long line of white stone tombs, containing the last remains of Bridget, Malcolm, Ninian, Erin, and Gwendolyn. They stood surrounded by thousands of flowers; Ariel gazed through her tears at all of them. They had all been lost to the world, and she had not been there, and felt the pain of failing the family that had been so good to her after her parents had died.

She walked slowly over towards the tomb of Bridget, and gave a sniffle as she saw the fine pathway through the white lilies to the side of her tomb. Ariel walked carefully through, and placed the small posy of flowers on top of the white marble lid, and then knelt before her queen.

"My Queen, and My Mother, I returned shamed for deserting you in your hour of need, and when you needed me the most. You were always there for me, I should have been here for you, I am so sorry I failed you." She lowered her head and wept.

Behind her, stood against the wall, stood a black robed figure in a tatty cloak, he watched silently as Ariel spoke her mumbled words of love to Bridget, and when she had done, he took a pace forward into the cave.

"You honour your queen greatly, but you are misinformed child of light." Ariel lifted her tear filled eyes, to see the shadowy figure of the White Lord.

"How am I misinformed, I was not here, and she suffered, and needed me?" The hood shook.

"That is your mistake. Yes, she did suffer, but it was of her own choosing. Bridget Violet was a great queen, as was her granddaughter, but Bridget knew of the tasks set for you both, for it was at her last meeting with your mother, that it was revealed to her. Bridget knew you would leave and go to the girl of darkness, and it was your mother who told her she must let you." Ariel could not understand.

"That makes no sense at all, why would my mother tell her to let me walk into danger?" A small chuckle came from under the hood.

"You are so like your mother; she had no issue with questioning the White Lord either. Child of Light, what I tell you is true, and I may add, it was necessary." Ariel did not understand at all, she shook her head and stood up.

"Why was it necessary?" He walked closer.

"Would it surprise you to know, that you were infected by your lover?" Ariel frowned.

"That is not possible." The hood twitched.

"Oh, but you were, the Merle tried to infect you as a protection from your light. Without your lover knowing, it passed from her into you, and it did infect your body, but your mother was very clever, and she placed a protection on you that enhanced your light and killed all of the darkness that entered you, and I may add, it also reduced the darkness within your lover. The kiss you so freely gave her, passed light into her, and it did help, it may have been what saved her. The girl Branna had some of your mother's protection, because you gave it to her, your light destroys the Merle, and from that the Redstone knew I could destroy it." Ariel walked towards him.

"And this was known by Bridget, and yet she never told me?"

"That is correct. Your mother placed the charm on you, but she had no way of knowing if it would be enough, after all, it took away her life, and all she wanted was you to be safe. Your daughter has the light within her also, it has passed into your line, if you do not believe me, then you have but a few minutes, so ask your queen." Ariel shook her head.

"Bridget is passed."

"Yet you are a mystic." Ariel shook her head again.

"No, I am not, I am a scribe, my mother never passed on her powers." The hooded figure lifted an arm, and he pointed with no visible hand behind her.

"Then Scribe, explain that to me." Ariel turned, and saw the faint figure of Bridget Violet; she opened her arms.

"Come to me daughter."

Ariel felt a huge surge rise up in her chest, as her eyes filled yet again with tears. Bridget gave a smile and walked towards her as she shook on the spot with her emotions, unable to move.

"Oh dear, my poor child, such trials you have faced alone. Your white lord does not lie Ariel, you were blessed by your mother in ways none of us understand. It is true, she told me you would run to a darkened soul, and through you she would find redemption. I knew you would go, and I was glad that you did." Ariel shook where she stood, as her tears flowed.

"But if I had known, I would have helped cure you, why did you not tell me, I would have saved you as you did me? I loved you like a mother, but when I asked, they told me you would not see me, I wanted to, I wanted to help you." Bridget gave a smile.

"Ariel my child, that was never your task, it was mine, and it was a task I accepted to save my people. Ariel, I chose it, and I chose it willingly, it was never for you to do, your destiny had other tasks, of which there are still some to come." Ariel swallowed hard as her lips trembled.

"I lost her, I lost Bran, she is gone forever, what task could I possibly do now?" Bridget's violet eyes shone with love, as she lifted a faint hand to Ariel's cheek.

"A new queen will come, and you will need to be beside her as she takes the crown, Sapphire is a good teacher, and the child Iona will learn much from her. Ariel, whether you believe it or not, the powers of Enaria live inside you, and within them is knowledge only a mystic or a queen can know. It will be your place to instruct her, and set her on a path only you can, for she will have a task of her own before she is crowned as all queens do." Ariel gave a loud sniffle.

"I cannot feel anything within me but pain, if I had known I would have cured you, and then gone to cure Bran. If my mother is within me, why can I not feel her?"

"Ariel, go to the whispering falls and stand as you once did with me, and open your heart to your mother. Ariel, let her out of you, allow her to come forth and release your true powers, for within you lies the power to be the greatest mystic of all lines of Fae, it is there, I feel it." She nodded, and wiped her eyes.

"I have missed you, there have been so many days when I spoke to you knowing my words would never reach you, and yet I still talked out loud to you, I guessed, I hoped you could hear me." Bridget gave a smile.

"I heard them, all of them, who do you think prompted the memories to come to your mind? I was always there within the knife that you carried, it is why I gave it to you, and now, I am also protecting your daughter. I was within the knife and the one who brought Crina and Bella to her aid. My dear precious child, I never left you, and I delighted in the happiness you had with Branna, it was right you left and learned to live, you sacrificed too much of your life to the house, why do you think I sent you to Avalon?" Ariel swallowed and blinked.

"I thought you sent me because you trusted no other?"

"It is true that was one of my reasons, but that was not the main reason, Ariel, the house was sucking your life away, you needed to taste the freedom of living, you were dying working with scrolls." She smiled a soft and beautiful smile at Ariel.

"I was right, you discovered such love, and it intensified the light within you."

"I still lost her, I could have cured her, and if I had known, I would have." Bridget shook her head slowly.

"Ariel, she had her part to play also, the love she gave you will help you as your powers reveal themselves, for it will be that precious love that strengthens them. Tell me, how could you use your powers, if you had not met and fallen so deeply in love with your Branna?" Ariel frowned.

"Are you saying that was her part to play in my life, she was just a pawn?" Bridget shook her head.

"No, I am not saying that, her love for you was real, and deeper than any of us thought, she was never a pawn, but she did have free will, and she made mistakes that could not be undone, and that ultimately cost her. Whether you believe it or not, in time, you will realise the power of Branna and how she enhanced your life and your abilities, nothing is ever written for no reason Ariel, you more than any should understand that."

The voice of the White Lord rung out into the cave, and Bridget's faint violet eyes moved to look at him.

"It is time, I cannot give you longer, speak your peace, time is short." Bridget gave a sigh and looked back at Ariel.

"Go to your home in Avalon and heal, knowing I loved you as my own child."

"I love you too, you were a mother to me always, and a rock in times of need."

She smiled and blew a kiss as her image broke apart and she faded into nothing, and Ariel felt the tug at her heart, and turned to look where the White Lord stood, but the cave was empty, and she was alone again.

Ariel sat alone in the cave for a long time reflecting on her time in Florae, and trying to work out if she had indeed wasted a large part of her life. She understood that she had lived life to the full in Avalon, the days there were busy, but even then, the work appeared to go faster due to the interactions and conversations she had with Branna. It was true, she had felt more alive in Avalon than at any other time in her life, and she had to consider the prospect. Would she live more fully if she returned, even though Branna would not be there?

Eventually, she stood up and left, she had made her peace and spent a little time by the side of each stone tomb, of the people who had become her family growing up. Once done, as she walked back down the long path towards the centre of Florae and the House of Scribes, her mind wandered, and she simply lost track of time, and walked slowly as she thought. When she arrived back at the house of Scribes, Bade was sat at his desk with a lamp lit, it was Gleefall, and the sun set early during the cooler days. He noticed her enter and stood up, she looked at him and gave a nod.

"Do not say it, I know, I am sorry too." He gave a smile, as she turned and walked towards the steps that would lead down to the caves that led to the Whispering Falls, Bade hurried over to her.

"Ariel wait… Are you sure you are ready for this, I upset you this morning, and seeing the tombs of your family can not have been easy? Are you really sure you can handle this?" Ariel gave her head a shake.

"Honestly Bade, I am not sure, I just know I need to do this today while I have the strength and determination to do so. To be honest Bade, it is either now or never, and so I am going to get it all over with once and for all." He stepped back, and gave a weak smile.

"Alright, I will be here if you need anything."

"Thanks, Bade, thanks for everything you have ever done for me, I have always appreciated it." He gave a nod as she turned, and headed for the steps.

Ariel stepped off the bridge, and walked onto the flat round plinth of stone, and looked around. Even though she had been here before, she still marvelled at the room, just as she had that first time on its completion, when she had stood here with Bridget Violet. The shelter under the water moved of its own accord, and slipped gently back, allowing the water to fall in a completed circle, and the room fell silent. Ariel turned slowly around.

"It is so beautiful, as much as I hated her, Rhiannon did a

wonderful job creating this."

She gave a gasp as a figure made purely of water stepped out from the wall of water, and stood in front of her. A shiver of shock ran down Ariel's spine, as she recognised the figure before her, and her voice dropped to a whisper.

"Mother?" The glass like looking figure smiled at her, and walked a little closer.

"Ariel my darling, just relax, I know this may be a shock, but I chose not to leave. I chose to stay close to our people, and when Rhiannon built this, I came here to continue using my gifts in the service of the queen, and to watch over you." Ariel felt her breath coming and going in rapid bursts, she could not believe what she was seeing.

"I was here before, why did you not show yourself then?" Enaria walked closer towards her, and held out her arms.

"Ariel, you know the rules of our line, you know how I too have to obey what was destined for me." She shook her head.

"You were my mother, you should have let me know, I have a daughter, and I would never hide from her." Enaria stopped.

"Yet you volunteered to be put in a glass box, and allowed your daughter to fend for herself?"

"It is not the same, I was protecting Ena, if they had found out about her, they would have killed me, and then hunted her down and killed her too. I bought her time, time to escape and find help, which she did." The glass like figure gave a nod.

"Can you not see; I did the same thing? Ariel, the Merle swarmed all over me, I had no choice but to protect you, I was filled with it as it tried to devour me. I could not risk it doing it to you, I had to send you away with the only woman I trusted."

It was too much to handle, it had already been such an emotional day for her, seeing her mother was just too much, she tried to clear her mind and focus her thoughts.

"I have no idea what is happening anymore, I have lost everything, everything I loved has gone, all I want is to get away and isolate myself away from everyone. I am in so much pain at the moment, they took her away from me, and it hurts so badly, Mother, I have to leave here, but how can I now, knowing you are here?" The clear face smiled.

"Ariel, your gifts are overdue, it is why you were told to come back, my power must pass to you, it is for you to inherit, as it will be one day for your daughter. Ariel, open your heart, feel my presence and let me pass my powers to you, it will keep you safe forever." Ariel shook her head.

"I am not ready, I am sorry, but I cannot, not yet, there are things I must do first, and then will be the time." Enaria gave a long sigh,

"Ariel, it has to be now, you can never return here, this is a chamber for only a queen, and she will need you to use the powers of our line. Ariel, please, it has to be now." She took another step back.

"And what will happen then, as quick as I find you, I get your powers and I lose you all over again? I cannot take anymore, does no one see that, I just cannot take it. Everything I love I lose, if I go away, and live alone, I cannot harm anyone, so please just bring back the bridge and let me go. Find Ena, give her your powers, she is your granddaughter, help her and protect her, just let me leave mother. Let me go where no one will bother me, and let me live in peace." Enaria shook her head, and the water she was made from, rippled across her face.

"Ariel, you do not understand, I gave you the gifts, they are already within you, all I want to do is awaken them. I will not be changed by it, I am tied to these waters forever, I cannot leave. You will never lose me, you never have, do you not remember my voice as you slept in your box, I was there inside you always?" She frowned.

"Wait… What… That makes no sense, if I already have your powers, why have they never surfaced?"

"Ariel my darling, you were not old enough, I had to bind them until you were ready, and whether you believe it or not, you are ready."

Ariel felt her heart pounding inside her, she was trying her hardest to stay in control, this was simply too much to deal with, and as she walked backwards, she bumped into the seat, she felt something behind her and turned to look back, her mother's voice sounded across the room of the falls.

"Take it, and when you are ready, drink it." Ariel saw the bottle filled with water on the chair.

"It is the only way, oh, you are so like your father, certainly as stubborn as he was."

Ariel lifted the bottle and looked at it, it was just a glass bottle filled with water, she turned back to her mother.

"How can this work?" Enaria smiled.

"I am these falls, all of the water that passes through this room, contains the power of our line, it is the key to the record it holds, as I am now a part of the house of scribes and can recall any fact within it to aid the queen. If you drink the water, it will release me into you and I will awaken all of your powers. When the time is right, drink it, now go, and do what you have to, I will be with you always."

Ariel lifted the bottle, and looked at it, she could see it was ordinary water, and yet there was something more to it. She could not quite place it, like it had a feeling, a presence, it felt strange to look at it. She turned to the watery figure as it stood by the bridge that had silently slipped through the water, and awaited her dripping.

"When I drink it, you will be with me… Always?" The glass like figure smiled.

"Always." She gave a nod, and walked towards the bridge.

"We will talk again soon." Enaria smiled and slid back into the water, and disappeared.

"I will be there inside you, have no fear.

Ariel stepped onto the bridge, and walked under the shelter carrying the bottle with her, she walked into the tunnel that led to the cave of the steps upward, and she suddenly remembered and turned to look back, the bridge had returned to its resting place, and the waters flowed down, Ariel breathed out and her voice was low.

"The stars, I forgot to ask about the stars, Bridget told me, I had to take them."

It was too late and she knew it, this had been her only chance, and she had forgotten, and she knew she would never enter the chamber again. With a heavy sigh, she turned and headed for the stairs upwards, and back into the House of Scribes.

When Ariel arrived back in the house, Bade had been called off to attend a council member. In a way, she was relieved, she knew he would ask too many questions. Ariel turned and headed for the doors, and made her way outside, Sapphire was leant against the rail, and smiled as Ariel walked out.

"How are you settling in?" Ariel gave a long audible sigh, as she looked at Sapphire.

"It has been an emotional day, I think I have faced more than I can take, but I am fine." Sapphire understood, her bright blue eyes shone out of her pale face.

"Crystal told me about Amethyst and her gift to you, I take it you will go there?" Ariel smiled; Sapphire was sharper than she looked.

"I am already packed, it may sound stupid, but that is the place I call home, no one understands that, but Sapphire, I will never settle here. I will come and go and help the queen to come, but in my heart, I feel that is where I belong." Sapphire did understand, had she not made a similar decision about Callanish?

"Then go Ariel, go there and find yourself again, take the time to think things through, and then when you know what you want and how you want to live, do that." Ariel smiled at her.

"I see you have done something similar, finally, a person who understands." Sapphire gave a small giggle.

"I know the turmoil, and I have seen it in you since we returned. Ariel, live for you, the way I see it, you have been in a glass box for a long time, so go, do what sets you free."

"Thanks Sapphire, I needed to hear that." She shrugged.

"Glad I can help, and if you ever need me, just reach out, I will be there."

Ariel gave a smile as she turned and walked the long deck back to her home, she stopped at the door and turned to look at Florae. In many ways it was the same, and in some things, it was very different. She smiled to herself as she unlocked the door, entered, then closed it gently behind her and locked it again, and leaned on the door and gave a long sigh of relief.

*O*ver the next forty minutes she gathered the things she would need, lifted her bag onto her shoulder, and then she closed her eyes and focused. With a pop, she was gone, and she reappeared in Avalon stood at the white gate, and looked at the house surrounded by fruit trees. Slipping her hand in her pocket, she pulled out her key and looked at it, it looked as new as the day Branna had given it her, and had been in her pocket for every moment since she had left, bound in the bracelets to prevent her from running.

Ariel pushed the gate, and it swung open with a creak, she walked towards the door and saw the small plaque of her mother's above the door. The path needed weeding, as it had become quite overgrown, the door looked weathered, and was in need of some paint, as she inserted the key, and the stiff lock turned with a loud click.

Ariel pushed open the door and looked inside, and her heart gave a thump, it looked almost exactly as it had been, except some chairs were tipped over and some of the pots lay strewn and smashed across the floor. The doors to the bedrooms were open, and her room looked almost unchanged, even the bed was still made. She remembered the charm she had placed on it, just in case Branna messed it up, and smiled. Branna's room looked the usual mess it had always been, but she also knew that this was where Ena had stayed and hidden for a long time. Ariel stepped in and took a deep breath.

"Branna my love, I am home."

She smiled, somehow it felt right, she walked into the house and closed the door, and took a deep breath, and closed her eyes for a moment. Breathing out, she quietly whispered to herself, and she felt the relief of the silence surrounding her.

"I did it, I finally made it home."

She walked through the living area into Branna's room and looked around, the closet door was open, and some of her clothes were still there in a pile at the bottom. The bed was a mess, but that was not unusual for Branna. Through the side door she could see Branna's desk, where she sat every day filing the reports of the progress of Avalon. She dropped her bag, and walked through, around the desk to her seat. She could almost hear the laughter of Bran, as they worked and made fun of the marshals, the desk was as neat as always. It was in need of a good dust, much of the house had a fine layer of it, which was strange considering it had been locked and sealed since the marshals had searched it.

It had always amazed her that she was so untidy, and yet her desk was always immaculate. Ariel ran her hand across the seat back, and moved round, her grey eyes taking every detail of the familiar sight from her day to day life here almost a thousand years ago. It felt crazy, as it felt like she had only left yesterday. She leaned forward and took hold of the drawer handle, and heard Branna's voice in her head.

"There is nothing there you would understand, one day you will open it and get the surprise of your life." Ariel smiled as the drawer came open, and there inside was a single piece of parchment where her black book used to sit, and in neat writing she read.

'Hey nosey, do you know how much I love you?'

Ariel smiled, and her eyes filled with tears, as she sat with a thump on the wooden seat, and slipped out the parchment, under which was a blue feather. Suddenly, everything she had been holding in for six weeks came rushing to the surface, and finally, now she was completely alone, she allowed herself to grieve for the loss of the love of her life, as she sobbed and wept onto the desk alone.

Amethyst Diamond, Queen of the Fae Ofmoon, sat at her table alone and watched as Ariel broke down and wept over the desk of Branna, she swallowed hard, for it was not an easy thing to see, and lifted her hand and wiped her eyes.

"It is good that you grieve, and I hope that you heal, now you have your home returned to you, for it is the least I could do to undo the wrongs of my grandmother. How I wish Branna could have found a way out, and been healed as the rest of my line have, for you have suffered enough Ariel. I can only hope, that eventually, your load will lighten, and you will find happiness in the house you both shared together."

She sat back and waved her hand across the table, and the picture faded, as she left Ariel alone to grieve privately.

It took many years for Ariel to really come to terms with the death of Branna. She woke the next morning lay across Branna's desk, and after cooking a small meal, she set to work, and for over a week, she scoured and cleaned the whole house. The gate was given a greasing, the door and windows were polished and repainted, some of the trees were pruned, the lawns cut, and the weeds removed.

It took over a month for it to return to how it had been when Ariel shared the house with Branna, and once she had finished and was pleased with her efforts, she gathered together the tools and supplies she needed. Ariel walked up the steep incline to the top of the high rock, where Branna's old weather worn table lay on its side, and she took a deep breath. Over the following days, Ariel rebuilt the shelter, and set the table which she restored and polished back up, straight below it. As she searched, she found the old lamp on the rocks to the path, and repaired it, polished it back up, and set a candle inside it. It had a few more dints in it, but it felt the same, and that was all that mattered.

On her days of distress, she would walk up to the shelter and sit on the edge of the high rock, wrapped in Branna's shawl, and talk as she used to, as she watched out over Avalon, and Branna worked at her table behind her. In many ways, it helped her to overcome her feelings of loss, as did shouting to her whenever she arrived home.

Her nights always felt the easiest, for she had spent many alone whilst Branna worked late high up on the rocks, and she would snuggle into Branna's bed, and stare at her closet, where her clothes were now hung up neatly. She found it a comfort, and it eased the pangs of pain inside her, and slowly over time, Ariel became accustomed to her life in Avalon.

Every four days she would return to Florae for a few days, and work in the house on her mothers' manuscripts, and spend her lunch times with Bade. They talked of the future and the preparations for the new queen, which was still a long way off. As Ariel knew well, Bade would as ever, be completely prepared, and in many ways, it was nice that he had changed little, for it became her means of stability.

One of her greatest joys, was that Gwynfor still lived, in many ways, he was the only family apart from Ena she had left, and she spent many days visiting him at his home on Sora, when he returned from Loxley for a break. They would sit on the steps as she had with Gwendolyn, and talk as the sounds of the sea rolling onto the beach softly echoed in the background.

One night, five years after her return to Avalon, as she sat with Gwynfor, she lifted the bottle of water out of her bag, and looked at him.

"I feel ready, but I am afraid, would you stay close whilst I do this?" The old Celt gave a cheeky smile, and took her by the hand.

"If what I have heard is true, it is probably better you do this out in the open, I am sure that you would not wish for your powers to stream down through my roof?"

He gave a chuckle, took her hand, and walked out towards the water, and the open space between the trees. He then stood a few feet away, as Ariel pulled out the cork from the bottle, and lifted it to her lips.

"It is time the gifts of my mother were revealed."

Ariel took a huge swig, and then drank the whole bottle down, and lifted the empty bottle from her mouth. She stood staring at Gwynfor, who shrugged.

"To be honest my dear, anything or nothing can happen, I must admit, I did think that being one of the greatest mystics, it would have been quite spectacular, alas, I feel it is not to be." Ariel agreed and gave a shrug.

"I suppose you are rig…."

*O*ut of the sky, twelve golden stars set in a circle, came hurtling down, and slammed into the floor around Ariel, and from the centre, a red five pointed star grew out of the earth. As Ariel looked down at it, she felt a jerk in her stomach, and the star erupted upwards in a column of bright red light. Ariel squealed with shock, and Gwynfor stood back and shielded his eyes as white light poured down from the sky engulfing everything. Gwynfor gave a resounding nod, and his bright blue eyes sparkled.

"Yes, that is more like it, now it feels sort of more official." Ariel's wails came out of the bright white light as Gwynfor agreed with himself.

"Oh yes, now that is completely what I expected, well done Ariel."

As the bright light streamed into the sky from the island of Sora, back on the main isle, Elgin sat on his balcony and watched, he gave a gentle smile.

"Good Girl, and not a moment too soon, there is much to be done, and you will be required to help train our future queen. Gather your power Mistress Ariel, for they will be very much appreciated when Iona sits and takes the crown. The time of the old is almost done, it is time for the young to take over and lead."

Chapter Three.

Loxley 2057.

"TEGAN, WILL YOU PLEASE GET UP, I WILL NOT SHOUT AGAIN, I WILL COME UP THERE AND DRAG YOU OUT OF BED BY YOUR HAIR!"

There was a heavy thump on the floor, and Iona smiled, she turned and walked across the living room, past the stairs and into the kitchen. Gailania looked up as she entered, her bright blue eyes sparkled as she lifted her spoon.

"She was up late talking with Fern; they are plotting again. That is the problem with sharing with those two, they keep waking me up." Iona gave a sigh.

"I will be glad when dad is back, she behaves for him. Where is Fern anyhow, her bed was empty when I looked in?"

Gailania flicked back her long copper hair, as she slipped the spoon into her mouth, and chewed.

"She went out with Thorn earlier to spring all the traps Grover and Willow set. Uncle Rowan got snared yesterday, and he was really mad about it. Aunt Jade had to let him down. She thought it was funny, but he was really mad about it, and cussed as he limped back to his house." Iona smirked, as she leaned over the sink.

"Those two are getting wilder by the day, I do hope you do not go feral, it is bad enough with Fern running wild, she acts more like a boy than a girl, and with Pandora due to arrive, we need to calm things down a little, you know how crazy she can make dad?" Gailania smiled.

"Pan is fun, we do some amazing things together. She promised me fencing lessons, Aunt Jade is going to make me a sword like mums." Iona looked up, as more thumps announced the arrival of Tegan on the stairs.

"Finally, she is up, be careful, Pan is scary with that thing in her hands, get Uncle Rowan to show you how to block, before you go anywhere near her."

Much had changed at Robbie's Mere, over the eighteen years of Iona's life, the house had been rebuilt, and the years had passed by in peace. Robbie and Rune settled into a normal life, and soon more children arrived, in the form of Tegan Cornflower, Fern Bluebell, and Gailania Briar.

Rune doted on her five children, as across the way, Jade gave birth to Yvee, Frayne, Grover and Willow. Like their mother, they were a little wilder than the other children, and at times a bad influence on Rune's children. By far the worst was Pandora, who was the child of Rafe and Jett Amber. She was small with jet black hair, cut with a sharp fringe like her mothers, and had the brightest blue eyes. At only the age of seven, Pandora was fearless, and better with a sword than most of the teenagers in the area. Rafe had made her a toy sword of wood that looked like the Sword of Truth, he had even drawn on all the designs, but Pandora terrified everyone with it, and few would fence with her.

In truth, it was understandable, she had been trained by Jett, and so was wild and aggressive, as she danced and twirled, swiping her wooden blade round like a guillotine. Like her mother, she was also very loud, and wherever she went, chaos ensued. Rune adored her, and Robbie avoided her, he had settled into a life that was quieter than most, and the chaos that followed Pandora, often saw him remark on how it was the most apt name ever given to a child.

The final battle before the gates of Loxley, had worn on Robbie, and he had hung up the Sword of Destiny, and vowed never to fight with it again, and turned to a life of peace. He was a proud father, who emulated his own, and many over the years had commented on how like Robert Lox he had become, especially in his manner for handling the farm, and the estate.

William had ruled as a good king, but on occasion had visited the house at the mere to consult with Robbie, who avoided court at all costs. He was not a man of political ambition, and preferred the simple woodland life, he left the affairs of state to Skip and Bear, who were regular travellers to the newly rebuilt city in London.

The country had changed under the control of William, currency had been unified and roads had been cleared, and law and order restored. Although there was little need, as most men wanted peace after the years of punishment, they suffered under the stone city rule of Mason Knox. It was normal for Runestone to disappear for a few days at a time, as she visited other towns and villages to help out with problems, or visit Fagan and Opal, and when she did, Iona assumed command of the household.

Iona was almost eighteen, and soon she would be crowned the Queen of Fae of Earth. For most of her life, she had been instructed in the ways of the Fae by Sapphire, who regardless of the doubt she once held over her own abilities, had grown into a powerful seer and mystic. Sapphire had been helped by Gwendolyn, who had placed a lot of what she had been taught by her grandmother Bridget Violet into Sapphire's table, and it had guided her in not just her own abilities, but also Iona in hers.

Runestone spent a lot of time alone with Iona below the house at her table, where she would instruct her in the ways of the Violet Circle, the powers that had been created from the core of Nature, and so as Iona was prepared for her reign, she carried with her a lot of power and authority.

Her twin brother Halbert Thorn, spent a lot of time with his father or Rowan, and he shared his time, either running the farm or wandering the woodlands with Rowan, and helping out with their management. He was intelligent, and thoughtful, with a mild manner, but he also had an infectious humour and could at times be heard roaring with laughter, as he pulled pranks on Willow and Grover to exact his revenge.

The land around Loxley had grown, villages had been rebuilt and new farms established, and for many it had become a large centre for trade. The market expanded as some of the training field was removed and replaced with a large gravel area, and Loxley now boasted over one hundred market stalls filled to the brim, on market days.

*O*ut in front of the water's edge close to the Mere, there was a bright violet flash, and an archway appeared, Iona turned at the sink.

"Mum and dad are back."

The kitchen door swung open and Tegan staggered in, and yawned, her long knotted brown hair sticking out at all angles.

"Morning… What is for breakfast?" She flopped down with a

bump, into the seat and Gailania giggled. Iona shook her head and turned, and placed a bowl of steaming porridge down in front of her.

"You will not be able to lie in when I leave you know, it will be up to you to take care of things when mum is away." Tegan looked up, her pale blue eyes looked dull, and just stared at her older sister.

"I can take care of myself, I am six you know, I am not a baby anymore." Tegan's eyes moved to look at Gailania.

"Oh yeah, beat Pan with a sword and I will let you fend for yourself, until such time little weed, I will be in charge." Gailania frowned.

"That's not fair, Pan is really good, why can I not fight Thorn or Fern?" Iona gave a giggle.

"I admire your bravery little sis, but Fern is no slouch, she spends way too much time at Aunt Jade's place." The door swung open and Rune walked in and smiled, she hugged Iona and turned to see Gailania's bright dancing blue eyes, she smiled.

"How is my little SweetPea, have you been good for your sister?" Her bright little eyes danced as she nodded her head, Rune smiled and looked at Tegan, and gave a sigh.

"Another late night plotting, who is the victim this time?" Tegan gave a smirk, and then yawned.

"We aim to snare Pan." Gailania rolled her eyes.

"Not again, when will you learn, she spots stuff quicker than any of us, huh, you call me a weed, at least I am smart enough not to try, she is way too quick for us lot." Tegan smirked.

"Oh yeah, Aunt Jade showed us a new way, have faith little weed, we will get her for sure this time." Rune gave a giggle as she turned to Iona.

"When is Pan due to arrive?"

"Tomorrow, I think?" Rune gave a nod.

"Okay, keep it quiet for now, you know how stressed he gets knowing she is coming." Iona gave a chuckle.

"Mum, he is a war hero, and saviour of our people, how come he is afraid of a tiny little seven year old?" Rune gave a loud giggle.

"He loves her to bits really, but like her mother, she is just too loud for him. You know, last month when we were at the castle, she curled up in his lap and fell asleep, and he just sat there cuddling her and stroking her hair all night." Tegan gave a smile, and spooned her porridge into her mouth.

"He only likes her when she is asleep, that is the only time she is quiet." Rune turned back towards the door.

"Right Girls, I have to unpack and sort some things out, Iona remember, Ariel is coming later, she wants some time with you, and it is important. Tegan, you are on loom duty today, we have to finish that new saffron yellow cloth for Mrs Benson. I will be there soon, I am trying to get the blue for Megan finished, she is completely refitting the Cheese Shop out, and I need to get it done." She gave a sigh.

"Right, I need to sort our room out, and then I will be down in the weaving room."

She breezed through the door, and left them to finish their breakfast, Robbie was stood in the bedroom going through notes, when Rune arrived, she dropped her bag and walked over to him with a smile.

"That was a wonderful three days." She leaned in and kissed him, and he slipped his arms around her with a smile.

"It was nice to get away, I had forgotten how wonderful those pools are, I needed to rest a little." Rune raised her eye brows.

"That was resting? We should rest more." She giggled as she snuggled into him, and he held her tight for a minute, and gave a contented sigh. She looked up at him.

"Busy day?" He gave a nod.

"Yeah, we have problems with the plough again, and the solar is playing up, I need to see John and Katie, and get both of them working again, and then I have to meet with the Towns Guild, Rowan wants to go over things with me first, so I have to meet up an hour earlier." Rune gave a smile.

"Back to normal, still my lord, it was nice having you to myself for a while. Go on, go do your Lord Loxley thing, I have weaving to finish, and Ariel is due today, so I will see you later, maybe we can have an early night."

When it came to the running of the farm, little had changed over the years, things broke and needed to be repaired, fields needed to be attended to, as the circle of life and the planting seasons came and went, and every day, there was yet another list of things to be attended to.

The day was just starting in Florae when at the base of the steps there was a bright blue flash, and Sapphire walked out of her window, followed by Jessica Sapphire. Jessica was six months older than Iona, and had grown into a woman of great beauty. She walked with an air of authority behind Sapphire, as they hurried up the steps towards the doors to the House of Scribes, where inside the council was debating a very serious issue.

Two guards barred the doors as Sapphire approached, she was in no mood to be trifled with, she glared at the guards as she approached.

"Open the doors." They stood resolute; one of them gave a slight bow of his head.

"I am sorry Lady Sapphire, but I have the strictest orders to not admit anyone when the council is in session."

"The council is making a grave error, and I need admittance with important evidence, now stand aside, I have not the time to be waylaid."

Sapphire had grown in stature, her face carried an air of authority, and as teacher to the future queen, she carried a lot of weight in Florae. The guard was caught unsure of what to do, he had the strictest orders from Alder, head of the council, and yet Sapphire had the authority of the future queen. He looked at his comrade who shrugged, and clearly wanted nothing to do with it, he gave a sigh.

"If you could wait just a moment My Lady, I will have to consult with my officer in command of this watch." Sapphire gave a frustrated sigh.

"Never mind, I will do it." She lifted her hand, and it flashed blue, and the doors silently swung open, she smiled at the surprised guards, and pushed her way through.

*I*n the large chamber of the council, the twelve councillors sat looking stern, as Tila stood with her head bowed, her hands bound in bracelets, as she spoke with tears in her eyes.

"But my Lord's, I was assigned this task by the Mistress of the House herself, I work on the specific instruction of the Lady Ariel. It has been my task to transcribe both books as a dutiful Scribe." She looked up as her tears ran down her cheeks.

"I have done nothing wrong." Alder banged on his gavel.

"Ten of the twelve disagree, the works of Branna of Fae will remain sealed and locked away, we will not tolerate the tarnishing of the reputation of a glorious Queen of Fae Ofmoon. What you have written is lies." Tila gave a loud sob and shook her head, as the doors at the end of the room burst open.

"NONSENSE!" Alder looked up in anger.

"This is a sealed session, you have no right to be here Teacher, as we pass judgement."

Tila turned and gave a sigh of relief as Sapphire, with Jessica, walked down the hall towards the twelve sitting members. Elgin, who had relinquished his title of head of the council smiled next to Bade. Sapphire's eyes burned with anger.

"May I remind you Lord Alder, that I have the total authority of your future queen, it is I who instruct her highness Iona Violet of Loxley on the affairs of state, and I am sure that you are well aware, that through me, her wishes are carried out prior to her crowning."

He fumed in his seat, and his face began to turn red with his annoyance.

"It is true to express her wishes, but this is a session of the council to the Fae of Earth, and I may add for those of Fae descent. You may carry the future queens wishes, but I believe constitutionally you have no power in this chamber. This matter has been deliberated on and settled, and all we have to do now is pass sentence for the false transcribing of documents." Sapphire looked to Elgin, sat to her far left.

"My Lord Elgin, as the longest serving member of this body, can you tell this fool of my lineage, he has apparently forgotten I am of Fae. Tell me honestly, that the document you have read as transcribed by Lady Tilla of Florae, is false and a distortion of the true facts?" Elgin shuffled in his seat.

"My Lady Sapphire, as granddaughter of Queen Gwendolyn, you are of Fae and have a voice here. Having read the document, and also been privy to the private correspondence of letters between Lady Ariel and our beloved Queen Bridget Violet, I would say that the books translated by Lady Tila from the journals of Branna of Fae are quite correct and accurate." Sapphire looked to Alder.

"So, who is lying here Lord Alder, are you seriously suggesting Lord Elgin and Lady Tila are in league to supply false documents pertaining to Queen Rhiannon?"

Alder looked very uncomfortable, and shuffled in his seat. Sapphire stared at him, her eyes bright blue, awaiting his response, it was clearly not going to come, Sapphire moved to Tila's side.

"I am a regular visitor to Avalon my lords, I visit with both Queen Amethyst who is a close personal friend, and the Lady Ariel, who as you know, I was instrumental in her rescue. I have talked alone at great length to the Lady Ariel about her life within Avalon and Saxony, and knowing her as well as I do now, as I do consider her a good personal friend, I can assure you, that she does not lie, and her writings are the accurate portrayal of events at that time. Lady Tila is innocent, she was assigned the task of transcribing both books of Branna, by Lady Ariel herself, which I may add, is because she is the most competent scribe in this house. Are you all going to sit there and tell me that the most powerful mystic the Fae have ever seen is a liar who created false documents, do you really believe a daughter of Enaria would do that?" Alder banged hard on his gavel, as the members of the council looked uncomfortable.

"This session has been finalised, the chance for testimony to defend the lady Tila was two days ago, where were you then Lady Sapphire? New evidence cannot be admitted once the proceedings have concluded, the defendant has been found guilty as charged." He banged even harder on the gavel, as the rest of the council looked more uncomfortable.

Sapphire gave a long frustrated sigh and took Tila by the hand, Tila shook in her shoes, and placed her head down and started to weep again. Sapphire looked to Alder.

"This is a travesty of a council. Lord Alder you may guide the council for now, but trust me when I say, your compass is well and truly off course. This council is supposed to be guided towards the welfare of the people of Fae, not your political ambitions. Your future Queen will know of this within the day, and Lady Ariel of Florae within an hour of that, and I will be strongly advising Her Royal Highness, Princess Iona Violet, to remove you the second the crown touches her hair. This is not over yet." She turned to Tila, and lowered her voice.

"Hang in there, I will get Ariel and Iona here if I have to. You will be back in Crystal's arms soon." Tila gave a sniffle, Sapphire spun around and stormed out of the chamber, followed by the smiling Jessica, as Elgin gave a little titter and looked at Bade.

"She has grown into a beautiful and powerful woman, I did rather appreciate the compass reference, as it does signify more as pointing to Avalon, I found it very eloquent."

The anger in Alder's voice was evident as he cleared his throat, and banged his gavel.

"Lady Tila of Florae, you have been found guilty of the charge of falsifying documents and slander to the reputation of the Queen Rhiannon of Moon. You will be stripped of your role within this house, and banned from writing forthwith. You will be taken to the Isle of Ada, where you will serve out your sentence of fifty years, before you may present a plea to this body to be considered fit enough to be allowed back into the population."

The gavel banged hard, and Tila fell to the floor and wept uncontrollably, Bade clenched his hand on the arm of his seat, and Elgin leaned over and softly patted it, his voice was low as the others all left the seats and gathered together to retire for refreshments.

"Do not worry, she will not serve longer than a month."

*B*ade left his seat, and hurried over to the weeping figure of Tila, as the guards tried to lift her from the floor, he pushed them back, and knelt down and pulled her close. She flung herself on his shoulder as she wept, Bade patted her back and spoke softly to her.

"Be brave, I will have you back in the house and fully reinstated within the month, Ariel and Iona will vouch for you. Tila, you did nothing wrong, I will fix this, no scribe in my house will ever suffer the same fate as Ariel did, as long as I am the Master of the Scribes." She sobbed, her lips trembling, and tried to speak.

"I did nothing wrong; I followed her instruction to the letter." He patted her softly.

"I know you did, you are my finest scribe, which is why Ariel picked you. I will get her here Tila, trust me, I will not let you down."

She gave a nod as he released her, and the guards lifted her up onto her feet. He stood up and took out his handkerchief and wiped her eyes, he gave a soft smile.

"No more tears, we will fix this, and you will walk free." She gave a sniffle and swallowed hard, and gave a nod. With the guards, she was turned, and escorted out of the house.

*T*here was a blinding flash of pure brilliant white, and Rune shielded her eyes with a smile. The light went out, and Ariel walked slowly up the grass with a bag on her shoulder, and gave a big smile as she saw the house and Runestone stood waiting. Ariel came closer and

Rune pulled her into a hug.

"It is so wonderful to see you again, it has been too long." Ariel gave a smile.

"I know, but you know how things are, I start to write and time simply slips past. It is nice to be back here. I was admiring the house, Gwynfor is so talented, it has weathered in well, he will be very pleased to see how the timbers have seasoned." Together they walked up the path, and Iona came to the door and gave a curtsy to Ariel.

"Mistress of the House, I am really happy to see you again." Ariel chuckled

"Iona, you are to be the queen of my line, I should be the one to bow or curtsy." She shrugged.

"I am not a queen yet, and you are the Mistress of the House of Scribes." Rune gave a chuckle.

"Sapphire has educated her very well indeed."

They walked up to the door, where Furry Face sat watching, Ariel smiled as she walked in through the door, and scratched behind his ear, he gave a playful whine.

Ariel would be staying for a few days; Iona was approaching her eighteenth birthday and there was a lot to do. Robbie had arranged a special celebration meal at the Mere, and there was a large guest list, as for the first time in a long time, Rune and Robbie's family would come together to celebrate the birth of the twins, Iona and Halbert.

It was to be a grand birthday, in advance of the big day, as the closer it got, the more preparation Iona would have, and so on the day, which would be the day of her crowning, she would have to be in Florae.

Ariel would spend her time in Loxley and Florae, as she guided Iona through the final process, and liaised with Bade, and so she would be a guest at the Mere as would a few of the other members of the family. Back at Lox Farm, Jess had cleaned the guest rooms with the help of Katie and Todd, and then moved over to help clean the other house, John Lox was feeling very excited, as Alice would be home with little Michael, Jacques was staying in York, due to the affairs of state.

In the last five years, a few yards back from the kitchen door, on either side of the large food steamer built by Harry, Robbie had built two small wooden cabins, and on their sixteenth birthday, Iona and Halbert had been handed the keys to them, and moved out of the house into their own small places. With Iona leaving for Florae, it was a hot topic with Tegan, as to whether or not Robbie would let her move in, as she was almost fifteen years old. Iona for now had made it clear that she would be returning home for periods to stay, but Tegan kept up the pressure, she wanted her own place, and some privacy from Fern and Gailania.

The three girls had always shared one room, due to the fact that for a long time, Iona had used the nursery, and Halbert had used the spare front bedroom, as Isolde had one of the larger guest rooms. After the birth of Gailania, who spent her first few years in the nursery, which was the smallest upstairs room, Iona asked if she could swap, so she could have some privacy as she started to have dreams and visions, and at first, they frightened her. It had made better sense to keep all the young girls together, and allow Iona the space, and it also made Robbie think about the future of his daughter and son.

He sat with Rune for a long time, and over the weeks and months, they began the process of preparing for Iona's powers to come, which resulted in Robbie suggesting they build the two cabins. When Iona moved out of her room, Isolde requested the small space, as she no longer had her sister with her, and felt she needed less room, and so the nursery became staff quarters, which provided more space for guests.

It had been the same around Loxley, Jay moved from the farm into the cheese shop with her sister, Katie moved from Harry and Magg's house into John's farm house guest room, when Alice moved to York, and Michelle moved out of the post office, into Judith's book shop, when she married Bobby, leaving Lucy in the small flat behind the post office. When John Styles married Jane, and had a son, Jess gave them Harry's old house, as he had become her most reliable farm hand, and supervisor on the farm. Louisa and Doc took over David William's house when they arrived back in Loxley after travelling for over ten years, and Doc took up a post in the hospital next to the barracks, and Louisa continued as a Commander within the ranks of the woodsman army, although these days, they were much smaller, and just handled security of the stockade.

That night, the family sat down for a meal in the main living room at the big table, and Ariel and Runestone did most of the cooking. They sat and discussed the coming crowning, and Ariel went over the ceremony. It had been almost a year since she had been back to Florae, and she was quite looking forward to it, as she talked of the realm and how much it had changed. Rune sat smiling as she listened, as she remembered the day of finding Ariel sealed in a box of crystal, and it was strange in a way, because when Ariel had left to meet Branna, Bridget had been on the throne, and eighteen years ago, when she had finally been set free, Bridget had passed on, and Gwendolyn had reigned for a thousand years.

For Ariel, her sleep had simply felt like a long night's sleep, she remembered nothing of that time and did not age at all, and yet the world she had come back to was completely different. Runestone more than most understood Ariel's story and her feelings. Rune could feel the sadness and loss inside Ariel, although she never asked about it, after all, she had played a big role in Branna's downfall.

*T*he children finished their meal, and excused themselves, and Rune began to clear the table. Ariel joined her in the kitchen, they talked of day to day things for a while, as Rune washed up, when Rune turned and looked at her, as she lifted the plates to dry them.

"How is Ena, I have not seen her for some time now?" Ariel smiled.

"She is good, actually, really happy, she and Max have done a lot of moving around, they came and stayed for a few months earlier in the year." Rune gave a nod, enjoying seeing the smile on Ariel's face.

"I am pleased to hear that, I will not deny, it worries me at times to think of you living there all alone with just your memories. I am happy to see you and Ena have each other." Ariel smirked.

"I am fine Rune, I know it is odd to many, but being there, helps me to cope better. Bade often lectures me on how unhealthy it is, but it is not really. I have my memories, I know she is gone, and she will not come back, but being there, in our home, and spending some time remembering brings me comfort. In many ways it helps me remember the love we shared, and I realise I did not lose it. I still have her love in my heart, and it makes a huge difference." Rune gave a guilty smile.

"I have often thought about it, and often wondered if there could have been another way."

"There wasn't, and both of us knew it. Runestone, I know what you feel, I sense it, but don't." Rune turned, and her bright blue eyes shone with sadness.

"If I did it again, I would think it out more, and try to do things differently." Ariel shook her head and smiled.

"How? Runestone, she fought it for years to try and suppress it, but it was too strong, the way I see it, she is free, and that was her dream. She knew she had made an error, and she spent all that time looking to correct it, but the simple truth was, she could not. She is free now, and that is all that matters." Rune gave a sigh.

"What about Ursula, has Ena found her yet?" Ariel gave a smile, and her eyes twinkled.

"No… She wears the veil to hide, but she too is free and living somewhere happily, and that again matters. The influence of Morgana has gone, although in a strange way, Morgana protected her and kept her safe. I think of it often, she could have corrupted her and attached her to a raven, but rather than do that, Morgana educated her to a very high standard. Ursula is doing well; she will not be found easily." Rune stared at her, and gave her a shrewd look.

"Do you know something you are not telling me?" Ariel winked.

"I have my mother's powers, not many can hide from me. Ursula for now is better left in peace, it is the best thing for everyone, including Ena. Ena has found happiness, and I want her to enjoy it." Rune understood, and put another plate in the sink to wash it.

"I will say nothing, I think you are right. It has taken a long time to recover from that awful war, too many good lives were lost, it is actually a relief to finally see it has faded from the memories of most of the people around here. Loxley took a long time to heal, I am glad it is over and my children have been raised in peace."

The door opened and Iona walked in, and pointed behind her with a thumb.

"Mum, Sapphire is here, and she is really angry, you are needed." Rune put the plate down, and lifted a cloth to dry her hands, as Ariel gave a shrug, and then followed Rune out and into the living room.

Sapphire was pacing in the living room waiting, she looked up as Rune and Ariel walked out of the kitchen.

"YOU WILL NOT BELIEVE WHAT THAT BLOODY IDIOT ALDER HAS DONE NOW!?"

Rune chuckled, some things never change, and Sapphire's particular dislike for Councilman Alder was one of them. They all gathered in the living room, and sat down, and Sapphire told them of what had happened to Tila. Ariel was outraged, as she got up and paced up and down, she turned and looked right at Iona.

"My Queen, have I your consent to rescind their ruling?" Iona looked surprised, and floundered a little.

"I am not yet queen, I do not know if I have the authority." Sapphire gave a cheeky grin at Rune.

"It matters not, once you are queen you can make a new rule and back date it. I believe Gwendolyn did the same thing, and I know for a fact reading the events of that time, she made rulings during the month between the passing of Bridget, and her crowning, I am sure Bade and Elgin would clarify that." Iona gave a nod.

"Then as future Queen of Fae, I grant you the permission to rescind this unjust ruling of the council, on the grounds that Tila was following the explicit directions of the Mistress of the House… Is that right, I did get everything correct, didn't I?" Ariel smiled.

"Your Royal Highness, I do believe your first ruling was eloquent and quite correct." Iona gave a huge smile, and Rune and Sapphire giggled. Rune gave a happy little chuckle.

"Okay, I think we need to present an image of power and authority, which can only mean one thing. Best clothes!"

Robbie came to the top of the stairs and was starting to move to the top step, when he heard Rune. Just the mention of best clothes was enough, he turned sharply, and hurried away back to the bedroom, just in case it involved him. Plans were made quickly, and Sapphire gave Iona a quick refresher lesson in the constitutional principles of Florae.

It was decided that a meeting was in order, and a show of force be made, and it was agreed, that the four of them would go straight away. Rune headed upstairs to change clothes and grab a few things, she walked into the bedroom, where Robbie looked up nervously, she gave a giggle as she saw him.

"You are safe, it is for us girls, you can remain tatty and smelly." He looked offended as he sat in his chair near the large glass doors to the balcony.

"I am not tatty or smelly." She gave another giggle, as she walked over to him in his seat, and poked a finger through the hole in his top, he looked down.

"Well yeah, I mean, that was an accident whilst teaching Fern to shoot, it was on the washing line, and her arrow went right through, apart from that, it is not tatty." She stroked his frayed collar and raised her eye brows. Rune grabbed some things and headed for the door, he got up and followed her out.

"There is nothing wrong with it, I find it comfy, I like it, good tops are hard to come by." The girls trooped up the stairs as Robbie stood and watched, Iona walked past and looked back.

"Actually Dad, you do pong a little bit, and let mum darn that will you?" He gasped, as she giggled, and he looked down and sniffed his shirt.

"It's not that bad." Rune walked along the landing.

"Tatty and smelly!" They all laughed, as Robbie raised his arm and sniffed, and then coughed.

After a quick sort through Rune's vast closet, and Sapphire jumped to her home to grab things and back, all of them stood looking at each other dressed in some very fine clothes. Iona was dressed in royal violet, and was secretly thrilled as she had been after the top and skirt for a while. Rune pulled her violet cloak with the golden tree emblem around Iona's shoulders, and stood back with a beaming smile.

"Wow, welcome to Loxley, Iona, Queen of the Fae."

Iona turned and looked at herself in the full length mirror, her cheeks reddened a bit as she saw them all looking at her, and felt a twinge of embarrassment. Stood there in all violet, she took a breath as she saw herself for the first time dressed in the robes of her mother, who was actually the Lady of the Woodland Realm, it was a strange feeling that rose within her. Ariel watched her with a smile, and lifted a finger to her crest on her robe.

"You truly look like the queen I expect you to be, but you need one more thing I feel."

Ariel placed her finger above the tree of gold embroidered on to her cloak, and slowly drew a circle, Iona looked down and gasped with awe, as twelve stars of gold appeared and encircled the tree. Ariel pulled her finger away and stepped back to view Iona. She gave a gentle nod, and then went down on one knee.

"My Queen, I swear here and now, my allegiance to you always, and will serve you to the best of my ability." Iona did not know what to say, as Ariel looked up and smiled.

"You hold the authority of Bridget, someone who was very dear to me, your rule will be long and fair handed, and My Queen, it starts today." Iona gave a nod and took a deep breath.

"I am terrified." Sapphire linked her arm.

"Good, you should be." Rune giggled.

"Okay, it is time, come on my daughter, in a month all of this will be for real. Remember what we have told you, and do not back down, it is time to make your mark, and show everyone you are ready for this."

Iona nodded looking absolutely petrified, Fern, Tegan and Gailania, peeped around the bedroom door frame, and all giggled.

Chapter Four.

The Mark of a Queen.

It was evening in Loxley, but still mid afternoon in Florae. The council had retired to their assembly room to relax after their deliberation, and the passing of sentence. They ate fine foods and drank wine, as they congratulated each other, and Alder swelled with pride, as they all gathered around him to congratulate him.

The doors opened and everyone stopped and turned, to see Sapphire and Ariel stood side by side, Alder gave a sigh and rolled his eyes.

"Lady Sapphire, not this again, may I remind you that this chamber is for members of the council only. If you have such an interest, may I suggest you apply, and until such time as you are accepted, stay out of this chamber." Ariel walked forward.

"Does that apply to the Mistress of the House as well Councilman Alder?" He smirked.

"Actually, it does, no one apart from members of the council can enter." Ariel frowned.

"Then what about a queen?" He gave a frustrated sigh.

"Lady Ariel, as I have stated very clearly, a defence was entitled to be given two days ago, and no one came forward, and so the trial was conducted. A majority decision was made, and I am sorry if you disagree with it. The decision is binding and cannot be revoked no matter what title you wish to use, the rule of the council is supreme." Ariel and Sapphire parted as Iona walked into the room beside her mother. Iona looked at Alder, and took a breath.

"I admit, I have much to learn still, but I am certain that a queen in waiting is allowed to overrule the council and set precedent, as I believe was done by the last queen, Gwendolyn White Circle. Master Elgin, would you care to confirm that for me please?"

*T*he room fell instantly silent as everyone apart from Alder bowed to Iona, Alder simply stood and stared at her with disbelief, Elgin gave a smirk and stepped forward.

"Your Royal Highness, I believe you are quite correct, if you would care to follow me, I will escort you to the royal apartments, where we may speak, and you can make your views known." Iona stood fast.

"That is very kind of you Master Elgin, but I believe I address my council, and so I feel here is quite acceptable." She looked at Alder, who had finally bowed to her.

"I wish it be known, that Scribe Tila, was given direct instruction by the Mistress of the House, so, if as you alleged, the work is lies, then may I suggest you place the Mistress of the House on the stand, and bring charges against her? I believe that would be fitting, especially considering she is the author, and it is her code that Lady Tila is transcribing." Iona turned to Bade.

"Master of the House, Lord Bade, please send word that I wish Tila of Florae to be brought to me in the royal apartments as soon as possible. Lord Elgin, I would be delighted if you would accompany me to the royal apartments, as the longest serving member of this house, I would have a care to talk with you."

Iona turned, and walked out through the doors; Ariel turned away smiling as Sapphire winked at Rune. The party moved swiftly down the corridor, as Bade rushed out behind them, and ran to the main hall to instruct the guards. Iona looked at her mother nervously.

"Was that alright?" Rune linked her arm.

"It was wonderful and word perfect, exactly as we instructed. Sweetheart, you must not worry, in time it will come naturally to you." Iona gave a sigh.

"Was it like this for you, I was terrified, and my legs were shaking?" Rune squeezed her arm.

"I remember the first time I addressed all of Loxley at the Beltane fair, I was so terrified, your dad stood behind me and rubbed my bum to relax me, and his mum slapped his hand, it was hard not to laugh. You will get used to it a little bit; I still find it daunting at times." Iona gave a nod and relaxed.

"I will not deny, it did feel a little fun." Ariel leaned in.

"Did you see his face?" Rune giggled with Iona, as Sapphire walked behind them.

"He is a pompous git, it is about time someone shrank his ego, I will never understand why Elgin stepped down, he was a first rate leader of the council."

They arrived at the royal apartments, where Master Elgin stood with the doors open, and gave a regal bow as they entered, Iona walked in and looked around.

"Wow, is this where I will live?" Elgin gave a smile.

"It is your highness, all of your rooms are connected to this one, so you may entertain, and hold meetings at your convenience. I do believe that Queen Bridget particularly liked this room, all of the décor was of her design, and Queen Gwendolyn liked it so much, she chose not to restyle it, but once queen, you will have a free hand to change anything you wish."

Iona loosened her cloak, and from nowhere a maid appeared to assist her, Iona gave a small startled jump as the maid lifted it off her shoulders, and withdrew with a bow. It felt strange, but she smiled and gave a nod back, and then seated herself. All the others took seats around her.

A door opened and an army of staff walked in with trays, and offered drinks and freshly baked cakes, Elgin smiled.

"You did catch us somewhat unawares, but we have things in hand, and diverted things from the council chamber here." Iona gave a chuckle, and patted the seat like she has done for her father a thousand times.

"Lord Elgin, please come sit with me and talk, I will need a lot of advice, and would wish you to be my advisor, would that be alright?" He sat down and gave a nod of appreciation.

"Your Highness, your principal advisor is usually the head of the council, which would be Lord Alder." She understood.

"Well, he will have to go then, I cannot take advice from a man who cannot clearly see the truth of the facts, I will need someone much more reliable. I am afraid Lord Elgin, you will have to take back your seat for a little while, until I can get to know everyone." Rune was quite enjoying herself, as she sat with Ariel.

"Is it always this much fun in Florae?"

*I*t took over half an hour to locate Tila, and transport her to the royal apartments of Iona. She walked in looking dirty, and scruffy, and went down on her knees before her future queen. Iona looked shocked, and turned to Elgin.

"What sentence was she given to end up looking like this?" Elgin looked at Tila, who had red eyes, and lowered her face to the floor.

"Tila was sentenced to hard labour, on the isle of Ada, it is basically one big rock pile. Those sentenced pick up all the lose stones and carry them to barges so that they can be used elsewhere. We do not dig, we just clear the surface of everything that is lose, and then use those for our stonework." Iona understood, and turned to Tila.

"Show me your hands." Tila lifted up her hands that were cut and scratched, Iona appeared angered.

"How can you write with hands like that?" Tila looked at the floor.

"My Queen. I am banned from all writing; it no longer matters." Her tears dripped onto the carpet; Iona shook her head.

"This cannot continue, I want no subjects of this realm to suffer such things, there must be better ways to deal with those who break the rules." She looked to Ariel.

"Her hands must be healed, she has important work to do, would you assist her?" She turned to Tila.

"Lift up your head, and look at me, I am a woman like any other." Tila shook her head.

"I am convicted of a crime; it is forbidden your Highness." Iona gave a sigh.

"As your future queen, I demand it, you have seen my face before, you held me as a small baby." Tila lifted her head, and looked at Iona with surprise.

"You remember that?" Iona smiled.

"I do, I have a memory for all things in my life, and I remember the oath you swore to me that day, do you still stand by it?" Tila held her hand to her heart.

"I do, I swore it and I meant it, and I have lived by it, and always worked hard to ensure the future of this realm for your rule, your Highness." Iona gave a nod.

"Then I rescind the sentence placed upon you, and offer you a full pardon, as I believe you were wrongly convicted, and did indeed write an honest account of the words written by Ariel, Mistress of the House of Scribes. You are to heal your hands and return to full duties, and please, accept my apology for the short-sightedness of my council."

Tila looked shocked, and stammered for words, as she rested on her knees before Iona.

"My Queen, you must not apologise, this was not your doing." Iona gave a nod.

"Nevertheless, as the future queen of this realm, I am ultimately the one responsible for everything within the realm, and it is not something I take lightly. Go with peace in your heart Tila of Florae, and live your life."

Tila rose to her feet and gave a regal bow, and walked backwards towards the door, and then slipped through, and ran down the corridor towards the doors. Ariel smiled at Iona and stood up.

"We are here now, I might as well give you the tour, after all, you will need to understand the workings of the house."

Rune gave a smile as she watched Iona stand, and at the side of Ariel, she walked down the corridor towards the house. Bade panicked and ran ahead of them to ensure all was well. Rune sat back and looked at Elgin.

"They will be some time I feel, may we sit and talk of what is expected of the family of the future queen during her crowning?" He gave a broad smile, and slid along the long seat towards her.

"I do believe that would be in order… Now, where do I start… Oh, yes, the crowning ceremony."

It was late when they returned to Loxley, Robbie was already in bed. Iona sat up talking with Ariel and Sapphire, who had decided to stay for the night, and Rune quietly slipped into bed, and snuggled into Robbie.

It was very early, and the sun was up, as the heat of summer moved into Loxley, Robbie lay fast asleep with the slender frame of Rune curled around him.

"LANIA… LANIA, WHERE ARE YOU?" Thump… Thump… Thump!

Robbie sat bolt upright in bed, and blinked, as he looked around the room, and the sound of thumping on the stairs reverberated around the house. Rune opened her eyes, and smiled up at him. He glanced down at her.

"Oh god, she is back, isn't she?" Rune giggled.

"Robbie, she misses everyone, so does Jett, they are here for a few days, and she wants to see the girls." He gave a long tired sigh.

"First it was her mother, and now it is her, I am destined never to have peace."

Happy screams echoed from the bedrooms, and then several pairs of feet pounded quickly down the hallway with wild screams, and thundered down the stairs, Robbie flopped back in his pillows.

"When those screams echo into the distance, I am making a run for the office and locking the door, just slip food under it, I will be fine." Rune giggled, and she rolled over to him and snuggled onto his chest.

"You do not mean it, I saw you at the castle, you think she is as adorable as I do." His eyes moved down to her bright blue ones looking up at him.

"Yes, I do, when she is unconscious." Rune gave a giggle, and sat up shaking her head.

"I will bring you coffee, you can drink it here and enjoy the peace for a little while longer." He gave a nod and breathed out a sigh of relief. Rune pulled on her robe and walked to the door, outside a familiar voice shouted out.

"HEY JADE… OVER HERE!" Robbie gave another long sigh.

"First the child, and now the mother, today is just getting louder by the minute."

Rune came down the stairs laughing to herself, as Jett and Jade came talking up the steps, and in through the door, Rune walked over and pulled Jett into her arms and gave her a huge hug.

"Jett, it is so lovely to see you."

She stepped back and took a good look at her, she was looking good, all of them had aged, and yet even at thirty eight years old, Jett still had that sparkle of a teenager, although, these days she carried a much greater air of authority about her.

As always, Jett wore all black, like her mother she wore tight fitting satin pants, and her usual long golden spiked boots, her tops these days were slightly different, she had taken to wearing a double breasted thin padded jacket with a high neck collar, that was edged with deep red piping, and had an almost military appearance to it. Her cloak was long, almost reaching the floor, and black, but the most notable difference was on the cloak, over her left arm, there was a large red lion on a golden five pointed star.

Her hair was longer with the long straight cut fringe, and she carried herself as a queen of power would, her golden sword of truth, hung on her hip, and just a snatch away from defence.

Jade never really changed, she still wore her boots and the green of a woodsman, but she had more of a look of maturity about her, her eyes spoke volumes, as they twinkled with bright green devilish delight. The only real change to Jade over the years, was her hair had grown past her waist, and fell down her back in a long shaggy mane of gold, and so most days, she would tie it back, into a thick wide bushy ponytail.

The three of them, were the most powerful women in the realm of men, and yet you would not think so to see them, as they laughed and giggled in the kitchen over drinks. Rune took Robbie his coffee, and returned to join in with the chat, which was as always, loud. Robbie sat quietly and drank his coffee as he came to life, but sadly one cup was not enough, so with a sigh, he slipped out of bed, and pulled on his pants and a shirt.

Walking bare foot with his shirt open, he made his way to the stairs, as he turned to head down, the back hallway door burst open, and the group of wild feral children came racing inside giggling and laughing. Fern led the way, and quickly grabbed the handle to the weaving room door, Robbie looked over the rail.

"What are you up to?"

Fern looked up and turned white, as the group bumped into each other, and Robbie stared down at all of them stood looking panicked. Willow looked up with bright green eyes from under her long blonde fringe, she was the double of her mother, as her face went as white as Ferns. Gailania hid her face in the back of Grover as he watched Robbie and swallowed hard, his grey eyes fixed on him, as he walked slowly down the steps, Pandora stood with a huge smile, and her bright blue eyes twinkled.

"UNCLE ROBBIE!"

She ran to the bottom of the stairs as he came around the post, and threw her arms around his waist, he looked down as she looked up at him.

"I missed you most, Uncle Robbie." His eyes narrowed, she was cute there was no doubt, but she was a combination of Jett and Rafe, and so he had learned to be cautious around her.

*T*he back door burst open and Yvee stood dripping in the doorway, her long blonde hair hung lank and dripping. Her eyes burned bright green with her anger and the group slowly stepped back, and took three paces closer to Robbie. Pandora let go of Robbie, and spun on her heels as the group came closer. Yvee took two paces into the house, her long skirt and top dripping on the polished floor.

"WHICH ONE OF YOU WOODLAND RATS DID IT?"

They all nervously swallowed hard as Robbie watched on, Yvee was scary. Pan pushed her way through, and pulled out her wooden sword, and stood proud in front of the group, in a stance of defence.

"I won't let you hurt them cousin." Robbie smirked, wow, she was cute and seriously brave. Yvee stared at Pandora with hate.

"It was you, little fungus, wasn't it, I know it, because there is no way they would be brave enough to face me alone, tell me Pandora Bedivere Rafe, was it you?"

Pandora stared at her with her fixed blue eyes from under her long fringe, a look of pure determination in her eyes, as Yvee took another dripping step forward. Robbie watched enjoying the spectacle and actually admiring Pandora a great deal more. She was so like her mother, even at seven years old, she had some stamina. He knew the powers that Yvee had, and even he was not in a rush to face her angry.

"What on earth is going on?" Rune appeared followed by Jett and Jade, who smirked as she saw her eldest daughter, Yvee looked at the three women.

"Those little Marsh Hounds rigged the door to the stable again, and look what they have done, it took me ages to do myself up for Kale."

Fern nudged Grover and sniggered, Gailania gave a giggle. It was common knowledge that Rowan was not a fan of Kale, and often referred to him as that 'wilted lettuce in the village,' much to the amusement of everyone. Pandora looked back at Willow and sniggered, Rune gave a sigh and looked at the children.

"Alright, which one of you came up with it?" They all put their heads down, except Pandora, she looked at Rune.

"We are woodsmen, we do not split." Rune gave a sigh as she looked at them all with their heads down, she lifted her arm and pointed.

"You leave me no choice then… All of you, my table, now!"

Gailania looked up from behind Grover looking absolutely terrified, and shook her head, as did all of them. Rune reached for the star symbol on the frame and placed her hand on it, and the door clicked open, Fern turned to her mum, looking panicked.

"Please mum, I did it." Rune stared at her and smiled.

"Really, Fern Bluebell, are you telling the truth or covering for your friends?"

She looked at the others, Grover shook his head, she looked at her mum, and was about to speak as Rune gave her that look, the one all parents had, that looked into her soul. Rune gave a nod knowing she was covering for all of them, and lifted her hand and pointed to the door.

"Table… Now!"

All of them jumped on the spot, and then with their heads down and looking terrified, they walked slowly and quietly through the door. Robbie gave a smile at Jett, she came over and slipped her arm around his waist, and half hugged him.

"It was Pan, trust me, I know her, Rafe showed it her last week and she drenched the cook." Jade giggled.

"What, no ants?" Jett smirked.

"Rafe is still angry with me for that, I mean, hell, it was a year ago, you would think he would be over it by now."

They sniggered, as they followed Rune down to her table, it gave a pulse as she entered and the lights came on, and the group of children all white faced, looked terrified as the bright violet twenty pointed star rose to the cool white surface.

Rune stood all the children in a line, and then went to her seat, she sat down and ran her fingers across the surface of the table, it sparked, and the children jumped back afraid. Rune looked up as her eyes went purple, and Fern swallowed and looked at Pan.

"We are done for, we are busted." Pan nodded rapidly, for the first time actually looking afraid. Rune pointed as her eyes blazed.

"Hands… Table… Now, and know if you lie, it will know, and the consequences will be dire."

Gailania's eyes filled with tears, Grover and Willow stepped back looking absolutely terrified, Jade tried to hide her amusement, as she looked at her children, and pointed. They looked terrified and shook their heads, Willow's eyes filled with tears.

Pan looked at the others, lifted her hand and placed it on the table, it stuck, she swallowed hard, and took a deep breath.

"I… Pandora Bedivere Rafe, future Queen of Caerleon, do solemnly swear that it was my idea to throw water on whoever walked through the door. I asked the others for help, and they did so, but I am the one to blame, please don't kill me table, I am sorry." Jett smiled.

"You deserve a punishment, it is up to the table, it is death or mucking out the stables, let the table choose your fate"

Jade gave a giggle as all the others gave a sigh of relief, but watched nervously as Rune swept her hand across the table, and an image of the stable rose up out if it, and there was a large steaming pile of muck. Pandora shuddered.

"I think death would have been easier." Robbie gave a snort, Yvee watched on with a smug look.

"Willow, for your part in this, you will wash and iron my clothes, and you young Grover, you can clean the workshop floor." Jade gave a nod.

"You heard her, go with her." They put down their heads.

"Yes Mum." Jade gave a nod as they followed Yvee up the steps to their fate, Pandora's hand came free, and she looked at the other two, her voice was quiet.

"I have got to go and clean the stable at home, I will see you soon." With her head down she walked up the stairs, Rune's eyes faded back to normal as she looked at her children.

"You two, go and sweep out all the bedrooms, and then there are veg to wash for tonight's meals." Gailania gave a sniffle, and wiped her eyes, and nodded, Fern gave a sigh.

"Yes Mum." With their heads down they headed up the steps, and Jett gave a smirk.

"Little Lania is adorable, honestly I just wanted to hug and protect her." Jade gave a giggle.

"Pan is a brave little bugger, wow, for her age, she has guts." All of them gave a giggle, and Rune stood up.

"Come on, we have a few hours of peace, let's use them wisely, let's go and have coffee."

*O*utside the stockade, in the clearing where Hearne's Rock once stood, was a large clear space of white flat stone. Iona sat in the centre as Sapphire and Ariel looked on, Ariel gave directions, as Iona sat with her eyes closed focusing her mind.

"Iona, you have the gifts of Gwendolyn within you, as she was the one to place them inside your mother for you to inherit, but you are also, a descendant of Eve, and so therefore you are also a power within the green circle. I am not sure, but as of yet, I feel you do not have the ability to transform, that may come with your crowning, but just in case, I want you to picture a window in your mind. Focus on it, as if it is there and you are waiting to walk through it."

Iona concentrated as hard as she could, but then stopped and opened her eyes.

"What does it look like, I know my mum's is a violet arch, and Saff has a blue orb, but what will mine look like?" Ariel gave a smile.

"What would you like it to be? Iona it will be your window, so choose it, just picture it in your mind and focus on it."

Iona gave a nod and closed her eyes. Sapphire watched with great interest, she remembered her time learning with Rune out on the Mere, and was curious as to what Iona would pick.

As they watched, in front of Iona, twelve golden stars appeared, and circled around each other. They were faint at first as they hung in the air, and then the lower ones moved to form the outline of an arch. Ariel smiled, and spoke softly.

"Hold it in your mind, focus on it and nothing else."

Iona's brow furrowed a little, and suddenly the archway filled in, and exploded with bright golden light, and Sapphire held her hand up to cover her eyes.

"Hell, that is bright." Iona opened her eyes and gave a gasp as she saw the golden glimmering arch in front of her, she stood up and looked astounded.

"Did I do that?" Ariel gave a chuckle.

"You did indeed, now look at it and concentrate, you can make it dimmer with your thoughts. There will be times when it will be prudent not to announce your arrival, so focus on it, and fade it so it is not as obvious." Iona took a breath and swallowed, she closed her eyes and tried to hold the picture of the archway before her in her mind. Sapphire looked at Ariel.

"I did not know it could be faded, hell, for years mine has been spotted, and got me into tons of trouble." Ariel smirked.

"Rune is a good teacher, but some aspects of Fae of Earth are known only to us." Iona focused on the bright golden arch in her mind, and as Ariel and Sapphire watched, it began to fade, until it was almost invisible.

Iona gave out a breath, and opened her eyes, and there before her, the archway hung in the air in front of her. It was almost transparent, and had just a slight ripple in the air with a golden hue. She smiled at Ariel and Sapphire.

"I have always wanted to do that, so, where does it go to?" Ariel gave a slight chuckle, and shook her head.

"Nowhere just yet, you now have to focus on it, and picture the place you want to be." Iona gave a nod and closed her eyes, she thought for a moment, and then smiled.

"I want to show mum." The air gave a ripple.

Jett was laughing loud, sat back on the chair in the living room, as Jade gave a giggle. Rune shook her head.

"Poor Harry, he had such a hard time with you two. You know he had spent weeks fishing in the Mere trying to catch a fish, and when he finally landed one, which I will add is the biggest fish I have ever seen come out of that water, he was so happy." Jade giggled and did the voice again.

"Hey Harry, you ain't too cosmic at the moment, I aint for eating, I am the king of the fish, your Karma will be chomped if you eat me." Rune giggled as Jett laughed so hard, she fell off her chair, she pointed at Jade and just roared with laughter. Rune shook her head.

"The poor man, he never had a chance with you two, you know he threw it back, and never ate fish again after that. I cooked a huge salmon one Yule, and he burst into tears and ran out of the house yelling at the Mere it was not him, it was all my fault. I think you scarred him for life." Jett wiped her eyes sat on the floor, and gave a sniffle.

"I miss him, I really loved him you know? He always had my back in a fight, I always knew you know, if anyone came at me, he would take them off me and I never worried, not once." Jade gave a sad smile.

"Yeah, he was special, really special, I really loved him." Rune gave a smile.

"He loved all of us, he was loyal, and he cared for us in ways I think no one will ever understand. My Dad has missed him a lot, I think that is why my mum rides with him, I think she understands how he misses the roar of a second motorcycle at his side."

Rune felt a strange sensation and smiled, she saw the twelve stars appear in the air behind the long seat, and then it gave a little ripple, and formed into an archway, Iona's head came out.

"BOO!"

Jett was up on her feet like lightening, and pulled out the sword of truth, she spun on her heels as a bright violet sword rose in the air, as Jett swung, and there was a resounding clash, as Jade jumped out of her skin with a shriek.

Jett stood looking down her blade at the violet sword, her eyes wide with amazement, she slowly leaned forward and looked, as she recognised Iona.

"Whoa girl, that is a nice blade, where the hell did you get that from?"

Iona stood staring at her hand holding a beautifully crafted sword of violet looking crystal, she shook her head as her eyes moved to Jett.

"I don't know Aunt Jett, I just thought I need to protect myself, and there it was." Ariel came walking through the archway, and looked at everyone, as Sapphire came through.

"She is Violet Stone, marked by the lord Hearne himself, that crystal around her neck is far more than just a jewel, it is a protection of great power." Jett gasped.

"Oh man, I have got to get me an onyx one of them." Jade nodded her bright green eyes twinkling with delight.

"Yeah, Me too, I want a green one."

Chapter Five.

Iona's Gift to Ariel.

*T*he following day, Rowan headed out on horseback with Halbert, to supervise a new area of planting. Timber was a growing commodity as new towns and small settlements were built, and Loxley had a lot at its disposal. As areas were cleared, they were replanted with new young trees, that were grown in a new tree nursery area near the village of Hope.

With Rowan busy, Robbie headed to the village, to meet with Peter Fairfax, who was the village representative from the newly established settlement near Bamford. Rune was busy on her loom with Tegan, Fern, and Gailania were hanging out with Isolde, doing homework from the school. The house was quiet, apart from the gentle rumbles that came from the sleeping Furry Face, as he lay across the door keeping guard.

*I*ona was walking on the moors with Ariel, up near the old stone circle. Iona took a deep breath, and glanced at Ariel.

"What is it like to live completely alone, I have often wondered as I have been surrounded by people all my life?" Ariel smiled at her.

"When you are surrounded by those you love, isolation is but a dream, the reality is not as wonderful, and yet it is at the same time, if you can understand that." Iona stopped and turned to her, her violet eyes were bright and filled with life.

"If I intrude, say so, but the truth is I have known you for most of my life, and you have always been alone, as has Sapphire. I know your story Ariel, and I understand why you live there, but would it not be easier to just go back to Florae and be surrounded by your own people?" It made sense to Ariel, she could see how Iona would think that, she looked into Iona's enquiring eyes.

"If I am honest, very few can understand why I have chosen to live my life as I do. The simple truth is that there are days when something triggers a memory with me, and it is such a happy one, I am glad to be alone and not have to share it." Iona gave a gentle nod, as the wind blew through her hair.

"What about the bad days, I feel them in you at times and it saddens me?" Ariel shrugged.

"Who wants company when they hurt so bad, I for one don't?" Again, it made sense.

"Are the memories still so strong, that they would do that to you?" Ariel started to walk again.

"One day Iona, you will find a love that is so strong, and so pure, it will completely captivate your life in every way, and if you lose it, only then will you understand its true power over you. I realise it may sound strange, but even in the painful memories of those blissful moments, there is a reminder of the wonder of its power, and so even in that, there is some joy. I think to still be able to feel as deeply after all the time that has passed, is in itself a reassurance, that it was right to feel that love in the first place. Memories no matter how good or bad, are a reminder that life was being lived to its fullest, and it is a good thing to understand that, and I may add, understand yourself."

Iona began to walk as she thought about what Ariel had said, in a way it did make sense to her, she considered it very carefully. Iona looked up and watched Ariel just ahead of her.

"So, if I understand what you are saying, then by looking back, you have gained the insight to understand your life and yourself, and from that you have learned great wisdom?" Ariel stopped and smiled.

"Yes, being alone gives me the space to really understand my life. Iona, none of us are perfect, we all make mistakes and errors of judgement in the heat of a moment, to be able to fully understand that, helps us gain a greater understanding. I have asked myself, what is my truth, what are the facts, not just my opinion of who I feel I am, for a queen, that is the most important question to ask? As a queen, you will do that, you will take time alone and consider everything you have done. I watched Bridget do it thousands of times, she focused and thought deeply about all that had occurred, and then she made her decisions. I have done the same, and I would advise you to do the same also." Iona frowned.

"I am still very young; I have not really done a great deal I can learn from." Ariel shrugged.

"All the queens of the past have had the ability of total recall, and look at your life. When you were but a few months old, you made a connection in a sealed realm with your mother. You also were present when the house was attacked by the Houlen. What are the truths of those times and what are your feelings, they are important, for they will influence every decision you make?" Ariel watched her carefully.

"I will also add that if your mother is right, you felt the star of the Merle and warned her of its danger, and you managed to travel to the hidden realm as a small child, and you did save your father in a cave after he was wounded. Iona, your powers have been active since the day you were born, which is the mark of a queen. If you want my advice, I would say, travel back in your mind and beliefs, and discover the truth of you. learn the facts of your life, and look at everything you have learned, see it for what it is. The way I see it, you have just under a month, learn all you can before you wear the crown, I think you will find there is wisdom to be gained from all of it. Open yourself up to the true power of a Fae queen, and let it flow through you, as you discover the truth of everything. Iona, knowing the real truth, that is where the power of a fair rule lies, trust me, I am living example of how the truth has been distorted, and its real meaning lost."

Iona stopped in her tracks, could she really do that, she had no idea, and yet somehow, she felt that Ariel was right? A thought crossed her mind, and she looked back up at Ariel.

"Is that why I dream so much, is it my past, or my truth trying to talk to me?" She gave a nod.

"It could be, Iona you are the Violet Stone, you will have the power of great sight, I can feel the mystical powers within you. Try and unlock them, and travel back through your life, and if there are lessons to be learned, now is the time to study them, and start your journey towards wisdom. All queens reflect deeply on all things in the run up to their crowning, and the fact you asked me those questions, tells me your process has started."

*F*or the young Iona, it was an interesting concept, she had not really given much thought to all her own or even others past experiences. She remembered all of them clearly, but had never considered that she could learn from them. She looked at Ariel.

"You say all queen's, does that even include Rhiannon?" Ariel gave a nod and smiled at her.

"Even her, yes. Iona, now is the time for you to look deep within yourself and understand your real truth. Who are you really, what sort of a queen do you aim to be, and how do you feel about the past, the present and the future? Those are the questions that will determine how you will preside over your realm, and it is important you understand the facts of who you are, before you are crowned. That is the process that will drive your instincts and intuition, and when you are the queen, those will be very important to how you will think of the future of the Fae people. Now is the time to prepare, and start the process."

Iona swallowed hard, it felt like a lot to consider, she looked at Ariel as something occurred to her. She was uncertain as to how to voice it, and yet felt it was something she really needed to understand.

"If you do not mind me asking, have you ever returned, you know, there, to the place you lived with her in her castle? It appears to me, there is wisdom in your words, but I cannot return to those places easily, as they are my past, the cave, the castle at Dunnottar, even to a degree the Hidden Realm, but the place she lived and built her home, it is still there is it not?" Ariel gave a smile.

"I returned to our home in Avalon, but no, I have never felt the need to return. Iona, that was the place I truly lost her, I am not sure of what purpose it would serve." Iona gave a shrug.

"I am not sure either, and yet something within me gives me the strong sense that you should, and I really have no idea why. I suppose, it is like Avalon, there must be some form of understanding to be gained from it." Ariel stared at her.

"Is this something that just came to your thoughts, or is it a strong feeling you have, like a sense of something important?" Iona frowned, and looked at the floor.

"I am not sure, I felt something, Ariel, I cannot explain it. It just came up from within me, like a sense of urgency, or something like that. It flashed into my mind, like it was important. Does this make sense because all this is new to me, and I am struggling a bit to understand it?" Ariel nodded.

"You are a true queen of the line of Bridget, I have seen Gwendolyn struggle with the same notions. Iona, I will take heed of your words, and I will go there." Iona looked up, and placed her hand on her stomach.

"Go now, I cannot tell you why, I just feel it. Ariel, go now, I am fine, I will call Sapphire, but I have no idea how I can understand this, I just know, you must go now. Ariel, I sense it, and it feels strong, this is important, you have to go back." Ariel gave a nod, as she stared with concern at Iona, and could feel the power within her surging up.

"Sapphire is coming, I feel her, thank you my queen."

There was a flash of the brightest white, and she was gone, Iona took a deep breath, and in front of her a bright blue orb appeared, Sapphire came through quickly.

"Are you alright?" Iona stood still, and the sense within her was fading, she took a deep breath, and let the air flow back out of her.

"Yes… I am fine now." She gave a nod and smiled.

"I am fine, everything is fine."

High up on the mountainous plains of Saxony, the trees flashed white, and Ariel appeared. Before her was an ancient tree, she gave a soft smile and turned to look behind her, and there was the other ancient tree. She had landed in what she had called their meeting place, it was a wide open circle between the two trees, and surrounded by large ferns. It felt strange, the place had not changed at all, it was just the same as it had been all those years ago. Her mind wandered as she looked around remembering everything, the night of her return came to mind, and she heard herself in her head.

"Is that really you, is all of this real, because if it is not, I am not sure I could take it?" Branna chuckled.

"You have not changed a bit? Yes, it is me; I told you I would let you know when I was safe."

Ariel stood for a few minutes, her insides swirling, was she really going to do this? She swallowed hard and walked from the clearing, as she had done so many times in her past, and headed for where she knew the castle once stood. Her mind was filled with the images of Branna, as she walked past trees, or turned onto a new path, everyone a moment from each place, all those years ago.

She was not sure why she was even here; she had always felt she would never return, and yet the feelings she had got from Iona were so strong, she knew this had to be done. The path came to an end, and there was the large white stone, blackened still by the scorch marks, from where her caravan was burned. Even after all these years, the pale grey stones were still marked, and they had not weathered away.

She stood for a moment, feeling the deep swirling inside her, how many times had she sat here waiting, or kissed Branna as she arrived, or left having spent the night making love to her? For years, this had been her special place, where she had written her journals of the life they lived together, as she documented all of Branna's life. Some of those books that survived, were at her home in Avalon, locked away from prying eyes. It was a significant place for her, and she lifted her sleeve and wiped her eyes, as her memories flooded her thoughts. The pictures came to her mind, as Branna lay naked in her bed inside the little caravan and looked back at her.

"I want my life with you, if I am honest, you are all that I want, I do not care about the castle and the gold and all those other trophies. When you left me in Avalon, it broke my heart, because in truth, I was so happy there. I wanted to spend our whole life sat under the apple trees, or growing food in the garden and swimming naked in the river. I was so content and she took you from me, and it twisted my insides and I hated her for it. My brother and my parents are still on the Moon Realm, and for all I know she has them locked away. Ariel, I want to be the person you see me as, but I am caught with a foot in both worlds, and in order to enjoy this simple life here alone in this caravan, I pay a mighty price."

Ariel took a deep breath, and turned to where she knew the castle once stood, and she felt her legs tremble, and her stomach filled with nerves.

"Oh lords of all the realms, I am not sure I am strong enough for this."

She took her first nervous foot forward, and made her way slowly through what had once been the centre of the Varisci world, the place where Branna had unleashed her bottle filled with smoke. This was where Berengar had killed his father, and where Branna had slipped out of the castle and come to her, instead of attending the Gathering. Here, Branna had confronted the soldiers and told them to hold off their attack, and where she had run to, in search of Ariel after Otto's vile attack on her.

Ariel came through the trees, and for the first time saw the large open space, covered in dusty old crumbled stone, set in the centre of a wide and vast circular valley. She stopped and swallowed hard as she was confronted with her past, in her mind she could see the long bridge, the guards at the gates, and the imposing castle that had loomed up to the tower, where she had shared her bed with Branna. Her breathing was a little faster, and matched her heart rate, as she walked towards the edge of the high wall, that fell thousands of feet into the canyon below.

Ariel stood frozen, and stared across the wide gap towards the ruins, in many ways it saddened her. Branna had worked so hard to create a family, and a home where she could be truly free, something she could leave as a legacy to her future lines. All was now gone, wiped away and left as rubble, her home, her life, her family, it was as if in a way, Rhiannon had won. There was nothing to even show she was here, and in a strange way, it felt wrong. In her mind she could hear Branna's voice.

"That is why it is important they build a family, pulling back from the fighting, and using the blood of this line is the only way to survive as a whole. Ariel, if one dies and there are others to follow, it will continue the legacy of what I have tried to do. I don't want the killing; I want them to live."

Ariel gave a sigh and lifted her hand to where her tears had run down her face, she took a huge deep breath.

"It is my fault Bran, if I had not forced you to put me in that box, Runestone would never have found you. Oh, Bran my love, I have such regret, but I also warned you, the line of men was weak, they fell too quickly to the darkness, they were never strong enough to resist. I wish so badly I had tried harder, maybe then you would have made it through, and we would be together again in Avalon. I am as big a fool as you, neither of us really understood everything. Even now I struggle, I should never have left you alone, I should have been braver, I wish so desperately I could have been at your side and lived through it all with you, so at least I would fully understand how it all had its effect on you."

Across the wide gap, something moved, and it caught her eye. Ariel stared across the void to try and work out what it was, not really understanding. It fluttered, it was a bird, an old one by the look of it. It appeared to be watching her, and flapped its wings, Ariel watched, as it hopped from stone to stone. It kept looking back at her, each time it moved, as if to ensure she was paying attention, her eyes strained to make out its detail so far away. Her voice was soft.

"Is that a raven… A white one?" The bird stopped and looked at her, and another memory flashed into her mind.

"That was really something to watch, you have got to show me how to do that, wow Ariel, that is really special magic." Ariel gave a smile as she saw what looked like a sense of relief on Branna's face.

"She is called Roack, treat her well."

The moment hit her, and she looked towards the bird and focused her thoughts, the bird gave a twitch, and spoke in her mind.

"Greetings woman of light."

Ariel swallowed hard, it had been a long time since she had been met with such words, she looked across the gap.

"Do you know of me, for I have no memory of you?" The bird nodded across the way.

"When last I saw you, you slept in my mistresses' box."

Ariel felt the air run out of her, her words felt desperate, and she had to swallow hard before she could properly speak.

"You knew Branna, you were with her at that time?"

"She is the lady of all ravens, I served her, and carried her words to others."

Ariel was astounded, she really did not know how to respond, she had thought everything touched by the Merle had been vanquished, it was almost as if the raven read her thoughts.

"I was never joined to her; I listened to her words and then carried them. When she died, the voice I used was taken from me, but because of my colour, she never tainted me with her darkness, she told me that like you, I would remain pure."

Ariel gasped, she had no idea what to make of it all, she closed her mind, and in a flash, she was across the wide gap, and stood a few feet from the bird, she opened her eyes and crouched down to face the bird.

"Why are you still here, the Lady Raven has perished, there is nothing here for you to remain?" The bird was very old, and Ariel sensed it's wing was damaged, and it could no longer fly, it looked thin and undernourished.

"She set me one final task, her dreams became real, so she knew we would meet and talk, and she told me I cannot pass until my task is complete."

Ariel gave a nod, she understood, she was aware that after giving Branna the light she had seen things. Ariel looked at the raven sat on the rock in front of her, it looked very frail.

"Tell me this task, and I will aid you if I can, do you have a name?" The bird flapped its wings, and settled.

"I am Jarron, her white messenger, I once carried her messages to and from the little raven. The Lady of Ravens, told me you would return here, she saw it in her dreams. She told me to wait for you, for there were charms here that no others would undo, and when you came, I was to show you the way." Ariel smiled, and felt hope in her heart.

"I am so glad to meet you Jarron, you have brought me great joy. Tell me of this way… The way to what?"

"Her chambers, they would not fall as the rest did, and she knew that within them, you would find many answers."

It was a huge shock, Ariel took a gasp of air and swallowed hard, just knowing that something of Branna had survived was startling to her, she reached out, and carefully lifted the bird from the rock.

"Ease your strength, show me."

As the bird spoke in her mind, Ariel picked her way through the piles of rubble, treading carefully between some of the huge chunks of rock. She recognised things, such as half a silver spoon with a raven's crest on it, old faded fabric from the drapes, and a piece of carved once highly polished wood. In her mind, she knew where each thing she saw had been in the castle, the raven told her to stop, Ariel came to a halt.

"Look to the floor, below are the stairs to her door, which is charmed, and holds back all destruction. Her chambers were never built, they were cut from the stone, so they did not fall when the rest of the castle did."

Ariel looked down at the floor understanding everything was buried, the stairwell had been filled with smashed and crushed boulders, she gave a long sigh.

"I am the wrong kind of Fae, my line have not the ability to cut through stone." The ancient bird turned his head to look at her, as Ariel stared at the rubble covered floor.

"She knew that, and told me, you know the steps, and how they turn, as they twist to the bottom. Nothing will pass the turn on the steps, she told me, if you remember their base. You can move there, and will be alone down there, and impossible to be discovered."

Ariel smiled, once again, Branna was showing her intelligence, she knew that Ariel could not cut stone, but she knew as a Fae of Earth, she could jump to any place, as long as she could picture it fully in her thoughts. Had she not just taught that very thing to Iona? Ariel held the bird and closed her eyes, and with a flash of white, she disappeared.

*T*he air around her changed and felt a little oppressive, but also familiar, Ariel opened her eyes and gasped in shock, the corridor at the bottom of the steps was clear. The corridor was lit by a thin slit in the wall, where the light seeped in, and she could see the dark shape of the doors up ahead, in the dim light.

"My task is finally complete."

The bird gave a twitch, and then flopped in her hand, and she looked down in the dim light, and gave a sad sigh, as the bird died in her hand. She carefully crouched down, and laid it on the floor.

"Rest well Jarron, you served your mistress to your end, and I thank you for her."

Ariel stood up and looked at the door, the corridor was stuffy, and she took a few nervous steps towards it, knowing that behind them lay her workroom, and her sleeping quarters. She came face to face with the door feeling nervous, she had walked through these doors a thousand times in her life, and never with any fear, and yet as she looked at them, she was afraid.

Taking the handles in her hands, she gently turned them, and gave them a gentle push, and as always, they swung open to reveal the large workroom, her crystal box, and the doors behind, with Branna's work tables. It was like nothing had changed in a thousand years, it was exactly the same as it had been in those weeks after her imprisonment, where she had lived below the castle and slept in Branna's bed. It was eerie as it was so silent, there had always been the sound of something bubbling away in the workroom, as Branna distilled some herb for a potion, but the silence felt oppressive.

Ariel took a step forward, and entered the room as her emotions swirled inside her, she looked at the window, where she had stood and watched out over many years of her life. The white rough walls of the cliffs as they plunged down appeared almost as they always had, and it felt familiar, and yet eerie now, knowing she was the only one left from those times. Ariel took a deep breath of clean air, and turned, the light was flooding in over the opened crystal box, and in a way, it felt odd, she had slept away hundreds of years within it, and she had been so disorientated for well over a week after being released, she had never actually seen it. In her mind, thinking of her last moment as she asked Branna to save them both, it had just been a bed made up of soft silken sheets.

Today, she got to see it as Branna had seen it for all of those years. The lid was lay on the floor, but she could understand how for Branna, she would have been able to look in and see her below the crystal. Looking at it and understanding it better, she felt it would be hard for her to see Branna inside it, and got an understanding of how difficult it must have been for her every day for all of those years alone down here.

She walked closer towards the crystal box, looking around the room, which even now was still so familiar to her. Her desk with her ink bottle and nibs, her old worn padded seat cover, her black hand stitched bag hung over the back of her chair, her small brass candle stick, with an almost burned out tallow candle. All of these things were so familiar to her, and each one held a precious memory of her of Branna. She reached the box and looked down into it, the shape of her body from her years of sleep was still sunken into the soft white sheets and pillow. It was exactly as she remembered it the day she had made it up ready, before asking Branna to do the charm.

There was just one thing, that was not as she remembered, she stared down into the box and saw the corner of a parchment sticking out from below the pillow. Ariel took a breath and reached in, she took hold of it and gently pulled, and a sealed letter came out from under the pillow. It had the dark red wax seal of Branna stamped on it to seal it. Ariel felt her heart beat faster.

"Oh Bran, what have you done?"

Ariel lifted it out and turned it over, she gave a gasp as she saw her name, she had no real understanding of how Branna knew she would find her way back here. Since returning to Loxley, she had always said she would never return, and yet here she was staring at a letter, and she knew within it were the final words of the love of her life, and even though a part of her wanted to know, another part of her felt great fear. Her hand trembled as she broke the seal, and unfolded the letter, and tilted it to the light to read.

Ariel my love.

Time has run out, the granddaughter of Eve, has taken you and Roack away, and the veil of protection is failing, and I know, that soon, Rhiannon will come to me as I am finally revealed to her.

I want to say so many things to you, I wanted to be the one to open your box and hold you again, even if just for a moment, but I have even been robbed of that moment with you, and I have a feeling, that I will defeat Rhiannon, but I do not think without Roack, I will live much longer, I know they will kill her to destroy me and all my family.

You are the only one who knows the truth, and if I kill her, there will be no other, as my family after all of my fights and struggles will end here on this day, my time now is short and so I have to act.

Ariel, do you remember how you used to stumble in my work room on the uneven floor? You threw the old mat over it to warn you to avoid it, well there is a reason, and if you are reading this as I have seen in my dreams, go to it, and remember the words you spoke of what you would do if you got free.

I am sorry to have to leave, I wanted to stay, and I was so close to my goal, but sadly, against all my calculations, time has run out. If I had only had a few more months, we would have been reunited, I was so tired and needed to rest first, to gather my strength, and then I knew what to do, I am certain of it. I am so tired and weary now, but you were right, having you near me helped, as I sat and spoke to you every day. You are the love of my life, and my whole world, never forget that, or me. I am sorry I could not live up to my promise, I so desperately wanted to, and I did try, and I lived as you would wish.

Live for me now my love. Live free.

I love you.

Bran.

riel's tears dripped onto the cold stone floor, as she finished the letter, and gave a huge sob, and wept as she hugged the letter to her.

"I love you too Bran, but I am not sure I can take much more, I really need you, and I have lost you forever, and I just cannot take more of my loneliness."

She leaned onto the box and wept, and through her bleary eyes, she looked at the work room, and the long table filled with bottles and jars, and for some bizarre reason, she noticed the hair brush, Branna had thrown there on her last day with her. She gave a huge sniffle and wiped her eyes, why had she never cleaned it up and used it?

She walked around the box wiping her eyes, and through the doors into the workroom, the only thing different, was there was no black book, the space it has always been on the table was empty, but everything else was the same. She lifted the brush, it still had a mass of black hair tangled within the bristles, and some of her own hair, she smiled as she remembered all of those times where she had convinced Branna to let her brush her hair. It was something she had always loved, Branna looked so good with her hair knot free and untangled. She slipped the brush into her deep pocket.

Ariel walked around the table, and there on the floor just to the side of the table where Branna always stood to write her notes, was the old badly woven mat, which Ariel had made for her. It was strange in a way, it was not the best, she had never been that good at weaving, but Branna had loved it and laid it on the floor by her table to keep her feet warm on the cold floor as she worked. It felt strange how the simplest of things made her so happy, Ariel had been embarrassed to give it her for her birthday, but she had loved it, and excitedly placed it down with a huge smile.

Ariel crouched down, and pulled back the rug, and there on the floor was a brass ring, she stared at it as she realised what it was, and the letter started to make complete sense to her. Ariel leaned forward and grabbed hold of it, and as she did, the floor lifted on a hinge and opened up a secret place, her breath caught in her throat.

"Her books!"

There below the floor, was two large black books, and also several others that looked like journals, one of them she recognised, it was the one she made when Ariel showed her the proper way to stitch a book, Ariel stared at them lay in the open space in the floor.

"Bran, did you write down your life without me?" She reached in, and lifted one out, and opened it.

'For Ariel.'

A deep grumbling rose up from below, and the floor shuddered, Ariel looked around alarmed, dust fell from the ceiling. She put the book down and lifted out the others, the floor vibrated again, Ariel understood, the column of rock the castle had been built on was shifting, it had happened before and worried Branna.

As the floor rumbled and shook again, she hurriedly pulled out the books, and stacked them on the floor at the side of Branna's secret hiding place. She pulled out the last book, and looked round, she needed to carry them, her eyes landed on her mat, she leaned over and dragged it over, and began to put the books in a stack on top of it, the floor shook again, and the stone lid of her hiding place fell, and closed, with a loud bang.

Ariel lifted up the books wrapped in the mat and staggered back towards the other room, where she knew Branna's large bag was still on her chair, she felt afraid. The floor vibrated shaking the glass bottles and jars, as she hurried past, trying to keep her balance. She staggered into the first room, and over to the desk, she put the books on the desk, and snatched the bag off the chair, and opened it up, then grabbing the books wrapped in the mat, she pushed them inside with all its other contents, and then pulled open Branna's desk drawer.

The ground shook and she leaned on the desk, and looked into the drawer, there was her comb made of bone, her hair trimming shears, and a hand drawn picture of herself, which Ariel remembered doing for her sat in front of a mirror, she snatched them up, and dropped them in the bag, then lifted it onto her shoulder, it was heavy.

Ariel took a huge breath, the dust was falling from the ceiling, as the room started to shake more, she had no idea how long she had, but one last thing occurred to her. The chances were, she would never get another chance to be here, she saw the door to Branna's private sleeping room, and staggered over towards it, uncertain as to if she had time. She pulled open the door and staggered in, it was crazy, but this place was her only salvation in a world empty of her, this was where her strongest memories were made, and she needed to know that it would not all be forgotten.

Ariel saw the bed, and ruffled sheets, the table and the small black box, it was where she kept the things Ariel had made for her, she staggered over towards it, and snatched it up, and threw it in the full bag, and then turned. The floor shook hard, and she fell sprawling onto the bed, and landed on the sheets, and suddenly she was overwhelmed by the scent of Branna, and she breathed in deeply, as her heart lurched. After all this time, that scent she missed so badly was all around her, and her head exploded with her memories of their close intimate love making.

She spread herself wide and felt the pillows on her right hand and just gripped at it, as the intoxicating scent of Branna washed through her igniting such powerful feelings and memories, it was as if she had only just left the bed. Outside the doors, she could hear glass falling from her work bench and smashing on the floor, and as much as she wanted to lie here, she knew, she had to go, but at least the last things of Branna would not be wiped away, she had at least saved a little of her.

She gripped the pillow as the floor shook, and stood up, and with a flash of light and a pop, she left, and reappeared on the edge of the rock looking out at the tall column, still holding Branna's pillow. Ariel watched as the tall wide pillar of stone, on which Branna had built her new world, shook, large chunks were falling away lower down, and Ariel stood still just watching as slowly it crumbled. With a loud whoosh, the pillar slipped, and fell into the bottom of the deep valley, thousands of feet below. Vast clouds of dust swept up the sides of the deep valley down below, and she gave a long sad sigh. Castle Berengar, or the last of the crumbled remains of it, had been washed away forever by the river deep down below. For over thousands of years, the river had slowly worn it away, and finally the bottom collapsed, and it all fell down. Ariel took a long deep breath; her voice was soft as she thought of Iona.

"Well my queen, it appears your powers are much further along than even I expected, but thank you, it is not much, but what I have is so important to me. Not only is it a memory, it is a bond, and a strong connection to her, and it will be important for the rest of my solitary life."

She turned away from what was the castle that had not only given her great joy, but also some of her deepest most painful memories, but in the end, she was glad she came back. It also gave her something far more precious, she had a small piece of the living Branna, trapped in her hair brush. She closed her eyes and thought of home, and in a flash of white, she appeared in the bedroom of her home, and looked at the bed, she gave a small smile and tossed the pillow onto it.

"Bran, I am home my love." She smiled, and walked through into the room of her desk to unpack the bag.

Chapter Six.

Other Truths.

*I*ona came down the steps, into Rune's table room, where she saw Rune sat back in her seat, staring at a picture of Branna, who was sat in her seat covered in blood, a sad look in her eyes. Iona walked slowly towards her, and Rune blinked out of her thoughts, and looked up at her. Iona smiled, and moved into her seat at her side, and spoke quietly.

"You too? I have thought of her today also, I feel Ariel has a strange effect on me at times." Rune gave a sigh.

"In what way?" Iona sat back, and considered it a moment.

"I know I still have much to learn, and Sapphire and Ariel have taught me so much, and my powers still have to fully develop, but I cannot help when I am around Ariel feeling like there is something more… I also felt it in Florae with Alder, almost as if there is another version of the truth, does that sound crazy?"

Rune turned and looked at her, Iona was watching her, her intense violet eyes wide, as if waiting for something that would give her the answers she needed, and yet for Rune there was nothing she could add. She smiled and took her daughters hand in hers.

"I understand what you say, I feel it too, but the truth Iona, is neither of us really know the full story. I will not deny, for a long time I have thought we could have done things differently, I just wish I knew what. Oh Iona, the council of the past made many mistakes, and we tried so hard to correct them, but I have to confess, at times I wonder are we making the same ones, and repeating history all over again?" Iona nodded.

"I am glad you feel it too, I thought it was just me. Mum, I want to be a queen who stands for truth." Rune smiled, and pushed her head back onto the rest.

"I believe Gwendolyn said the same, as did her grandmother

Bridget." She smiled and turned her head towards her daughter, her voice was soft and reflective.

"I remember the day your father got the sword of truth, I was so in love with him, he had no idea how deep it was. I think I have loved him since I was a tiny little girl, and I looked out of my mum's gate, and saw him there in the street. When that sword came to him and he lifted it up, wow, I will never forget that. I saw the way it shone in his eyes, oh, what a moment that was, I knew then I would never leave his side, because he stood for the one thing that I wanted more than anything, he stood for truth."

Iona smiled, as she saw the love in Rune's eyes, and nodded her head softly.

"He is a great man; I am actually going to really miss him when I go to Florae. I want that Mum, I want that truth, that power of standing and letting others see that I stand for what is right. I want to be like my father."

Rune smiled, Iona had no idea how much Rune understood that, she too had felt the same as a teenager standing at his side. She squeezed Iona's hand.

"I think you will be, and he is a good role model for anyone, it is a hard path though Iona, it is not always easy to know what is the right thing to do. I will not deny, I have struggled with it at times, and this is one of them." She looked to the image above her table of Branna, and pointed.

"I think there is more to this Branna's story, and her influence on everything, but sadly I have tried in the past, but it is hard to talk to Ariel about this. The truth is Iona, I killed the love of her life, and that really bothers me. How can a woman of such darkness and evil, be loved so deeply by the purest of all of the Fae? Ariel has such beauty inside her, such power for good, I feel it and it overwhelms me. I also feel the depth of her loss, and honestly, I feel such dreadful guilt, it has eaten at me for years Iona. I cannot help but ask, could we have done things differently?"

"What does dad think?" Rune smirked, as she looked at her daughter.

"Oh sweetheart, he does not want to talk about those times, they are still a deep source of pain to him. I honestly do not think he ever got over the death of his father, and also Ruby. She was a really special person and he really cared about her, I think in a way, her innocence, her childlike ways made him feel more responsible for her. When she was killed in that bunker, it cut him so deep, it is still there, I am not sure he will ever let go of it. That bloody awful war, still lingers inside so many, it was such a horrible time for all of us."

"Okay… So how do we find the truth? If I am going to be the queen who stands for it, how do we get to the full truth, because looking at Tila, it is clear, no one really knows for sure what the real story of all this is?"

"The problem is Iona, which truth?"

She leaned forward in her seat, touched her table, and pictures started to appear, and Iona watched as they all rose out of the table. Rune sat back and looked at them all.

"I have spent years studying all of the stories, and I still feel as lost as I did back then. Everyone has a story, and they are similar but different."

Iona looked at the table where there were pictures of Ena, Gwendolyn, Merlin, Rhiannon, Una, Melanie, Maddy, Fagan, Rayne, Ariel and Branna. She looked at her mother.

"What about Morgan, what was her story?" Rune frowned.

"She was the Dark One, she was evil, I know, I faced her." Iona agreed and nodded.

"I get that Mum, but she was not born evil. Look, if I am going to start my reign with the truth, then it has to be everyone including her. Mum, she was a daughter, and at some point, a child of innocence. No matter how you look at it, she was not always the Dark One, she had to be something else before that? Mum, from what we know, she was close to Branna, they shared something, they were family. Branna must have known her before her evil days, so what was she like then?" Rune shook her head.

"That is the problem, Branna is gone, and I doubt those who knew her, will want to talk to us about her. This is the problem Iona, Una hated her, and from what I remember so did Mel and Maddy, and they were alive at the time. I doubt they would say anything different. Rhiannon is gone, but could we honestly trust her? Gwendolyn was married to Merlin, so she would have met her, but she too is gone, and Ariel was in her box." Iona nodded at her and looked at the table.

"So that leaves Ena, Fagan and Opal, and possibly Rayne." Rune took a deep breath and held it in for a moment, before letting it flow out of her.

"I will warn you Iona, all of these people suffered because of her and Branna. Asking questions and digging for the truth of Morgan, will not make you popular, if anything this close to your crowning, it could make you very unpopular."

*I*ona stood up and walked slowly around the large table, as she looked at the images hanging in the air. Rune watched her as she thought it all through, she looked up from the table, as she stood opposite Rune sat in her chair, and her violet eyes sparkled with her intelligence.

"I remember being told that the hardest thing anyone could do was make a stand for the truth, because most of the time it was a lonesome task with no rewards. They told me, the real reward was knowing you made the stand." Rune gave a giggle and stood up.

"And you are so like him, but he was right. Iona, if you aim to do this, you have to understand, even your father may object when it comes to digging around in Morgan's life. This family suffered a great deal of loss because of her." Iona took a breath and nodded, but she looked serious.

"I know Mum, but I have to know if I am going to rule, I want all of the facts. It appears to me, everyone has a truth, but when you compare them to the facts, all of them are tainted. Mum, I want the pure facts." Rune smiled, and walked around the table, and took her daughters hands in hers.

"Then my daughter, you will continue the work your father and I started twenty years ago. It will not be easy, so where do you want to start?" Iona looked at the table.

"Start with what we know, we start with Morgan, and work backwards." Rune nodded.

"Alright my daughter, we will do that, and we start now, and will do it together, for in a month, you will be crowned. I would think, after that you may not have as much free time as you want." Iona nodded, and took a deep breath.

"Thanks Mum, I really want to do this, but I am terrified of doing it alone." Rune gave a chuckle.

"Oh dear, you are so like him, he has that way of winning me over, and then all hell breaks loose."

"AUNTIE RUNE, I FINISHED THE STABLES, CAN LANIA PLAY NOW!?" Rune gave a sigh, and turned to the steps.

"DID YOU WIPE YOUR FEET?"

"YES, AUNTIE RUNE!"

"ALRIGHT THEN, SHE IS IN HER ROOM!"

"THANK YOU, AUNTIE RUNE!" Rune turned back to Iona.

"See what I mean?" Thump! Thump! Thump! Rune looked up, as above them, Pandora headed up the stairs. Iona giggled and linked her arm.

"Come on Mum, let's have a drink and work out how we will do this."

Rune swiped her hand across the table as she passed it, and all the images sunk into its cool surface, and together they headed up the steps, and towards the kitchen.

In Avalon it was getting late as Ariel sat at Branna's desk, and looked at the journals and books she had recovered from her workroom. Bran's bag had a few things in it she remembered, like her roll of herbal cures, which she could not believe she had been carrying it around for all these years. She put her brush on her cabinet in Branna's room, knowing she would never use it, but knew she would hold it often.

Her small black box of precious things she had not opened yet, she knew that would be a pull on her heart, and so saved it for later. Once she had finished, she shook out the mat she had made Branna into the garden, and banged it out. She then placed it in front of her desk, where she had often seen Branna stand to make a quick revision on her documents. It was not much, but felt like a lot more than she had started with, and was grateful she had such close personal things of hers, to remember her by.

Ariel looked at the stack of books, the most obvious being the one she knew the best, it was Branna's precious black book. In many ways, it was this book that brought about her downfall, her research that drew her into the merle. It was the work Rhiannon allowed her to do, because Rhiannon saw her as expendable. She knew she would never really be able to read it, because it was in her own private code, and Branna had never shared how to decipher it all with her. Ariel reached down and pulled open the draw, where the blue feather rested, and slipped the book back in.

"This is where you will stay, it was where she kept you, and so I will too, but I will never open you, for as much as Bran loved this book, I hate you, I hate what you did to her." She closed the draw, and looked at the stack of books still left on her desk.

It was hard to believe that for all of her time alone, whilst Ariel had slept in her box, Branna had written a journal. It was not really daily, it was just updates, added when she could find the will to write them, as Ariel would find out as she read them, they would be emotional and filled with pain. As Branna struggled with her fight against the merle, new entries were written as she tried to keep her connection alive to Ariel. It spanned a thousand years of heartache, grief, and pain, and on many of the pages, there were ink blots where her tears soaked the pages.

One book appeared different, and she picked it up and opened the cover, the first page read, 'Tell the world.' Ariel frowned, and turned over the page, and read. 'Countess in the shadows, Morgana's truth." Ariel turned over the page, and started to read what Branna had written.

'*I* spoke often to Ariel of how Maud was a disappointment, of how vile she was becoming or how her hateful ways repulsed me. I told her, how I had always wanted a daughter who was more like me, and less Varisci. When I met Morgana in secret in her bedroom of her home at Tintagel, I knew then, she was my double, and my one chance to set straight the mistakes of my own life.

Morgana looked so like me, she was like looking at my younger self, and she was so incredibly intelligent for her younger years. I cannot deny, meeting her changed my life, and I had no idea of the joy she would bring to me, to help me through these dark days of loneliness. Morgana had suffered in a way no one really understood, at just four summers of age, she saw Uther Pendragon enter the castle, and walk into her mother's bedchamber, and watched as he raped her mother. Hours later, she received the news that her father had been killed in battle with Uther's men, and as noon arrived, she saw her father carried from the battlefield with a Fae sword still sticking through his gut.

I have no idea how a child of such early years, managed to grow up and survive as she has, and all I can add, is that her inner strength and ability to deal with such things of a terrible nature, made me respect her. The fact she has come through that, and has lived a life alone since, having to accept Uther Pendragon, the man who raped her mother and killed her father, as her adopted father, astounds me. Yet today, at just fifteen summers old I met a bright intelligent and caring girl, who although filled with extreme sadness and anger, has managed to become a person of such high quality and value.

I cannot deny, meeting her has touched me deeply, and tonight I am filled with many deep thoughts about my own life, and similarities between her and myself, and what we have endured living under the eye of the golden queen. I watched as she bravely told me her tales of her life, and wept as she did, and yet somehow, I feel it helped her, as it has me. I know as I sit here tonight looking at Ariel encased in her crystal box, she would want me to protect her as any parent should, and knowing her mother is not able, as she is ruled by Uther, I have sworn my vow to ensure that I will bring aid to her whenever she needs it.

I feel this is my chance to do something of value, I see in her the person I was, and I want to help ensure she remains that way. I will embrace her and bring her into the family, but as I look at Ariel sleeping before me, I swear, I will never allow her to be corrupted. I will never let the darkness eat her as it has me, Morgana of Berengar, will never be tied to a raven.'

Ariel gasped, and sat back, her head swimming with questions, as she looked at the book on the desk.

"But Bran she was, how is this possible? I know you Bran, I know you would not break your oath, and how important that would be. Bran my love, Morgana was tied to a raven, she did things of great evil, how did that happen, how could you have allowed it?"

Ariel took a deep breath and turned the page. The page was added long after the book was finished, and she could see how Branna had glued it in place, but it was a different piece of parchment to the rest of the book. Ariel looked down at Branna's neat handwriting.

It is my hope that if anything happens to me, my words reach out from these pages to touch the life of Ariel, for I know in my heart, that she will read what I write, and tell the world the real truth of Morgana. I know this, for Morgana was pure in spirit and lived true to her vow to be a full fellow of the Whitelines, and not walk the same path of darkness as I find myself on. I felt I could guide her with wisdom, to ensure she never repeated the mistakes of my past stupidity. I have paid a high price for the mistakes I have made, and I vowed to ensure, that Morgana stayed on the road of light. It is after suffering a cruel twist of vengeance that Morgana has fallen, and I find myself lost and in pain, as I failed her, as I failed myself, and Ariel.'

Ariel breathed in and swallowed hard, she had no idea what to think, she had no idea how this happened, she leaned forward to read on.

'The following is Morgana's story, as witnessed by myself, and documented on the day after every occurrence, I have detailed every conversation we have had, and every experience she was forced to live through by a hateful queen. No story will rival this, for it is truth in its purest form, for as I have seen at the will of the golden queen, that the real truth has been bent and distorted to match her wishes. She is surrounded by her puppets who she spoon feeds her truths to, and they lap it up greedily to stay in her favour. Having said this, I know Gwendolyn tried to find the truth, and she was diverted in all of her attempts to find it. I hold no judgement on Gwendolyn, she was kind to Morgana at a time when she really needed it, and I was always grateful to her for that. As the days passed, I saw Morgana, who was so like me, to be more and more like the daughter I had always desired. Morgana had the dark look of me, and yet knowing her, she had the spirit and goodness of Ariel.

This is the truth, as written by Branna, daughter of Vinella and Brandle, The Lady Raven of Berengar.

Ariel sat back in shock, she stared at the book on the desk, and felt her breath coming in bursts she was so surprised. Ariel took in a deep breath before she could even speak.

"How could that be, Bran my love, how is that even possible, Morgana was even darker than you?"

*R*une smiled as the children ran through the house, and Robbie looked panicked.

"Robbie are you sure you will be alright, we will not be long, if it gets too much, get Tegan to calm them down?" He looked at her, and frowned.

"She is the worst one of the lot; she makes Fern look and appear innocent." Iona sniggered behind her mother; Rune gave a sigh.

"Okay then, I will get Jade to send Rowan over, I am sure two big war heroes should be able to cope with a few kids, you dealt with the Houlen with no trouble." Robbie looked back as the door banged, and Pan and Gailiana came running in.

"This lot makes the Houlen appear quite pleasant and sociable." Rune reached up on her tip toes, and kissed his cheek with a smirk.

"We will see you soon, Rowan is on his way."

Rune turned, and her archway opened, and giggling she stepped through with Iona, and walked straight into Avalon in front of Merlin's cottage, Una was in the garden picking tomatoes, she stood up with a smile.

"Rune, Iona, what a lovely surprise." They walked through the gate, and Una pulled both of them into a hug.

It took a few minutes to do the pleasantries, and Una brought out juice and cakes, and they sat out at a table Wilson had built, Una was really happy, she looked at them both sat at her table.

"Okay, an unannounced visit, I am old enough to know you both are up to something, what are you up to?" Iona gave a smile.

"Aunt Una, your mother swore an oath she would be a queen for truth, and I also wish to swear the same oath, and yet I have had feelings that there is still a lot of thought that there is a gap in what really happened in Avalon with Morgan le Fey. I want to know all the facts." Una frowned.

"I thought you did, and to be honest Iona, I see no purpose to this, she was a wicked evil person, and that is truth enough for most of us." Iona gave a nod, and then looked at Una.

"You are sworn to protect, you have gifts that reveal the purpose of a person. Yet, here in Avalon, she lived amongst you, and you felt nothing. Aunt Una, if she was so evil, then why didn't you feel any of it?" Una sat back and looked angry.

"Do you not think I have not thought of that all my life, I gave a child to protect my mother? I saw her when that witch hit her with a spell, and wounded her, and then when she was pulled from her glass tube of hell, and was close to death?" Una stood up, and her eyes flickered.

"How can you call yourself a queen of truth, if you cannot see the evil she did? Leave my home, I will not sit here and tolerate such insults to my glorious queen and mother." Rune stood up.

"Una, no one is implying anything other, we know what she did, and that is not what we are looking for, please, listen, and please be calm." Una looked at Rune, and her eyes teared up.

"You should know better, you know the sacrifice I made Runestone, you know the pain of that." She took a deep breath.

"I am sorry Runestone but this is not something you should be doing, we dealt with her, and it cost me two sisters." Rune nodded, and her voice lowered.

"I know Una, I often think of them, but you have to understand, we know what she did, what we seek is who she was before all of this started. Who was the girl, that became Morgan le Fey? That is all we seek, and you were here, you met her, we just need to know what that person was like." Una wiped her eyes and gave a slight nod; she sat back down and Iona reached out across the table.

"Aunt Una, I would never hurt you, my family means everything to me. There are so many versions of events, and I want to know what is truth, and what is not. Look, there was a time when she was simply an ordinary girl, and then something happened, that is what I need to know, what was it that turned her, what was the ordinary Morgan like?" Una took a sip of her drink, and calmed down a little.

"Eleanor thought she was boring, to be honest I never had a problem with her, she was quiet, and a loner. I always thought she was sad, Maddy did too. Iona, you have to understand we moved in different circles, Morgana did not want to be a part of that, she tried to stay away from all of it, and on the few occasions she attended, she would sit alone." Iona understood her.

"Rhiannon accused her of the death of Eleanor, do you know why she did that?" Una shook her head.

"Iona, you will be my queen, but I must tell you, you walk a fine line, this will not be met well. I can say with no doubt, she did not kill Eleanor, she was nowhere near her when it happened." Iona leaned forward on the table.

"How can you be so sure, every record states clearly it was her?" Una shook her head.

"It was not possible, I was stood fifty feet away from her as she talked to my father, as much as I hate her, that is one crime I know she did not commit. Iona, she was quiet, well read, and I heard very intelligent. I know people who thought she was actually very polite, some even said she was a lovely girl. My father spoke fondly of her, and I always thought he admired her, he certainly praised her willingness and effort to learn the best she could from him. I know my mother visited her, and even helped her, she was down there completely alone, and yet she managed to survive better than many. I did not know her that well, around Eleanor and me, she was very quiet and said little. I did not mind her, at the time I often thought we would get on, because she did use her words well, it was clear she was well educated." Iona sat back, as she thought, her eyes moved to Una who was watching her carefully.

"I am grateful to you, I never meant to upset you, just answer me one more thing. If she was innocent of Eleanor's death, what makes you so sure she did all the other things that Rhiannon accused her of?" Una shrugged.

"Who else would? Iona, she killed Eve, I mean seriously, who else would do that, and how, she was life, how did she even do that, everyone knew it was her?" Iona nodded.

"Thank you, Aunt Una, and you make a valid point. All I want is the facts, nothing more."

They spoke with Una for a little while longer, and Iona talked of her nervousness over the ceremony that she faced, and after a while, it was time to leave, and Iona thanked her and gave her a hug. Una had mentioned the cottage Morgana had lived at in her final comments, and Iona felt, that whilst she was in Avalon, she wanted to see it.

Rune walked at her side down the road, she had never actually seen it herself, and was interested in seeing it, as they walked, Rune looked at Iona.

"Would you like to share your thoughts, I thought that went better than I expected. Iona, can I ask you something? I feel that this is very important to you, more important than I think I realised. Why is that?" Iona stopped and turned to look at her, and she appeared very serious.

"I don't expect you to fully understand this Mum, but I have a feeling, and it is so strong inside me, and I will say I do not understand why I feel this way, but I have had dreams and images that make no sense to me. I just feel this is something only I can do. I cannot explain it, but I feel very strongly that there has been a great injustice, and if there has, I cannot settle with that, I am sorry. Everyone I know and respect has been touched with this and it goes back a long time, but my instincts are telling me I must do this before I take the crown." In a way Rune understood, she knew the power of these feelings, she understood how they took over until they were resolved.

"Alright Iona, if this is something you are compelled to do, I will support you, but again, I will say be wary. You saw how Una reacted, I could feel her restraint, she respects you, but not everyone will."

Iona understood and turned back to the road; the remains of the cottage were just ahead surrounded by weeds. Both of them walked slowly up to it, most of it was gone, all that remained was the chimney, and the stone slab floor, with two burned down door stumps. The gate had rotted and fallen off, and parts of the fence had fallen down, Iona walked slowly onto the site.

"She lived here alone, grew her own food, chopped her own wood, and grew plants that she used to create cures. I feel no evil here mother, there is nothing dark, if anything I just feel an overwhelming sadness." Rune looked around the place.

"All I really know is that when Fagan came here on orders of the queen, he managed to see some of her feelings, that is how he knew she was Fae and tied to a raven." Iona turned.

"How?" Rune frowned.

"What do you mean, how?" Iona waved a hand and then breathed out.

"Tell me, is there anything you can see?" Rune frowned.

"I cannot, you just slipped on a veil." Iona smiled.

"I remember Ena saying Morgana always wore a veil, so how did Fagan see into her?" Rune shrugged.

"Maybe back then she did not wear one, perhaps she felt safe, she was in Avalon, so at no risk." Iona considered it, and then shook her head.

"She was a student of the Whitelines, being taught by Merlin in the realm of Rhiannon. Tell me Mother, as the creator of the Violet Circle, have you shared your achievements with the Fae?" Rune shook her head.

"Well no, we all have certain secret spells and things." Iona turned and looked at the chimney, with bits of wood and burnt things on it.

"I may be wrong, but if I was teaching anyone as Sapphire has me, that would be my first lesson as it was with Sapphire. I am sure Merlin would have done the same, so if that is right, how could Fagan see her thoughts and feelings, she should have been veiled?" Rune had never considered it.

"You have dreamed it haven't you? Iona Violet, I sense you hiding something." She smiled.

"How, I am veiled?" She giggled, and winked at her mother.

"I have dreams I do not understand, except one, which Una just made clear. I saw her with Merlin when Gwendolyn came to him, I saw that, it happened right up there." Iona pointed, and Rune turned around to see the top of the mount.

"I can see now why you wanted to do this, but honestly, I am still trying to understand why all this matters. Morgan was dealt with; she is no longer a threat." Iona nodded

"I agree, so this has more to do with who she was here in Avalon, and nothing to do with who she became. Mother, at this point, I feel it is safe to say that there were two Morgan's. One was Morgana of Cornwall who lived here, and the other was Morgan le Fey, and I think both of them were completely different people, and if I am right, they had opposing views." Rune shook her head.

"Iona, I have to say, I find that really difficult to believe, I understand we all change, I did when my powers came, but here in my heart, I am still the same person."

"Yes Mother, you are, but you have not been corrupted by the merle, and that I think is what makes all the difference. If I am right, Morgana of Cornwall, was just a normal girl, working very hard to learn her art from the guardian of the Whitelines. How she drifted away from that, is what really matters, because that could teach us a great deal. Not just about Morgan, but also about Branna.

Chapter Seven.

Casting Doubt.

Alder sat in his seat, and viewed the room. Nine of the council sat with him, all listening to him, as he spoke with authority, Bade and Master Elgin were elsewhere. Alder looked slowly at all the council members, understanding he had attention.

"My dear friends, it is very simple, we are either the council of this realm, or we are not. We have followed very strict procedures for the entire length of this realm's existence, and yet now I feel we are being undermined by a princess who is a stranger to our customs and traditions. The case of Tila is a glowing example, of how unskilled and uneducated the princess is, and it concerns me deeply." Heads nodded around the room, Cullen leaned forward in his seat, he had served with Alder for many years.

"Lord Alder, all new queens have made changes, Queen Gwendolyn made several before her crowning, this is not unusual." Alder nodded.

"I understand that, but never has a queen undermined her council once the vote has been passed, not once. This is my point, and I may add one of my greatest concerns."

Alder had great authority, and it was true, Iona had to a degree made him look foolish in front of the rest of the council, and he was very unhappy about it. Nerissa appeared to be confused.

"You say one of… Lord Alder how many concerns do you have, it was but one incident?" Alder cleared his throat, and looked seriously at everyone.

"It grieves me a great deal, but I cannot deny, I have some fundamental concerns as to the legitimacy of Iona Violet, to even take the crown."

All of them gasped and sat back in their seats, to even voice such a thing was very dangerous. Borak took a deep breath; he was feeling very uncomfortable.

"Surely you do not mean that Alder, that is a very dangerous idea to hold?" Alder nodded.

"And yet, as much as I am stricken to my stomach to even suggest it, I feel honour bound to the oath I swore to raise it, in the only place I could, the Council of the Elders." He leaned forward in his seat.

"It is our responsibility to ask these questions for the sake of this whole realm, it is why we hold these seats. If truth be told, and consider this very carefully, how do we know that the Great Queen Gwendolyn White Circle placed the line of her succession into a member of the Green Circle, tell me, what facts do we have?" He stared at them all, but they were silent, not one of them wanted to even contemplate it, Alder leaned back in his seat.

"In days past, we would have sought the council of the greatest authority, the Magnificent Queen Rhiannon, but sadly that day has past, and I will remind you, was due to the very person who claims that the Queen of Fae has come from her line, Runestone Sapphire. It is a known fact that Queen Amethyst is deeply aligned with Runestone, and so we cannot seek wisdom there, which is why the duty of question is upon us, we are the Council of the people of Fae of Earth. Queen Gwendolyn has three surviving females of her line, and yet they have been passed over for this child of a Green Circle, would it not be more prudent to look to Una, Citrine, or as much as I have no tolerance for the woman, even Sapphire would have more legitimacy than Iona Violet?"

There was stunned silence, Alder was talking treason, and all of them knew that just to comment or even suggest this, would cause chaos. Gullveg, who was a middle aged, balding Fae, looked at Alder with bright blue eyes.

"Alder, what you are suggesting is treason, an act that has never been committed in any of the years of this or our other realms. Just being here implicates us all, this is very unsafe ground. I can understand your thinking, and do not think that there are any here, who when we first heard the news of the coming of Iona Violet, did not question her eligibility to start with. Alder, what you are suggesting is that within the month, a replacement is found from the line of Gwendolyn. That is no easy feat, and also begs the question of what would happen to Iona Violet?" Cullen looked around.

"This must be brought to Elgin, he is the most senior and long serving member, his wisdom is needed here, this is a very dangerous consideration, the people have embraced Iona, they want her as queen." Alder nodded.

"And if she is illegitimate, what then, it will show at the crowning? The people will rise up against her, and then what, we all resign?" Cullen sat back, he looked very worried indeed, and was not at all at ease with this topic, Alder looked around the room.

"With a month to go, we must consider this now, and if we find that Iona Violet is an imposter, placed to advance the Green Circle, then it is the responsibility of every true and loyal member of this council to act, time is slipping through our fingers. As much as I am saddened deeply to ask, and will do so with a heavy heart, I feel that we should draft a proposal to declare Iona Violet as questionable, and consider the suitability of the other three."

*T*here was a deep silence all over the room, as the members who looked sickened, looked at each other, Borak gave a nod, as he looked at the others.

"This sickens my stomach, but I believe you have raised a point worthy of consideration Alder. There have been doubts, possibly not spoken, but I know from the few conversations I had eighteen years ago, no one is completely in agreement with the lineage of Iona Violet. I will back a motion to consider her suitability, but I will also advise to walk softly, this will bring great unrest. If we can prove Iona Violet to be the rightful heir, I will rest better knowing we acted in the best interests of our people." Several heads nodded, and Alder smiled. Lord Gelsey had been sat quietly listening, he gave a deep sigh.

"As possibly the most learned historian here after Elgin, I would have to say, if your suspicions are correct Alder, then Sapphire is already invalidated. She is the centre of the Circle of Sight, a role destined for her, and I may add, embraced by Queen Gwendolyn. She did indeed write it in her journals when Sapphire was born, and so if you really mean to do this, then only Una or Citrine should be considered. I am not convinced you are correct Alder, but I will go along with this, for no other reason than to remove all doubt once and for all about Iona Violet." Others appeared to agree that was a good point.

One by one, Alder swung the motion in his own favour, and after several long hours of debate, the council rested to take refreshments, with ten votes and signatures to the motion, which under Fae law, was a vote cast, and approved by the council, as a majority of ten.

*I*ona walked around the property of Morgana of Cornwall, her senses flowing inside her, she had never felt such strong feelings in her life, and she felt light headed, she stopped stood by the chimney, and breathed in, Rune watched her carefully.

"Are you alright sweetheart?"

Iona had gone very quiet and swayed slightly, her eyes started to flicker, Rune understood it was the power of her line, and stepped back. Iona gave a gasp, and her eyes suddenly turned deep purple, as she froze on the spot, and Rune gasped and looked around as the walls began to grow out of the floor.

They were slightly transparent, Rune could see through them, and yet they were dull and there, all around her the cottage was appearing, shelves with jars, a table, flames in the fire place, she had never seen anything like it. Iona swooned and her hair began to turn black, and Rune's eyes opened wide as Iona morphed into a young woman, in a black dress with long dark hair.

Rune could not believe what she was seeing, Iona had become Morgana, she was younger, certainly prettier, but it was definitely Morgana. Morgana turned and snatched a figure off the shelf on the chimney, she appeared to be in a rush, and had two bags from each shoulder. Rune jumped, as the door crashed open, and Fagan charged inside with his scythe. Morgana looked white faced and terrified, she stared at Fagan as he lifted his blade, and Rune tensed, and then Morgana spoke.

"She is wrong, it was not me Fagan, I would never do that, I believed in Eve, I am innocent."

The scythe came around, grey smoke funnelled out of the floor, and as the blade met where Morgana had stood, it swept clean through, dragging the smoke with it, she had gone. Rune swallowed hard, and gasped, and suddenly everything was back to normal, and Iona stood blinking, as the flickering in her eyes flashed on her cheeks. She took a huge deep breath.

"That scared the hell out of me, did you see it?" Rune was so shocked, she could hardly speak, and she nodded, as she breathed her words out.

"I saw it… What the hell was that?" Iona looked pale.

"I think that was the past revealing itself Mum." Rune lifted her arm, and leaned on the old chimney to steady herself.

"I think it was, and honestly, there was no doubt that was Morgana, but that was not the woman I fought, what in all the realms is going on Iona?" She smiled.

"No idea, but it is sort of freaky and fun." Rune looked at her in a strange way, Iona appeared to be enjoying it.

"Are you alright Sweetheart?" Iona nodded.

"I could feel her Mum, I could feel the truth of her, and she was not lying. I know you don't want to hear this, but she was pure Whiteline, and powerful, there was not a shred of darkness in her."

*T*hat made no sense at all to Rune as she looked at the conviction in her daughters' eyes. Rune had no idea what to think at all, she looked at the floor and shook her head, her voice was almost a whisper.

"She was my greatest enemy; I killed her Iona. I hunted down that lair where they all lived, and I removed every one of them. This makes no sense at all, absolutely none. She was evil, she did such wicked things." Iona walked over, and slid her arm over her shoulder.

"Let's go home, we have made a start, and we have progressed well… Come on." The violet arch opened, and holding her hand, Iona walked her through.

They had hardly stepped through, as Gailania came screaming down the grass, with tears in her eyes.

"MUM SAVE ME, DON'T LET THEM GET ME!"

She crashed into Rune's leg, and snatched it tight, as Robbie and Rowan appeared around the side of the house in hooded cloaks. Both of them held up their bows, and had big stuffed pom poms on the ends of their arrows. Iona gave a giggle and Rune sighed, and looked down at her daughter who was as white as a ghost, and shaking.

Robbie slipped back his hood and lowered his bow with a smile, Grover hung from a tree by his leg, and Tegan and Fern were knotted in a large net hanging from the big tree in the garden. Pandora was staked out on the lawn, with a cloth stuffed into her mouth, and appeared to be loving it. Rune gave a sigh as Robbie approached with a limping, but grinning Rowan.

"Robbie, you were supposed to look after them, not hunt them, and trap them." Gailania nodded.

"I got Thorn to help me, and they hung him up in his cabin, they don't play fair."

Rowan sniggered, as Robbie chuckled. Rune gave a sigh, and walked towards the house holding Gailania by the hand as the two laughed, Rune looked down at her daughter.

"They are worse than all of you, honestly, do not encourage them." Gailania nodded.

"Be careful, Aunt Jade is still hunting, she put Yvee in the horse trough and, put a board over it, because she tried to help us, she is scary!"

Rune walked up the garden and flicked her wrist, the net swung loose, and Tegan and Fern fell to the floor with a squeal, Grover dropped from his tree. Pandora was up on her feet with a huge smile, she snatched up her sword.

"THAT WAS GREAT, LETS GO FOR BEST OUT OF THREE!" She ran to help Fern and Tegan untangle themselves.

Rune walked inside with Iona, as a pair of green eyes watched from above.

"Jade, game over." She came back into view with a big smile, holding a wooden knife, Iona just laughed as they entered the kitchen.

"Shouldn't we cut Thorn down Mum, and where is Willow?" Gailania skipped over to her seat.

"Willow hid in dad's clean clothes closet; I told her he never goes in there."

Rune laughed, as she pumped the water into the pan for the stove. Behind her smile, she was unsettled, what she had seen and felt, had shocked her, and her doubts were growing.

Master Elgin was sat in the Scribe room, two desks down from Tila, as he read several parchments he had specifically requested, they were both reports Ariel had tended to the Queens private archive. Alder walked in and approached him slowly, Tila noted it but kept her head down. She had only just got back to service and was reading, as her hands were bandaged and still not fully recovered.

Alder passed her at a fast pace and walked up to the side of Master Elgin, he was holding a piece of parchment. He gave a polite cough to gain Elgin's attention.

"If I may have a moment of your time, I would appreciate your private attention for a document I have." Elgin looked up, and lifted his hand for the document.

"What is the problem, let me have a look?" Alder held on tight to the parchment, and leaned into him and lowered his voice.

"I would prefer your private audience in this matter." Elgin shrugged.

"This is the House of Scribes Alder, everything at some point ends up in our archive, hand it over and let me see it." Tila glanced to the side, she could see that Alder was resistant to the idea, he leaned in again.

"With respect Master Elgin, this is not something we wish to do here."

Elgin frowned and turned in his seat, he saw the parchment and snatched it out of his hand, he unrolled it and looked down at it. Tila was trying not to look, but she could not help it as Elgin's chair slid back on the polished floor, and for his great age, he stood up surprisingly fast. With the squeal of the chair on the floor, every scribe in the house looked up, which was two hundred of them. Elgin turned looking outraged, and raised his voice.

"HAVE YOU LOST YOUR MIND, WHAT IN ALL OF THE REALMS ARE YOU THINKING!?"

Alder stepped back, and took a deep breath, Elgin held up the parchment containing the royal seal.

"WHY WAS I NOT CONSULTED ON THIS, YOU HAVE NO RIGHT TO DO THIS WITHOUT A FULL COUNCIL PRESENCE!?" Alder stood firm, and smirked.

"Master Elgin, may I remind you, that you stepped down, and I was appointed to run this body? I have no need to justify my actions to you, I answer only to the queen."

Elgin looked very annoyed, and Tila was riveted, as she sat up straight and watched, Master Elgin looked like he was going to explode.

"ANSWER TO THE QUEEN, PLEASE REMIND ME OF WHICH ONE, THE DECEASED EX QUEEN?" He looked at Tila and all the other scribes watching.

"OR THE ONE YOU ARE CURRENTLY TRYING TO OUST!?"

There was a massive collective gasp, as two hundred scribes all sat with their mouths open, and their eyes wide. They all gave the same collective response.

"WHAT!?" Alder looked around, every eye in the house was upon him, he turned back to Elgin.

"The council has doubts as to the legitimacy of Iona Violet of Loxley as a suitable future queen of this realm, after all, she is not born of Fae."

No one in the room could believe what he was saying, and murmurs broke out all around the room, as flabbergasted scribes looked to each other in complete shock, what Alder was suggesting was unthinkable. Elgin leaned into Alder; he was red with anger.

"You have no right, do you hear me, no right at all, Robert of Loxley is a descendant of Gwendolyn White Circle, he is related, do you hear me, you idiot? He is a direct descendant of Gwynfor, of the house of the White Circle, who I may add, was the son of Queen Bridget Violet, have you lost all of your sense, you fool?" Alder looked angry, as his eyes narrowed and he tried to bite his lip.

"That is not a direct line, the most suitable candidates are Princess Una and Citrine. I am aware of this situation, and the council has debated it fully, and the motion has passed, Iona Violet will not be queen until we are satisfied."

He snatched the paper out of Elgin's hand, turned, and stormed out of the room, bumping into Bade as he arrived down the corridor. Elgin stood staring and shaking where he stood, he was deep red with rage, as he lifted his fist.

"I WILL FIGHT THIS EVERY STEP OF THE WAY ALDER; DO YOU HEAR ME…. EVERY STEP OF THE WAY!?"

He swayed, and Tila jumped out of her seat and hurried over and grabbed his arm, and helped him, as he breathed heavily, and sat back in his seat. He gave a nod of thanks as he tried to catch his breath, he swallowed hard, and took a deep breath. Tila was worried, he did not look good.

"Master Elgin are you alright, I am worried about you?" He gave a smile, and nodded his head as Bade hurried over, but looked up at Tila.

"Scribe Tila, you must leave here, I fear for your safety, go to Ariel, tell her what has happened, and to await for my word." He reached up and took her arm.

"You are an asset to this house, but Alder has overstepped the mark. Tila, he intends to prevent Iona Violet from taking the crown, he has ten of the council on his side, this will divide the realm. We have to act, and you will be in danger, he will move to reimprison you. Stay with Ariel and work with her, we cannot allow him to prevent the rightful queen from ruling this land. Tila, he is drunk on power, that is what this is about and Iona Violet challenged him, he will not forgive that easily, and you will be his first target, now hurry, go." He pushed her away as Bade looked at Elgin.

"Surely you are not serious, that is treason, there is no way he can do that?" Elgin looked at him.

"Bade, he has done it, the other ten are backing him, it is done. Bade get Tila out of here, she is in danger, now both of you move, this will happen fast now it has gone public." Tila nodded, and leaned in a placed a soft kiss on Elgin's cheek.

"I am going, Master, please do not die, you are the biggest asset of this house, try to live." She moved back, grabbed her bag and some fresh sheets of parchment, and in a loud POP! she was gone. Bade looked white as a sheet as he looked at the old master.

"We need to prepare, this is unprecedented." Elgin gave a long sigh.

"Bade, if this was me doing it, I would arrest you and I, and then empty the house and seal it. You need to leave, grab the three volumes of constitutional law of Fae, and go to Sapphire. If you are not here, they will not use you to break Ariel… Go on Bade, go, I need you safe, you have the skills that will be needed by Sapphire and Ariel to help Iona Violet."

*A*s Bade turned to leave, he heard Alder coming up the hallway with the rest of the council, Bade gave a PoP! And was gone, Elgin sat back and took a deep breath, as Alder came around the corner with two guards and the rest of the council, he spoke loudly as he walked.

"Arrest Tila the scribe, as her sentence will now stand." He walked right up to Elgin with a smug smile.

"Master Elgin, will you sign this document?" Elgin sneered at him.

"I sign nothing handed to me by a puppet of Rhiannon, you will suffer for this Alder, I will see to it." Alder turned to one of the guards.

"Master Elgin is to be confined to his residence until further notice, please escort him out." He turned, as Elgin looked up and laughed.

"So predictable, I studied how Rhiannon clung to power, don't waste your breath Alder, Bade and Tila are gone."

Bade was on the top floor of the archive looking down, holding three large volumes. He watched as Master Elgin was helped out of his seat, and walked slowly towards the doors, he stepped back to avoid being seen, and waited. Down below Alder raised his voice.

"CLEAR THE HOUSE, ALL SCRIBES ARE TO LEAVE, THE HOUSE IS NOW CLOSED." Bade shook his head slowly and whispered.

"You are a disgrace to the house, you will pay for your treachery Alder, I will assure it." There was a loud PoP!, and Bade was gone.

Chapter Eight.

The Unthinkable.

Ariel had been sat all night, as Branna's candle holder sat on her desk, and she read through the night. Having been sealed in her box for the entire time, she had no real idea of who Morgana was, and yet deep down inside she felt a strange stirring, almost as if she had met her. She had sat all night and for most of the day as she headed towards the end of the book, and was so involved with the story, she did not hear when Tila arrived.

Tila knocked, and waited, as she looked around at the beautiful garden, filled with birds and buzzing insects. There was no response, and she was already panicked. Thinking Ariel was out, she turned, and sat with her back to the door, so she could wait. Inside the house, Ariel sat, her eyes locked on the book as she reached the final pages, and as she read, she felt a strong pull inside her, and her eyes filled with tears.

'Morgana used her intelligence, not great powers from the lines of old, and in doing so, she outwitted them and out smarted them. She ultimately removed them from the lives of the rich and powerful, and in doing so, she removed the one thing all those who craved power and greed needed most, the support of the Ruling Council. No matter what her future holds now, in that one thing, she should always be remembered, for she was without doubt, an unsung hero of her people. She was the daughter of a great queen, and it showed.

Morgana never wanted the darkness she has now within her, or to be seen as evil, she never wanted to act evil. All she wanted was justice for the murder of her father, and the rape of her mother, and to most, if it was any other person, that would appear to be fair and proper. She wanted the truth, and questioned all who confronted her, for she saw two truths, the facts as they happened, and the stories told by those of influence who craved greed and power, but which truth was right? She fought for what she thought was right, as did, Rhiannon, and even Maud, all of them believed in the truths they held.

Morgana had many choices in her life, and she chose what she felt was the right path, which was to become a white raven for good. In her lack of understanding of the hate she faced, she suffered a cruel last act of vengeance, and it cost her the very core of whom she was. Morgana became in the eyes of others, the very thing she hated the most. Today, she is still called evil, and yet as I sit here, knowing her as I did, I have to ponder, and I do have to ask… Was she really?'

The final act of revenge from Maud, combined with Branna's heartbroken writings about what she saw, and her final closing passages of the book had her sat back in her chair as she wept. She closed the book and wiped her eyes, feeling the pain that Branna had experienced, and noting where Branna's tears had landed as she wrote and cried. Ariel took a deep breath, she remembered all of the nights they lay together in her caravan, as she spoke of what it would be like to have a daughter who was like her in every way. Ariel could see, that for Branna, Morgana had been exactly that, and it broke her heart to know that what Maud did, was far worse than killing her. Branna had to watch this young woman who was in every way like a daughter to her, slowly be corrupted by the darkness that had eaten at her, and she had fought all her life. Ariel could not imagine how painful that must have been for her.

"I am sorry my love, I should have been there with you, if I had been, maybe we could have saved Morgana, and prevented so much pain in this world, and in your life without me."

She got up from her chair, and her legs were stiff, as she lifted her pot beaker off the desk, she was tired, and felt very emotional. Branna's account of how she felt about Morgana, and how she had taken her under her wing and cared for her, was very tender, and loving. She had seen Morgana as a daughter, and had been happy to see that Morgana had found a way to finally be free, and had wanted to follow in Merlin's footsteps, and be as she commented, a 'White Raven for Good,' made all of her story feel harder to accept.

Her final accounts of the heartbreak she felt, as Morgana turned colder and darker, were so devastating for Branna, as she honestly wrote down her thoughts and feelings of it all. Ariel's mind was filled with thoughts as her insides swirled with emotion. She came through the bedroom and into the front area of the house, and placed her beaker on the table, as she turned to the fireplace.

$\mathcal{S}$he needed wood for a fire, so turned and walked to the door, and pulled it open, and jumped back in fright, as Tila fell backwards into the house with a squeal. Ariel looked down at her sprawled out looking terrified.

"Tila… What are you doing here?" She looked up from the floor covered in parchment.

"You were home all the time… I sat here for ages?" Ariel shook her head.

"I was in Bran's office, reading important papers." Tila sat up, and then twisted as she stood up, and looked closely at Ariel.

"Have you been crying?" Ariel sighed.

"Tila… Why are you here?" Her eyes went really wide, as she realised.

"Mistress Ariel, we have huge trouble, they want to ban the queen, and we need you." Ariel frowned.

"Tila, have you been drinking mead, you cannot ban a queen, what is up with you?" Tila took a huge breath, and flapped her bandaged hands.

"Mistress Ariel, Alder has passed a motion to say Iona has no right to the throne, he has ten on side, and they are talking of Una or Citrine to be the next queen." Ariel gave a small laugh, and shook her head.

"Don't be ridiculous, that is not even possible." Tila nodded.

"Well yeah, I know that and you know that, but it does not look like Alder does, and I think he is going to put Master Elgin in prison, because Master Elgin went crazy mad and shouted at him." All of this felt like insanity, Ariel stepped back and allowed Tila inside.

"Okay, I think you need to come in and tell me everything that happened, because honestly, none of this makes any sense at all."

$\mathcal{R}$une could not relax, all through the meal with the family, she felt more and more unsettled. When the meal was over, she left the girls to wash up, and walked down to her table, and placed her hand on the table to store the memory within it, and then sat down. Her memory appeared and rose out of the table, and she sat back and watched as the cottage built itself, and then Iona morphed into Morgana.

"Freeze."

Rune sat back and looked at her, she was nothing like the person she knew, almost as if she was a completely different woman. Rune leaned forward to study the image, and could see she was around mid thirties, although she did have an air of youth to her, and the creases by her mouth showed she smiled a lot. Under her eyes looked a little dark, she knew that well, it was caused from late nights reading. Rune sighed and sat back.

"How can you be Morgan, if I was to meet you, I would think nothing of it, you are just an ordinary person? You are nothing like the person I know as Morgan." The steps clattered and Iona appeared, she smiled as she saw her mum looking at the frozen image.

"I was hoping you would be here, I am not sure about you, but I cannot stop thinking about today, I think we made some headway." Rune was feeling very uncertain.

"I am not sure about headway; I am really feeling disturbed by all of this. I was hoping to resolve a few things, but what I saw today, has created more questions, and we have not even looked at Branna yet."

Iona sat down next to her and looked at the table, where the picture was frozen of Morgana looking towards the door, and she looked really afraid.

"I wish I could describe what it felt like to be in her shoes, I had such a strong sense of the person she was, and it did surprise me. Mum, I have heard the stories of her all my life of the evil that was Morgan le Fey, but standing there and feeling her emotions, that was not the person I expected at all. Mum, she was really afraid, I could sense her thoughts, and all she could think about was they killed my father, and now they will kill me, and I am innocent." Iona turned to her mother.

"I know you do not want to hear this, but Mum, I absolutely believe she had no idea about who killed Eve. Mum, she believed in Eve, she believed in the Earth Faith, and the fact Eve was dead, terrified her to the bone. Mum, Morgana was wearing a veil, but she dropped it to show Fagan who she trusted, she was innocent." Rune turned and looked at her.

"What?" Iona nodded.

"She trusted him, she saw him as a friend, and she tried to show him her innocence." Rune shook her head.

"No, that cannot be possible, Iona, I have talked to him of this moment, he saw her with Branna and tied to a raven." Iona shook her head.

"There was no raven in her being, she was completely free of anything dark. I am sorry Mum, but I know what I felt, she was without doubt, pure Whitelines. I hate saying it, but that young woman there, the one in that cottage, she was a good person. She was kind and caring, and also very saddened by the loss of her family, and another thing, she was with child, and nervous about it."

Rune leaned forward and put her face in her hands as she tried to think, she felt like everything she had believed had just been ripped out of her. Iona lifted a hand and rubbed her back.

"Mum, we will work all this out, we know two things which will help us, Eleanor and Eve, were not killed by Morgana, so I have to ask, why was Rhiannon so convinced they were?" Rune sat back and looked at Morgana frozen above the table, looking terrified.

"Oh Iona, I have no idea, I mean look at her. That person is no threat to anyone, she is just ordinary, she lives in Avalon in that cottage, and she is absolutely unremarkable."

Both of them looked up at her, and Iona took note of all of her demeanour, and how she was dressed, and her skin.

"She is slender, a little undernourished, and looks tired, her normal living conditions are harsh, I have seen women in some of the local towns that look like her. It is hard to believe that this person we are looking at was the daughter of a queen, and would become one of the most feared people in history." She turned to look at her mother.

"Mum, how does that happen?" Rune sat staring at her with bright blue eyes.

"Sweetheart, I have no idea, I wish I could answer, but I simply have no idea. At the moment, the only thing that makes sense to me, is that in the centre of everything is Rhiannon, and that bodes ill for anyone near her." She looked at the table, and then back to Iona.

"One thing I do know, is if she trusted Fagan, that means he met her before this day, and if that is the case, we need to talk to him."

*A*riel sat at the table with Tila sipping her herbal tea having listened to everything that she had said. She thought carefully, her grey eyes taking note of everything Tila did.

"Where was Bade?"

"Master Elgin was talking to him when I left, I think Lord Elgin wanted him to leave too, and Mistress, he should, Alder is full of power and I think he is going crazy. Mistress, Master Elgin is the nicest person in the house, and I am worried about him." Ariel gave a smile to try and reassure her, but she was concerned.

"Tila, I am sure that Master Elgin will be fine, he has seen many challenges, and the one thing he knows, is how to make his way through the rough times, and yes, he is the nicest person in the House of Scribes."

Ariel got up from the table, she had paced a lot when she had been stuck in Florae, and as she had all those years ago, she paced as she thought, and sounded out her thoughts.

"Iona cannot be told this just yet, I set in motion something very important for her, and I do not want her distracted. I assume Bade was sent to Sapphire, she already hates Alder, so her reaction is easy to predict, let us hope Bade can keep her calm. If Alder intends to do this, he will need to keep the council tight and together, I cannot see all of them being in complete agreement with this. If he wants Una or Treen, he may find that difficult, both of them are very loyal to Runestone and Iona." She stopped and looked at Tila.

"Where is Crystal?" Tila looked up at her.

"Here, she is seeing her sister." Ariel suddenly understood everything, and stamped on the floor.

"Oh no, I just realised, he intends to seal the whole of the realm, that is why Master Elgin sent you both out. Yes, of course he will, because he knows, not one scribe in the house will support this. He will seal the realm, clear the house, and lock the doors, that way if the people try to stop him, he is in his own fortress, I know, I designed it." Ariel looked back at Tila.

"This is not a recent thing, Alder has been planning this for some time, if you ask me, neither Una or Treen will take the seat, and he knows that. Alder intends to create an argument against Iona Violet, and only because he knows they will refuse. There will be no one to be seated, that will leave it vacant for his rule, Alder is going to rule Florae by default." Tila gasped, she could not believe her ears.

"But that is against the Fae creed." Ariel nodded at her.

"That it is, and that could be his undoing, because that will turn Amethyst against him. Tila, you must go to Crystal and tell of all this, but make sure she does not tell Amethyst, at least not yet, we need time to prepare before this blows up. Then Tila, I want you to do what you do best, I want you to write down everything that happened, exactly as it happened. I want this most recent event writing down immediately, so the record of this cannot be altered." She nodded.

"What are you going to do?" Ariel looked at her.

"I am going to get Bade and Sapphire into Florae." She frowned.

"How, it is sealed?" Ariel smiled.

"Not to a mystic it is not, especially one who owns rooms in the royal apartments, and whose mother was Enaria."

*T*here were two pops and both of them disappeared and the house stood empty, as Ariel headed towards Sapphire, and Tila to see and speak with Crystal. Below the house at Rune's table, Robbie came down the steps looking for her, to discover Rune and Iona talking. He heard little of the conversation, but what he heard was confusing, they were talking about the innocence of Morgana.

He stepped out not understanding, and saw the frozen picture of Morgana hanging over the table, he had seen enough of her to last him a lifetime, and had to ask, what for him was the obvious question. Neither Rune or Iona had noticed him, as they stared at the picture and spoke quietly.

"What are you doing, you are not talking about her are you, because innocent is not a word you should apply to that witch?"

Rune took a breath and turned with her daughter, she stood up to face him, she could see he did not understand, and looked very confused. Iona stood up in front of her mum, and faced him.

"Dad… This is something I am looking into, and I have asked mum for advice and some guidance." He nodded as he walked in, Rune watched him carefully, he looked at the table and then glanced at his daughter.

"There is no purpose to looking in to her, we killed her, it is old news, and should be buried and forgotten forever." Rune went to speak, but Iona put her hand back to her, as if to stop her.

"It is something I need to know, something I need to do before I am crowned." She took a step forward towards him.

"I want to know the truth of her and Branna, and I mean the full truth and how two intelligent people can be drawn into the merle and become corrupted. I feel it will serve the people of Fae better." He glanced at Rune, who he could see was watching his every move, he looked at Iona.

"You do? All you had to do was ask, I would have told you the truth of her, she was a vile sadistic evil woman, who has played her part in the death of members of this family and our friends. There, now you know, you need to drop this, and forget about her, and let the dead stay resting in the peace we gave them." Iona shook her head.

"I am sorry Dad, I cannot do that, I have to do this, I have to look at her past and discover the full truth of everything, because I do not believe the full truth has been told." His eyes widened as he moved to Rune.

"Seriously, you are helping her, what the hell is wrong with you two? You know the truth Rune, you were the one that helped kill her, you were the one that put your life on the line to walk into that sick castle of depravity and wipe out all of her ravens. Why the hell are you digging this all up again, did we not suffer enough?"

Rune could feel his anger rising, and the pain he felt, and she went to move towards him, but Iona beat her, and took a pace towards him.

"Dad, I understand how you feel, but…." Robbie felt his temper rise rapidly, and cut her off.

"DO YOU!?"

She blinked and caught her breath, as his eyes narrowed, and he pointed at the picture of Morgana above the table.

"IF YOU UNDERSTOOD HOW I FEEL, YOU WOULD UNDERSTAND THAT THIS… THIS SITTING AROUND QUIETLY CHATTING ABOUT HER INNOCENCE IS THE MOST OFFENSIVE THING YOU COULD EVER DO TO ME!" Rune felt the emotion flow up in him, he took a breath and fought his anger. His voice went very soft.

"I am glad she is not in this world; I am glad she is dead and I helped to kill her, I wanted her dead, I hated her. She took my father, and Beth, she corrupted my brother, and took Ruby, and I watched her monsters tear one of the kindest and most caring people I have ever known into pieces… Pieces, right in front of me, not ten yards away. DO YOU KNOW WHAT THAT DOES TO A PERSON, DO YOU UNDERSTAND HOW THAT FEELS IONA, BECAUSE I DO, AND IT DESTROYED ME?"

His eyes filled with tears, and Rune felt his pain within herself. He took a deep breath, and looked at Iona, she stared at him with watery eyes, and he lowered his voice.

"I am glad that my daughter, and the rest of my children are now safe. I am glad that within a month of your birth, I stood on that island whose name you carry, and I slaughtered her monsters as they came at me, looking to kill you, and I slaughtered the lot, because that gave you the life you have. If you want to know the truth of that dark hearted witch, walk into the Village Hall, and look up. That wall has the name of everyone who gave their life to allow you to live here safely. Take a good long look daughter, because you will notice, there is a long list of our family up there with them." His eyes burned with fire as he spoke, and it scared her a little.

"I was forced to fight an enemy who did not even know me, and I watched as his men tried to destroy everything I cared for. I never thought killing was the answer, but her son was adamant he would kill everything for no other reason that he wanted it all for himself. His men did not want a war, they were forced to, for no other reason than his vanity. I learned one thing from that vile war that all of us had in common, and that is no matter what, all men bleed the same blood, and it is red. You will stop this now, I will not allow it, not in my home. AM I CLEAR?" He turned, and stormed up the steps as Iona stood with tears in her eyes.

Rune slipped her arms around her, and Iona turned and buried her face in her shoulder and wept.

"He has never ever shouted at me before, not ever Mum." Rune held her tight as she wept, and gave a long sigh.

"He is upset, he will calm down. Iona, he suffered so much with the burden, he was glad when it was over, but every death in that war he still feels the responsibility of. I will talk to him."

Iona pulled her head out of her mother's shoulder and sniffled, she shook her head, and her violet eyes twinkled with her tears. She lifted her arm and wiped them, as she sniffled again, and looked at her mother.

"I am going to be a queen; I have to stand up as one. Mum, this is something I am going to do. No one has the power to stop it, because this is what I need to do to understand everything, and then give up my life here and become a queen of my people. I am Violet Stone, and that means I face everything, including the fact I have hurt my father who I love dearly." More tears welled in her eyes.

"I will talk to him, and explain it all." Rune smiled, and lifted her hand to her tears, and wiped them away.

"You are so like him, and you will make a wonderful and caring queen of your people. I love you Iona Violet, you will be a loving queen, but you will always be my daughter, and in this, we will continue together." Iona smiled.

"I love you, Mum." Rune pulled her back into a hug.

"I love you too, my precious daughter."

"MUM… CAN PAN SLEEP OVER WITH ME?" Rune gave a sigh, and looked to the steps.

"HAS HER MUM SAID IT WAS ALRIGHT?"

"YES MUM, WE ASKED HER FIRST."

"ALRIGHT THEN, I WILL BE UP IN A BIT TO MAKE UP A BED."

"IT'S ALRIGHT AUNTIE RUNE, ME AND LANIA DID IT ALREADY." Iona pulled back and giggled as her eyes still sparkled with tears, Rune looked up at the ceiling.

"ALRIGHT THEN, DON'T STAY UP TOO LATE, I WILL BE UP IN A BIT TO KISS YOU GOODNIGHT."

"THANKS MUM…. THANKS AUNTIE RUNE!"

Rune and Iona headed back up the steps to the kitchen, which had been trashed by the kids, and there were crumbs and dirty pots everywhere. Both of them got stuck in, and cleaned up, and then Iona hugged her mum and headed out of the backdoor to her cabin.

*R*une went up to the bedroom where Pan and Gailania had made a bed up on the floor, and were both lay together colouring, and talking. They looked cute together, and reminded her so much of her and Jett when they were younger, she kissed them goodnight and walked softly down to the bedroom. Robbie was sat on the balcony, as she peered around the glass doors at him, he glanced to the side, and then looked forward out over the mere.

Rune walked out and sat at his side, he pretended to ignore her, and she understood he was angry and hurt. Her voice was soft.

"Rob…" He turned and looked at her, his eyes dark and still angry.

"It is wrong Rune, we…." 'SNAP!'

He went instantly silent, his lips sealed as she looked at him, her eyes sparkling with the most beautiful blue, she smiled as his mouth moved, but he could not say a thing.

"You listen to me Lord Robert of Loxley, I do not care what disagreements you have with your daughter, but if you raise your voice to her like that again, I will have my table suck you into it, and hold you there for a year. Am I clear?" He frowned as his head bobbed as he tried to complain. He looked funny and she smirked.

"Robbie, our daughter is going to be a queen of Fae, and in a month, she will leave here forever and go to live in Florae, and whether you think so or not, you are going to really miss her, and she is going to be homesick and miss you. She is to be a queen, and she is very afraid, because for the first time in her life, she will be alone. Robbie, Rhiannon was the same, and just as Branna and Morgan were seduced by the darkness, she was seduced by the power she held, think about that. Power can corrupt, and it matters not whether it is dark or light, our daughter is afraid it will happen to her. Iona needs to find out the truth of Morgana the young woman, who I may add, was around her age when she looked into the Whitelines, and she needs to know the truth of her, and why she became the person we faced. It serves a purpose, actually, it serves a very important purpose, because it will show her how not to use power."

She smiled and leaned in and kissed the end of his nose, he snorted with his frustration. Rune stood up and walked towards the doors, she turned and lifted her hand.

'SNAP'

Robbie gave a huge gasp and breathed in, and she walked through the door, and he slouched back on the seat with a frown.

"I hate it when she is all smug and smart, with her snappy fingers." In the bedroom Rune giggled.

"I can hear you." He gave a sigh.

"Bat ears as well." Rune giggled as she lay on the bed.

"I love you, Lord Loxley." He appeared at the glass door, and she looked at him and smiled.

"Pan is staying over and the house is quiet." He looked at the door, and then back at her, he took a step forward, and the door opened.

"Mum, will you tell those two little fungi to go to sleep, they are keeping us awake." Robbie gave a sigh, and Rune looked up at Tegan.

"Your dad will sort them out, he needs to say goodnight to them." Robbie looked at her in disbelief.

"Why me?" Rune winked.

"I want to make myself extra sexy for you." He looked at Tegan, and she smirked.

"Come on Dad, the little rats won't shut up." Rune gave another giggle, as he walked towards the door sulking.

Chapter Nine.

The Face of Fear and Truth.

As dawn rose, at Callanish in the small cottage, Sapphire, Bade and Ariel read through the laws of Fae, and talked of what their plan could be to remove Alder using the laws of Florae.

Rune was still asleep with Robbie, Pan was curled around Gailania and Fern, who had climbed in with them, had her arm around both of them. Tegan was flat out, lay across her bed, with her head hanging off, and her hair hanging down to the floor. Tila was up, cooking as Crystal dressed, and Iona was not in Loxley.

Iona stood on the cliff top, wearing her veil, she had not slept much after her father's outburst, and her mind was filled with questions, and she wanted to answer them. Behind her just down the hill, were the remains of an ancient castle, and on the headland, the crumbled remains of Morgan le Fey's new complex. The town behind her lay in ruins and deserted. In the final days of the war, when the Dark One fell, and all her buildings fell with her, the people fled in fear, and never returned.

The wind blew through her long brown and golden hair, and her violet eyes looked out to the sea as she softly spoke into the winds.

"I believe Morgana of Cornwall, was innocent of the murder of Eve and Eleanor, but knowing that makes all of this harder. Why release Merlin and Opal into the hidden realm, and yet Lord Hearne and Gwendolyn with her family were sealed in crystal tubes, it makes no sense to me?"

Iona turned slowly, and her eyes followed the sea back to the land, and high clifftops opposite, where the crumbled remains of an ancient church stood, surrounded by the long grasses that swayed in the wind. She breathed in deeply, and felt her senses connecting to something, and a picture flashed in her mind. She blinked, what was that?

She closed her eyes, and felt her way back into her inner most self as Ariel had taught her, and once again, the feeling began to grow. Iona breathed slowly, and her mind relaxed and started to focus. There was another flash, and suddenly in her mind she saw Morgana stood near the church, and two graves. One was old, and one was new.

Iona breathed in, and could feel the pain and devastation within her, Morgana was crying as she stood before them looking down. Each grave bore a name, Victor and Medraut, Morgana gave a sniffle.

"What am I to do now father, they have taken you, and my son who I loved dearly, and once again I feel the emptiness within me? It feels like the cruellest twist of fate, as I am again alone, is this my destiny?"

She gave a sniffle, turned, and walked onto the cliff path, Iona followed her, as she walked paths she knew well, almost as if she had walked them all her life. She was older than her last vision, maybe a little older than her mother Runestone. Iona in her mind walked at her side, unsure of where she was going, and why she was walking away from the castle and church. It became clear, as up ahead on the path, another woman walked, she was older, much older, although they looked a similar age, Iona could feel it. Morgana walked up to her, and Iona suddenly realised who it was, and breathed her name quietly out.

"Branna!"

Branna opened her arms, and pulled Morgana into them holding her tightly, and Morgana broke down and wailed into her with utter grief, as Morgana sobbed.

"He was my son, and I loved him so dearly, and I have lost him too, what do I do now, how can I carry on without him?"

The smoke funnelled up, and they disappeared, and Iona took a deep breath and opened her eyes, as she swooned slightly. She stood breathing slowly, all of the feelings of that moment washing over her, and trying to understand what it was that had happened in her vision. Iona looked across the bay, she could see the exact point where they had met, but it was slightly obscured by two ancient trees. Her mind played slowly back over the memory.

"So much pain, how can anyone be filled with so much grief and pain, was all of your life pain Morgana, was there no joy in your life at all?"

*R*une came down the stairs yawning, she had not slept well, she walked into the kitchen, where Pan and Gailania sat eating bread with big blobs of jam on it, she frowned as she looked at them both.

"Where is your sister?" Gailania shrugged.

"Tegan is still asleep with her head on the floor and her legs on the bed." She giggled and Pan giggled with her.

"I meant Iona, she told me she would be up early and make you something to eat." Gailania shrugged, her blue eyes dancing, and jam smeared all around her mouth.

"Fern said she was crying last night, maybe she is still sleeping." Rune gave a sigh as she turned.

"She was crying?" Gailania nodded.

"It is probably love, Yvee cries all of the time too, Fern said it was because she was love sick." Rune smirked, as she turned around to the sink.

"Yvee would be better served helping her mum, and spending less time with Kale."

"It is probably because Uncle Rowan hates him, he says that wilted lettuce will never have her hand, he will kill him before that happens. Does dad want to kill someone too?" She looked at Pan.

"I am never getting married, my dad says there is no man good enough to outshoot him, and that is what they have to do. That is probably why Iona was crying, no one is as good as my dad." Pan nodded.

"If I want to get married, he will have to beat my mum with swords, and my dad says if he wins mum, then he will have to win my dad in an unfair fight, cause my dad will bite his face off, and I am not marrying a man with no face." Gailania looked horrified, and nodded really quickly.

*R*une came out of the kitchen chuckling with her cup, and walked across the living room, to sit in the peace, as she focused her mind to find her eldest daughter. Rune looked deeply, but there was nothing. She gave a sigh, Iona was veiled, and too far away for her to get a proper fix on her. Robbie appeared at the top of the stairs, he trudged down, and then saw her and stopped. She smiled as he stood there, in bare feet with his shirt out.

"Be wary, your nemesis is in the kitchen covered in jam, so she will be loud, and sticky." He nodded.

"I will head to Thorn's cabin, and make a drink there." She giggled.

"Thorn does not drink coffee; he won't have any." Robbie sighed.

"Okay, Iona does, I will go there, I do need to talk to her."

"She is not there Robbie, she left in the night wearing a veil. It appears she feels she must hide to achieve something very important to her." He turned back and looked at her, Rune lifted her hand and pointed.

"It is jam and sticky, or no coffee for you My Lord, that is the price you pay for raising your voice." He gave a desperate sigh, and his face dropped.

"Rune, do I have to?" She sat back, and lifted her cup.

"Yes… You can forget asking me… Off you go Uncle Robbie." He walked across the living space like a man convicted, and pushed open the door.

"UNCLE ROBBIE!" The door swung shut, and Rune giggled.

"Awe God… No, stand back, what the hell have you been doing, you are both covered!?" Rune sat back and chuckled into her cup.

*I*ona stood on the headland and looked back at the ruins of the castle; it did not take much to work out how it must have been impossible to storm it. This is where Morgana's story began, it was a time long since lost, and yet the energy here still lingered, she could feel it, as she looked slowly around talking to herself.

"It is funny, this place was built by your father, it was he who laid the stones, and you were born here, and started your life here. Yet, this place has not been remembered for you or your father." Iona spent a moment just looking across at the old ruin.

"It has only ever been remembered for Arthur, how did that feel Morgana, what was it like as a young girl, having lost your father living here in a castle that was no longer yours, but given to a king?"

Iona closed her eyes for a moment, as she felt the earth around her, and could almost feel the sadness of the site. Was this her legacy living deep under every stone, the power of a sad and lonely young girl? She opened her eyes and took a deep breath.

"Were you driven by pain and sadness to become the feared figure you became? I wish I could talk to you, I wish I could hear your story, for I feel there is more to this than has been said. What is your truth Morgana, would you answer me if I asked you?"

Behind her there was movement and she turned, and her breath trapped in her throat, as she saw Morgana facing her, and behind her a figure in white and blue appeared, it was Gwendolyn. Iona watched as Morgana stood with her back to Gwendolyn, and Iona sensed she was waiting to be struck down, which made no sense at all, why would she not turn and face her? Morgana spoke.

"Come to kill me have you, well my back is turned to you, so take a shot, that is the usual way the council act?" Gwendolyn stood still; her bright blue eyes focused on her; Iona watched with great interest.

"I did not come to fight you Morgana, your mother has died, and I believe that is a time of truce. You are not easy to find, and yet I knew you would be here, and I want to talk." Morgana turned and faced her, Iona noticed as her long black hair swished across her back, lifted by the wind.

"I would not tell your sister the golden queen, she will curse you for not killing me the moment you saw me." Gwendolyn looked her in the eyes, Iona sensed her desperation and sadness.

"All I want is the truth, every lead I have, crosses the path of you, I know that you know something, and I need to know how to find my family members, my daughter's need their children back." Morgana gave a small laugh, as she looked at Gwendolyn in her long thick white robes, her blue cloak, and her long golden hair flowing behind her in the wind.

"You talk of truth, which truth, the facts as they are, or the words of the great golden queen, for it appears to me, only her words matter, and my voice is silenced?" Iona pricked up her ears, was it not that very same thing she had said to her mother?

"Morgana, all I seek is the full truth, your words do not have to be silenced, tell me."

"Then what, you will go to the golden queen and set things right?" Morgana laughed.

"You look at me and see evil, would you truly believe anything I say? The golden queen has smeared my name, and accused me of every wrong in the kingdom. Just because it is the great and glorious golden queen, everyone bows down and agrees with her. Are you honestly telling me anything I say will be believed, for if you are, then you know you speak lies?" Gwendolyn stared at her with hope in her eyes, she took a step forward.

"I know you know something, and what you know can help me, Morgana, please talk to me, and I will listen." Morgana shook her head.

"Gwendolyn, I know you to be a reasonable person, but have you any idea of what my truth will do? She will destroy your kingdom, and tear down everything to hide what the truth of her is. If I told you what I know, you would not live long enough to listen, do you not think she is watching you now, and is ready to pounce the moment you leave? I already sense her guards approaching." Gwendolyn looked round, as Morgana smiled.

"Her hand is long, and even you are not safe. I am not guilty of the sins she has given me, but that matters not to her." The smoke swirled up from her feet, and Gwendolyn reached out to grab her.

"Please Morgana no, I need to know what you know!"

*I*ona gasped, and Gwendolyn looking desperate faded from view, and Iona stood alone again, the grass blowing around her feet, and wind lifting her hair, and once again her emotions swirled within her. She moved her hand, and her faint window appeared, she stepped through and walked out onto the top of Citadel Mount, and Amethyst smiled as she saw her.

"Iona, you are a princess and very powerful, and even under your veil, it is not easy to hide from a queen more powerful than my grandmother. Tell me, how can I help a wandering princess?" Iona smiled; she should have known better.

"I have a wish to see the grave of Igraine."

"See it, or sense it?" Iona frowned.

"How do you mean?" Amethyst gave a chuckle.

"All queens have a quest before they take the crown, I thought mine was to reopen Avalon, I was wrong. It took me some time to work out it was also to right the wrongs of my grandmother." Iona was interested.

"It was?" Amethysts eyes shone with bright violet, and Iona sensed that she had some idea of what her intentions were. She lifted her hand.

"Walk with me and I will show you the way." Iona turned to see the large block of stone known as 'The Rest.' They started to walk slowly side by side.

"I heard about Tila, Crystal was very upset, I owe you my thanks for stepping in on her behalf, you acted quickly, and it meant a lot to me to see you go to her aid. Crystal is very important to me, and Tila is to her. Iona, my sister spent a lot of time alone unable to touch anyone, so she suffered the fact that she could not embrace those she cared for, one of which was Tila. I have always felt I owed a great debt to your mother; it was her gift that allowed them to hold each other. It is something so simple and yet so important, I have had great joy seeing my sister so happy." Iona smiled.

"I did not know that, I know they are together, I just did not know about my mother's gift to her." Amethyst stopped, and looked at her.

"Iona, I feel I know something of your quest, walking around old burned out buildings with your mother, is something a queen will notice, and if I did, others will also." Iona gave a nod, and let out a long sigh.

"My father knows, and he is angry with me." Amethyst appeared to understand.

"If what you seek is the truth of Morgan le Fey, you may find many will resist you, and few will want to talk with you. I feel from one queen to a future queen, I should warn you, but I will also add, if you uncover more of the truth of my grandmother, you would seek me out first, and show me what you have learned, for I have worked hard to undo some of the things she did."

Iona could understand that, it made sense to her, and also felt fair that she should inform her first, considering all of the things that she had heard of that time stuck in this realm.

"I will… I realise the sensitivity of this, and suffered my first telling off. My mother has offered to help me, but I feel in allowing her to do that, it will cause a rift between her and my father, and I do not want that. Their love is strong, I do not want them to fall out over me. Amethyst, this is something I must do, I have no idea why, I just feel very strongly that if I am to rule as a queen of truth, I must do this." Amethyst smiled.

"Out of all the people you could talk to, Iona, I am possibly the only person who will understand that feeling and power to act. I was the same, allowing Ariel back into her home, gave me a sense of peace like no other. It saddens me that my race was cleansed, and yet we could not cleanse Branna. I would have wished that, but the White Lord took her before I could fully understand all that had happened." She smiled and pointed.

"It is right there, I am not sure what you will learn from it, but her mother lies within, Morgana was taken, and even if she had been given a place to rest, it would not have been here, this was the one place she never wanted to rest, that much I do know."

Amethyst watched as Iona turned to walk towards the doorway, and Amethyst looked up at the top of it, and then turned back to look towards the Citadel.

"You know Rune, that was one hell of a shot, I doubt I would have hit a small star at that range."

*I*ona entered the rest, and saw the tomb of Igraine opposite Uther's, whose tomb was filled with flowers, she turned to Igraine's, where there was a single posy of wild flowers on top of it. She walked towards it, and could feel the power that emitted from it. She stared at the small bunch, wrapped and tied in a small piece of lace. It was similar to so many she had picked for her own mother as a young girl, and Gailania still did for her mum. She gave a small smile, and yet again, she saw a tenderness, a love from a daughter who really loved her mother.

"Such devotion Morgana, I find myself confused, as the more I hear and see, the less like the woman you became you are. How did you go from the young woman who picked these for her mother, to the figure of horror I have always heard about?"

There was a faint scent in the air, and she leaned forward as she looked closely at the small posy. It contained lavender, sage, chamomile and wild rose, they still had their scents intact, she could smell them clearly.

"If you look hard enough, you will see they still sparkle where her tears fell upon them."

Iona gave a startled jump and turned, and there before her, stood a figure she had never seen before, although she could see little, as he wore a long black tatty hooded cloak. What frightened her the most, was on his shoulder was a large black raven, which stared at her.

"Who are you, and why do you know such things?"

He moved a little closer, and she could sense a great power within him, and from under the hood came a little titter of a laugh.

"Your senses serve you well young Violet Stone, for I see you have reasoned out your answer, and have guessed correctly." Iona dropped to her knee.

"My Lord Albanlin, forgive my stupidity, I should have known straight away." He gave another little laugh.

"Rise to your feet young queen, it pleases me to see you here, the

Mistress of Light has set you on the right path." Iona slowly rose from the floor.

"She has?" The hood twitched.

"She has indeed, for the search to know the truth is a search of great importance. I feel seeking the truth, is the path to true justice for all, and if that is to be your rule, Bridget Violet would be very pleased to see this." Iona understood that.

"My Lord, my search is going to hurt people, for I feel what I am learning, is not what they want to hear, and yet I feel it is important they hear it. Am I wrong to follow the path I am on?" His hood moved, and she felt he had given her a nod.

"A queen who panders to every whim of her people will eventually lose respect, and a queen who panders only to her vanity, will lose respect much faster. Both paths lead to failure of a sort, whereas, the middle road of truth, will not always be appreciated, and at times make you feel good, but it will always garner respect. You have a path to follow, and as I once told a young student, it is your own choice to take the path you deem the right one. I had high hopes for her, for she had everything to be a light for great good." Iona sensed he meant Morgana; she looked back to the posy.

"Are you talking of Morgana, because she did not choose a path of light?"

"Actually, young Violet Stone, you are wrong, she did choose the right path, and it was the brightest of lights." Iona gasped.

"How… My Lord, no disrespect, but she slaughtered thousands." Albanlin walked towards the tomb, and stood before the small bunch of flowers.

"I cast a spell on these, for they held the truth of who she truly was, and I wanted that preserved for all time. You can clearly see the tears she shed as she wept for the loss of her mother. Let me show you something my young queen, and then I will tell you what I know."

*I*ona stepped back and looked down, as Morgana appeared breaking her heart, as she wept before the tomb, the small posy on the floor below her face. It was painful to watch, made even harder, as Iona felt the deep bitter feelings of loss within Morgana. Iona swallowed hard, as she stared at her, feeling overwhelmed by the power of the feelings. Morgana slowly calmed down, and wiped her eyes, and then spoke.

"Have you also come for me, to punish me for the sins of my accusers?"

"No… I am merely a spectator in all things, although, you stand on a fine edge young Morgana, and it interests me in what you will do next." Iona saw the White Lord stood over by the far wall, Morgana stood up, and turned to face him.

"I am white line, so you are indeed my master, as you are Merlin's. Do you wish also to command me?" His hood moved slightly, as she looked at him.

"It may surprise you to know, that to this date, you have honoured your oath that you undertook as a student of my guardian. I see only one life that weighs heavy on you, and in that I feel you judge yourself harshly, for it appears your life was in great peril, and your need was to defend yourself." Iona was confused, how could she have honoured her oath to the Whitelines? She watched on as the images continued, unable to understand how she had honoured her oath, and trying to work out everything. Morgana looked at her lord.

"My belief is to preserve life, I am not so casual in the way I deal out death, unlike others you are allied to." That shocked Iona, of what did she speak?

"Indeed, I admire the sense you hold for the injustice you see, my interest now lies in the path you shall walk, as I see many roads, of which some are shrouded in darkness." She gave a slight laugh.

"You care about me whilst your council destroy whomever they choose to get what they want. What about those who have suffered at their hands, tell me Lord, what of the deaths and wrecked lives that grieve for the actions of your so called superiors who wield the power?" Iona could not believe what she was hearing, she was questioning the white lord, how could she do that?

"That is exactly my point young student, I have given free will to all, even you, and I will not step in to stop you. You have the power of your own choice, and it is in that, the way forward is paved. I see the choices you have and the lengths you have gone to, I am not as blind as you think, but I will add, that you alone took it upon yourself to act, and speak out against the injustice you see. That was the path you started, all I ask is will you continue straight, or deviate onto darker roads?"

"All I can do is fight for what I have seen as unjust, and yet I fight the corruption of those you support, and you stand here and question me?" She gave a slight laugh, and turned and pointed behind her.

"There lies my mother, laid out in a box, next to the man who raped her, tell me wise lord, can you not see how insulting that is to her memory? She was a queen of those dedicated to the faith of the earth, a faith that celebrated you, and those who came with you. She was a woman of the highest standing in this realm, and yet you have sat idle and allowed Arthur and this rapist to bring forth a god who betrays her and all of us. You seat a queen in this first realm and call her glorious, whilst she hurts the very people who have toiled in this land to create her realm of power. How can you stand before me and request what path I take, when you have never cared of the path of those you have aligned yourself with?" His hood twitched.

"Yours young student, interests me the most." She gave a sigh.

"Your priorities appear to me to be somewhat off balance, for I am meaningless, as all I want is to live in peace, and yet no matter how hard I have tried, since the day I was born, I have been attacked for a reason I still do not know. My Lord, do not waste your time on me, I have nothing left, my father and mother have gone, and I feel empty like a barren wilderness." The White Lord turned, and walked slowly towards the door.

"The time to choose your path will soon come, and the choice you make will be of great importance. You have never been meaningless young student, the path you take will be a great bearing on everything. Think with care of your road from this day, for if I am right, you will bring about great change." He faded away and she stood alone, and lost, filled with grief, and shook her head.

"You know it all, and still do nothing, does everything have to burn down before you finally take note?" Her voice echoed off the walls, he was gone. Morgana turned and looked one last time at her mother's tomb.

"You are better off now, you can be with father, and I must continue this miserable existence here in this dying realm." The smoke swirled around her, and she was gone.

*I*ona stretched out and leaned on the tomb of Igraine as her head swirled, and her eyes flickered, and she felt breathless.

"My Lord, what have you shown me, why does she feel the Ruling Council is corrupt?" His hood moved.

"Because they were, she was right." Her eyes opened wide with shock, and she gasped.

"My Lord, this cannot be right, I am sorry, but I am struggling to accept this."

"As your father struggled to accept your truth, you now struggle to accept mine, whereas Morgana understood and acted to stop it." Iona could not believe what she was hearing, it challenged every belief she held, and she breathed in to try to even understand it.

"My Lord, she imprisoned Merlin and Opal, and also Gwendolyn and her family and Lord Hearne." He gave a titter.

"She did, she was gifted, it impressed me, as for most of the time she used little of her powers and used her mind to outwit them, I admired her." Iona looked up as she breathed in, and saw him stood next to the wall.

"And yet she still turned dark and slaughtered thousands."

"Would it surprise you to know that even in her darkness, Morgana caused few deaths compared to that of her son, who was the truly evil one? Morgana was not innocent in the end, but all through her life she never needed to kill if it could be avoided. The truth was that she could project terror in such a way, often times death was useless to her, for keeping people alive to do her bidding served her better." Albanlin turned, and walked back to the tomb.

"The council went too far; she was right about her father and her mother. All of the council agreed to it, and all the council helped plan it, and to a degree, she was right, they were all complicit in the fall of her father, and others in their rush for a One True King. Tell me young queen, will you slash freely at others in your journey towards becoming a queen?" Iona shook her head.

"My role as queen was preordained, it is agreed and will be so." He gave a small laugh.

"Alright, if it was opposed, and you confronted an enemy who was determined to prevent you, would knowing Morgana, who was not powerful compared to the council, still stood up for her beliefs, and stood her ground and confronted them head on and worked to prevent them? Would you do the same, or would you slaughter all in your path?" Iona stared at him in the dim light.

"I would state my case with the truth of who I am, and I would win my position on that ground." His hood moved a little.

"That is what Morgana did, it is why I admired her, her fight was hard, but she won in the end." Iona shook her head.

"No, she didn't, because she went dark and ended up destroyed by my mother and you." Albanlin walked slowly towards the door.

"Young Violet Stone, she did win, and is still winning, that much I have seen today, her darkness is a different story altogether, but I think that is a part to play out yet. I have played my part and I am pleased with your progress. You have won my respect, I look forward to the coming month, I find like young Morgana, your story is becoming the most interesting." He faded away from view, and she stood staring at the wall.

"That makes no sense at all." A quiet chuckle echoed around the room.

"The voice of a queen, and her consent, can change everything, it makes far more sense than you currently realise."

Chapter Ten.

A Fond Old Memory.

Master Elgin sat on his balcony, with a stack of parchment and ink, as two guards stood at the bottom of his steps. He watched as the people of Fae began to gather in the centre circle of the realm, below the House of Scribes steps. He knew that the scribes of the house would not be quiet, and smiled as he watched from his apartment house at the side of the large building. For Elgin, he was perfectly placed with a front row seat to watch, and record anything that may happen.

At Callanish, Ariel walked up towards the large circle of stones, in her mind a plan was forming, she closed her eyes as she walked.

"Runestone, hear me."

On Sora, Gwynfor sat on his bench on the deck in front of his cabin, as the sea rolled up the sand onto the beach across from the grassy front of his home. He held an axe and drew a wet stone over the blade, as he fine tuned the cutting edge. On the floor at his feet a line of sharpened chisels, worn from years of work, awaited his hand to guide them again.

There was a flash and he looked up, and through the window of light, walked Ariel, Runestone, Sapphire, and Bade. Ariel smiled as she walked towards him.

"Greetings Lord of the Isle, I have need of your wisdom."

Just behind them another flash erupted, out of which walked Tila and Crystal, and then a bright yellow flash brought Ena and Max onto the grass. Gwynfor gave a smile and stood up.

"I expected this, there are dark deeds on this day in this land, never has such a thing been considered, come, we have work to do." He looked at the group.

"I have room, come on, there are plenty of beds, and I will put on a pan, and we shall sit and talk. My word this is fun, I have not had such company in years, it will be like a holiday week, come, make yourself at home."

Ariel was clever, Sora was the one island that was slightly separated from Florae, and not under the rule of the council, as it had always been the property of the royal house, a private estate for the privacy of the family. Gwendolyn had taken many months in her life to recover and rest here, as it was an island no ordinary Fae would ever travel to.

*A*cross the realms, Iona Violet wandered through Avalon, unaware that she was walking in the footsteps of Morgana, as she walked through wild meadows of lavender and chamomile. Lost in her thoughts, as she considered the words of the White Lord, along the base of the high giant's shoulder, and eventually into the trees.

She was tired, and had not slept much, her mind constantly filling with thoughts, and the images that she had seen, as she searched for the truth of what had happened in this land in times long since passed. Without really understanding, she walked through the trees, and found herself stood in a large area, up against the high rock, where the waters fell into a large pool.

Iona stopped and looked around at the sea of green, and noted an old heavy built arbour, which was covered in climbing vines of green. She walked over to it, and felt the power of the charm that was upon it, and as she investigated, she pulled back the curtain of growth, to reveal a silken bed. Iona looked back to the pool, as she began to realise where she was, she had walked by accident into Eve's Garden. It was a place she only knew about as her mother had told them all of it as children sat on the nursery floor. Knowing it was no longer occupied, she slid into it and lay back, her body was weary and her mind exhausted. Within minutes she was asleep, curled up on the bed, and sleeping deeply. From out of the pool, a red mist flowed towards her, and surrounded the arbour, and as Iona dreamed, the mist settled around her.

As she slept, her dreams were filled with images of a time she never knew. She found herself walking through Tintagel, or around the cottage in Avalon, and all of the voices, and conversations she had witnessed spoke in her mind. She lay back as she slept, and through the mix of all the other voices she heard something she had never heard before.

"They are beautiful are they not?"

"My Lady of life, please forgive me, I was distracted by the wonder and enchantment of this flower."

"The White Star, is the only thing my brother gave to this or any other realms. It is a flower of great beauty and enchanting to behold. I do not blame you for admiring it, I often do myself. I know of you little Morgana; I have heard of your woes in the land of the Queen of the Moon. I take it you came here to collect plants to furnish your garden?"

"No, My Lady, I would never take what was not given, I awoke feeling a sadness in my being, as the past overwhelmed me, and I wanted to walk to clear my thoughts, and I am not sure why, but I ended up here."

"The forest of my husband is indeed a place of great beauty, and I feel you were drawn here out of need, for within this realm, you will find the peace to ease your heart. There is much here that would aide you, and all but this one plant, could be harvested for your garden, this sadly only grows within the boundaries of this forest, and to move it, would bring about its demise."

"I would not do that to something of such great beauty."

"You may take some of the flowers, for I hear you wish to aide those who live within the Moon Realm with tinctures to ease their ills. They are very potent, so use them with great care."

"I am grateful, and yet, I do not wish to spoil this place, for I feel it would lessen the beauty of it."

"Then hold out your palm, you show such respect for my husband's forest, and it will be rewarded."

The image of a hand flowed into her dream, almost as if she was looking at her own hand, and she watched a plant with two leaves grow out of it. As Iona dreamed, in her mind the plant grew, filling her mind with leaves, and she heard a soft voice almost whisper to her.

"I will care for you, for you are beautiful, and I feel the power of your goodness. Grow stronger my little plant, for we shall do great good for those who have need of you. May the blessings of this earth, forever hold you and care for you as you grow stronger." The plant exploded into flower, and they were the purest white, and shaped liked stars.

Iona gave a gasp, her eyes snapped open, and she sat bolt upright on the bed, and took a huge intake of air.

"That flower, I have seen it before!"

*U*na stood outside the burned out cottage of Morgana of Cornwall, as the sun started to sink down in the sky, it was late evening and since Iona's visit, she had been very unsettled. She stared at what was the cottage hoping answers would come, which would help ease her inner turmoil. She gave a sigh.

"So much pain has been caused, and yet my queen to be, has stirred much of my feelings of the past, feelings I had thought I had left behind me all those years ago. How I wish I could still leave them behind, and yet once again I find myself standing here for the hundredth time, looking for answers I know will never be answered."

She stared into the darkened ruin of Morgana's cottage, lost once again, as her mind played the memories, she wished she could forget, feeling utterly alone and betrayed. As she was staring ahead, she noticed the twelve faint stars, circle in the air and then drop to the floor creating an arch, and suddenly through it walked Iona, and their eyes met. Iona looked surprised.

"Aunt Una, what are you doing here?" Una stared at her, and took a deep breath.

"I am unsettled and have been since your visit. Iona, I held much back, and I feel guilty because I should have been honest with you. You will be my queen, and you showed that clearly in the way you defended yourself. I know of the quests set to all queens; my mother spoke often of them. The truth is, I have been here many times looking for answers I can never answer." Iona gave a soft nod, and smiled.

"Then we share the same purpose, for I have returned also to seek out something that may answer my questions." Una frowned.

"You have?" Iona turned, and looked to the apple tree, and she smiled and lifted her hand.

"What do you know of that plant?"

Una walked through the gap where the gate had fallen off, as Iona turned and walked over to the tree, and Una followed her. Iona came to a halt and crouched down, and there growing in amongst all the grasses, was a plant filled with bright white star shaped flowers. Una gave a gasp as she looked down at it.

"I cannot believe it, it is the white star, the flower of Albanlin." Iona suddenly understood, and stood up with a smile, as Una stared at it almost in shock.

"Eve gave this to Morgana and she planted it, and here it still grows, because she blessed the roots in the name of the earth, as the old ways always did." Una turned slowly to look at her.

"Iona, that plant only grows in the Forest of Time, apart from one other." Iona nodded.

"It grows at my home, I have seen it many times but had no idea as to what it was, for it is not in any book I have read." Una nodded.

"Well, it won't be, but the thing that has shocked me, is this will never thrive where there is evil, and yet here it is growing in Morgana's garden." Iona smiled.

"Morgana tended this plant with great love, I feel her presence all around it, and yet, she is called evil. Una, the girl who lived here and the woman she became are two different people, and something happened to her of which I have no clue. I just know that when she lived here, she was a dedicated student and true to the Whitelines, so I have to ask, how can a person who grew this plant, become so tainted, she turned from the light into darkness?" Una shook her head.

"That is a question I cannot answer, but I am starting to think I would like to." Una turned to her.

"Are you free, I feel there is something I need to show you, it is something that you must see for yourself to understand it?" Iona shrugged.

"I have not made any plans, and I have been avoiding my dad, so yes, I have nothing better to do." Una took her hand.

"Come with me, we will walk and talk."

*U*na took Iona down the road, and turned at the fork, heading towards the marshes, and as they walked, she talked.

"Iona what I am going to tell you is painful for me, and a source of shame. I am not sure if you know, but as a young girl, I became involved with a married man. His name was Kane, he was good looking and wealthy, and I was very naïve, and believed all he told me about him leaving his wife. What I did not know at the time, was he was not quite as wealthy as I believed him to be, it was his wife who had all the riches." Una stopped, as they walked onto a wooden bridge, and turned to her.

"Iona, we had the most terrible row, and I refused to see him for quite some time. He sent me letters and pestered me for a long time after, and I eventually relented, and met up with him in Glaston. He sweet talked me, and apologised, he even brought flowers and wine, and we spent the night together again. When I awoke, he was gone, and I was so angry with myself, as I had sworn to myself beforehand, I would not stay with him. I came home, and not long after I found out I was with child. He never knew the child was his, I never told him, and the next time I met him we had another argument about his wife, and we parted company forever." Iona gave a nod understanding what Una had told her.

"Aunt Una, you do not have to tell me this, your life is your own." Una looked serious, and took a deep breath.

"Iona, I have not told you why we had an argument to begin with, and I feel it is important."

"Alright, I am unsure as to why this matters, but tell me." Una looked like this was really difficult for her, and her voice lowered.

"Iona, the reason we argued, was he told me he had been sent to Tintagel by the queen. Kane was given the task of seducing Morgana to find out what she knew about Rhiannon. It appeared that Morgana had far more knowledge than most about Branna and Ariel, and Rhiannon wanted to know everything she knew. Kane was supposed to seduce her, win her confidence, and then inform Rhiannon, when she was heading back to Avalon, at which point, she planned to have her killed on the road whilst travelling here." Iona gasped, and Una nodded.

"We argued, because he returned angry that Morgana had deflected all his advances, and turned him down flat before he even got a chance to try and seduce her. I was so angry, especially as he told me he found her quite pretty, and thought she had a very lovely body, and he was disappointed he did not get her disrobed to see it." Iona nodded her head.

"He actually told you that, I hope you slapped his face?" Una smiled, and gave a sigh.

"I was a foolish and jealous young girl, and I learned the hard way. To be honest, even though I was angry, I knew she was not to blame, and she did reject him outright. As I told you, I have always thought, had we been in different circumstances, I am sure we would have been friends." They started to walk again, as Iona thought about it.

"Rhiannon really hated her, well, she must have if she wanted her dead."

"I have often thought of it, because when you take into account that, and I know for sure she did not kill Eleanor, then you start to wonder. Iona, Rhiannon blackened her name and reputation, she had friends, until Rhiannon made it impossible for her. I want you to meet someone, who was here at the same time as she was, he is old, and has suffered terribly, but I think you need to hear his story." Iona gave a nod, there was something very sincere about the way Una spoke.

*U*na led her across the marshes, and when the road split, they took the left hand road, which came upon a village. They walked up the main street and out the other side, and walked for another ten minutes, until they arrived at an old stone-built house, surrounded by a beautiful garden. Una turned.

"Iona, this is the house of the retired Commander Stenlow, he was the commander of all the marshals when Morgana lived here, and he knew her. Stenlow defended Morgana over the death of Eve, and as a result he was shipped back to the moon realm, and suffered in the deep prisons where he served his term until Amethyst took the throne and pardoned him." Iona understood, and together they walked down the path.

"I will warn you, his wife was a terrible woman, she was not well liked at all, and when he was sent back to the moon realm, she left him, and took everything he owned. He returned here with little; he is the older brother of Fagan. He stayed with Fagan for a while, and we helped him get on his feet, Wilson and myself have helped him a great deal."

Stenlow sat on his porch, he was a great age, his hair was snow white and very thin, his elegant moustache he had once been so proud of, was now unkempt, badly trimmed and was lost to his long beard. He walked with a stick, and was slow, Iona felt sorry he had been disturbed by them, and yet she saw a kindness to his eyes, if not tinged with a little sadness.

Una explained why they were there, and told him that they were looking for the truth of who Morgana was when she lived in Avalon, and the sheer mention of her name appeared to fill him with light. He looked at Iona, not really knowing who she was. He gave a soft smile and a contented sigh.

"She is who I think of when I look at the sunsets, I have often wondered about her, she was such a lovely innocent girl. Strong willed mind you, she stood her ground, and spoke her piece, she could be quite the little powerhouse when defending herself. We did not get off to a good start, and I will admit, I think that was my fault, but once I got to know her, she was such a lovely girl." Iona saw his face, and felt his emotions rise inside him.

"I have thought of her often over the years, as I was stuck in that awful place up there. It may sound strange, but in a way, she kept me going. I never talked to my sister, we had little in common, and yet Little Morgana gave me some very good advice, and I took it, and it made that awful place bearable, because I found a common bond with Lumi because of it. Over the years we spoke often as a result, and I learned such a lot, and found myself very close to my younger sister." He gave a smile; it clearly meant a lot to him.

"Morgana had such a lovely smile, I can see it now as I speak, the queen was not good to her and I never understood why, because to be honest, she kept herself to herself, and was always sat reading. Whenever I rode past, she was always there with her head in a book, or chopping wood and attending her garden. I must admit, I did not agree with the queen, and I grew quite fond of her, she had no one to look out for her, and so I did what I could to ensure she was safe. It broke my heart when they burned down her house, I was most vexed at my brother, I told him, shame on you for what you did, she was innocent, I know, I was with her when it happened." Iona frowned and looked at Una, and she nodded in agreement.

"Iona, when Eve was killed, Morgana was just outside my cottage on the road, with Commander Stenlow." He gave a nod.

"Poor girl was terrified…Well, to be honest, I was too, no one had ever heard a wail like that before. It was a terrible thing, she was so afraid and shook from head to foot, poor girl was as white as a spirit and shaking. I told her, run home and I will watch, I could see her cottage just down the road. She was so scared she ran like the wind, I watched until she reached her fence, and then went to discover the source of the matter. I saw the Queen up on the top of the shoulder, so I turned around and rode back to make sure she was safe. When I arrived back, her cottage was ablaze and our Fagan was stood there, and I asked him what in all the realms was happening. That was when he told me, the queen had said she had seen her kill Eve, and I knew then it was not true, so told him."

Iona sat back in her seat, it was clear to work out, this must have happened after the incident when she had dropped her veil. Iona looked at him.

"What did your brother say?" Stenlow gazed at her, as if remembering.

"He seemed really preoccupied, kept talking to himself, and staring at the apple tree, he has always been strange, but I felt he was stranger than normal. He then just blinks and tells me to go to the queen and tell her what I knew, which I did, and to be honest, I soon wished I hadn't. She called me a liar and sent me up there to that awful place." Iona was starting to understand.

"What happened to her after that?"

He looked even more saddened, and he leaned forward in his seat, and leaned on his walking stick, his eyes stared in a most serious way at her.

"That is what bothers me the most." Iona looked at him, not understanding.

"Why does it bother you?" He took a long deep breath.

"My mother had gifts, she had the sight, and our Fagan has them too, not me or Lumi though. One night as I lay in my bunk after a long day, and I had sat with our Lumi, I had talked to her of little Morgana, and I suppose I had her on my mind. I lay there not able to sleep, because it may sound strange, but she was such a lovely girl, that I worried about her. She lost everything in that fire, and I cared to know what had become of her. I suppose talking all day of her, I had her in my thoughts, and as I dozed off, I had the most terrible dream." He shuddered, and it looked like he had gone quite pale. Stenlow looked visibly shaken and drew a long breath inward.

"Terrible dream… It started off with me seeing a white raven, so not so bad really, but then it got dark and sinister, and I could see her, pinned to a wall and screaming, and she was covered in blood. It was awful and scared me to death, and then suddenly, this big black bird loomed in front of me. I woke with such a fright, I fell clean out of bed, and lay on the floor shaking and panting I did. Oh, it was terrible, even now it gets my heart racing." He sat back looking shaken by just the memory, and shook his head.

"I will never forget the look of fear in her eyes, and the sound of her screams. I tried to talk with Fagan to find out if he could help, but he refused to talk about it. I would love to know what happened to her, she was such a lovely girl, so kind, gentle, and really caring, she helped a lot of people you know with her cures?" Iona smiled.

"She sounds like she was lovely." Stenlow smiled a beautiful smile.

"Like me, she loved the sunsets, and she often told me she thought Avalon was a beautiful place, as I said, she was a lovely girl, I have such beautiful memories of her."

They sat with Stenlow for a while longer, and as the darkness came down, they both helped him inside, and made sure he was fine, and once he was settled, they thanked him and left. Iona was quiet as she thought of all she had been told; Una walked at her side.

"I knew none of this Iona, I only found out once Amethyst pardoned him and he requested to return, it is his wish to spend his last days here. By then, Morgan had been destroyed with Branna by the white lord, it did not appear to matter any longer, the deed was done. Iona you were right, at that time, we all believed she had done it, all of us were convinced that what Rhiannon told us was true. You have to understand, back then, she was considered to be the wisest of all, she had vast knowledge and powers, she was a queen of Fae. Think about it, honestly Iona, who would not believe her or trust her?" Iona glanced to her side, to see Una's face.

"That is what worries me most Aunt Una, I will be a queen of Fae, everyone will see me as they did her, and I want to be true to my people. I want to ensure that I am informed of facts, not tainted truths, which is why I feel I have to do this." Una appeared to understand that.

"You remind me of my mother at times, she was the same, all she wanted was the truth, but back then, everyone was afraid to tell it. It is funny really, because Morgana was the only one I think who ever stood up to her. She had a powerful presence; it was clear to all that she had been raised to replace her mother. It was sad really, I did think at the time, she would make a powerful queen."

They walked back to Una's cottage and stood outside the gate, and Una smiled at her.

"I am sorry about my treatment of you the other day, I was foolish, and afraid, and it was wrong of me, I should have been more open with you. Iona, it has not been easy for me, I was taken in to the sleep realm, and when I came out the whole world was different. You wake up and nothing is real any more, and everything you knew is gone. The language had changed so much, it was like learning another language, and like I had to learn to speak all over again. I lived alone with my son, and had just the help of a few good locals and Opal to understand the world and all of the changes. Opal was a young wild girl when I knew her, and when I came out, she looked as old as Eve, I was older but looked younger than her. I struggled to adjust, but it was only when I came to Loxley that I really found my stride, as I had my sisters and we all helped each other, losing them was a mighty blow for me." Iona shook her head.

"It is fine, I really understand Aunt Una, this is not something people want to talk about, all of you suffered because of her. Especially your mother." Una took a huge breath.

"It was bad for her and almost killed her, and yet the thing I do not understand is that she did nothing to my sisters or me, or our children, we were completely intact, untouched and unharmed, and I still do not understand that. To find out it was Morgana was not easy, and it left a lot of unanswered questions for all of us, but the truth was, we knew little of her apart from her being a quiet and somewhat isolated lonely girl. Maddy always called her the sad one, she felt her sadness and loneliness, and I cannot deny, there is a part of me that felt guilty, because, I knew she was not that bad. I could feel her goodness, I have often thought I should have spoken to her, I lived literally just up the road, and yet I did nothing to help her." Una stopped and looked at Iona.

"My father talked of her and he said she was a pleasant girl, and how he admired her, he grew quite fond of her. He told me many times I would have much in common with her, and how I should visit her and befriend her, and yet I ignored her because the queen was dead set against her. Iona, I feel so guilty for that, had I befriended her, would things have been different?" The truth was, no one could really know for sure.

"Aunt Una, you cannot blame yourself, I am not sure, but I do not think anyone really thought what happened would. The fact remains that the girl who lived here, somehow changed, and we still do not know why. Something happened, but we have no idea what, but I do think it is clear, there is far more to this than we currently know." Una took a deep breath and it was clear, her emotions were high.

"What will you do now?" Iona, looked down the roadway, and thought for a moment.

"I aim to seek the truth, so I intend to keep going until I know all of her story, because I feel strongly that somehow knowing will help, and what I discover will help me to be a better queen, and I want that, I really do." Una pulled her into a hug.

"It is late, you know, you can stay if you need to?" Iona smiled, as she stood back.

"No, there is somewhere I need to be."

*U*na turned to head to her door after saying goodnight, and Iona opened her window, and stepped through. She stepped out into the old ruins at Tintagel, and walked slowly up the weed riddled path, and felt the wind blow through her hair. Looking out to sea from the old broken down wall, she took a long deep breath of the air, and watched the sun slowly set, as the land fell into darkness.

"I can understand why you loved this place, Morgana; I think I too would have loved to have grown up here. I am closer, and I will learn the truth of you, and if as I sense there was an injustice, I will correct it, to reflect the true record of your life. Anyone who nurtures the White Star as you did, should be recognised for it, and it still grows strong and has flowers, which I know must mean something, I am just not sure what yet. What became of the sad and hurt little girl who lived here, and became the student of Merlin who excelled in her studies, what changed you so much, you could do so much harm?"

She stared out to sea lost in thought, as the waves crashed up onto the cliffs below her, a young queen to be, filled with power, and at the start of a long journey into her future. She was not fully aware of it, but this time was important, because, she was in the process of change, she was becoming the Violet Stone, Queen of Fae.

Chapter Eleven.

New Candidates.

*T*he day began slowly on Sora. In the early hours, scribes appeared with news, and Gwynfor having been fully filled in on the latest information, had a picture in his mind of what was happening. It appeared the crowd that had gathered, had not left, and spent the night sat outside the House of Scribes and Royal Palace, and as a result, an address of the crowd was planned.

The whole group was awake eating and drinking ready for their day, awaiting the return of Runestone. She had jumped home to inform Robbie of what was happening, and was disappointed to find Iona had not come home again, and was still wearing her veil. She had to sort out the children as they were back in school today, and rushed around, screaming at Tegan to get up, before sitting quietly and sorting out Gailania's ponytail.

The plan of action was to blend into the crowd and listen to what was announced. Gwynfor was thoroughly enjoying having guests, as he made the most of his hosting skills, and cooked everyone a hearty breakfast. He cooked on a huge flat skillet, and insisted everyone tried the waffles, with their bacon, eggs, and tomatoes. Rune arrived looking worried, and was handed a plate, she had already eaten, but decided to eat outside on the step, Ariel sensed her concern, and followed her out and sat beside her.

"Do not worry, she is fine." Rune breathed in to try and calm herself.

"I will always worry about my children, she has never stayed out like this before, Robbie was far too hard on her. She does not need that kind of behaviour, he has always sat with her and talked. Ariel, I know what she is trying to do, and I know there are some that will not like what she asks them easily." Ariel understood.

"I know this is hard for you Runestone, but Iona needs to do this.

Like you, I have felt her doubts and fears, this is something only she can do, the point she wants to prove, can only come from a Queen of Fae. Iona needs to now understand which part of her that is, and then bring it to the fore."

The time finally arrived, and Gwynfor gathered everyone before him. They pulled up their hoods, on their long green Fae cloaks, and were ready, his eyes twinkled as he looked at them all with a huge smile.

"Such fine company, my word, I feel quite honoured, some of you are quite famous you know?"

There were giggles, he was a lovely old man, ancient, and yet filled with such life, he waved his hand. There was a tiny little pop, and everyone blinked, and looked around, they were in the heart of Florae, behind what was a very large crowd. Sapphire frowned as she looked behind her to Ariel.

"How did he do that?" Ariel smiled.

"He is Gwynfor, the prince of this realm and brother to the queen, he looks old and frail, but mark my words, he has more power and life in him, than we do."

Elgin sat on his balcony, like all of Fae he waited for the announcement. He pulled himself up from his chair, and walked to the balcony rail, where he stood in full view of the crowd. To his side, he could see the peace gardens, and then the long deck and the steps down into what was named the Royal Circle, in the centre of which, was the Whispering Falls.

Rune stood at the back and watched, for her this all felt very unnerving, her daughter was to be crowned queen, or in this case maybe not. She could not understand why all this was happening, she had spent years with Iona and Sapphire covering what was expected, and she had thought everything was a done deal. It now appeared, Councillor Alder had a different idea, and she felt her anger rising for wasting her daughters time, and putting her through the nerves and worries that she was facing currently.

The time was approaching and they gathered together, they were close enough to the crowd to not be noticed, but far away enough to not be overheard, as they watched whispering comments to each other. Sapphire peered out from under her hood at the tall House of Scribes, as she stood next to Rune.

"I am glad I brought my bow, if needs be, it will be an especially great pleasure pinning Alder to a wall." Rune turned, frowned, and looked at her.

"You brought your bow; I cannot see it?" Sapphire smiled.

"It is where no one will think to look." Rune smirked, and glanced down.

"Wow, I am impressed!" Sapphire looked down at her tight pants, and then back up looking shocked.

"It's not in there… Hell Rune, have you seen the size of it?" Rune sniggered, as did Tila.

"Size of what, I am assuming the bow?" Sapphire looked shocked.

"Well yeah, I only show that to a select few." Rune looked at her, and raised her eyebrows.

"Few?" Tila sniggered, and Sapphire smiled as she leaned in.

"It has not been neglected, I can assure you, and you know what, Opal was right, although I do wonder how she found out." Rune giggled.

"From what I have heard, my grandmother was wild in her youth. I am happy to hear you have the attention of the Fae men, although, standing here there are quite a lot of them." Sapphire sniggered.

"That is my secret, but I will tell you this, sometimes it is nice to have a whole island to yourself, living alone has its perks." Rune giggled.

"I am happy to hear it, I had wondered."

*O*ver the top of the crowd, high up on the large balcony above the large doors to the House of Scribes, the large windows opened, and five soldiers of the Fae walked out, holding their bows, which were pre-loaded with arrows. Ariel scowled next to Ena.

"That snake, he would raise a bow to a Fae, oh how low he has sunk."

A member of the council walked out towards the rail, and looked down on the masses gathered below, all of the chattering instantly ceased, and the whole of the centre of Florae fell quiet. It was Council Member Borak, he was holding a large rolled up parchment. He cleared his throat, and then unrolled the parchment, and held it out in front of him, at arms length. His voice was loud and as clear as day.

"People of Fae, and Florae. On this day, I give notice, that in a majority vote of the Council of Elders, of ten votes to two, a resolution was passed calling into question, the legitimacy of the line of Iona

Violet of Loxley."

Hushed voices spoke quickly, and many of them were shocked to have the rumours confirmed. Borak looked down at the large circle of people below him.

"It has been stated, that since Iona Violet was offered up as queen, with no clear proof that she is of a worthy line, as her roots are firmly Green Circle. No written word exists to confirm the wishes of our dearly beloved past Queen Gwendolyn, and as the Council chosen to protect the interests of this realm, we have chosen the path of reasonable question." Rune looked around.

"Oh hell, where is Tila?" Everyone looked around, there was no sign of her, Borak continued.

"This is not a case of refusing to accept her, it is more a case of ensuring she is the right choice, after all, there is an unbroken line also in the candidates of the line of the White Circle. We have requested that Princess Una of Florae, and Citrine of Morbihan attend a meeting with us, after which time, we will call forth Iona Violet of Loxley, to account for herself. The council feels this is the right approach, and have voted such. In the meantime, all business of the house will remain under suspension, and our loyal leader of the Council of Elders will assume a custodial role, as the leader of Florae, and the Fae of the free realms and matters pertaining to the Fae of Earth."

There were gasps, as he looked out, and a flaming arrow fired up, hit the parchment and dragged it out of his hand, and it shot up in the air. Borak jumped as the archers lifted their weapons, and he looked down, as the crowd roared out with approval. Tila stood, staring up at him with hate, she lifted her bow, with another arrow fitted.

"TELL YOUR MEN TO STAND DOWN YOU TRAITOR TO FAE, IONA VIOLET STONE, IS MY QUEEN, AND OUR QUEEN. HOW DARE YOU AND THAT TREASONOUS WORM ALDER, DARE TO CHALLENGE HER!"

There were loud grumbles and objections throughout the crowd, Crystal gave a sigh, and clicked her fingers and her bow appeared.

"Oh hell, I should have known she would cause trouble, come on." Borak pointed down at her, and looked at the guards below on the front deck.

"There is a warrant for her arrest, send out the guards and get her."

Tila took a step back, as she looked up, her bow on Borak, and the crowd parted. They pulled her back into them, as the doors opened, and more guards came rushing out.

The guards came down the steps and the crowd joined together, jeering and shouting their dissatisfaction, as members of the Fae pulled Tila back, she noticed many of them were scribes. A white gloved hand gripped her hood and dragged her backwards.

"Come here you, I might have known you would stir things up. Come on, we have to go, it is getting dangerous, this is not what we planned." Sapphire shrugged at Crystal's side.

"I am up for it, show me where that worm is, and I will go and get him, I have a spot already picked out for my arrow."

The guards had long poles, and came down the steps at speed, and pushed into the crowd, and the jostling began, as scribes from the house who made up a lot of the front line, grabbed the poles and started to push back. It was descending quickly into a volatile situation; the people of Fae were showing a discontent never seen before in Florae. It was getting out of hand, as several people fell to the ground, Ariel was about to move forward where from nowhere there was a very loud voice.

"STOP THIS ALL NOW…. ENOUGH!" It boomed out loud with authority above all the noise.

Everyone stopped and looked up at the long deck, where Elgin walked slowly with his stick, and stared out over the rail at the guards holding the poles against the citizens of Florae. His face was filled with anger.

"No soldier or guard has ever raised a weapon to a fellow member of Fae, stop this all this instant. Never in my life have I seen such a disgraceful display, we are all Fae of Earth, and we serve our queen and our realm with equal respect to all." He stared down at the guards.

"Lower your weapons and withdraw, you swore an oath to serve your queen, and protect your people, not attack them or intimidate them, now stand down and withdraw."

High above him, Alder watched from the doors, as the crowd moved back away from the guards, who felt their loyalties torn. Master Elgin was an imposing figure, even in his greater years, and if anything, he commanded more respect in the realm than any. The sergeant at arms gave a nod, and the soldiers stepped back, up righted their poles and withdrew.

Elgin eyed them as they came up the steps back to the house, and then turned to the people, he looked out over the masses as the crowd parted, and a single figure in white walked to the front, and bowed to him, he smiled to see Ariel, and then looked to the crowd.

"I believe the Council stands in error, but I also believe we are all duty bound to the creed of the Fae. We debate, we consider, and we show respect, that is who we are, and who we will always be. As Master of this House, of which I have served all my life, I believe with every scrap of my being that Iona Violet is to be crowned the queen of this realm. I have met her, spoken with her, and I have felt the power within her, and she will be equally as powerful as both Gwendolyn White Circle, and Bridget Violet, of that in my mind there is no doubt."

The crowd all started to chatter, Ariel looked up with pride and smiled. She gave a soft nod to Master Elgin, he noted it, with a soft nod in return. Elgin looked to the crowds.

"All of you, I know in your hearts where your loyalty lies, and at this time, it is more important than ever before, that you have a strong faith. In a month, we will be crowning Iona Violet Stone, she will prove herself the true queen of this land, have faith in her. Go home, kneel before your altars, and make your wishes known to this land."

The crowd started to slowly disburse, and Elgin turned, and looked up at Borak as he looked down at him from the balcony, Elgin took a deep breath.

"I expected better of you Borak, your honour lies in tatters, with your kinsman and conspirator Alder, you will answer for this."

He turned, and using his cane, he walked slowly back towards his residence. As he arrived at the steps he looked back, and Ariel stood alone waiting for every last person to leave, a little way down the road, a line of hooded and cloaked individuals waited for her, one of which, was Tila, she waved, and he smiled, as he turned to the steps.

"She had better live through this, I am far too old to teach another to her standard." The guard stepped back, and allowed him back into his home, and Elgin patted his shoulder as he clumped up the steps.

"Thank you, Elmer, lives were spared today, it is a good day for the history of this realm." The guard gave a quick nod, and stood to attention.

Ariel stood alone, and looked up at Borak, she walked forward towards the steps, and came slowly up them, her eyes fixed on him as she stepped up each one. At the top she stopped.

"I remember your father; he was a good man. I held you in my arms the week you were born, Griselda was so happy, and your father so proud of you. He looked at me as I cuddled you in my arms, and he told me, Ariel, one day my son will be a council member, and he will be honourable and just in his judgements. On this day young Borak, I am glad that your parents no longer live, for the shame they would feel, would destroy them. Go home Borak, light a flame, and burn herbs on your altar, and beg for their forgiveness and make your promise to your ancestors, that will correct the evil that was done this day, for you have shamed your family."

She turned and walked along the deck towards the quarters of Master Elgin, and reached the guard and smiled.

"Elmer, it is nice to see you, how is your wife?" He looked nervous.

"Mistress Ariel, please do not do this, the master is under house arrest." She smiled.

"I am Ariel, daughter of Enaria, and daughter as adopted by Queen Bridget Violet. All of your guards with all of your weapons, have not the power to stop me, so stand aside. Tell that to your captain, or, if you insist, I shall hit you with a dream charm, where you will cheat on your wife repeatedly, and have a very good time." He shook his head as Elgin gave a chuckle.

"Please Mistress Ariel, she would never forgive me." Ariel smiled.

"Alright then, shame really, I was going to throw in her two cousins, you would have had such dreams."

He swallowed hard, the thought was most tempting, he moved quickly out of the way, and with a smile, she walked past with a titter. Elgin gave a hearty laugh and opened his arms, and Ariel walked into his embrace.

"I feel your guard would take my offer, as long as his wife did not find out. How are you Master Elgin, I am glad to see you well?" He pulled her close with great fondness.

"All the better for seeing you, the realm needs you my dear, I am delighted you got in, but there again, I knew you would. Alder is skilled, but not skilled enough. I see you brought back up, although I feel my little scribe is still as fierce as her manner on the battlefield." Ariel gave a little chuckle.

"Tila was here for one reason only, she was here to ensure your safety, she is worried about you." Elgin gave a happy chuckle as he turned towards his door.

"She really is quite a remarkable scribe, and I feel feistier than most Fae, but loyal. Come we must talk; I shall tell you of my thoughts."

*I*ona woke, she had fallen asleep sat in the corner of an old ruined wall, and she ached. She was huddled in her cloak, and pulled it off as the sun had risen behind her, and she was warm. She stood up, stretching the aches out of her, and turned around, realising somehow, she had ended up inside the ruin of the old church. Her head was hazy, and did not remember leaving the castle, where she had been sat thinking out everything that she had learned so far.

She continued to stretch and looked around for a way out, there was a large window, which must have been the way she climbed in, as everywhere else was overgrown. She climbed out, and walked slowly around the church and came back where she had stood to watch Morgana and the two graves. They were really overgrown, in her vision they were clearer, but that was a very long time ago, and since the Red Death, everything in this region had grown wilder. She turned around, and looked out over the sea, as the seagulls screamed high above her as they glided across the sky, and she had to decide what it was she would do next.

After Stenlow, there was only one thing she could do, but she was uncertain, Stenlow had told her that Fagan had refused to talk to him, which did not fit her idea of the man she knew. It had been five years since she had last seen him, but he had always been warm and friendly towards her, although saying that, her dad had not taken well to this, so maybe Stenlow had a point. Staring at the sea she tried to puzzle out her choices.

"Come on Iona, to be a queen you have to stand tall, you know he has the answers. He talked to your mother, he should talk to you, and if not, you still have to try."

*U*na was up and walking around, this was her last day, and she would have to return to Loxley, and she was trying to get her head in gear to head back, but her thoughts kept slipping back to the previous night, and Iona. Two hands came around her and pulled her back, and she closed her eyes and leaned back, his voice was soft.

"Una, she is going to be a queen, stop worrying."

She turned in his arms and looked into his hazel eyes, he pulled her close, and smiled, and she breathed in, and felt calmer. Wilson had changed her life in so many ways, he was so different from his days in the Specialists, and not the hap hazard and accident prone Woody they all joked with. Alone with her, his deeply caring and soft side showed, and she found him so wonderful to be around. She leaned back and looked at him, she knew the story of the pain he felt at the death of his mother to the Cutters, he looked at her.

"What?" She chose her words carefully.

"You know, I helped her last night to learn more about Morgana?" He nodded; she considered things carefully.

"Mason's Cutters changed your life when they raided your home. I know it was quite some time ago, but have you moved forward, is it behind you now, because you never really talk of it, and I wondered, you are alright now, aren't you?" He breathed out, a long soft flow of air, as he held her.

"I am not sure you get over it, so much as learn to cope with it. I still think of her Una, she was not an easy woman, but she was my mother and I vowed I would take care of her." Una felt his sadness and understood.

"I am sorry for asking, I would never hurt you Wilson, but you know, she was four, and they murdered her father. I guess I never considered it as a girl, and now, I am trying to understand how that feels." He gave a soft smile, he understood.

"It is never easy, and I would think only being four would make it harder, be honest, who would know how to sit with a tiny girl, and put that in a way she would understand? Una, it happened to me, but I was a lot older, and I am telling you, I would have no idea what to say to a girl that young. I am not sure there are words that would have helped her, I am really not."

It made so much sense to her, and in a way, she found she admired Iona even more, because somehow Iona had already worked that out, and she wondered if that was what drove her. Una suddenly understood something massively important, and she gasped as she looked at Wilson, he stared at her.

"What?" Una's eyes filled with tears.

"I just realised, when Robbie was lost, Iona went to him, and she was the same age. Wilson, had she not been a queen with the gifts that she had, Robbie would have died, queens of Fae have the power to travel using their tables. When she was four, she got a fever, and everyone except Rune was worried. She told me one night, not to fear, because Iona had gone to help Robbie. It was at that time in her life, she understood who she was, and at just age four she travelled back in time to that cave and saved him. Oh Wilson, they were the same age, Iona understands Morgana in ways none of us ever will." He smiled at her as two tears ran down her cheeks.

"You see, it was right that you went down there and spoke with her." She gave him a nod.

"I do feel better because of it."

$\mathcal{H}$e leaned in and gave her a soft kiss. The front door banged, and he sighed and slid out of her arms and walked to answer the door. Una turned lost in thought, and lifted a towel, she folded it ready to pack in her bag, there was movement behind her, so she turned. Behind her stood a messenger of Florae, he gave a regal bow.

"Princess Una."

She smirked, it had been a long time since she had been called that, he handed her a rolled parchment. Not quite understanding, she took it and saw the seal of the council, she frowned.

"What is this about?" The messenger looked at the document, and then lifted his eyes to her.

"Your highness, you have been summoned to Florae on urgent business, please read the document." She looked down at it.

The document looked very official, she broke the seal and unrolled it, and started to read. It detailed that there had been some concerns raised as to the suitability of Iona Violet, and the council requested her immediate attendance in the high chamber as quickly as possible. It told her little more; she lifted her eyes from the document, and Wilson leaned into read and frowned.

"Is that normal?" Una shrugged.

"I am not sure, I did some constitutional law but not that much, and the last time a queen was placed on the throne, I was not here, I came later." Wilson nodded.

"You had better go, I will wait here, I would like to see Fagan about some better hinges for the big gates, his nephews are good, but they do not match his standard." Una looked at the parchment and gave a sigh.

"Alright, I will get my things, give me a minute."

*E*lgin sat and sipped his tea, as Ariel sat opposite him, he sat back, and studied Ariel, she was as always present in the moment and paying him great attention.

"I naturally assume, you have worked Alder's game out here?" She gave a nod.

"He is a fool, I cannot see Una or Treen playing into his hands, Una is far too smart, and he should be wary of Treen, she is loyal to Loxley in a way he will never understand. At this moment, I am not sure he is the one to judge Iona worthy, I would even say, he will exclude her and take the seat for his own." Elgin smiled.

"Good, we agree. Ariel, you and I know, Iona has the force of a queen inside her. I have read the writings of Una, Melanie and Madelaine, as well as Runestone, from that moment of discovery, and I have spoken at great lengths to Gwynfor. I hold not one doubt that she is the only candidate that this land will accept, but Alder is determined to build a case against her."

"I understand that, Bade is currently working on this from the legal standpoint, I wish to look into other avenues. Master Elgin, Iona is not aware of this at the moment, she is engaged in a matter that will be massively important to her reign. This is her time of trial, as she seeks out the sort of queen she is going to be, and finds her confidence, I cannot and will not have her diverted."

Elgin had more than a good understanding of the process, he remembered the young Gwendolyn, who sought her answers in Avalon.

"I cannot deny, when you returned, and you were restored back to this house, I thought all the loose ends of those times of the Queen of Fae and her ways was over. It now appears to me that in his time as ambassador, he learned far more from her than even I realised." Ariel sipped at her tea, her grey eyes taking note of him.

"Let's be honest, as head of the council he has had power for some time, and like his mentor, he is now reluctant to relinquish it to a queen. I feel the incident with Tila in a way awakened him, I feel he had it in mind that a queen who was not raised here, would not understand the culture of this realm. Her performance that day, showed clearly, she was better trained and schooled than he imagined, and his plan to rule by proxy through the new queen, was shattered.

Sapphire has done an excellent job of training her, which may even explain his dislike of her." Elgin sat forward in his seat.

"I think I also felt your hand in that night, her constitutional precision, can only have come from a scribe of high talent. Ariel, we must oppose Alder at all costs, because I fear if we do not overcome him, it will cause permanent destruction to every aspect of Fae life, and undo every tradition of our culture. We cannot let this happen." Ariel understood, but in many ways, she was not afraid.

"I have great hope that the truth of Iona will win over the day, Master Elgin." Outside the apartment, a trumpet sounded, and Elgin gave a frown, and looked up.

"What in all the realms is that?" He pulled himself up from his seat, as Ariel rose up with him. Both of them walked to the door, and stepped out.

*O*n the deck in front of the Royal Circle, two heralds stood with long trumpets of bone, and played a fanfare, Elgin shuffled forward with Ariel at his side, and leaned on the rail. Down the long white road that led to the coast, was a rider, who wore a long burnt orange cloak, that ran from her shoulders and down to cover the rear of her horse. She was alone, as her horse casually walked towards the centre of the realm, as she looked from side to side.

Her long golden blonde hair flowed down her back, and her eyes which were the softest browns took in every detail. Ariel gave a happy nod as she watched down the long road, and saw the two cloaked figures step out, and the horse came to a halt. Rune looked up and smiled.

"Hallo my sister, it has been too long since we saw each other." Treen smiled as she looked at Rune and Sapphire stood side by side.

"Hallo Rune, it ezz been a long time, but it ezz not always easy these days. I ave not forgotten you, and my Skippy, is already with the preparations to come for the seeing of Iona and her taking the crown." Rune felt a little bit relieved to hear it, Treen looked at Sapphire.

"You my sister, you ave been the naughty girl, you ave left me with the love sickness of Jean Paul, he is dithery dathery all the day, thinking of you instead of doing his work. He pines away, and ezz not of the right head." Sapphire looked embarrassed, and turned a little pink, as Rune raised her eyebrows, and looked at her.

"Yeah, I am sorry about that, he got a little clingier than I wanted him to." Treen gave a chuckle.

"You were off with the clackers and did not say bye bye, shame of you." She giggled.

"I ave to see this man, Older, he ezz talking the nonsense, and so I must go see, but we will see each other soon, yes?" Rune smiled at her.

"We are staying on Sora with Gwynfor, let me know when you are ready, and I will open a window." She gave a nod, and pulled tight on her reins.

"I will be soon; I feel this will be quickly, I talk little to the fools."

The two women stepped back, and Treen moved her horse forward, and Sapphire stood and watched at Rune's side.

"She has not changed much, although, she commands great authority as well as her mother did."

Rune watched with a smile, she knew Treen well, and somehow, she felt Alder would encounter his first hurdle today. She turned at the side of Sapphire as they walked towards the farm house on the side of the road, where they were all waiting for Ariel.

"So, Jean Paul, you kept that quiet."

"Treen has a big mouth."

*R*une gave a giggle as she glanced at her, and saw her cheeks flush. Elgin watched with great interest, as Treen rode up to the base of the steps, and the large doors of the house opened, and Alder walked out to the top of the steps. She looked up as she slid off her horse and he gave a regal bow.

"Princess Citrine, I am delighted you could make it." Treen suddenly understood as she walked up the steps.

"So, you are this Older, I remember you from Avalon, you are the one the queen of the moon hated, are you no?" Elgin smirked with Ariel, Alder looked a little put off, she reached the top of the steps.

"What ezz all this being about, I am busy, no?" He offered his arm looking a little down hearted.

"If you would care to come this way, I shall present you to the council to talk."

She nodded, and strode ahead, leaving him behind, her long orange cloak flowing behind her. Elgin gave a little chuckle, as Alder scurried behind her, and the large doors swung closed with a bang.

"Well, that did not go so smoothly." Ariel gave a little chuckle.

*I*ona walked slowly through the trees; her mind filled with the pictures of Stenlow. The truth was, hearing his words and feeling the sadness in his heart, she felt sorry for him. She sensed how hard his life had been, and it had taken its toll on him. The lines of the Fae were notorious for holding on to their youthful looks, and yet, he looked double the age of his brother Fagan. Stenlow's words echoed in his mind.

"I tried to talk with Fagan to find out if he could help, but he refused to talk about it."

It made no sense to her, every story she had ever heard about Fagan, was about how kind and helpful he was. She could not understand why he would deliberately avoid talking to help his brother, when it was so obvious, he could have simply spoken, and eased his brother's mind. The path turned as she walked, without really looking where she was going, she simply followed her instincts, and found herself walking out into the wide glade, that housed his cabin, barn, and newly rebuilt forge.

Fagan stood on the steps of his cabin, the old owl Brooke on the window sill at his side, she should have known the old owl would have warned him. She walked slowly up towards him, and stood at the base of the steps, and looked up, he was tall and stocky with his white bushy hair, and she smiled.

"Master Fagan, I have a deep need to talk with you, on a matter that I feel is important."

"Aye, I am aware little Violet Eyes, the thing is, ole Fagan has no wish to talk with ye. Be off with ye, I left that life behind me, and have had done with it."

Chapter Twelve.

A Question of Trust.

Rowan was feeling frustrated, as he looked at his daughter stood weeping yet again in the workshop. Jade walked up to the door and stopped, as she heard Rowan sigh.

"But I have not done anything to him, do you think if I had any intent of harming him, he would be alive now… He wouldn't?"

Jade smirked, and put her hand to her mouth, to hide her giggle. Rowan gave another long frustrated sigh, as Yvee stood weeping.

"Grover told him you hate him, and he is a wet lettuce, and now he is afraid to come over to see me." She wailed once again.

"He is afraid to love me."

Jade bit her knuckle and shook, as Rowan stood useless, unable to even comprehend her. Her eyes were blotchy, and red, as she sniffled, and her voice went squeaky.

"Why don't you like him?" It felt like a trap, and Rowan knew it, and panicked.

"Yvee, your brother has a big mouth, Kale can visit you here safely… Well, when I say safely, I mean, I am not about to pounce on him, but… Well… You know, your brothers and sister can be a little wild, honestly, he is afraid of me, out there somewhere Pan is lurking, that is the real threat, and not just for him." Yvee gave another sniffle.

"So, you don't hate him then?" He sighed yet again.

"Look Yvee, I honestly mean him no harm, as long as he is respectful and keeps his hands on all the appropriate places, he is safe." She nodded, as he turned back to the bench.

"What if he touches me elsewhere?" Rowan's head snapped around at high speed.

"HAS HE?" She looked appalled.

"NO!" Rowan nodded.

"Good!" She gave a deep sigh and stared at him.

"God Dad, I cannot believe you would even think that!"

She gave a loud huff, spun on her boots and stormed out, as Rowan stood staring not even understanding what just happened. Jade leaned in the door, and giggled.

"I think that went well." Rowan turned and looked at her.

"You were not like that, why is she?" Jade smiled, as she walked up, and slipped her arms around his waist. She looked at him with her green eyes dancing below her long shaggy fringe.

"You knew you were mine, and be honest, I can go invisible, and have knives. Seriously, who would have been mad enough to try?" He smiled.

"They would have failed, all I wanted was to look into those beautiful green eyes." She smiled, and reached up and kissed him.

"See, when you try, you know all the right words." He gave a sigh.

"If she did not wail the house down, I would be fine, why do they always have to wail?" She giggled as she slipped back.

"Willow says it is love sickness." He nodded.

"Find her a bloody cure will you, it is driving me nuts." She giggled, as she headed towards the door.

*T*reen stood up from her seat and looked angry, her eyes burned with a bright orange.

"What eez the wrong with you, ave you taken the loss of your brain? Not a queen, ave you been drinking the wine, this eez stupid no, of course Iona Violet eez queen?" Alder gave a frustrated sigh.

"SHE IS GREEN CIRCLE, NOT FAE." Treen marched across the floor, which was forbidden and she came up close to Alder as her eyes smouldered orange.

"Listen with your ears Older, this thing you say, this not queen, not Fae, this ezz the words of a silly person. My Mama, if she was here, would kill you for just saying it. She ezz the Violet Stone, and she will be queen if I ave to make her stepping over your dead body to crown her. I will be of hearing no more of this stupidity, as heir of Gwendolyn and Bridget Violet, I am using the words to tell you, Iona is queen. You ezz in the need to hear me Older."

Treen turned and stormed across the floor back towards her chair. She snatched up her cloak, and swung it around her shoulders, as she marched towards the doors. Alder sat back and gave a long frustrated sigh, as he watched her walk away, his face red with anger.

"IT'S ALDER!"

The large doors swung open, as Treen marched towards them, and as they did, Una stood looking confused, Treen smiled, and pulled her into a hug.

"Hallo Auntie Una, watch this snakey, he ezz talking the stupidity. Rune ezz here, and I am going to meet her with Saff, come and see me soon, yes?" Una smiled.

"I will, I have to meet Councillor Alder first." Treen huffed, and looked behind her.

"This man eez no brain, and needs to be hit harsh to make im work better, he ezz the fool." Una looked through the doors, as Alder slipped from his seat, and walked forward with a huge smile. Treen glanced at Una.

"The only thing of this man that ezz real, ezz his teeth, and all of the everything else, ezz the silly person, he makes me mad, and want to kill im."

Una looked at Alder as he approached her, and Treen gave another huff as she saw him, and walked out. Una watched Alder approach.

"Princess Una, please, come in and we shall have refreshments as we talk."

Una gave a violent shudder, and then followed him where he directed her to a seat, as the other nine members of the council all watched. She sensed something was not right, and thought she should be cautious.

*I*ona stepped back, and looked up at Fagan, he looked resolute, and it was clear he was not going to allow her in to talk. She turned and walked five paces as he watched her, and then she turned back to face him.

"Master Fagan, I am Violet Stone, and I will rule as a queen, and I will rule through truth." He nodded.

"Queens tend to visit here a lot, even dead ones, and that has always been the problem." She understood, she could feel how unsettled he was.

"Alright Master Fagan, I understand, and I will leave, but before I go, answer me one thing, why would she do this?"

Iona stood still and closed her eyes, and as she stood still, slowly her appearance changed, as she became Morgana, and stared at him, then spoke.

"She is wrong, it was not me Fagan, I would never do that, I believed in Eve, I am innocent."

Iona reappeared, and looked at him with bright violet eyes, he was clearly very shaken, and she felt the jolt of pain inside him, he looked at her, and shook his head slowly.

"Ye does not fight fair little Violet Eyes." She understood that.

"She took off her veil, she trusted you when she trusted no one else, and that means something. She saw you as a friend, and I need to know why she took off her only protection from Rhiannon. Please talk to me?" Fagan's eyes teared up, as he looked at her.

"If ye knew what ye asked of me, ye would not ask, ye would spare the pain." Iona felt the huge surge of emotion inside him.

"I would still ask Master Fagan, for I feel what you feel, and you know of the injustice she suffered. Only you can bring the true resolution to this… Master Fagan, you know me, you know how important you are in my life, and also my mothers. Like Morgana, I am placing all of my trust in you, do not fail me. I want to right the wrongs of the past, for only a queen of Fae can do that, and it will be me." He took a deep breath, and swallowed down hard.

"Ye better come inside, this is for only ye ears, and them trees can talk, it will be a time in the telling." Iona nodded, and walked slowly towards the cabin, as Fagan went indoors to put on his old metal kettle to boil.

*U*na sat in her seat and listened to the elaborate case being made by Alder, with the additions of a few of the others, although she noted four of the others stayed quiet and looked uncomfortable. Alder was elaborate and eloquent, and he laid out his case well. He arrived at his summery, and brought all of his arguments together, and in truth, did a wonderful job of trying to encourage Una to take the throne.

Having listened attentively to all he said, she sat back as he stared at her, and she took her time to collect her thoughts. It was a very long pause as he leaned forward in his seat awaiting her response. Una lifted her eyes, and all of them were watching her closely.

"You make a good case council leader Alder." He smiled, and sat back and relaxed.

"However!" He frowned.

"Firstly, I would ask how long has this plan been in your mind, because it is clear to me, having listened, that a great deal of effort and preparation have been put into this. I commend you, for the eloquence in which you delivered it, I was indeed impressed at your ability to bend truths away from their true meaning." He leaned forward to speak, and Una shushed him.

"I have not finished; show me the respect I showed you, and allow me to speak. I am Una Holly Rimmer, daughter of Gwendolyn White Circle and Merlin, guardian of the White Lines. I realise I spend little time in Florae, as I split my time between Loxley and Avalon, but nevertheless, I do spend time in Florae, and I am not quite as ignorant to the running of this realm as your presumptuous proposal suggests. I am the great granddaughter of Bridget Violet, of whom her son, Gwynfor still lives and is a regular guest to my home. I am sitting here, having being told by the Council of Elders, that I am to appear before the council, and yet I see only ten. I was educated by a queen, and a very sharp and well reasoned one, and so therefore, I am aware that in order to be presented, twelve must sit. This Councilman Alder, is not a full sitting, and so therefore constitutionally irrelevant, thus backed up by the lack of a scribe to record the minutes of this session." She took a deep breath as her violet eyes stared into him.

"This is an act of high treason, and if, as I suspect, because be honest, my mother did not name me, and so therefore it is already noted I am not legally entitled to the position of queen. I would imagine, when both Treen and myself turn you down, which we will, you will use this trumped up argument to disqualify Iona, and seek to possess the throne under your own domain, using the title of custodian. However, I feel you have made one error, which will be your downfall." She sat back as he looked at her.

"I have, and what may I ask would you consider that to be?" It was an understandable question.

"Four of your members are not fully on board and will turn against you, and withdraw their vote, thus bringing the total to an even balance of six for and six against, because I am sure the lack of the presence of Lord Elgin and Bade shows their inability to support this." Alder was resolute.

"The vote is cast, and that is supported by constitutional law, I am afraid Princess Una, you should have spent more time in Florae." She smiled.

"I understand that, but answer me this Councilman Alder, which tier of the constitution?" He frowned as he looked at her, and some of the others leaned forward in their seats, Una was relaxed and happy, she had done this many times with her mother growing up.

"It is a clear fact, there are two tiers to constitutional law, the first was the law as written by Bridget Violet, and the second was as amended by Gwendolyn White Circle, my mother. I know for a fact that she amended the rule of the voting system, to a rule that stated the council could only pass a vote if all twelve were present. The fact that I am sat here, proves beyond doubt that Master Elgin, and Lord Bade were not, because they are far too loyal and dedicated to the people of Fae to even have allowed this to be brought up. Gwendolyn White Circle changed the rule. I know this Lord Alder, because I wrote it, with the guidance of Master Elgin." She sat back and smiled.

"That was how my mother taught me constitutional law, she forced me to do it, and I hated it, and yet, now I am thankful to her. I feel this conversation is now over, for that is all this is, a conversation, this meeting is not official. If you would care to, I would be happy for the two other members of the council to be brought in with a scribe, and we can start over again, I have time."

There was utter silence as Una sat and watched, she waited a few moments and smiled, then stood up.

"I did not think so… Members of the lesser council, for that is what you are, I will bid you good day."

Una turned, and walked slowly towards the door, as she arrived, she turned and looked back, where all of them sat watching her.

"If you do this, and try to remove the legitimate Queen, the daughter and granddaughters of Gwendolyn White Circle, will declare war on this house, and we will not stop until it burns with all of you inside it. Be warned members of the council, I may not be here much, but I am her daughter, and will fight to ensure no one ever takes away everything she gave her life for to protect this realm, even from you ALDER!"

The doors opened, and she walked out into the sunshine, and took a deep breath, and smiled.

"I miss this place; I should visit more."

As Alder tried to quieten the voices of concern in the house, high above them the cave that had been hollowed out of the mountain for the tombs of Bridget Violet, and her husband, had yet again seen changes, as it was expanded by workers of Amethyst, Queen of Fae of

Moon.

Next to Gwendolyn's tomb, there was a long altar, all elaborately carved straight out of the wall, on which were set a row of statues to honour the fallen. Una walked quietly into the cave, where she saw Treen on her knees, in front of the statute of Alexandrite, set between the statues of Madelaine and Melanie. Treen quietly wept, and had placed flowers at the feet of each statue, Una came up at her side, and knelt beside her, and lifted her arm up her back to comfort her. Treen swallowed hard, and lifted a small handkerchief to wipe her eyes. Her voice was soft and a little strained.

"I miss them." Una gave a soft nod, and pulled her closer.

"I miss them too." Treen took a deep breath.

"Alley, was not just my sister, she was more, it eez like she was part of me, no? It eez gone now, and I miss it, I miss her. This eez all I ave, they never left me anything to rest in the ground. I come here to talk, and feel closer."

"Mel was my twin, we were parted for so long, and I missed her so much, and yet the moment we met at Loxley, it was like we had never been apart. Losing her again has not been easy, at least before we could talk in our minds, I do not have that now. Your mother Madelaine, was my big sister, she always took care of us when mother was busy. I trusted her so much, she was a good sister, Maddy was the first one I told about Kane, and she did not shout, she listened, then told me I was an idiot." Treen smiled, and sat back, and spoke Fae.

"Mama was my hero also. She was a fighter, and had a hard life at times, but she never let me down. I want to be like her, I try, and her land is now safe under my care."

"She was proud of you Treen, we talked a great deal everyday about our children, and she was proud of who you had become. You know, there were a few times on those awful front lines, where she stood watching over you, and watching you in command. I stood with her often and saw the pride she held because you were her daughter. It meant a great deal to her to see you with Skip, seeing you happy and living your life, after all that happened to us, that was what made her the happiest."

"She was a good Mama, who loved her family."

Una lit the herb sticks and placed them in the small polished trays, and took a few minutes to quietly say her thoughts and prayers in her head. Once they had finished, both of them stood and bowed, and then bowed to their past queens, and walked back up the passage together, out of the cave. Both of them stood on the path looking down on Florae, below them at the base of the mountain, stood the rear of the Royal Apartments, and the House of Scribes. Treen looked down at the house.

"I am not with comfort over this council, Mama would be very much against this plan. It eez in my mind, a screen of the smoke, to hide what this man Older wants." Una nodded.

"We were just pawns in his game Treen, this is a power play to prevent Iona Violet from completing her destiny, as was deemed by my mother. It has been too long between queens; I still think Gwynfor should have sat as consort until Iona was ready. I did try to talk him into it after the battle, but he felt at that time Elgin was a safe pair of hands. Had his health not suffered, Alder would never have got his hands on the seat, and that was the one mistake all of us have made." Treen nodded.

"No one who served in Avalon, can be aving the seat, it ezz to me clear, her rule was not a good thing for Florae. I am of the thought I should spend more time here, just to watch things. We still ave rooms here, and they are inside the house, to keep our eyes on this snakey of a man." Una nodded.

"I am going to go to Gwynfor's, I need to talk with him, I know he will know what we can do, I think my stay here will be longer than I thought. I will send a message to Wilson to let him know." Treen nodded and smiled.

"He has been a good man to you, yes?" Una smiled.

"I am very happy with him Treen, he is a very caring and kind man." She gave a big smile.

"This ezz pleasing for me to be hearing, my Mama worried many times about you, she always told me all she was of the wanting, was your appiness." Una took a deep breath and held it a minute, as the emotion swept over her.

"As I said, she was a wonderful sister, and I know how she felt, she talked often to me in father's house in Loxley. Treen, my only regret is she did not fully see us together, I know she would have been so happy. Your mother was always there for me, she was the rock below us when we lost our mother, I will always hold her deeply in my heart. My biggest regret will always be, I was too far ahead on that awful bridge to save her when she needed me most." Treen took her hand and gave it a squeeze.

"My Mama died doing what she did best, fighting for the all of us, it eez the way she would ave wished it."

Una gave a sniffle, and nodded, as that moment of her holding her arrow, and waiting for the soldiers to reach her played in her mind. It was painful for her as she remembered the explosion as they got her, and the bridge disappearing. It was one of the most painful moments of her life, and was still part of her dreams.

*I*n the House of Scribes Alder sat alone lost in thought, as the others had all dispersed and gone to their quarters. Una and Treen had both made threats, and Alder had spent a lot of time talking to convince the council. He tried to explain, it did not matter, as they still could hold the realm in their control until a new heir came along, after all, neither Sapphire or Citrine had children yet, and one could come from their line. He felt weary as he sat alone sipping wine. The door behind him opened, and he gave a sigh.

"I am fine, thank you, you can retire for the night."

The figure in white walked past him, and walked to the seat in front, she sat down and smiled, and he gave a sigh, and rolled his eyes.

"What are you doing here, and how did you get in?" Ariel leaned back in the seat, and made herself comfortable.

"I am the mistress of this house, I own apartments here as gifted to me by my adopted mother, Queen Bridget. No matter what you may try, you cannot keep me out." He sipped from his glass, and eyed her cautiously.

"What do you want?"

"To talk, nothing more."

"I am not in the mood." Ariel understood that.

"Alright then, I will talk and you can listen." She gave a sweet smile.

"You are wasting your time, she is not a legitimate queen, I will die before I allow her to be crowned." Ariel nodded.

"This is true, especially when you consider how many members of Florae are currently plotting your death as we speak." He gave a tired sigh, and lifted his glass.

"Oh please, spare me the rhetoric, this is Florae, and I may add this is the House of Scribes, it is more secure than Avalon." She nodded, as she looked up at the beams running across the ceiling.

"I must confess, it is that, I designed it that way, however, Lord Alder, your fear is misplaced, everyone out there is indeed loyal to Iona Violet, but can you say the same for everyone in here?" He frowned.

"What are you saying, a council member is a threat, be serious, those idiots have not the capacity to think it, let alone do it? All of them are afraid of their shadows, it is why little gets done here." Ariel gave an agreeable nod.

"I believe you may be right, however, there are guards and servants within these walls, are they all loyal to you?" He looked at her, he had clearly not thought of that, she smiled at him, and shrugged.

"Not all death is through war Alder, I would say in the world of men, there have been some spectacular deaths, and not one of them involved a traditional weapon." He looked at her, unsure of what she meant, and sat forward.

"Like what?" Ariel was enjoying herself, she smiled as he stared at her.

"Well, for arguments sake, let us say, oh, I don't know, the maid. The one I spoke with before she served the wine. Can you be sure that she is completely loyal to you and not Iona Violet? Poison can be such a terribly painful way to die."

Alder's eyes opened wide, and he jumped back in his seat, dropping the glass, as he swallowed hard, as he watched the wine soak into the rug, a look of terror on his face. Ariel gave a chuckle and stood up.

"I would wipe that up, it will leave quite the stain." She walked to the side of his chair and stopped, as Alder stared at the floor his heart beating fast, and she leaned in and spoke quietly.

"We would not waste good wine on you, as you are not worth it, you are quite safe this time, but mark my words, if I want you dead, you will not see it coming, but it will come. Enjoy your drink, knowing this night you are safe. Mark my words carefully Alder, I will do anything to protect this realm and its queen from your greedy little hands. Sleep well, enjoy the wine, it could be your last, and I see there is still some left in the bottle."

Ariel walked out of the room, and with a pop! she was gone. Alder sat breathing hard, his heart racing, and he knew she was right, he did not know who was, and who was not loyal to him.

*I*n Gwynfor's cabin on Sora, there was a happy reunion, as

everyone sat around talking and laughing, there was a loud pop! Ariel appeared with a large smile, Bade looked up with hope.

"Well?" Everyone turned, to see her grinning as she came across the large room.

"The seeds of doubt are planted, I enjoyed that, he was more than a little nervous when I left." Gwynfor gave a giggle as he looked up at her.

"See, I told you… All we have to do is wait, now the seeds of his own greed will germinate and eat him away from inside as his fears take over. Once he sees everyone as a potential assassin, he will find himself more and more isolated, and that will eat at his soul and he will drive all of them out. My sister was a genius, I remember well when we made up the plan, I am not sure she ever used it, but she spent a lot of time thinking it through and perfecting it. She told me, the simpler and more subtle it was, the better it would work. I am glad we have not wasted it, I felt she did a rather splendid job of perfecting it." He smiled, and Tila gave a giggle.

"You have a devious mind My Lord Gwynfor." He gave a little chuckle.

"You know, travel, that is the key, I have taken many holidays and you would be amazed what you can learn, travel is good for the mind and sharpens the wit. You mark my words young Tila, it is in the watching of others we gain the greatest wisdom."

Gwynfor was not far wrong, Alder had become corrupted, and it was that which shaped his thoughts. Ariel had only made a suggestion, but as he retired for the night, already her words had seeped into the darker parts of his mind. She had simply posed the question of who could one really trust, to a man, who had violated the trust of everyone. As Gwynfor had explained, over the coming days, Alder would allow the thoughts to grow in his mind, and his distrust of others would grow, and through that, in his self imposed isolation, he would begin to unravel. He had made himself a prisoner of his own mind, and the House of Scribes, and he had nowhere to run, and Gwynfor understood, that as his own mind worked against him, eventually he would break. When that happened, all those supporting him would abandon him, for it was Alder who was the glue to this problem, and as Gwynfor rightfully pointed out to the group earlier.

"Unstick him, and everything falls apart, it is simple really… Did I tell you my sister was a genius?"

Chapter Thirteen.

The Darkness of Fagan.

Fagan sat and watched as Iona tucked into her meal, he was shaken and needed time to settle, so cooked some food. Iona had not eaten much for two days, and he was surprised to see her tuck into the food.

"Ye is as slender as ye mother, and yet I feel, has the appetite of ye father." She took a sip of her tea.

"I have not been home, and not really eaten much. I am in your debt; this is fine food." He smiled, and gave a nod.

"I regret being harsh with ye, I hope ye knows, I care deeply for ye, and I am sorry." She smiled.

"I know… Master Fagan, it is so important I learn the truth. I know she was your queen, but Rhiannon was not truthful, and I think a great deal of what she did, is what created much of the troubles we have all faced. I will not ask you to speak ill of your queen, but I do want the truth of Morgana of Cornwall. I will show that what she intended and what happened, are two separate things. I know of the evil she has done, and that is why it is so important that I know the truth of the person she was here, living in Avalon. Master Fagan, it matters, the truth must be known."

He gave a soft nod; he knew she was right, and this one subject had been haunting his thoughts for most of his life. It was the reason he moved into the forest, and left his Fae race behind. As he sat there looking at her, just a young girl, almost with the same hope in her eyes as Morgana had, he felt the pressure build inside him. Fagan looked up with sad eyes, his voice soft, and filled with regret.

"I betrayed her, I let her down, and I have had to live with it, and there has not been one day it has not haunted my thoughts, she deserved better of me." Iona felt the power of his deep emotions.

"Talk to me Master Fagan, show me that I am right, and her truth has been hidden."

Fagan took a deep breath, and leaned on the table, Iona had never seen him like this, all of his usual bright optimism had gone, and he looked like a man who had been crushed.

"Tis not a good tale Little Violet Eyes, and I am not right sure where to start." Iona looked at him, her tone was soft and caring.

"Start at her arrival here in Avalon, and then go from there."

*I*ona was almost eighteen, and her future would lie in a realm she had never lived in, and she was to be a queen of a people she only half knew. Ariel had set her off on a task, and without really understanding why, as she sat with Fagan, deep inside the Forest of Time, she was not even aware of how much she had changed. Fagan sat with her, and to him, she already had the power and stature of a queen.

Fagan began his tale of Morgana's first days alone in the cottage with nothing but an old table and bed. He talked of her days collecting her herbs and plants and drying them out, and all while studying her books for the old wizard. He would pause to smile.

"She was lovely, had a smile as bright as a freshly opened daisy she did, and such dark deep eyes. Oh, Little Dark Eyes was special, there was no doubt of that, she made me laugh, she made her bags for her tea out of an old dress, she had no money ye see." He smiled, as if the memory was one of great joy.

"Traded me she did, for a bit of old rope, I was going to burn it, but she runs in to her little cottage, and out she pops with that big smile, and some tea to trade. Aye, she was a lovely girl, used the rope to make new souls for her shoes she did."

Fagan gave a little chuckle, and his eyes lit up, and it was clear to Iona how fond he was of her, he looked up and they danced and sparkled.

"I will never forget her first day of trade, took her weeks to gather that stock. She turns up bright as a button, and gives me her penny, and off she went to set up her first stall. I watched her from off yonder, she made me laugh she did. She put a cloth on the table and put everything out just right, and she had neat little signs on all of it, even now, I could see she was raised by a queen. Attention to detail, I told all of em I did, but not her, she knew, and she did it, I was as tickled as a harebell to see her sell her goods." Iona smiled at him, he looked so happy, and then his faced clouded over.

"Next time were different, tis not a good story." Iona watched his whole demeanour change, and he sagged to the table.

"She turns up with a big smile and sets up with cheer, and then her highness sends our Stenlow over, and he tells her he does, she cannot trade, cause she is not Fae. Oh dear, tis heart breaking, his soldier comes over and starts smashing her bottles and rippin up her tea, she were devastated. I missed most of it, but when I comes back, there is the queen sat on her horse, right there in front of her." He shook his head, and looked so sad.

"I walks up at the back, and all of em are on their knees, but not her, stands there proud, with tears in her eyes and she stares at the queen, and I will never forget it, I know it word for word I does."

He took a deep breath in, and Iona watched him carefully, feeling the pain surface inside him. Fagan stared into space, as if he was seeing it happen right in front of him, and his words were quiet and soft.

"You are right, you are the queen of the Fae of Moon, I am Morgana, daughter of Igraine, widow of King Uther, the one true king. I am a countess, and by right of birth, Queen of the Britons of the realm of men. I am apprentice to Merlin, guardian of the Whitelines, as appointed by the White Lord himself, who by rights, is a superior within the ruling council. It appears we are equals, queen of Fae." He took a deep breath and shook his head.

"Ye does not talk back to the queen, but she did, and the queen was really mad, oh dear she screamed at her she wanted her out of the realm. She were brave, Little Dark Eyes stood there, her fists clenched and tears on her cheeks, and she stared at her sat on her horse, and she says. I do not live in your realm, I live in the property of Merlin, which he owns in its entirety. It is his and is not classed as your land. It is independent from Avalon, as it is white line territory, and as long as he gives me the right to live there, I shall." Iona was really surprised.

"She said that, what did the queen do?" Fagan shook his head.

"She screamed at the top of her voice, and points to the road, and told her to get off her market, she was trash. It was in that moment I became real frighted for her. No one faces her out and defies her, and I will give her something, she stood tall like an oak, and she says. As you wish, queen of the fair, I see now why Ariel never returned." Fagan shook his head slowly.

"It were a bad move, I should have known then she would suffer, that was one subject no one talked of, well, not near the queen. The queen were madder than bees on a busted hive, I should have seen it really, me brains were full of bindweed back then, I know better now."

Iona watched him, unsure of what he meant, Fagan stared into the space as if seeing something, she moved her head to try and get his attention.

"Know what Master Fagan?" His eyes moved to her.

"That were the day she marked her, after that, for the queen it was war. She gave the order and I spent the week after that fencing in her land, she were upset, but she were sweet." He sat up a little and gave a smile.

"Made me barley crackers and tea everyday she did, and they were good, best I ever had. Aye, she was sweet, spent all week sat with me chatting, she were clever and no mistake, and interesting, said things only I ever thought about. The traders really stood by her, they sent food, new jars, and cloth for new bags, made her cry it did, she had no idea folks could be so nice. It made me sad to see that, touched me deep it did." He gave a huge sigh.

"Bless her kind heart." His eyes teared up again and he took a moment, and his voice cracked, as he shook his head.

"I failed her I did; I knew what would happen and I were right, she come after her and blamed her for everything she did." He looked at Iona and swallowed hard.

"There were good folk here, they stood up for her, next market, Morgana had left, and gone home, but they stood by her, kept her stall empty. Seth paid me a penny to keep it free as a mark of respect, and when the fair haired folk come, all of em stood by her and refused to serve em." Iona was amazed, and sat back as Fagan lifted out a big rag and wiped his eyes, he gave a reassured nod.

"Good folks the Fae, decent, she were seen as one of em, and for the first time and only time in me life, they stood their ground. I admired that; it took guts." His eyes filled with tears, and he looked down and shook his head, as his tears dripped onto the table, and Iona felt a huge pull at her heart, as he wept.

"She got em all, had em all killed, every last one of them." Iona gave a gasp, she could not believe what she was hearing, she had no idea what to say, and it just sort of slipped out.

"What… All of them?" Fagan looked up, he was finding it hard to speak as his tears fell, and he nodded, and gasped his words through his tears.

"Over a hundred, women, children, and men, their whole families, she slaughtered em all… They were good folks, kind folks, but she took the lot of em out. I didn't have the heart to tell little dark eyes, she was already heartbroken."

He gave another gasp and lifted his rag to his face as his shoulders shook, and Iona felt her own tears in her eyes. She could not believe what she was hearing, it was impossible to even comprehend, as she watched Fagan weep for the people he knew were his friends. Fagan lifted his head and looked at Iona, and through his tears she could see the fire in his eyes.

"I am shamed to say it, but I hated her, let all the gods take me, I hated my queen." He sat back and took a deep breath, and wiped his eyes, and breathed in and out as he calmed down.

"After that, Little Dark Eyes hid away, our Stenlow told me that after the White Lord visited her highness, she wrote a pardon for Little Dark Eyes, and let her back on the market, but she never came back. Folks got scared of her, because they feared for their life, and then all the rumours started. It were after she had left for good he told me, she started them to make it as hard as possible for her. I knew she was lonely, Stenlow told me, he has a soft heart, he is a good sort is our Stenlow, not a man of bad deeds, he told me he felt sorry for her and was worried about her. I reckon he grew to care for her, his daughter died at birth, and I think in a way, he sort of thought that Little Dark Eyes, who was about the same age, is what his daughter would have been like. Aye, he watched over her, made sure she was safe." Fagan smiled.

"Our Stenlow, is a better man than me, I should have done more for her, I liked her, she were a good soul." Iona nodded, and smiled.

"I have met him; he does appear to have really cared about her." Fagan smiled, and gave a soft nod, and Iona understood the pain he was feeling, and quietly asked.

"She was with Stenlow when Eve was killed, wasn't she?" Fagan looked at Iona, and his eyes went dull, she could instantly see his pain.

"Tis the darkest day of me life, haunts me it does."

He got up out of his seat, and walked over to the cabinets. He bent down opened the door, and pulled out a large stone jug. He reached up for two glasses, and turned to her.

"Tis not a good thing I did, this helps oil the words and kills the pain." He walked back to his seat, and put down the glasses, then pulling the cork, he poured out two glasses of a slightly golden liquid. He slid one across the table towards her.

"Sip it, ye folks will not agree, but ye will need one when I am done, I will need a few to get this out." Iona looked at the glass suspiciously. He lifted his glass, and swallowed the contents whole. Fagan gave a little shudder, and then poured another and sat back, and looked at her.

*F*agan began the story of the day of Eve's death, he talked of how he had seen Morgana on the road towards the shoulder when he was out delivering. He returned to his shop and got on with his work, it was mid afternoon when the first wail came, and he ran out of his shop still holding the scythe he was sharpening. Fagan described the plume of red shooting into the sky, and the clouds as they rolled in, and then from nowhere came the rain.

Everyone was terrified, none of them knew what was happening, and time slipped past in horror, until the second wail came, and he knew that was the queen. He jumped to her and she was wounded, and screaming that Morgana had killed Eve, she had seen her do it. Rhiannon told him when she confronted her, Morgana had attacked her, and burned her with a curse of dark evil. She pointed at the cottage as guards started to arrive, and he ran at the door, and broke it down, and saw her stood with her bags ready to run. Fagan shook his head, and lifted his drink and swallowed it, then poured another.

"I shamed meself, I knew down deep it were not her, but when she told me she had seen Little Dark Eyes kill Eve, I were so angered I was, I thought she had turned and gone dark." He looked up as tears filled his eyes.

"I dint want that, not for her, she were sweet, but I were as angry as a hornet on a busted nest, and lost me thoughts. I never should have listened, I saw it in her eyes, she were scared of me, poor soul, I terrified her, but she stood there and she faced me. She were a brave un, I admired that." His tear dripped onto the table, and Iona could feel the surge of pain flow through him.

"She turned and looked at me, and blow me, she dropped her veil and said it." Hc stared into space.

"She is wrong, it was not me Fagan, I would never do that, I believed in Eve, I am innocent." Iona watched as his faced changed, and he shook his head and bit down hard on his lip. He took a huge inward breath and looked at her.

"I believed her, I knew her to be true, and yet I swung for her, and she went, gone in the smoke, and all her pictures hit me, and my mind filled me head with parts of her life." He lifted his glass.

"May the gods forgive me, I knew she were true, she had never lied. I saw her truth, she showed me."

Iona lifted her glass and took a sip, and her throat filled with fire, and she coughed as Fagan stared at the wall, and his tears flowed down his face, but he just sat there, sagging, almost broken, as she coughed and spluttered through his silence. A few minutes passed by, and he breathed in, and his eyes moved to Iona.

"I saw the big raven sat on the window of a building, and I could feel the spell of connection. Then I saw Little Dark Eyes walking up steps with the raven on her shoulder, and she met Branna. I saw her pleading with a woman, and Little Dark Eyes was begging her to stop, and then darkness came, I saw a white raven land on her arm. What really shocked me, was I saw Ariel's face looking down on her." He sat back and looked at Iona, the front of his top bore a large damp patch from his tears.

"When Stenlow told me, I knew he was true to his word, I already knew she was innocent, I believed her. I will not say I know all, her pictures baffled me they did, and even now they still do. I have spent me whole life here alone trying to work out what she showed me, and half of that wondering why me, why drop the veil for me? Even now it haunts me dreams." Iona looked at him.

"Stenlow told me his story, he told me you refused to speak to him, why Master Fagan, you could both help each other?" Fagan nodded, took a breath and rubbed the bristles on his chin.

"Aye I know, and I know what he saw. He were talking one night, and told me he thought of her, asked if I knew anything. I shook me head and says no, then he leans over and pats me hand, and tells me he knew she were a good person. Thing is, as he touched me, I got his dream in me head, and I saw it, I saw what he saw. I pulled me hand back and shouted at him, I never meant to, but what I saw terrified me, and I have never spoke of her since."

Iona could see the horror on his face, and she understood that as a mystic, Fagan saw and read more into it than Stenlow fully understood. She took another sip of her glass, and could feel her heart was racing, her words were soft, as she looked at him filled with deep sadness.

"Can you speak of what you saw Master Fagan?" His eyes moved to her, and filled with tears, he just stared at her, and then gave a gasp as the tears ran down his cheeks.

"My dear sweet Violet Eyes, I cannot… I do not have the words in me." Iona understood, she had some idea of what he saw, her mother had talked of it.

"It was the ritual wasn't it, the one only a queen of the moon can conduct?"

He breathed in and gave a small gasp, and nodded a yes. Fagan took a deep breath and poured another glass, he lifted it up and swallowed all of it in one, and then looked at her.

"What I will say to ye is this. It was not her doing, it were forced upon her, it were not of her choosing."

Iona suddenly realised what he said, and it felt like a punch to her stomach, and she took a deep breath and lifted her glass and took another sip. It burned down her throat, as she fully understood what he had told her, and all she could think of was.

"Was it Branna?" Fagan breathed out, and lifted his rag to his eyes and wiped them.

"No… She tried to stop it, but were too late. I saw her try, I do not understand all I saw, but I know Branna was not the evil in the room. I could feel it, but could not see it, and it has haunted me since." He refilled his glass and took another drink, and calmed himself a little.

"Ye will be queen, ye has the power to speak truth. I do not know all of it, but this I know, Little Dark Eyes was white, I saw it in her, and I saw it in her garden, she was not dark, not here." Iona understood.

"You saw the white star too?" He nodded.

"I saw it that night, I stood there as her house burned, and I leaned on the fence in the rain, and as I looked at it, it burst into bloom. Listen to me Little Violet Eyes, and know this. That plant will not grow where there was darkness, and it grew in her garden, she planted it, and it took. There was no darkness in her, she looked dark and dressed dark, but there was not one bit of it in her. Little Dark Eyes was a good soul, she was kind, and she were lovely, I were her only friend at the end, and I failed her. Tis me burden, and I have carried it, I lived here alone to be at peace with me thoughts, and this burden is heavy, but I will bear it to me death. That is the darkness in old Fagan, and I learned from it." Iona smiled.

"I am very grateful that you have shared this with me, Master Fagan, it answers many questions, and I need to have them answered. What you have done, is a good thing, I am not sure if it will help you, but knowing the truth is what matters." He nodded.

"She went dark, and she has done things that folks have suffered by. It was right she was stopped, and if what I saw was true, stopping her brought her the peace she yearned for. I felt her, I felt her fear, and felt her hatred of the darkness, and her fears of what she would become. She did not want it, she did not want to be dark, that I know is the truth."

He sat back and sighed a heavy sigh, and in a way, Iona thought it had helped him to share it. He closed his eyes and rested a moment.

"She was a lovely girl, proper dignified and brave, and pretty too. I liked her, we were friends."

Iona watched as he drifted into sleep with a faint smile on his face, and although it had never really appeared obvious to her, she noticed how like Stenlow he was. She lifted a thick blanket off the chair by the fire and laid it over him, and smiled.

"Thank you, Master of the Forest, you are a man of high honour in my kingdom, and you always will be. Morgana would be pleased to know she still has her friend here, thinking kindly of her." Brooke flew in, as Iona lifted her cloak, he landed on the window as she walked to the door, and she smiled as the owl watched her with big eyes.

"Watch over him for me, he is precious to all of us." Brooke gave a hoot, as Iona pulled his door closed, and walked into the twilight.

Moments later, she walked out of her window, and onto the cool stone of the old burned out building, that had once been Morgana's home. She stood next to the chimney, which was starting to crumble, and leaned against the rough brick, as she looked around.

"This was not much Morgana, and yet, I find I can really understand you. I too have a small cabin, it is wooden, but has a brick chimney, and I suppose if it burned down, it would not look much different than this." She smiled.

"I remember my first day moving in, I was so excited and so happy, I hope you felt like that too? I spent my day scrubbing and sweeping, and I rearranged all my furniture, which is silly because I had so little really. I suppose just knowing it was mine was what mattered. Is it strange that I feel I completely understand you, and I know it may seem odd, but I wish that I had known you. I wish I could have met you; I am sure we would have been friends."

Iona stood in the growing darkness lost in thought, as all the pieces of the story of Morgana started to come together, and she felt she had a more accurate idea of who Morgana was, and the life that she had lived. She gazed up at the mount, with its tall white citadel, and large silver dome, it was impressive, of that there was no doubt. Avalon was almost a mystical paradise, a utopian oasis, even in these times. It never appeared to age, and back in a time when the world was young and life was simplistic, it must have felt even grander than it did today.

"You certainly showed your power Rhiannon, but to rule with such fear, is it worth it? Amethyst is so loved by her people, they do not fear her, and she is gracious and kind. I have seen her rule as I grew up, spoken to her people, and seen the devotion they have to her. Why throw all that away Rhiannon, why target half of your population? I do not think I will ever understand you, my father could be so much more powerful than he is, there was a time when he was younger, when it was him who the people wanted to rule. Yet, he chose not to, all he wanted to do, was come home and love my mother and his children. Morgana should have been an asset to Avalon, she cared about the people, she was a healer, why is it that through history we have always persecuted those with the ability to heal?"

She gave a sigh and leaned off the wall, and walked slowly back across the blackened stone floor, through the gap where two of the old door frame stumps stood worn and charred down to but just a foot high each, on either side of the old doorframe. She stepped past, and onto the path to where the gate posts stood, and the old gate lay broken and decayed in the grass at its side. In her mind she could see the pictures, as her memory of the night played back through her thoughts. Fagan sat up on his cart and looked down at her.

"What were ye up to as I rode up?" Morgana smiled, and pointed behind herself with her thumb.

"I was looking to repair my shoes, the soles have worn out, I was wondering if I could sow some cloth to them." Fagan nodded.

"Have ye heard of rope?" Morgana frowned.

"Rope, why rope, how do you fix a hole with rope?" He shook his head, and lifted a piece out of the back of the cart, and then he skilfully wound it around itself, forming a coil.

"Look, ye coil it like this, and sew as ye go." He made a circle with a hole in the centre, and then pushed it together flat so it created an oblong.

"Sew it firm mind ye, and then ye can sew on the sides, and the rope becomes a thick sole. I used to line mine with fabric, they are soft and comfy, and hard wearing." Morgana watched fascinated, and gave a smile as she understood, he grinned at her, and handed over the coil of rope.

"I have plenty of rope, here take it and try it, ye will find if ye is clever, ye can sow those old shoes to the rope and put a hard wearing new sole on them." Morgana took the rope with a smile.

"How much do I owe you?" Fagan waved his hand.

"Tis old rope, and I have plenty, take it." Morgana shook her head.

"If you do not mind, I want to pay or trade you for it. I decided the day I moved here I would stand on my own feet. I collect flowers and leaves and dry them to make tea to sell, what kind of tea do you like, I will mix some if I have it?" Fagan gave a shrug and considered the point; he scratched his bushy white hair.

"I does like rose hip, and I am partial to rose petal." Morgana grinned, and gave a proud smile.

"I have both, wait here a moment I will get some to trade you for the rope."

Fagan watched her, and gave a chuckle as she turned and rushed into the house, a few moments later, she returned with a hand sown small cloth bag, containing the dried ingredients.

"I have mixed them both together, I think you will find they blend well, and make for a refreshing drink. I am happy to trade this for the rope."

Fagan took the tea and gave the bag a sniff, it smelt divine and his eyes sparkled. As Morgana took the rope, she looked at him on his seat, her shoulder length hair blowing behind her in the soft breeze.

"I feel we have made a fair trade, and I am happy with it, Master Fagan." He gave a nod.

"Aye, I reckon I have too, I respect that Little Dark Eyes, I will commend ye to ye teacher when I see him. I shall also try this tea, and if it is agreeable, I will tell folks how good it is." She gave a big happy smile.

"I thank you Master Fagan, as soon as I have enough dried out, I will bring it to the market." Fagan sat up, and flicked the reins of the horses.

"I will look ye out, take care of yeself, and mind that blade, it has a fine crafted edge and is sharp." She nodded.

"I will." The cart gave a lurch, and he trundled on with a wave, and Morgana stood and waved as she watched him ride on down the road. Iona came out of her thoughts, and sighed.

"It is hard to understand why some people can see such love in another, and yet others are blinded to it. I wonder if power can be like the blinkers covering the plough horse? Does it narrow the vision of those who wield it? I think maybe it does in some cases."

It was time to go home, she was tired, and needed her bed, she had been away from home for too long. Her window opened, and she stepped through into her cabin in Loxley, and took off her veil. She felt emotional and exhausted, and walked through to her room dropping her cloak on the chair, and loosening the ties on her dress. Iona climbed wearily into bed, and lay back, her head was swimming with what she had learned, and she now knew she was much closer to the truth. She closed her eyes.

"So much pain, so much hate, and all for the want of a woman blinded by her own idea of who she should be. It should never have been like that, it was needless." She turned over, and blew out the candle, then lay back in the darkness, her eyes closed, and she drifted off into sleep, and knew she would dream of walking in Tintagel.

*R*une leaned on the door frame of the kitchen doorway, and looked out towards the small cabin, and saw the light go out, and smiled.

"Welcome home Iona Violet Stone, I feel the changes within you, the power you hold, works for justice. Sleep well my precious daughter."

Rune turned and closed the door, and walked over towards the table and the large oil lamp, the kitchen door opened and Gailania walked in rubbing her eyes.

"Mum, I cannot sleep, my tummy hurts." Rune gave a smirk, and lifted her eyebrows.

"Did I not tell you about eating too much gingerbread?" Gailania looked up with a sad face, as she rubbed her tummy, her voice was sad and quiet.

"Yes, but Mum, it was so nice, and Pan loves it too." Runestone smiled, as she lifted her daughter into her arms.

"Come on, I will sit with you and rub your tummy better, there is just too much in there and it is stretching you sideways." Gailania put her head on Rune's shoulder as she walked slowly up the stairs.

"Thank you, Mum."

Rune rubbed her back, and her hand began to glow with a soft violet light. She gently lay her daughter back into her bed and sat on the side of it, and smiled as she placed her hand on Gailania's stomach and rubbed as it glowed. Gailania settled and closed her eyes, and Rune softly stroked the hair from her face.

"Sleep deeply Sweet pea."

Gailania turned on her side, and Rune pulled up the covers with a smile, and looked around at the two other beds, where Fern slept in a tight ball, and Tegan lay sprawled out, her head hanging over the side of the bed. She quietly got up, and walked to the door, and turned back to watch for a moment, with a soft smile on her face. Her voice was soft and almost a whisper.

"This was all I ever wanted, just this, Robbie and me, and my beautiful children. No matter how dark or hard it was, this was worth the fight."

She turned, and walked down the long corridor, she was Runestone Sapphire, Lady of the Woods and Eve in a human form with the power of life, and yet, none of that mattered to her, because she was also called Mum.

Chapter Fourteen.

The Hidden Truth.

"I forgot my bag!"

The steps thumped, as Gailania ran like crazy up the stairs, Tegan with her hair sticking out everywhere stood by the door impatiently waiting.

"Hurry up weed, or we will be late." Rune frowned at her, as she came out of the kitchen with a cup.

"GOT IT!" Tegan shrugged, and leaned out the door.

"FERN, WAIT UP!"

Gailania came flying down the stairs with her cloth bag, and skidded to a halt at the bottom, as Rune stood watching.

"What have I said about running on the stairs?" Her bright blue eyes twinkled.

"Not to, sorry Mum!" She was cute, Rune leaned down, and kissed her head.

"Go on, get yourself to school." She gave a big smile, and hurried over to Tegan, who rolled her eyes.

"Bout time!"

Rune watched as they waved good bye, and then headed out back to the cabin behind the house. Iona was still asleep, she sat on the bed, and put the cup on the side, and then gently stroked Iona's hair back from her face. Iona disturbed, and moved under the covers, she opened her eyes, and turned to look up at her mother. Rune smiled.

"I brought you coffee, the house is safe, the children have left for school."

Iona pushed her arms out of the covers and stretched the aches out of her body, and groggily sat up. She rubbed the sleep out of her eyes, and blinked as she looked at her mother. Rune smirked and lifted the coffee and handed it to her.

"Did you sleep well?" Iona sipped, and lifted her eyes to her.

"You always ask that, but I know you sense me, I feel you, so you already know I did a lot of dreaming." Rune smiled.

"Mum's like to check." Iona gave a soft chuckle.

"I am fine, I have learned a lot about her life, and about what it was like to live in a realm ruled by Rhiannon. I think I have learned how not to rule a realm, Morgana had a rough time there, Rhiannon did not hide her hatred of her. I was right to a degree, which I feel happy about." Rune looked at her.

"How so?"

"The way she intimidated everyone to make sure only her version of the truth existed. Morgana stood up to her, showed her for what she was, and that was what caused all of this."

Rune leaned back, Iona looked tired, she had dark lines under her eyes, and it worried her.

"Iona sweetheart, do not push yourself, you look tired." She gave a nod, and sipped more coffee and blinked.

"I have not slept well, but I really think that this is meant for me, I am not sure why just yet, but I am getting there. I think I have most of the story of her life in Avalon, I now have to work out her connection to Branna, and how that happened, and then how she ended up as the person you knew. I think I know parts of it, but they do not make full sense yet." Rune understood this process, she herself had gone through many trials.

"I can help if you still need it." Iona shook her head.

"No, I do not want this coming between you and dad, and I think that if I am going to understand this all, it has to be me alone. You really helped me get on the right track, but from here, at least for now, I will carry on solo." Rune smiled and slipped off the bed.

"Alright sweetheart, but I am here if you need me." Iona smiled.

"I know that, and thanks Mum." Rune got up to leave, and Iona looked up.

"Where is Ariel?" Rune turned.

"Something came up that needed her attention, she told me to tell you, she would be in touch soon." Iona gave a nod.

"Okay, thanks."

*O*n Sora, the group had reached the point where they knew this would become a waiting game, as until Alder made a move, they would not be able to act. Crystal was staying with Tila at Gwynfor's, and Una and Treen had decided to stay, so Sapphire jumped to Callanish to consult her table, and Ariel headed back home to Avalon. Having read Branna's version of Morgana's story, she wanted to look deeper into everything, and since Iona had removed her veil, she was aware of the direction Iona had gone on, and found it interesting she had chosen to look into the same things as her.

*I*t was quiet at the Mere, and Iona sat out with another drink, on the bench outside her cabin. She had spent several days learning new things, and she relaxed and enjoyed the peace. The backdoor of the house banged and she looked up, to see Thorn, he saw her and smiled and walked over. He had changed a great deal, and he was starting to look very much like his father's son, with his long dark bushy hair. His main difference, was his bright blue eyes, which were very much like his mother's, and showed the power of life within him. He and Iona were close, and out of all her siblings, she spoke most to him.

"Hello, you, I wondered when you would surface, you have been illusive of late, how are you?" She smiled, as he walked up and slipped on the side of the bench.

"I am okay, I have been busy, there is a lot to do in the next month." He nodded.

"I have heard, Dad was a little ruffled by your choice of subject matter."

Iona had pretty much worked out everyone would know, keeping secrets in Loxley was not easy. As always, he was simply him, it did not matter that she had angered their father, he was her brother and in that he had never changed. She felt very close to him, he was in many ways her best friend, and had always stood by her and supported her, especially when she was a younger teenager and had doubts. They had spent many nights together talking at that time, and he always had that happy way of finding the right words to help lift her up. She gave a sigh.

"I was trying to look into this in a way that would not hurt anyone, I know it is not a popular subject. Thorn, I know this sounds crazy, but she was two people, she started off one way, and then in a way I am not sure of, she became what mum and dad faced. Both aspects of her are complete opposites, and mad as it sounds, I feel I need to find out what was the reason she went from one thing to another." He turned his head and looked at her.

"The change was that different, she was not like a spoilt horrible rude teenager?" She looked at him, and nodded at him.

"It is absolutely one extreme to the other, and it is looking like it was not her choice." He frowned.

"How do you mean, someone forced her to be evil, because that makes no sense Nona?" She gave a little titter.

"Welcome to my life." She sighed.

"The way I think it happened, was there is this Fae of Moon spell, where you tie your life to an animal, and it forms a connection that enhances your life. Hers was a raven; you know, we have both heard the stories." He nodded and was clearly following her.

"Thorn, somehow, and I am not sure yet, but she was forced to be tied to a raven, and it was one that was connected to the merle. I can only guess that through that, the darkness or the evil of the merle had an effect on her… It turned her bad." He sat back.

"Okay, so that is creepy, because that means it is possible to create evil people, and no one wants that." She nodded, and loved he just accepted something she had struggled with.

"I know right, but can you see my problem, dad knows the evil one, and I am learning about the nice one? He will never accept she was once actually from what I hear, a good person? Thorn, Merlin taught her the white lines, and she was good at it, if she was bad, why did he not see it?"

"I am not sure we can second guess that Nona, without him being here it is hard to say, because you would have to talk to him. From what I have heard from gran, because he was her dad, if she was some sort of evil person, he would have seen it. What do your gut instincts say?" She sat back, and looked up at the trees, and gave a sigh.

"I believe Morgana was just an ordinary girl who suffered the loss of her father at an early age, and she was sad inside, but as a person, she was kind, and she was helpful. From what I know, she was really intelligent, and very independent, she made cures that really helped people. I think if she lived in Loxley, we would be friends." He gave her a slight nod as he thought, his eyes moved to her.

"Then go with that, I know you, love it or hate it, you are the most like mum, you have her ability to look deeply into people, you always have. Nona, if you tell me someone was a good person, I accept it without question, because I know you, I know how you work. You think she was different, nicer, then honestly, I think she was." She gave a small smile; he winked at her and then patted her knee.

"You worry too much, in that way, you are also like dad." He stood up with a smile.

"Thanks Thorn, I am glad you were around today."

"Anytime, I am always around Nona, just yell." She nodded.

*I*ona sat and watched as he waved and headed off, he was working trees today with Rowan. She sat and sipped what was left of her drink. Talking to Thorn woke her mind up and she felt more confident, she got up and headed inside, and thought about her next step. Her one thought, was she knew Morgana left Avalon, but where did she go? All she knew from the stories her mum had told her was that she had a castle in the Hidden Realm, the problem was, she had no idea how to get there, and her mum had left to go shopping. Although, she stopped as she washed her cup.

"Sapphire dream walks, which means she has access to the realm, she knows how to get in."

Iona could sense that Sapphire was at home, and so she packed her shoulder bag to be more prepared, and jumped to her cottage. The door was always unlocked, Sapphire lived alone on an uninhabited island, she never worried about locking it. Iona knocked on the door, and opened it and leaned in, Sapphire was on her bed wrapped in a towel, having washed, and was brushing her hair.

"Hi, is it okay to talk?" She looked up, and then cringed as she found a knot in her hair.

"Yeah, what's on your mind?"

Iona walked in, she saw Melanie's old hat hanging over her bed, which was yet another reminder of what all of them had suffered, at the hands of Morgan. She sat in the only chair in the room and stared at it, and she realised something, Sapphire was looking at her, she smiled.

"I know what you have been doing, Rune spoke to me, it is alright Iona, you can talk. I am actually interested in how you see things."

Iona felt a little guilty, she understood this was possibly the one subject, most people would go against her on. She looked again at the hat, and then back to her, Sapphire turned and looked at it.

"It was my father's, when Morgan tried to take us, my mum grabbed it, and it never left her from that moment on. She still had it on when Morgan got her, and it stayed with her for all that time. It sounds odd, but having it hung there, is like having my parents together and with me." Iona nodded.

"I forget you were in Avalon at the same time as she was. I know some of your story, I am sorry Sapphire, you like many others suffered, it must feel strange to you that I am looking at this. Una was not pleased at first." Sapphire smiled.

"You do not have to apologise Iona, it is part of the story of all of us, and not your fault. I was a small baby, I do not remember much, just fleeting moments of my father. I never realised most of my memories were as a baby. I guess as I grew up, I took them out of context. Even now, when I hear his voice in my mind, it is like he is talking to me as a grown up, which obviously he wasn't." Iona nodded.

"I didn't realise you were so young; I suppose I do the same, and think of you always as you were when you first started teaching me. I never realised you were so young… Weird question, but do you remember it, you know, being in that state?" Sapphire smiled, and shook her head.

"No, I have only ever known this time, which in a way is a blessing, Jaz sort of remembers a few things of Florae and Avalon, but not much." Iona took a deep breath.

"Sapphire, I know this is not popular with everyone, and I am trying not to upset people, but it is important to me that I do this." She pulled her hair back into a ponytail, and tied it back with a ribbon.

"Iona, I am a centre of a circle, I understand what you are doing, it was expected. Well, we knew something would drive you on a journey of self discovery, and to be honest, the fact that your inner senses sent you on this particular line, shows that you are ready to take the crown." It surprised Iona.

"So, you don't mind?"

Sapphire stood up and reached for her pants, she dropped the towel and slipped them on, then lifted her blouse off the bed.

"Iona, I understand how the powers work, there is obviously something to be learned from this, which is why your sense of self sent you on this." She nodded as Sapphire pulled on her fitted jacket.

"I am glad you are okay with it, because I wanted to ask you some things, but was not sure of how you would react." Sapphire nodded, and walked into the kitchen space.

"I will make a drink, come on, we will sit and talk."

*I*ona sat at the table as Sapphire boiled a large copper kettle on the stove. She watched Sapphire as she moved around her kitchen space, and noticed things, like she made her own bread, and had rows of tall jars on the shelves filled with dried foods. She saw the axe in the corner, and a bow saw with a rough jagged blade, and she realised, Sapphire lived in the same manner as Morgana.

"You know, I have never really thought about it, but you live here completely isolated and alone. You chop your own wood, and grow and make all your own foods, is it very hard?" Sapphire sat down and shrugged.

"It is all I know, I have grown up living here, well for most of my time. This is how I lived with mum and with Jaz for a while as a kid. I suppose my mum taught us everything. I grow a few things, not much, and there are wild foods all over the place, and then there is Loxley. I cheat and buy fresh veg and meat there, and Jaz visits once a month and spends a few days, he cuts peat, and helps me haul up drift wood from the beaches for the fires. I have a log shed around the back which is full, which gives me two years' worth of wood, and don't forget, I am not here full time, I bounce around a lot."

"Do you not get lonely?" She lifted her cup, and smiled.

"Iona, people like us who have gifts, we need isolation at times, strange as it may look to someone who has grown up in a family house, this for me, is a necessity for my kind of life."

Iona had never thought of it, and yet she realised that it was probably the same for Morgana, the isolation helped her focus and study. Her life looked hard to those who did not have to live that way, but in a sense, Morgana must have adapted and become accustomed to it. She smiled at her.

"If I get lonely, I jump to you, or Rune, be honest, your house can be really noisy at times?" She gave a little giggle.

"Yeah, it can be mad, especially when Pan visits." She lifted her tea, as Sapphire watched her.

"So, what were the burning questions you had for me that had you use a window to come all the way over here?" Iona looked over her cup.

"I want to know how to get into the Hidden Realm, I know you dream walk there." Sapphire gave a nod.

"In dreams or in person?"

"In person, I do not dream walk, or at least I don't think I do." Sapphire sat back, and thought about it.

"It is possible for all centres, and some queens, apparently, it was the one thing Rhiannon could not do, but I think Bridget and my grandmother could. I sometimes dream walk there, and at other times I have gone in person, I just use a window into it."

"How, I have never been there so I cannot picture it?" Sapphire understood.

"Actually, you have, just not physically, you went there when you were four, do you not remember it?" Iona shook her head.

"Not enough to navigate it."

"Okay, I understand that, it is a big place, I knew what it looked like because I dream walked there. It is not a huge problem, I can take you, and then you will know a point you want to go to, so you can focus on it for the future. What part have you got in mind?" Iona took a deep breath.

"I want to see her castle." Sapphire frowned.

"How, it is not there, everything she built fell when she died?"

That confused her, in her mind, Morgana must have built the castle before she was forced into the ritual. So, in her thoughts, technically, everything she did before should not, if she understood the magic, have crumbled. She had thought everything she built as the evil Morgan was destroyed, after all, the plants she planted and raised flower beds she built were still there, they were decayed and over grown, but they remained. It made no sense to her.

"I want to visit where it stood, I could sense things in the cottage ruins, so I have wondered if I would sense more on that site." It made sense to Sapphire, she had the limited ability to sense things, just not the past.

"It is not a problem, finish your drink, and I will take you there. I have seen it from a distance, it will be interesting to see it up close."

Arriving in the Hidden Realm, was a real eye opener for Iona, she stood on the road and looked both ways, it stretched for miles and blurred out of sight in the distance. Behind her was another road, not as wide, and that appeared to bend and weave. In front of her was a huge wide space, where the trees had been cleared. The floor was filled with a black sand like dust. There were occasional pillars of smooth black polished stone, about a foot high scattered all over the site, almost as if they were markers. Iona looked at them, and held out her hand, as Sapphire walked along the edge of the black sandy dust.

"There is not much really, I remember seeing it from a distance, it was huge, with a tall tower on which was a raven, it was double the size of Dunnottar."

Iona was focused on one of the pillars, and in her mind, pictures began to appear, of Morgana alone, walking around and pacing out areas, and then lifting the small pillars out of the floor, it confirmed Iona's thoughts.

"Morgana made these before she was dark, which is why they are still here, but I also sense another presence mixed in with the dust. Sapphire, I don't think she built this alone." Sapphire turned, and looked across the wide gap between them.

"Someone helped her?" Iona nodded.

"I think so, but it is hard to tell, things here seem blurry." Sapphire looked around the trees and roads.

"This whole realm is blurry, nothing here makes sense, they say it has doors, but they constantly move. Only the dream spirits can navigate here, which by the way, you have never met Cal have you?" Iona frowned.

"Cal, who is that?" Sapphire smiled, and waved her hand.

"He is shy at times and hides, he says your power is big, and it worried him." Iona turned around looking but saw nothing.

"He… Who is He?"

Sapphire gave a little giggle and pointed, and Iona followed her direction, and saw the grass move. She stood still and watched, a little hand appeared, and the tall grass parted. A small face with giant eyes peered out at her. She gave a big smile, and waved.

"Hi, my name is Iona Violet, you must be Cal?" He blinked, and Sapphire gave a giggle.

"He is very shy, but thinks you are nice, but the black dust scares him, so he is hiding." The grass slipped back together, and he disappeared, Sapphire looked at the large area of black dust.

"So, what now?" Iona walked slowly around the edge.

"I am not sure, there is something here, something I need to see, I just don't know what." She looked at the dust on the floor, and then lifted her foot, Sapphire appeared nervous.

"Not sure you should step on it, looking at it, no one else has, that could be a sign." Iona understood.

"If I am right, there is nothing to fear, she built this first, and I think with help. She must have done this after she left Avalon, or just before."

*I*ona stepped onto the black dust, and felt the change of energy instantly, Sapphire watched her nervously, not convinced walking on it was a good thing. Iona looked at the floor, and her eyes appeared to brighten, almost as if they had an extra light in them, all Sapphire could do was watch, and hope nothing horrible happened.

Iona was lost in thought, focusing on her inner self, moving very slowly with her palms held out, as she felt the energy of Morgana, and also a lot of pain and sadness. She took another step forward and stopped, she lifted her face and looked at Sapphire.

"I feel something."

Sapphire jumped out of her skin, as Iona appeared to freeze, and then a huge castle rose out of the floor, and thundered up into the sky. She could not believe her eyes, the castle was there, and not at the same time. It was see through, like some sort of image held in place of what had been real. It was dull, and Iona was not clearly in view, it was almost like looking through heavy smoked glass. Iona stood still, and Sapphire saw her eyes were filled with violet, something she has seen Rune do many times, it was clear she was her daughter.

Above them was a scream, and Iona looked up, Sapphire followed her gaze. High above them, she could see the small figure of a person, a naked person, hanging in the air and they were screaming out something. Sapphire moved forward and lifted her foot, and suddenly, she was yanked back.

"Don't be stupid, leave her, she needs to see this."

She looked to her arm, and the white sleeve that contained the hand that was holding her, and followed it up, to the face of Opal.

"Connect to her, you need to see this."

Sapphire turned to look at Iona, she had gone, another scream above her echoed down, and she looked up and saw Iona high in the air floating. She focused on her, and the connection was made, and as it joined her, she gasped out in shock, and felt a sickness in her stomach.

*M*organa was hung against one of the wide pillar walls, naked and spread eagled, as she fought and struggled. In front of her a silver knife hovered, but what frightened her the most, was from the table, to just below Morgana was a smogget. Those she knew well, but she was uncertain, because it looked different than the ones she had encountered, or at least what she had seen. It was small and squat, and had a hideous and contorted face. The back of whatever it was stretched back to the black book on the table. The smogget chanted in a cruel and crude language, and then the knife plunged into Morgana's breast, and Sapphire jumped with shock, as Morgana screamed for all she was worth, begging and pleading the thing to stop.

Sapphire stood filled with horror, as what she knew was the young Morgana, screamed she did not want it, but what really shocked her, was she was screaming out that she was Whitelines, and did not want to be dark. The hideous thing laughed and cackled with delight, and chanted more, as another symbol was cut out in her skin, and Sapphire felt sick to the stomach, unable to fully understand what was happening. It felt violating, repulsive, and terrifying to watch, as another symbol was carved into her, and she felt useless as she could not do anything to stop it, and felt forced to watch.

Morgana screamed out 'BRANNA' and in an instant she was there, as she cut through something and stretched out for the table, and Sapphire understood as she saw her rip out the page and burn it. Everything stopped, and Morgana fell to the floor, the knife in her heart. Iona was floating right in front of her, holding her own heart and weeping, as Branna rushed over to her and pulled Morgana close and wept, and Sapphire felt herself swallow, as tears filled her eyes, it was heart breaking to see. Sapphire took a deep breath, and suddenly the castle was gone and Iona knelt on the floor weeping bitterly. Opal held her arm, understanding Sapphire wanted to go to her, and Opal spoke softly.

"Leave her, she needs to do this, she needs to feel all of it, this moment marks the coming of a true queen."

It felt hard to talk for Sapphire, she still felt so emotional, as she turned and looked into Opal's eyes, and spoke quietly, as if not quite believing her own words.

"That was Morgan le Fey, and yet, I found that a terrible thing to see. I found it heart breaking and I want to cry." Opal nodded as tears filled Sapphire's eyes, as she watched Iona.

"That was Morgana of Cornwall, not le Fey. The one we named

the Dark One, she came because of what you just witnessed. I cannot deny, I have thought of it often, because that is how I remembered her from my youth in Avalon. I never understood what happened to change her, I tried to find out but could never see it, and now I have, and it all makes sense." Sapphire was struggling to understand any of this.

"It does?" Opal nodded.

"Poor girl, it was never her choice, no wonder she was always angry." Sapphire did not know what to say, as she looked at Opal.

"You sound like you feel sorry for her." Opal looked at her with pale blue eyes, that held great compassion.

"I do Sapphire, all those others tied to ravens, they chose that, she didn't, she did not want it. For the first time ever, I understand why Leenard could never understand, or come to terms with her sudden change. This was the piece he too could never find, the piece that told him how a bright young girl and exceptional student, who he grew to admire and care for, turned so dark. He always thought it was his fault and carried that with him, he blamed himself, and now I know, he was wrong to do so, he was blameless."

Sapphire gave a nod and wiped her eyes, she could understand that, she turned back to Iona who had stood up and was also wiping her eyes. Both of them waited for her to walk slowly towards them, and as she stepped off the black dust, Opal pulled her into her arms.

"It is a painful path seeking the truth, but what you saw, answers many questions. Are you alright?" Iona looked at Opal, and gave a nod, but it was clear, what they had seen had impacted on her a great deal.

"I will be Great Grandmother." Opal pulled her back into another hug.

"You are a brave girl, few could have endured that, you will be a remarkable queen."

Chapter Fifteen.

Two Sides of the Raven.

Luminaria came down the steps from the deck, and smiled as she walked towards Fagan. Like everyone, she had aged a little, and the golden hair that used to flow down her back in waves, was now silver, and tied into a long plait down her back. Fagan nodded as she walked up.

"Alright, he has eaten, and is in a good mood today, a little more his old self, so, try not to upset him. I am grateful you are doing this, and I cannot tell you how happy I will be to see the last of that beard, it has never suited him. Right, I need to get back, I will come back after sunset and help him to bed." Fagan gave a nod.

"Alright our Lumi, don't ye go worrying none, I will sort him out." She smiled as she climbed up on her horse.

"Go easy with that razor, his skin is old."

She smiled, pulled on the reins and the horse turned, and then galloped off, and Fagan turned, and walked up to the deck, where Stenlow sat watching. Fagan leaned on the post at the top of the steps and looked at him.

"I will get the water and soap, and soon have ye back to rights, and then Stenlow, tis time we talked."

Sapphire sat on the large log in Opal's circle, as she sipped from her drink, as Iona stood just in front of them, lost in thought. The pictures of what she had seen, were still flashing through her thoughts and feelings. Opal could see that she was struggling to understand it all, and she got up and walked over to her. Iona took a deep breath, and tried to smile, as Opal took her hand and patted it.

"Your task is not an easy one, and I feel the impact it is having on you. What I saw today answers many questions for me, and I am grateful to you." Iona swallowed; she was very emotional.

"How does it help you, you are so wise, even my mother seeks your opinions? I feel so emotional, nothing I have read or heard of, would frighten me as that did. Grandmother, Morgana was begging not to have that done, she was forced, and I felt her absolute terror, she wanted to remain white." Iona gave a sob, and her eyes filled with tears, Opal took her hand.

"Come my child, walk with me." Opal pulled her hand softly, and walked with her out of her circle, into the trees, as Iona tried to compose herself.

"You have a powerful ability, much like Bridget's. Iona, Merlin never understood how the girl he knew and made a fellow of the Whitelines, became the force of evil your parents fought. I had many talks with him in our time together, and he tortured himself, because he truly thought she was filled with light. It is sad he is no longer here, because today, you showed the truth, and it changes everything." Iona looked at her.

"But how, everyone hates her, no one is ever going to believe this? She may have started out good, but she still turned dark and did great acts of evil, and that is all people will remember." Opal smiled.

"Listen to me Iona Violet, future queen of Florae, it is your truth that matters. There are many who still believe in the story told as her truth by Rhiannon, but it matters not if they think that. Iona, you know the facts, that is your truth, and when you rule, it will be your truth that matters, it is what makes the difference. Like you, Amethyst has adopted the facts, not a tainted version of them, and if you take your seat with the same heart, then the world of Fae will have fair rule. In time, the truth will be known, and that will be your part in this." She let go of Iona's hand, and smiled at her.

"Go… I feel your need to be alone, so go, worry not about Sapphire, we will have a good chat as always." Iona gave a slight smile, and nodded.

"Thank you, Grandma, yes, I would like some time alone."

Opal understood, and thought how like her mother she was. Opal gave her a hug and stepped back, and Iona turned and opened her window, and Opal watched as Iona stepped through, and the window closed.

"So like Runestone, so powerful and filled with love, good luck Iona Violet, difficult days will come, but somehow, I feel great hope."

*I*ona did not leave the realm, she reappeared at the castle site, and stood once again alone on the cross roads, looking at the dark sand. Her mind was filled with pictures, Morgana's face, which was filled with fear and pain, her pleading voice echoed through her thoughts, and she could feel all of the terror that Morgana was filled with. Her voice echoed in her head, and she felt weak and sat down on the floor, as she felt the fear inside herself, and wept.

"No… No, I do not want that, I am Whitelines, I do not want any more darkness. Maud please, I do not want any more, I have had too much already."

Iona looked at the floor, as her tears dripped down, feeling helpless, she could not imagine being torn from her family and forced into a life of darkness.

"I am so sorry Morgana, you did not deserve that, after all you endured, you deserved better."

Iona sat for a while, much of which she cried as she began to fully understand the full implications of what had happened, and it felt cruel and unjust, but there was little she could do, it was a long time ago. The feelings had been so powerful, she felt drained, as pictures she did not understand all mixed together with what she had witnessed, and the exhaustion overcame her. Iona closed her eyes and lay back against a thick lump of tall grass, and her mind drifted.

*A*s Iona slept, the pictures came together, and the life of Morgana flowed through her thoughts. Her anger and frustration, her outbursts, as the weeks past and she screamed into the tower of her castle, or curled up weeping on her chair, lost and alone, as she tried to fight the changes inside her. It was sad and painful, and one set of pictures, disturbed her as she saw Morgana fall down on her hands and knees in front of her fire, as she clenched her fists, and screamed out, as her eyes exploded with red light.

"NO…. NO…. I WILL NOT LET YOU WIN!"

Iona could feel her fight against the darkness, as she fought with all she had, but she also felt her sadness and anger, as she knew she was losing to the power of the darkness. As Iona dreamed, she witnessed Morgana slowly become seduced by the darkness, and felt her heartbreak as she finally accepted her fate. As she slept, another selection of pictures came to her, and she felt a wave of hope pass through Morgana, as she met a young lord, named Hesketh.

He was a distant cousin of the Pendragon line of Arthur, and for a time, she felt hope grow within Morgana, and she became calmer, as she was romanced and shared moments of what felt like love. It was an unusual moment, and she felt that the love was actually helping Morgana claw back control. She saw her married at Tintagel, and Hesketh working on rebuilding the castle. Morgana appeared to be happy, and Iona mumbled in her sleep as she dreamt, a part of her was happy to feel the happiness within Morgana. The life of Morgana was flashing through her mind in her sleep, she got pregnant and had a son, and once again she felt her happiness, and then her mind flashed, and Iona jerked in her sleep, as the pictures became clear.

Morgana turned and looked down the hall at her son Gawain. Behind him his wife Phillipa, who was holding a child in her arms looked afraid, as Morgana screamed at her son.

"How dare you wear that thing around your neck in my home. Have you any idea of the history of our people, do you know of the damage that crucifix has done to the people of this land?" She glared with hate at him, as he looked nervous.

"Mother, we believe in this faith, both Phillipa and I have embraced it, and we have begged to be forgiven for the sins we have committed." She stared at him, and her eyes flared with red.

"Our land was carved from the stone by my mother and father. He built his castle with his bare hands. I watched our people slaughtered by the hundreds; in the name of that god, you hang around your neck. How dare you turn your back on the blood that flows in your veins, you are no better than that Arthur, he turned his back on us, and he suffered for it."

She stormed across the hall, her eyes red with her anger, and grabbed it, then tore if from his neck, as she stared in to his eyes, and he shook his head as his anger rose.

"You may be my mother but you do not rule me, I have the right to live my own way Mother, you have not the right to rule me." Morgana snatched at his throat, and stared at Phillipa.

"This is you isn't it… He has never spoken back to me, and has always understood the importance of the line of our ancestry. You are the reason; you brought your god into this family, and you have poisoned his mind." Phillipa looked afraid, as she held the child.

"I never hid my belief, and I will not deny my god, not even for you, he is my saviour." Morgana pushed, and Gawain was flung into the wall. Morgana stared at Phillipa her temper was flaring, and her voice sunk low.

"He is your saviour, tell me, where is he, show me, let me see this almighty god that you so dearly cling to?" She stepped back, her eyes widening with fear, as Morgana advanced on her.

"He will lift me up, and deliver me from evil." Morgana snorted.

"Arthur thought the same, and yet, his god did not appear to lift him up. As I remember it was the maiden daughters of Gwendolyn, and I should know, they sleep in my cellar as we speak." Phillipa stepped back.

"I will not deny my god, I will die before I do that, and no matter how powerful you may think you are, you will not defeat my god, unlike you, I walk in the light."

Morgana's eyes opened wide, Phillipa hit a very raw nerve. Her arm shot out, and she grabbed her by the throat and pulled her with power. Phillipa was dragged up close in front of Morgana as she choked, her nose almost touching Morgana's. Her voice was cold and cruel as she squeezed her hand.

"What would you know of the light, I have known the purest of white, purer than your god could ever be. Now little Christian, I know the darkness, and it is deeper than you will ever know of, so show me, my darkness against your god's light."

Phillipa struggled to breathe as Morgana squeezed, and Phillipa could see deeply into her eyes, and saw the depth of the darkness within her. Her body started to spasm and tears filled her eyes. Morgana watched her as she gasped and fought for air, she stared into Phillipa's eyes.

"You come into my home, you dine with my family, I let you marry my son, and you whined so much, he turned his back on Berengar and changed his name to Knox. I tolerated the insult, and I allowed him to be called that ridiculous name, but now you corrupt him to this god, who has still not appeared. Where is he, I am waiting, I met Eve, I saw Hearne, and spoke with Albanlin, so I know my gods are real? Eve's daughter lives in my woodland with Albanlin's wizard, so where is your god, why is he not here?" Morgana gave a snort.

"I thought so, he does not exist, he is yet another myth created by man."

Phillipa flopped, and her child started to slip. Morgana let her go and snatched the child out of her arms, and turned and walked away holding the child, as Phillipa crashed dead onto the floor. She walked up the room cradling the child, and looked down at his small face.

"You will be safe, there will be no raven or crucifix for you, I will ensure you live as a free man, free of her, and free of the darkness."

Behind her, Gawain wailed on the floor as he dragged the body of Phillipa into his arms, and wept. Morgana gave a sigh, and turned holding the child.

"Stop your blubbering, you are free of her, you call me, and yet you allowed her to rule you like Rhiannon rules all those other weak and feeble minded idiots. You sold us out to their fake unseen god, well that is what you get for betrayal. I gave birth to a man, and yet all I see is a blubbering woman… Stop your whinging, you are free of her now." Gawain looked up with rage in his eyes.

"I LOVED HER, AND YOU MURDERED HER… I HATE YOU… DO YOU HEAR THAT, I HATE YOU?"

Gawain released Phillipa's lifeless body, and got to his feet, as Morgana walked down the hall towards her seat. He pulled out his knife and ran at her, screaming, holding up the knife to try and plunge it into her back.

"I WILL NEVER LET YOU TAKE MY SON; YOU WILL DIE FOR WHAT YOU HAVE DONE!"

Morgana spun around in an instant, and her free arm came up and exploded with light, and Gawain was lifted into the air, and flew down the room. He crashed into the floor at the side of his wife, his body bent and twisted, dead. She sat down and cradled the child close to her, her face white, her eyes dark, and her lips almost a bluish colour and she smiled.

"We have no need of them, they are weak, and in this family, we are strong, aren't we Mason?" There was movement, and Morgana lifted her eyes, and the young girl stood filled with shock and fear as she stared at the two bodies on the floor. Morgana gave a sigh.

"Ursula, get someone to clean that up, and then come help me, we have a child to raise."

The young girl stood trembling, her eyes filled with fear, she looked up, and appeared to look right into Iona's closed eyes. Her voice was shaky, but soft.

"Get Ariel, I need her… Save me!"

*I*ona's eyes snapped open, and she jerked forward as she breathed in. She sat forward breathing fast, her heart was racing, as she looked around, and realised where she was. Her breathing slowed a little as she took deep breaths, and swallowed as she tried to compose herself.

"It was a dream, just a dream, nothing more, just another of many."

She wiped her face with her hand, her mouth was dry and she was a little disorientated, she knew it would pass, and sat breathing as she slowly awakened, and understood she was still in the hidden realm. Iona took a deep breath, and looked at the large area of black sand like dust in the clearing in front of her.

"Oh hell, Morgana, you killed your own child, and who was that girl, I have seen her before, but who the hell is Ursula?" Iona got to her feet, and felt a little unsteady.

"I need to see Ariel, that girl could see me, but how, it was years ago?"

*T*hrough the reeds and grasses, and along the path known to few, outside of the Hidden Realm in Avalon, Stenlow had spent his day being shaved, and having his moustache styled by Fagan, and he was looking a little like his former self, albeit much older. He walked slowly with his stick into the house, and placed a pan over the fire to boil, and caught a look of himself in the silver polished plate over the mantle. He gave a smile, it had been a long time since he had looked so well groomed, and remembered fondly his routine every day, as he prepared for duty.

He had spent most of the day talking with his younger brother, about days long since passed. Fagan confessed to his mistakes, and admitted, his brother was indeed quite correct, and Morgana of Cornwall, had indeed been innocent, and how he felt deep regret for his actions. There had been a wedge between them for too long over it, and as Fagan shaved him and styled his moustache, they healed the bond between them, it made both of them feel happier as a result.

Once Fagan finally left, and feeling very sentimental and nostalgic, he sat back and remembered the young woman with the long dark hair and dark eyes with great fondness. He smiled as he remembered her embarrassment, when he found her in the hot springs. He gave a little chuckle.

"She was such a lovely girl, so kind and full of life, I hope she was alright after she left. I do wonder what became of her, she was quite shy and sensitive, and yet so full of goodness and life, I do hope she did well."

Stenlow turned, as the water heated, and walked slowly to his bedroom, where he opened the door to his tall cabinet. There inside hung to one side of his few clothes, hung his prison guards' uniform, and at its side, the royal blue of his Marshals commander uniform. It was as always, in peak condition. He kept it orderly always, with the buttons polished to perfection. He had so many memories of his time as commander, none more so than the time when young Morgana lived there in her cottage. He lifted out the uniform and looked at it.

"Such strange times, and yet even though tinged with sadness, they also held some happy memories."

They were for him, memories he knew kept him going in that awful prison. The memory of her face and her smile kept him going, he would lie in his bunk, reliving their conversations, and it was probably the only reason he made it through. They were for him a happy time, but it always bothered him that he never saw her again, and had often sat thinking, and hoped she escaped the realm to freedom. He looked at the uniform, and thought just for one more time, after all, he had done his moustache, so why not?

Stenlow had lost weight, and yet as he slipped on the uniform, he was delighted to find it still fitted, it was looser than he remembered, but he stood and looked in the mirror as he fastened the belt, and smiled. It felt strange after all this time, but it still looked good, and he felt the same pride he always had, as he admired his moustache and the fit of the uniform, and perfectly done hair.

He slid his hand in his pocket, and felt something soft. He frowned as he fingered it, unsure of what it was, and when he withdrew his hand, he was more than a little surprised and gave a chuckle.

"Well, I never, it was the last one on her stall, the only one not destroyed, all these years it has been there after I picked it up. I cannot believe it."

He lifted it up and looked at it, and admired the quality of the work, and the way the small cloth bag was sown so neatly with the smallest of stitches. He pulled it close and sniffed, it smelt as fresh as the day he picked it up, rose petal, and honeysuckle, with just a hint of chamomile.

"Such skill, you were indeed quite a remarkable young woman."

Stenlow walked slowly back to his bubbling pan, and looked at his pot beaker, and with a chuckle, he dropped the small hand made sack of tea into it, and then poured in the water, feeling most uplifted. It was almost time, and so he turned, and holding his cup in one hand, and using his stick with the other, he walked through the open door, and sat in his chair ready to watch the sunset. He sat back, looking and feeling a little like his old self, and remembered that day, and gave a small chuckle and smiled to himself.

"COMMANDER STENLOW…. I AM UNDRESSED!" He realised, and turned his head quickly.

"Oh… Er… I apologise, I can assure you, I was not staring, I am not a man like that."

He flustered on his seat, as Morgana looked back for her dress and cloak behind her, she was right in the middle, and afraid to move. Stenlow flustered even more, as Morgana slipped off her rock and tried to crouch down behind it to hide, with the water touching her chin.

"I am most sorry, and I deeply apologise, one of the villagers saw you turn on this path, I did not realise you came here to bathe." She was crouched low, with her hands hiding her breasts.

"I may live alone in a small cottage with a small well, but I can assure you I keep myself very clean. I like to soak, and I was enjoying sitting back for an hour or two, and watching the world in peace, even that is not a crime in this realm. Close your eyes, as I am caught in view, and I have a need to get to my garments." He shut his eyes tight, looking even more flustered.

"My young lady I assure you, I only had to check things out for the queen." Morgana eyed him carefully, her cheeks reddening, as she stood up.

"Well, you most certainly did, I am sure you… Well, I am sure you checked all of my things out." He felt offended, opened his eyes, and turned to her.

"I am not like that."

His words died in his throat, as Morgana stood frozen completely naked right in front of him. She saw his eyes open, gave a slight squeal, and dropped back in the water behind the rock, disappearing for a second, before coming back up spluttering, and coughing. Stenlow had his head turned away apologising profusely.

"I am apologising my dear lady, I thought you had exited the water, oh … Dear, I am most certainly very sorry…. Very sorry indeed."

Stenlow sipped his tea and gave a little chuckle, as he remembered her, and he had to admit, even though as a gentleman, he should not think it.

"I found her to be a most captivating lady, and a really stunning and attractive young woman." He gave a happy sigh.

"I kept your secret, I never divulged what happened that day, I feel I owed you that, and felt bad I took advantage of your vulnerability. I have protected your modesty, have no fear."

Stenlow lifted his tea and sipped it again, it really was a remarkably good cup, she had talent, of that there was no denying. He gave a happy sigh, the sun was starting to fall, the sky was starting to colour, as his mind slipped back to her, and he remembered that walk back to her cottage.

"I think Avalon suits me better, I have a desk with a window, and most nights I see the sun set in the sky. It is funny really; my younger sister often told me of how she would sit there and watch as I do now. I think of her most nights as I watch it, in a way, I feel I am watching it for her. We never had much in common growing up, she was always far more organised than I was, and very grounded, which is why when she told me of the sun sets, I felt there was a hidden part of her I had never seen. It probably sounds foolish, but watching as I do most nights, I feel closer to her, and I miss her."

Morgana smiled, as she walked slowly at his side. He could not help but glance at her, and watch how she looked down in thought. The pale white of her soft skin, the gentle shape of her nose, and the shine to her hair as it brushed her neck softly, before falling down her back. She was remarkably beautiful, and yet he felt something else, a calmness within her, that gave him a deep sense of ease, she glanced to him, her eyes so dark, and yet filled with such life and kindness.

"I do not think that is strange, you clearly love your sister a great deal, I think that is nice." He looked at her, feeling a little surprised, and yet happy.

"You do, you think I love her, for I must admit, I have often wondered, we are so different and find it hard not to argue with each other, it makes me wonder?"

Morgana could see the hope on his face, it was clearly very important to him. He listened to her softly spoken words, and felt the depth of who she really was, and it was nothing like what had been said about her.

"Maybe the next you see her, talk of the sunset, and tell her how you watch it and think of her. Let her see that part of you, I am sure she loves you too, but maybe like you; she hides it. I would say it has to be worth a try."

It made a great deal of sense to him, and he smiled. The path widened and Morgana could see the cottage, and was feeling much less embarrassed now. Stenlow came to a halt with his horse at the end of her fence line.

"You are home safe now, I have to go this way, so I shall wait until I see you enter, and then I will be on my way." She turned with a smile, and started to walk along the fence. He climbed up onto his horse, she turned to look back and waved.

"Thank you, Commander."

He nodded, it was odd really, but in a strange way, it really cheered him up, and he felt a strong sense of connection with her, and he liked it. He liked her, she was a pleasant and decent young woman. Had his daughter lived, he would have wished for her to be like young Morgana.

"It was my pleasure." The sky was filled with reds and yellows, and he smiled as he watched it.

"I do hope she too still watches the sunsets; they really do remind me of her; I hope she is safe. She deserved so much better than the way she was treated, it would be nice to know that she found peace."

*S*tenlow felt a soft warm hand slip into his, and he turned, and Morgana was sat at his side. She smiled, that warm radiant smile, and her eyes shone with life, she had hardly changed. She was still as beautiful as he remembered her, and he gave a sigh of happiness, and was so pleased to see her again. He squeezed her small soft warm hand.

"I do watch the sunsets, and I think of you too, I was always grateful you watched over me." He smiled a big smile, and nodded.

"I have worried about you more than you realise, I am glad you are safe." She gave him that wonderful smile, with her eyes so dark, and yet filled with such love and life.

"I am safe, and I thank you." He nodded.

"The sunset tonight is the nicest for a very long time, I am sure my sister will take a moment and watch, you were right, she did love me."

She nodded, and turned to watch it.

"I am happy you two found each other. I love to watch the sun set over Avalon, I love living here, it is such a beautiful place."

Stenlow smiled and nodded, and then breathed out his last long happy breath. Morgana slipped her hand free, and stood up, and looked down at him with a sad heart.

"You were a good man commander Stenlow, I always appreciated it, thank you, my old friend."

When Luminaria arrived to put him to bed, Stenlow was still sat in his seat, wearing his uniform with pride, and wearing a happy and peaceful expression. She swallowed hard, as she looked at him, but felt some relief, as her eyes filled with tears.

"You are free of her now and her awful ways. She made life so hard for you, and yet, it was her cruelty that helped me find the love in my heart for you. I love you Stenlow, you got me through with your stories of your young dark haired girl. Without you, I am not sure I would have made it. Rest well my dear brother, in a realm free of Rhiannon, you earned it the hard way."

Stenlow was well thought of by those who lived close by, he was always regarded as a fair man, and many were shocked to hear of his passing, for they had seen him that day sat with Fagan, and also as he sat drinking his tea alone watching the sunset.

When Fagan arrived to help his sister, and take care of his brother, he noticed the chair at his side, and lifted up a feather that was lay on the seat. As he held it up, he was baffled, for not only was it the purest of white, it was also the feather of a raven.

Chapter Sixteen.

A Dilemma of Daughters.

Ariel was sat on her bench in front of her house, when the window opened, and Iona came through. She stood up and walked towards her feeling the sadness that surrounded her, and opened her arms. Iona stepped into her embrace, and pushed her head into her shoulder, and wept. Ariel felt the pain within her.

"Did I not tell you that the path of the truth was a difficult one?" Iona gave a huge sob.

"I know she is hated; I know what she has done, but Ariel, it terrified me, she did not deserve that." Ariel held her tight.

"I agree, this is why the truth is more important now than ever. Iona, it is easy to twist and misrepresent the truth, for like gold, it is something that we have to dig deep down for, and we uncover each layer that has been added to change its true meaning. Rhiannon failed because she tried to varnish over it with her own veneer, but like all things, varnish fades and veneers peel, and what is underneath is always exposed." Iona gave a sniffle, and stood up, and wiped her eyes.

"How will knowing this truth help me, when so many will never believe it?" Ariel gave a slight shrug.

"Will denying it make it less truthful?" Iona frowned.

"No, the facts are the facts." Ariel smiled.

"That my young queen, is entirely the point. Iona, Bridget Violet once told me, a queen has to know the full truth, and no matter what others think, that is what she must use to rule. Bridget was a great queen, and not always popular, her rift with Rhiannon made great waves of discomfort, but she never changed her core belief in that truth, and she saved her people because of it. That is the mark of a great queen." Iona understood.

She was still so young and inexperienced, and yet Ariel could see that already, she had changed a great deal, as her powers began to seep to the surface. Ariel took her hand and led her inside, and made them something to eat, and they sat at her table, and ate and drank wine. Iona sat, and told her of everything that she had learned about Morgana, and considering Ariel had already read the journal written by Branna, she knew most of it.

"I have some of Bran's journals, and so I know some of this, I knew about Gawain, your mother told me, she discovered that when she was fighting her. Mason was her grandchild, not her son, I did not know the reason though, and actually it makes a lot of sense." Iona frowned.

"It does, how so?" Ariel lifted her wine and took a sip, and then looked at Iona across the table.

"Love her, hate her, Morgana was a fierce defender of the Earth Faith, contrary to popular opinion, Morgana believed in Eve and Hearne. Her objection with them and the whole of the ruling council, was that she felt, if they had given free will to the people, they had no right to meddle in the affairs of man. If you think about it Iona, it was their meddling and their attempts to appoint a one true king, that caused her the greatest pain in her life." Iona thought about it, and Ariel could see her understanding grow.

"It may surprise you Iona, but Bran admired Morgana, because she wanted to stop the council from hurting anyone else, the way she had been hurt. Morgana's goal was never to kill the council, it was to contain them, in a way they could never meddle in man's affairs again. If you think about it, in a sense, she wanted to preserve them, but remove them from society, and she was successful. I am sure your mother has told you, that what she did was to undo the mistakes of the past? Well, Morgana was a result of many mistakes, and in a sense, your mother was like many, blinded by the lies of Rhiannon. Her end was met when she faced Bran, it was the one thing that never changed in all the time I was with her, she swore to kill her and remove her, and she did." Iona nodded.

"I can understand that, and why. I saw how she manipulated the truth of Morgana, to a point where everyone was afraid to be near her. Rhiannon's gossips isolated her more and alienated her from the population. Fagan told me it got so bad, people lived in fear of being seen near her, as they believed she was dark and meant harm to all. That still does not explain why she killed her son." Ariel nodded at her.

"It does to me, it actually makes a lot of sense, and the answer is simple… Arthur."

"Huh?" Ariel smiled.

"Iona, Morgana's mother was a Celtic queen of great power, and was a high born who was deeply respected, her father was seen as a saviour of his people, and raised in the same faith. Both of them worked hard to encourage the rituals, and gave land they owned with a sacred site to their followers. Their influence was so great, that Arthur, when he was revealed as king, used their influence to bolster his authority. It was the reason his transition was so easy; he had the support of all the believers of the faith." Iona smiled and nodded at her.

"And he converted to Christianity?" Ariel raised her glass.

"He turned his back on them once he was established as king, he even tried to outlaw their sites and ban them from them, as heathens and heretics. Morgana took issue with it and confronted him, and it was the spark that led to a war of words, and then ultimately actions. Morgana showed no fear in her confrontation with him, she accused him of the betrayal of his people, and named his god false, and he was greatly angered by it. The rift between them never healed, and ultimately led to his death, and that of her son Meudraut. Morgana devoted her time to gathering the followers of the Earth Faith around her after the death of her mother, she literally rebuilt the faith from the ground up. She allowed them the use of Tintagel to practice their faith and rights against the wishes of Arthur, whom she banned from ever stepping foot in the castle again. In a sense, she was very like her father, and denied a king his wish." It suddenly made complete sense to Iona.

"When Gawain converted to Christianity, she saw it as the same level of betrayal as Arthur. In her eyes, he turned his back on her, and her father and mother, and denied the legacy she fought for." Ariel gave her a soft nod.

"Lord Hesketh was a distant cousin to the Pendragon line, and a high priest of the Earth Faith. In a sense, her son turned on him too, and Morgana could never accept that. I cannot say for sure, but for her, there could not have been a bigger betrayal of everything she had fought for all her life. Even as the Dark One, she was a devout follower of the faith. Gawain must have dealt her a crushing blow when he told her. If you think about it, she never forgave Arthur, and must have seen it as yet another Pendragon betraying their ancestors. Gawain had a slim chance of winning her over, and he failed."

"It feels so harsh, and over what, a religious belief?" Ariel gave a shrug.

"If you consider how many of the Earth Faith have been slaughtered in the name of the Christian god, it makes a lot of sense Iona. The trail of blood is long and vast, and I may add, has even touched the lives of all of your family. Mason used the church as puppets, because he knew they were greedy, which he exploited, but as the Dark One, Morgana had no tolerance for them, even here in Avalon, she ordered the death of thousands of monks. Your mother and father saved them, and yet they turned on them for more money from Mason. It may not be appealing to hear, but Morgana would have felt justified, and seen it as matching up the numbers. If you want to have a good conversation, talk to Jett Amber, she has made her views of the church well known."

*T*hey finished their meal and cleaned up, and then headed back outside as the afternoon waned, and Ariel relaxed and breathed the air, as Iona sat lost in thought. In her mind she was putting everything together and building up what she saw as the truth of everything. It was a very different story to the one she had known growing up, and she could really see why it would be so challenging to others. She gave a sigh, and Ariel gave a little giggle, she turned to her.

"What?"

"I can almost hear your thoughts, it is like the wooden puzzle you get as a child, and have to lock all the pieces into place before you see the full picture." Iona smiled.

"I feel I almost have the full picture; I just have a few pieces to find to complete it all."

"So, what is missing, do you know?" Iona turned to her, as her mind swirled.

"What do you know of a young girl called Ursula?" Ariel took a breath, and appeared startled.

"You know of her?" Iona nodded.

"I know she was young, a sort of assistant, almost like Morgana was to Merlin. Apart from that, I know little, except I have this strong feeling inside me, and I am trying to work it out." Ariel sat back and took a deep breath.

"Alright… Tell me of this feeling." Iona sat back, and gazed forward as she remembered the moment.

"I told you about her son and him being killed, well what I did not tell you was she came into the room, and Morgana told her to get someone to clear it up." She turned and looked Ariel in the eyes.

"Ariel, it is like she knew I was watching, she looked at me, and I know this sounds crazy, but our eyes met. Even though this was a dream, she could see me, and she told me to get you, and save her." Ariel gave a gasp, and Iona nodded.

"It was years ago Ariel; how could she have known I was dreaming it?" Ariel sighed.

"Oh Iona, you are to be my queen, and you have no idea how much you have grown, and how right you are for the throne. The truth truly is your gift, I cannot lie to you, although you are going to be very surprised by the truth." Iona frowned.

"Do you know her?" Ariel turned and looked at her.

"I have never met her, or spoken to her. Iona, she is Ena's daughter, my granddaughter." Iona's eyes opened wide, and she gasped.

"WHAT…. How?"

"It is a long and complicated story, and the reason why Bran and myself had to separate for a while. Iona, the simple truth is, I was raped by Otto, and had a child who you know as Ena. Ena escaped the realm with Dorin and married him, they had a child who was named Ursula, and during the uprising against the boat people, Dorin was killed, shortly after he got Ursula away. She was told to go find her mother, and on route, she ran into Morgan le Fey. I am not sure of all of it, but the general story is Ena returned believing everyone had been killed. Their boat the Magpie, was in flames just off the dock, what Ena did not know, was le Fey took Ursula in and saved her. The cost of that is she became an assistant to Morgan."

Iona could not believe what she was hearing, and took a deep breath, as she considered the facts, but it was easy to understand how Ursula had been able to penetrate her dream, she was after all, of the line of Enaria. She asked the only question she could.

"Where is she?" Ariel gave a sad smile.

"Hidden from Ena, who has vowed to kill her. Ena feels great shame, can you imagine, she escaped and spent her life trying to stop Bran, and then Morgan, and it was Ena who led Runestone back into the sealed area and eventually brought the demise of all the family. Iona, Ena will never forgive her for betraying my family." Iona looked at her feeling the mixed emotions of Ariel.

"Ariel, I have no wish to upset you, I really do not, but I have to find her. She has important answers, and she knows the other side of Morgana." Ariel gave a soft nod and smiled at her.

"I do know where she is, and I have watched over her. She cannot hide from me, although, I have never approached her. Iona, you should know, after Dana's death, she took Raven and moved away from where they were. Ursula has tried to raise her as her own with an ex soldier of Mason's army. From what I can tell, Raven Merle knows nothing of her family line, she was just a baby when her mother was killed. Iona, Ena can never know of her life now, she has stayed away from all connections to the Knox lines and has lived a simple life, I believe she is glad to have a free life, I do not think she is evil." Iona understood.

"Ariel, I do not wish to harm her, I need to talk to her, she has answers I need." Ariel understood.

"I want her safe and protected, she was to a degree innocent of all that was done. She was held captive, but also, Morgana never harmed her, or tried to corrupt her. I think in many ways, there was a part of her that saw a little of herself in her from her youth, and she shielded her from a great deal of what happened in the castle. Morgana taught her to read and write, and transcribe old documents, nothing more. I believe that as my light protected me around Bran, her light was a protection from Morgan le Fey, and I think Morgan knew that."

It was a lot for Iona to consider, she sat thinking as the sun hovered lower in the sky, radiating warmth on her face. If Ursula was related to Ariel, she must have known of her danger, and yet she had stayed with her. Iona remembered her mother talking of the time when Morgan took control of Avalon, and how Ursula had been with her and helped her, and it made no sense to her.

"Why did she stay with her, why did her sense of danger not alert her to Morgana? Ariel she is of your line, she must have some abilities to sense darkness, it makes no sense to me, why did she stay?"

"That is a question only she can answer, I cannot say, I have not thought about it a lot since I found out where she was, and I honestly do not know." Iona watched her carefully, and could feel a sadness within Ariel.

"If you found her, why did you not go to her, she is your granddaughter? How did you find her anyhow?" Ariel smiled.

"Sapphire… She searched for Dana for a long time and found her living in the region of what we now call Spain. She had a house there, and it appears that Ursula had caught up with her, I am not sure why, I felt she had something to pass on. Sapphire told me and we both went there and watched from a distance. Ursula was with a male and it looked like she was in a relationship, I worked out he must have been a soldier, as he still had a soldier's coat."

"So Dana was there with the child, so was Ursula taking care of it?" Ariel thought for a second.

"I formed the opinion that because Dana was a high up who was used to ruling over others, she would naturally have taken her in to work for her. Iona, the way I saw it, was she must have had nothing, or at least left the castle with little. If you think about it, then the most obvious thing to do, is go to what family remained for help."

It did make some sort of sense, she would probably have left in a hurry, but there again, she could not have had that much, as she never left the castle. Iona felt Ariel was right, knowing Dana lived, it made sense to go to her and get aid.

"Dana died under mysterious circumstances, so that would leave her alone with the child, it would be logical she would take care of it." Ariel nodded.

"There was no mystery to her death, Sapphire was there." Iona stiffened.

"She was?" Ariel nodded.

"Sapphire kept an eye on them, I will not deny, Sapphire had no love for Dana, she despised her for her part, especially the orphanages. Dana went for a long walk on the beach alone, and that was her mistake, she stripped naked and went into the sea, and there were others she was not aware who watched her. The problem was, Dana was always covered in gold jewellery, she flaunted it freely, in an area of great poverty. Sapphire was alerted by her table, and when she looked in, Dana had come out of the sea naked and was attacked by three men. They abused her against her will, and then slit her throat and stole all her gold, when Sapphire realised and got there, Dana was dying. She was badly beaten, sexually abused, her throat was cut and she was almost dead. There was nothing that could be done, so Sapphire left her and came here to talk to me." It was a chilling tale, and Iona gave a shudder.

"Some people think Sapphire killed her, I have heard talk of it, are you sure she did not?" Ariel smirked.

"She did not kill her, she was as mad as hell someone else had done it, and beaten her to it. Iona, the only reason she was alive was that Sapphire realised she was protecting my granddaughter. We went back to check all was well, and when Dana's body washed up, because the tide did come in and swept her out. We went to the house, but it was empty, Ursula had gone, and took the child with her, which was probably a good thing as the house was raided and robbed a week later."

"So, she disappeared, how did you find her again?"

"She is my granddaughter, and the moment I accepted my mother's powers, I felt her, and she was back in this country, so I looked her out, and have been keeping a watch on her since."

It felt difficult, and Iona felt uncertain of what to say, she could see that it mattered to Ariel, but could not understand how knowing all this, she did not go and help her.

"If she was my granddaughter, I would help her, why have you not spoken to her?" Ariel gave a sigh.

"Iona, I have a dilemma of daughters. If I go to her, and Ena finds out, she will go after her and kill her. I realise this probably makes no sense to you, but keeping a safe distance protects her. Ursula has a new life and a new start, as does Ena and myself, I want both of them to overcome the darkness of those times. I want them to live in the light, and I am watching over both of them to ensure that happens."

"So, what are you saying, should I leave her alone?" Ariel smiled.

"You are a queen who seeks the truth of her people, her mother was half Fae of Moon, and half Earth, and she is too, as Dorin was Fae of Moon. She is one of your subjects Iona, or she will be. If you talk to her, it will appear normal, go to her, talk to her, and learn what you must if she will answer."

"I will."

*I*ona sat with Ariel as the sun began to set, and Ariel told her where Ursula was and how to find her. They sat for a long time as Ariel filled in what she had found out about her living in the castle, which she told her was not easy. Ariel used many of her skills and powers to discover the truth, of how she ran away after the death of Gawain, and was lost in the Hidden Realm. Morgana found her and cursed her, into the image of an old woman, which slowed her down. At some point she relented and freed her of her old form, restoring her youth, and from that day on, Ursula had shown loyalty.

As Ariel grew tired, Iona thanked her and left. Once again, she jumped to the burned out cottage, and stood in the darkness staring at the old ruin. She felt closer, and yet, like she still had far to go, she leaned on the fence and looked over at the apple tree, even in the light of the moon, the white flowers could be seen glowing in the dark. She gave a sigh and spoke to herself.

"It only grows where there is truth, and yet for years, everyone has forgotten to notice it. You showed them the truth Morgana, and no one believes you, even now, how do I overcome that?"

Chapter Seventeen.

Ariana and Rae.

*T*he cart rocked from side to side, as it rumbled along the old worn track, and the lantern swung and bobbed with the motion. Fagan sat up in his seat with a heavy heart, as he watched the road, the moon was high and the lantern added a little extra light. As he approached the old ruin of Morgana's cottage, he noticed the outline of a figure leaning against the fence. He pulled on the reins, and the cart came slowly to a halt, as he realised who was standing there, and looked down on her as she turned to him.

"Ye should be home in bed, not staring at old ruins." She gave a nod up to him.

"I am going home shortly Master Fagan; I just need somewhere quiet and peaceful to think." He gave a heavy sigh.

"Tis a night for it, my brother walked into the other realm this night, and sitting here alone, gives me the space with me thoughts." Iona looked saddened.

"I am sorry to hear that Master Fagan, I met him only once, but could feel the kindness of his heart. He was a good man, and served his queen well, I hope one day I have the loyalty of a man such as Stenlow." He took a breath; he was clearly choked with emotion.

"I have to thank thee, ye opened my eyes, and I spoke with him, and we parted on good terms, tis a thing I is grateful for, it was a good thing we did it." Iona smiled.

"I am pleased you could do that; it must have meant a great deal to him, I know he felt bad about it, he told me." Fagan nodded.

"Tis good it was done, the road is long, tis time to roll on, and gather the thoughts, like wheat." She understood.

"Take care Master Fagan, I will give your regards to my mother."

He gave the reins a jerk, and Iona stood in the darkness as he rode off, and she could feel the sadness that surrounded him, as she watched the cart disappear. It felt like another witness to the life of Morgana of Cornwall was gone, and with him, she felt like it was another part of her goodness lost to the knowledge of the realm. She opened her window, thinking a time would come, when only those who remembered the bad would be left, and she felt time was running out, she needed sleep, and then she needed to talk with Ursula.

*T*he following day, Iona rose early, and the house was the usual madness, as the children flew around grabbing their things for school, Rune smiled as she saw her enter the kitchen, and turned to her.

"How are you doing?" Iona sat down at the table.

"I have progressed, I just have a few parts to add, and I think I will know the full tale, and have all the facts." Rune watched her carefully.

"You mean to complete this and not let me help you, you are my daughter, I am here." Iona smiled at her as Rune placed a cup on the table.

"I know Mum, but I think it is better this way. I have really started to understand things, and there are a lot of people who have the story wrong, but I do not think I will ever get them to believe it. I am doing this for me, for I want to know the truth, I doubt I will share it, dad was right, it would serve no purpose to those who believe her fully evil. If she was still here, and brought before me to be judged, because I know the truth of it all, I feel I would act fairly as queen." Rune smiled, and leaned down and kissed her head.

"I think you are right, and in that you show great wisdom, follow your instincts, I have watched, and they guide you well." Iona lifted her cup.

"They have certainly shown me things, and taken me to places I was never sure I would go." Rune smirked.

"That is not instincts, that is life Iona Violet."

*T*wo hours later, Iona stood on the edge of the coast, and looked out over the beaches of Whitehaven. It had once been a popular location in the days of old, but now it was deserted, well, almost. A lone figure walked along the beach, picking up driftwood, her hair short and dark, and her clothing worn over the years and patched.

Ursula was used to the solitary life, it suited her, she had spent so much time alone in the castle, she had become accustomed to it. Her life with Tom had not been easy, both of them worked hard to fix up the old run down cottage, but over the years it had become a home she loved, and she was happy. Tom had been her only comfort, apart from her daughter Rae, but in recent weeks, she had left, she was nineteen and wanted to discover herself, and as much as Ursula had tried to convince her it was dangerous, Rae had left in a storm of anger. She paused as she lifted more wood, her mind on her daughter, and the worry it had brought her, and that was when she noticed the young woman stood on the sand watching her.

Iona walked slowly towards her, the violet of her eyes fixed on the woman she knew was a great age, and yet looked only in her fortieth year. Ursula stood frozen watching her, and Iona could feel her nervousness. Iona smiled as she got closer, and Ursula gave a slight nod.

"Can I help you mistress, are you lost?" Iona stopped, and looked at her.

"Do you know who I am?" Ursula shook her head looking worried.

"Should I?" Iona gave a smile.

"Not really, my name is Iona Violet." It was clear she knew now, and she felt the apprehension grow inside her.

"I know you know of me Ursula, but I am not here to harm you, I am only here to talk. You have answers to questions, if you help me, I will thank you and leave, and you will be protected by your queen." Ursula nodded, and swallowed hard.

"I want no trouble, I live peacefully, free of it all, and have nothing to do with it. My life is pure and wholesome, and I am no longer her, I am now Ariane." Iona nodded.

"It is nice to meet you Ariane, can I help you, your load appears heavy?" She looked shocked, and shook her head.

"You are a queen; it is not your place to carry my burden." Iona smiled, and took a step forward.

"I grew up in Loxley, I have chopped and carried my own wood for many years, I am not incapable." She took three large pieces off her, and looked around.

"Lead the way, and we will talk."

Ursula gave a frightened nod, and turned towards the path that ran up from the sand, into the dunes and fields, where her home was. Iona followed her as she walked across a large field, to where a low line of bushes marked the edge, behind which was a small cottage. It was not huge, and had just two sleeping rooms, and one large room downstairs, with a large wood stove to cook on. Ursula, or Ariane spoke as they walked.

"I left that life behind." Iona understood that, but she knew there were insights she had a need of.

"Ariane, I know the story, actually, I know all of her story, apart from a few small pieces which I hope you can fill in for me." Ariana gave a long sigh.

"I have grown weary of it all, I feel her shadow follows me. I find peace, and then ugliness arrives. I just want an end to all of it, I have served my time of darkness; I just want to be free in the light." Iona nodded towards her, and understood that.

"You will be, this will be the only time you will see me, unless you need me."

*I*ona helped stack the wood, and looked around, it was a small home, but was comfortable, she liked it. Iona sat at the table as Ariane made her a cup of tea. She came over to the table and sat down opposite Iona, and looked worried, Iona took a breath.

"You were young when she found you, and she took care of you, I know that much, and in a way, I understand why she did that. I know you ran away after the death of Gawain, and she locked you into an old body, and then at some point she restored you. I know you suffered with her, and I understand the fear of her…" Ursula cut in.

"It was never fear." Iona frowned, and she shook her head. Ariane fingered the handle on her cup.

"I know this might sound odd, I know of the fear she instilled in people, but I was never afraid of her, the truth is, she was good to me in a strange way." Iona was a little surprised.

"She was?" Ariane nodded.

"When my parents were killed, I was only nine summers, and I was alone and scared in a place I did not know. She did take me to the market to find my mother, and then two days later back to the dock, and I saw our boat burned. After that, she took care of me, she was nice to me and helped me. She was never bad to me, which I know sounds odd, but she was different with me than she was with others." In a way Iona understood that.

"That to me makes sense, I know of her early life, and I have thought that deep down inside of her, there was a small part of her that the darkness did not touch, and it is within that, your relationship with her is important." Ursula lifted her cup, and sipped from it; her dark eyes watched her carefully.

"I know this is hard for those who fought her, it is why I changed my name and have hidden, but the truth is, she talked to me at times, she had moments when she was different." Iona pricked up her ears.

"Tell me about those." Ariane appeared to relax a little, and gave a small smile.

"She could be funny at times, she did make jokes, and she smiled. At night she would get out her other book and sit by the fire to read, and it probably sounds weird, but it changed her. It made her happy, and she would talk to herself and occasionally with me. My mistress would tell me of Avalon, and how she lived in a cottage, and chopped wood for her own fire. She told me of how she lived alone and was happy, and her mother was a great Celtic queen, and how deeply she loved and admired her. She missed her mother and father, and I understood that, which I think she knew, as I missed my family." Iona could tell that she was being honest, and also that she did actually feel some affection for her.

"Do you know of her past?" Ariane shook her head.

"Not that much, just the small things she told me when reading her book." Iona smiled.

"If I was to tell you that when Morgana lived in Avalon, she was a kind and caring person, who helped many people with her cures, would that make sense to you?" Ariane nodded and smiled.

"I can believe that, I really can, I saw that in her at times, she was really advanced with potions, she made many of her own recipes. You know, she loved Lord Hesketh, and he loved her too, he got ill a lot as he aged, and she would sit on his bed, hold his hand, and I helped make cures for him. I did the same for Lord Knox, after his fight with the hooded man. My Lady, she had a gentle side, I saw it, and so did Lord Hesketh." It actually made some sense to Iona, she thought carefully.

"Considering that, you ran away from her." She nodded.

"I was scared… Have you seen a dead body, because I hadn't? There were two of them, her son and his wife, and she did that, I never thought she could. She had a temper at times, especially when she wanted to do something she would call the right way, and her book did not let her. It made her so mad; she would yell at the roof that it was not fair, she could do it better that way. She would scream to stop messing up her spells, you know, she was a little unhinged at times. I saw the bodies, and I got so scared she would do that to me, so I waited, and when I got the chance I ran, but I did not know where I was, and got lost, she found me again and punished me."

That interested Iona, she worked out that Morgana was talking to the Merle, and she was accusing them of messing her spells up. It posed the question, was she trying to use the Whitelines, and the Merle stopped her?

"She used a spell to transform you?" Ursula gave a nod, and looked frightened.

"She could do that, her book showed her, that is where she learned it. She made me old and understood my dreams, so after that I stayed below in the cellar, and it was terrifying. She had things down there that really scared me, they were locked up, but I could hear them at night. Lord Hesketh, I think understood that and gave me a cat, which helped, I would curl round him at night and talk to him. The sound of my voice in my room helped cover some of the sounds." Iona thought carefully.

"You say the book taught her those spells, I thought it was her book, tell me about it?" Ariane instantly looked scared, and her voice shook a little.

"It frightened me, when I came upstairs after, you know, when I was me again? I told her I was afraid of it, and she would lock it with the other book when she went out. I had bad feelings about it. I know you will think me foolish, but I felt the book was alive, it only went quiet when she wrapped it in the velvet cloth." Iona frowned.

"Went quiet, what do you mean?" Ariane swallowed hard, and lowered her voice more.

"When I was alone, and please don't think me crazy, but the book would make a laughing sound, and it really scared me. She once forgot to put it away, and I was so scared, I ran to the table and threw the cloth on it, and then hid under my work table. It went quiet after that, and I was glad, because I was really afraid of it, I still am."

"What do you mean you still are?" She looked very nervous and scared.

"I had to hide it from Rae, she wanted to see it, and I knew it would hurt her." Iona suddenly understood, and gasped.

"You still have it?" Ariane swallowed really hard, and took a breath, her eyes were wide with fear.

"She told me to hide it, she had a secret place at the old cottage, she told me Rae would find it, but I did not want that. I did not want her hurt, but it was hurting her, it is why she left." Iona was not sure what to think.

"Where is it, is it here?" She shook her head.

"Not in the house, I got Tom to bury it. It was hurting Rae, and I know she was not my daughter, but I raised her. Lady Knox was not interested after the fall; she was too busy carrying on with the chieftains in the area. Rae was raised by me, and she was raised the same as my mother raised me. That book was getting into her mind and telling her things, so I did the only thing I knew from what my mother told me about my grandmother, I put it in a box."

"You know about Ariel?" She nodded.

"I met Lady Raven five times; I know the story. My Mistress talked often about it, at the time I had no idea she was my grandmother, but I knew power could be contained with crystal. When I was a small girl, my mother and Bella showed me how to make small boxes, Bella would place little glowing balls of power in them that hummed, and when I sealed the box, they were silent. I worked out, that if the balls went quiet, the book would too. My Lady, it was talking to Rae in her dreams, it was telling her to do bad things, and rebuild the castle." Her eyes filled with tears.

"She was like my daughter, I am blighted and cannot have them of my own, and it was hurting her, and I had to stop it. Her nightmares were horrible, she would scream in the night and cry such a lot. I hated seeing it, I wanted her to grow up normal and good, like I should have done. I was trying to protect her." Iona reached out across the table and took her hand, and gave it a gentle squeeze.

"Ariana, you did your best, where is Rae, because I expected to see her?" Her eyes screwed up more, and she broke down.

"She ran away… Tom has gone after her, she has been gone for a week and I am so worried about her. She wants to know the truth, she wants to know about her family, and I refused to talk about them because I don't want her to know what they did." She took a deep breath, and tried to wipe her eyes.

"I am sorry My Lady, I miss her, and I have heard nothing, I just want her home safe."

Iona gave her a smile, and could see the fear and concern she had for Rae, it was clear to her, that Ariane really did see her as a daughter, and like all mum's, she was really worried about her. Ariane calmed a little, and wiped her eyes.

"I am sorry My Lady."

"It is very understandable, your daughter is missing, I would imagine my own mother would be equally the same." Ariane nodded.

"Your mother is the Runestone, I am sure no one would dare to hurt you. I saw her once in Avalon, and her power overwhelmed me. She lived in my stones, and I was afraid of her. Your mother never understood that deep down inside, my mistress was a nice person, it was the book that made her that way. I hated that book, and I did not want your mother to kill my mistress. If she had come for the book, I would have opened the doors and let her take it, I hated it, just not my mistress. I know people will not understand, but my parents died, I had no one, and in a strange way, she tried to be a mother to me. She sat for hours and taught me to read, and then showed me how to write properly. On my birthday, she snuck into Avalon, and she would get me an apple off her tree, she was not all bad, there was good in her." Iona smiled.

"That is why I am here, because I think that too. Ariane, all I want is the truth." She gave a small smile.

"My mother told me I was white Fae, and I felt her goodness. When she argued with herself, I always thought that was her goodness trying to fight the book. Does that make sense?" Iona gave a nod and sat back in her seat.

"You have no idea how much sense that makes to me." Ariane nodded.

"I cared about that side of her, she was good to me."

Iona smiled, she had no idea how much of what Ariane said made complete sense to her, she looked at Ariane.

"Give me the book, I know who can destroy it, let me take it so if Tom finds her, she will always be safe here. A daughter should be safe at home always." Ariane stood up, and took a deep breath looking relieved, and gave a nod.

"It is outside, follow me."

Ariane grabbed a spade, and Iona followed her, then went around the back of the cottage where there was a vast vegetable garden, and a beautiful orchard, not unsimilar to a smaller version of the one at the farm in Loxley. Ariane stood next to a patch of bare earth, she looked at it, and Iona lifted the spade out of her hands.

"I have protections, and I grew up in Loxley, I may be destined for a crown, but my father insisted I learned a good way of life first, and that was Loxley life."

She smiled as Iona stuck in the spade and began to dig. The box was just over a foot down, and together they cleared away the sides and then lifted it out of the hole. The box was crude, she had seen her mother make a few over the years, and compared to hers, this one was rough and not the best it could be. Iona understood that she had never been fully taught, as Ariane wrapped it in a large piece of cloth.

"Keep it covered, it helps to keep it silent, how will you dispose of this?"

"It will need a source of powerful light, and I have two that I know of, both of which will make sure this never hurts anyone ever again." Ariane looked at it wrapped in its cloth.

"Good… Get rid of it, no good can come of that book."

*T*he moment came that Iona was not looking forward to, she had no idea how she was going to pose this, but she knew it had to be done. She stood holding the crystal boxed book and looked at Ariane.

"I am not sure how to say this, it is not easy. Ariane, when you ran as a small girl to find your mother, she had heard of the raid on the boats, and was making her way back. She arrived to find your boat on fire, and your father dead, she also thought you like so many of the other children, had been slaughtered. Ariane, your mother survived believing you to be dead. It broke her heart, and started her campaign to find and destroy Morgan le Fey. It was your mother Ena, that showed my mother how to find the Lady Raven, and in doing so, that started the fall of the family. It was later that she discovered that you had been the assistant to Morgan le Fey, and she was heartbroken. Ariane, she swore an oath to find you and remove you, for she believes you to be dark."

Ariane stood with tears in her eyes, as the tears ran down her face, her voice was broken and shaky.

"She lives?" Iona nodded.

"She does, her efforts to help my mother, helped to release your grandmother Ariel, she is alive and living in Avalon. Ariane, Ariel has been watching over you, she wanted to meet and talk with you, but she fears if she does, your mother will find you, and she wants you to live free. Ariane, she wants you to be happy, she knows about Tom and Rae, and she was relieved to know that you had light in your life. I came here to learn the truth, and I want to leave knowing that I also brought the truth, only you now can decide what you wish to do."

"Thank you, My Lady." Iona smiled at her.

"You have a lovely home, and have found peace, I hope by taking this, your daughter may return, and if she does, guide her. What you now know, may guide you, but know in your heart, you will forever have my thanks for what you have told me this day. Morgana of Cornwall was a nice person, she suffered a cruel fate, because her goal was to become what she called a white raven, she wanted to do good. Morgana never chose to be tied to the raven Rajani, it was forced upon her, and I have thought for a little time, she was trying to fight it and overcome it. I think her treatment of you, showed that she was, and what you have told me has convinced me that she never stopped fighting it. It matters Ariane that this truth is now known, and I feel that your ability to look inside her and see the good she was fighting to pull back, proves, you were right to care. It actually, would have meant a great deal to her. I am sure in her own way, she really did see you in the same light, because the facts stand, she never harmed you or turned you dark." Ariane, dried her eyes and gave a weak smile.

"I will not deny, I was afraid when you arrived, and when you told me you were her daughter, I thought you had come to kill me. I am grateful to you, for talking with me, it was not easy, but I find it has helped me. I have always thought she had another side; I was around her for the largest part of my life so far. On those nights when I have thought of her, it has always been the moments where she read the other book, and I felt her heartbreak. My Lady, I believe she was angry at what happened to her, I am glad you told me she wanted to do good, for I saw that. I will always remember her sat on her red chair by the fire, talking quietly to me, that I believe was the real Morgan. I have no idea what happened to that other book, I hope she took it with her, for if she did, she will be free of the darkness, because I honestly believe, it was a book of light." Iona nodded at her, she understood that.

"As you spoke, I think I realised, the other book was the one she wrote in service to Merlin, I think that was her true book, the one she believed in. It was her book of the Whitelines, and the path of a White Raven, which was her hearts desire. Ariane, she was not always evil, and I truly believe she never wanted to be." Ariane smiled.

"I think so too." Iona took a deep breath, and looked around the property.

"You are well set up here, I think it is a good place to be. I must leave you now, but should you ever need me, close your eyes and think of me, and say my real name, Violet Stone. I will hear you, and I will come to you, for you are Fae of Earth to me, and as so, I will serve also you as queen. Fare thee well Ariane, live long and walk paths of green in peace." Ariane gave a bow.

"Farewell, My Queen."

The window opened behind her, and with a smile, she turned and walked through, and as it closed behind her, Ariane stood alone in front of an empty hole. She turned and walked slowly back towards the cottage, and spoke softly.

"Please hurry back Tom, and please find her, I need to know she is safe."

Chapter Eighteen.

Final Conclusions.

*I*ona Violet of Loxley, walked out from her window onto the top of the cliff at Tintagel, and the moment she did, the wind lifted her hair and blew it around her shoulders. It was strange how much this place had grown on her, as she had come to love it a great deal. Standing on the edge of the cliff, and breathing the air, filled her with joy. It felt like simply breathing in the world, and the freedom that came with it.

"I could live here Morgana, I think I could find a satisfaction here, I really understand why you fought so hard to protect here, I would too."

"It matters not, it fell to the world, and yet I feel her spirit still walks here." Iona turned, and saw the hooded figure behind her, she held the box out in front of her. Albanlin stepped forward.

"Tell me future queen, what have you learned about your chosen focus for the truth?"

She watched him as he came closer, and there was a part of her that worried, as she had heard many stories of him lifting his hood to show Morgana the truth, and it was really windy here, and his hood flapped around.

"My Lord, I have discovered many things, the young woman I know as Morgana of Cornwall suffered at the hands of Rhiannon, but you know that. Morgana was a good student, she studied hard and learned the craft as taught her by Merlin. She was vocal about your treatment of her people, which she saw as wrong and immoral, and she stood against Arthur for selling out those who placed him in power. I have thought deeply about her points of view, and considered everything I have learned about her, and I feel I have found the truth of who she was." His hood twitched.

"Would you care to share that with me?" Iona shrugged.

"Is there any point, you know what I discovered, and you were aware of Morgana? You have watched us both, you know that when her choice came, she chose to be a White Raven, not a black. She wanted to continue the work of her mentor Merlin, but do it in such a way that she considered the lives of others. Morgana was innocent, and you sat back and watched as Maud planned her downfall, by leaving a part of herself in this book, and against her will, Morgana was tied to a raven. You allowed her to become everything she hated, when what you should have done was save her, I have no need to tell you, you know already."

He lifted his arms, and slipped the box from hers, and turned to walk away, and then stopped, she stared at his back.

"Did you know about the two books, and how one possessed and controlled her life, and that Maud was still in the book, and not destroyed by Branna?"

"No!" She gasped out loud.

"How is that possible My Lord?"

"It matters not, the fact was, I did not, and you uncovered the truth. Queen Violet Stone, this was never about what I knew or did not know, this was about knowing if there was one person apart from Ariel, who would honour the truth. It pleases me to see there is. What do you intend of Branna, for you still have to know the truth of her?" Iona gave a sigh.

"I need to think, I need to rest, and in a strange way, I want to spend some time and make my peace, and remember Morgana of Cornwall here. I feel had I met her, we would have found common ground, in a way, it is sad I never did. This was never Arthur's place, he was born here, but he was not devoted to it. History should be changed, and Morgana should be given the credit, for she was the real saviour of her people of Earth Faith, not Arthur, he sold them out to Christianity." The black hood gave a twitch.

"Maybe one day she will be." He faded from sight, and she sighed.

"I doubt it. Much has been done since that time, there is too much hate for her now, and those who mattered are long gone."

*I*ona turned back to the sea, and watched the waves rolling towards the shore, a storm was coming. She took one more deep breath and turned, and looked down on the ruins of what was once a home, filled with a loving family. Two parents, one of Germanic origin, and one a queen of the Celts, and a small daughter with long dark hair, who loved to laugh and scream with joy, as her father threw her up into the air.

It was hard not to see how similar her and Morgana were, she was devoted to her father just as Morgana had been, and she loved and deeply admired and respected her mother, who was of the higher status than any queen in any realm. She could not imagine the pain Morgana must have felt losing them, just the thought of losing hers was something she could not even contemplate.

She walked slowly across the top of the plateaux, and her window opened, and she stood before it, and turned to where she knew, once many years ago, Morgana of Cornwall, sat alone and living in grief. Iona looked up to where Morgana probably sat looking out of her window, and smiled.

"Rest well Morgana, and know that your truth will be written, in the journals of a new queen."

She stepped through the window, and walked out onto the long expanse of grass that was home, and smiled as she saw the house on the edge of the trees, it was good to be home. Half way between the mere and the house, she stopped and looked at the trees, and as she saw the grass next to the tree line, the memory flashed into her mind. She swayed with the power, and closed her eyes, and in her mind the pictures grew, as she walked towards her father sleeping with her mother under the blankets.

"I told you she would find you." In her mind, Iona smiled, he looked so young.

"You are real; I thought you were a dream."

"I am a dream Daddy, but not for much longer, Granny Opal and Granny Gwen have helped me." She handed him a bundle.

"Victor died, but he left you this. The dark woman has made bad things and this will protect you. He told me to tell you, there is one more who can do his work." Robbie took the bundle, and looked at her as Rune stirred.

"Am I really your daddy?" Iona stood swaying feeling that moment from when she was four, and her heart was so filled with the love that flowed from him.

"Oh yes, I am your daughter, can you not tell?"

"How is this possible when you have not been born yet?" She felt her face smile at him.

"I will be... I am in mummy's tummy waiting to grow, Granny Opal showed me how to share mummy's power to help you. I will begin to grow soon, and then we will see each other again." Iona felt a huge surge inside herself, as a tear ran from his eye.

"You are Iona, aren't you?"

"I love the name you gave me Daddy."

The power and energy flowing through her was immense, as she just stood still feeling her whole body filled with a huge force, and reacting to the power of the moment. She breathed in deeply, and just held the feeling within her, for she had never felt such a surge of power in her life before. Rune looked out of the glass doors and saw her daughter and smiled, she could feel the power of Robbie all around her, and understood what Iona was seeing. She turned and walked into the room, and headed to the kitchen to put on some water to boil.

Robbie sat at his desk going over the farm reports, when he heard the stairs creak, and looked up. Iona was stood on the stairs watching him, her violet eyes shining through the rails of the top banister. He leaned to one side and looked at her, she moved, and slowly came up the stairs, stood at the top, and took a deep breath, she looked sad, which was not like her. She had grown so much, she was no longer a child, she was a little taller than Runestone, with brown hair streaked with red, and yet even though they were violet, to him, she had her mother's eyes.

They held so much life and love, her facial features were definitely her mother's, her soft gentle curves, to her cheeks and her jaw, and there were a few freckles just dusting her nose. She stood there, just like Runestone, tall and slender, and she was very beautiful, he smiled.

"Are you back for a while, or will you be leaving again?" Her eyes filled with tears, and he took a deep breath, it was not something he wanted her to do, her voice was soft and a little crackled.

"I am sorry, I hurt you. I didn't mean to Dad."

He sat back in his chair, and she walked over to him, and he pulled her down to him. He pulled her close and she slid onto his lap.

"Dad, I love you, I hope you know that, I am going to really miss you?" He felt her tremble as she wept into him, as he held her tight and turned into her.

"You are my daughter, and I love you deeply too. Iona, I will not deny it will feel strange not having you around all the time, but you will be able to come back home, and we will be visiting you as well." She gave a sniffle and pulled away, and looked at him.

"Dad, you shouted at me, you have never shouted at me before, not ever. I am so sorry, I know you did not agree, but I had to do what was right for me. Dad, I need to know the full truth, all of it, and I have learned a great deal from it, and it is finished now." He gave a nod.

"Are you going to tell me what you found out?" She shook her head, as she looked at him.

"I am not going to tell anyone, I needed to know, I needed the truth, it mattered to me, and I know it now. I will write it down, and record all I learned, and then if people want to read it, they can, and if they don't, that will be fine too. Dad, I want to be a true queen, I want to help the people of Fae as you have yours, but I do not want people to die or suffer because of things I have done and said." Robbie gave a sigh.

"Iona, that is not easy, trust me, I have tried, and there are times when you may have to. Some people will not stop, Mason was like that, and in the end, I had to face him, it was always him or me." She nodded as she understood.

"Dad the ruling council helped Uther overthrow Morgana's father when she was four, and he died. Uther took her mother for his own, and it was wrong, it was a long time before she turned dark. I never want things like that to happen, the council has not the right to dictate who should and who should not live, no one has that right, not even a queen." He gave a soft nod, and smiled.

"I will always stand at your side and support that; you will never stand alone. Iona, a lot of good men lost their lives for the freedom we have, but there has been enough blood spilt. We have to learn to live in other ways, and work out problems without the use of a weapon. That is the path we must walk, one that heals, and does not injure." She smiled, and leaned in, and hugged him tight.

"I love you, Dad." He gave a smile.

"I love you too, I always will Iona Violet."

She slid back off his knee, and smiled at him, and she felt so much better, she turned to walk towards the stairs, stopped, and turned back to face him.

"I remember that day Dad, I will never forget it. I have always loved the name you gave me. I will never forget that moment, and I am glad to have been able to come to you." He nodded.

"Yeah, me too, it was a defining moment of my life, everything changed for me after that day."

Iona came down the stairs feeling better, Rune looked up from her seat, and watched her, she noted the red watery eyes, Iona looked over towards her.

"I have spoken with him, and I hope fixed it, I do not want any division with him, or you and him either. Mum, you and dad, are the ground I am rooted in, if you crumble, I will fall, never let that happen." Rune smiled, and gave a soft nod.

"Your roots are deep and strong, and they also hold together the earth they stand in, you will not fall easily. I take it, you have learned the truth?" She nodded her head.

"I will now write down all I have learned; I want it recording for the house. In time, others will be able to read it. I need the time to sort everything out, I think I will rest first, I have a lot to consider."

"Alright sweetheart, you know where I will be if you need me." She understood that.

"Thanks Mum."

While Iona entered her small cabin and rested, in Florae Councillor Alder, had spent a few days falling apart. He became highly paranoid, and made his serving staff taste his food and wine before he ate. He had even started spending more time in his private study, which looked out across the steps of the house and over the centre of Florae. He trebled the guard, even though he knew that it would be impossible to breach the heavily fortified House of Scribes, and all of this was predicted by Gwynfor.

It was without doubt raising eyebrows with the other members of the council, who were starting to wonder if the pressure was just too much, and there were quiet discussions going on in secret. It appeared to the council; Alder was starting to fall apart.

Knowing Alder was watching, and in order to enhance the process, Una with Treen, or Gwynfor took it in turns to walk around the Royal Circle at the base of the steps, and stop and talk with guards, always ensuring they were in full view of his windows. They knew full well, his imagination would start to spiral out of control, and they were right, his paranoia grew deeper and deeper. He would stand for hours doing nothing but muttering under his breath, as he stared out of the window.

"What are they saying, I know they are planning something?" He would fidget, and point at them from a safe distance.

"You cannot fool me, I am on to you, I know your game, well, you will not bribe my guards, I will not be easily got by assassins in the night."

He shook his head as Treen and Una walked slowly around, stopping and talking occasionally, and then smiling and looking up at the windows. Alder seethed as his assistant stood on the opposite side of the room.

"Why are they still here, they came to be interviewed, why have they not left?" He lifted his hand and shook his finger.

"I don't care what anyone says, this has Elgin stamped all over it. He is behind all of this, he has never accepted my way of running the house, he is jealous of my success. That is what this is, he is trying to undermine me, but I will show him, I will prove this imposter queen is not worthy of her seat… I will show her for the fraud she has always been."

*O*utside, Treen looked at the guard standing to attention at the bottom of the steps, as he stared ahead trying not to be seen to be fraternising.

"This uniform, it eez comfy, no? I have a liking for the texture of the cloth, it allows more movement, no?" The guard stared ahead, and spoke quietly trying not to move his lips.

"Your Highness, I am not at liberty to comment." She gave a giggle, and then looked up at the window.

"Your council man Older, he watches, yes, I see im, he a snakey of a man, your queen will soon come, no?" She nodded her head, as if agreeing with him.

"It eez fine, I play game, nothing more, Older will not be in the charge long, and Queen Iona Violet eez a good person, this I know, eez true." She stepped back, and looked back at the window, and gave a sly smile, then turned and walked over to Una. Treen leaned into Una, and whispered.

"He eez watching, this I think is a hoop." Una giggled, and looked at her.

"Hoot… It is hoot dear." Treen gave a laugh.

"I ave been gone too long no, I am forgetting the words of the people who live local yes?" Una smiled, and looked back at the window.

"To be honest Treen, I actually love the way you phrase the sayings of the locals, and they do too, because it implies you are interested." She nodded, and then frowned.

"I ave much of the respect for the men, to me, they talk funny, but I learn it so they see I am as you say, one with them." Una gave a nod.

"That is how we won the war, you commanded from the front, and to be honest, you are braver than me." She shrugged.

"If I had ave the senses, I would ave runnered away, it was scary for them, and for me." Alder screamed at the window.

"WHAT ARE THEY SAYING, WHAT DID THAT GUARD TELL THEM, I WANT TO KNOW?" His aid looked at him nervously.

"Master Alder, I do not think that would be wise. I do not wish to anger you, but that could make you look weak and afraid."

He stared at her from the window, and gave it a moment of thought. Alder nodded his head as he thought, he lifted his finger and waved it at the window, and appeared to calm down.

"You make a good point… That is what they want, they are trying to scare me into changing course, and that is because they fear me… Yes… They fear me, they know I am right, they know she is fake, you made a good point… A very good point indeed, they are trying to wear me down, but I will not be beaten, I know now, how right I am."

As Alder ranted at his assistant, Treen and Una walked away down the road towards the farm they were temporarily staying at during the day, laughing and joking between each other. They were swapping stories from their time with the Specialists of Loxley, but Alder, who was stood on a chair watching, he was convinced they were mocking him, Gwynfor's plan was working perfectly.

*I*ona had lay back on her bed and closed her eyes, and yet she found sleep was not going to come, her mind was too active, as the images of Morgana at the cottage, Stenlow at his home, or Fagan as he opened up flowed into her mind. She drifted in the peace of her house, and tried to relax, she felt weary, but also felt some cheer, as she had discovered more about Morgana than had ever been known before. There was also some sadness, as she now understood that Morgana to a degree had been scapegoated for all of Rhiannon's anger.

She used her network of gossips, to influence those within the realm, ensuring false stories of Morgana made it into the general population. She was accused of poisoning people, controlling people's minds, killing people, and stealing husbands, and then Rhiannon made it known, she had killed Eve, and Eleanor, and run her out of Avalon and ordered her property burned down.

She had no idea how Morgana had been able to endure all of it, and yet she had, and had still gone from Avalon, and chosen a path that would follow in the footsteps of Merlin. She knew deep inside; she would not be able to deal with that amount of pressure from a queen as powerful as Amethyst. In truth, even if it did clash with the beliefs of her whole family, she felt sympathy for Morgana. She lay back with her eyes closed.

"How do you survive that, was there anything in your life to show you love?"

As she breathed out, her mind exploded with images, and she gasped, as pictures of Morgana she had never seen before played in her mind. Images of her laughing as she walked through a woodland next to a river, or high up on battlements with a tall knight, she even saw her sat in her room eating beside him, as they laughed and tasted each others food. The speed of them flowing through her slowed and settled, and she saw Morgana sat at her table in her cottage, with her eyes closed, as she rubbed the side of her head. There was another voice, and the image expanded to show a man in fine clothes who she knew to be the knight, he was stood looking at her.

"I can offer you much, even the freedom to do this… Whatever it is that you think you are doing. I have rooms Morgana, you could fill them with bottles, and whatever these things are. Would it be so awful to share your time with me?"

Morgana opened her eyes, and leaned back on the wall with a frustrated gasp. Lot stood looking at her, and she really did not want to do this, not now.

"Lot, I hate to point it out, but I have freedom already, I come and I go as I please. What you want is not for me, I would not be happy in the way other maidens would be. You think you know me; you assume you know what I want, but apart from living here and being something to liven up your bed, what else do you really know about me?"

He stood staring at her as she watched him, she was right, he knew nothing about her. He took a deep breath, and looked a little hurt.

"I care for you; I am happy when I am with you. I have means for a life of comfort, and would share them with you."

She smiled, and slipped from her seat, and walked over to him, and took his hands in hers. He towered above her, and he had a chiselled, yet kind face as he looked down at her. Morgana smiled again.

"Lot, you are a good man, you are honourable and brave with a good heart, but I have chosen a life of solitude dedicated to my studies. If I had made a different choice early in life, then maybe things would be different and I would be flattered by your offer, but I did not. I understand you see no value in this life, but be assured, I want this, I chose this, and this is how I intend to continue." She could see the hurt deepen in his eyes as he tried to smile.

"You are an amazing and beautiful woman Morgana, and I do not ask this because you liven up my bed. I ask because it is heartfelt to me, I care for you deeply." She smiled at him, he was so sincere, and she knew he meant it with all his heart. She squeezed his hands.

"Thank you, it matters to me that you said that, but I still cannot take what you offer. Lot, you deserve better than me, and if you knew the truth of my life and my feelings, you would understand better. Just know, that for a time I felt cared for deeply with you, and it made a big difference, but trust me when I say, you will thrive in the arms of another."

He stepped back, and was clearly emotional, Morgana could feel the surge of emotion swirling within him. He swallowed hard and gave a slight nod.

"If that is your last word, I have no choice but to accept it. I shall leave you to your solitude, and ask you pardon my interruption. Goodbye Morgana."

He turned abruptly, and walked towards the door, and she felt the sadness mix with her frustration, creep up inside her. She walked slowly to the door, where outside he pulled himself up onto his horse. Morgana stood at her door, wrapped only in her cloak, and watched as he gave a nod, sadness painted across his face.

"Live well."

She nodded, he pulled round his horse, and bolted off up the track at speed, and she felt the two tears at the bottom of her eyes, even though this was her choice, watching him ride away was not easy for her. Quietly she turned, and walked back in, locking the door with a long heavy sigh. As the fire crackled in the hearth, she entered her bedroom, slipped off her cloak, and climbed back into bed, pulled the blankets up over her, where she gave a faint sob.

*I*ona lay still, her breath coming slowly, as she felt the power of Morgana's emotions, she sat up and breathed out, as her eyes contained tears, and whispered.

"Morgana, he loved you, and you loved him very deeply, I could feel the power of the love you held, why… Why refuse him, you were deeply in love with him, why let him go?"

"Rhiannon or Arthur would have destroyed him. She knew what would happen, and she was right. Lot lived a good life, and eventually married another, and he found happiness, and she wanted that for him." Iona turned to see Ariel stood in the doorway, she frowned.

"I thought you were tired?" She walked in and sat on the bed at her side, and gave a smile.

"I am, I asked your mother and will stay here tonight, I wanted to talk to you first." Iona nodded, she understood the way Ariel just appeared and then vanished.

"Ariel, Morgana was deeply in love, pushing Sir Lot away tore her apart. He was her first and strongest love at a time when she had a pure heart, but she could not risk his life, and she knew he was in danger so spared him, by breaking her own heart." Ariel smiled and took her hand.

"Many who walk in our world have made similar choices, Sapphire being one, she shared something similar with Keith, and like Morgana, she understood that he would be harmed by the world in which she walks. There are times when the life we choose is not suited to others, and in those times hard choices need to be made, Morgana made hers. You are right, her love for him was deep, she cried a few times with Branna, but be honest Iona, Rhiannon had marked her, Lot would have been used to hurt Morgana, and she understood that. Pushing him away, protected him."

It felt hard to accept, she could feel the power of it, and it felt wrong that she should have to go against a feeling so deep. She pulled up her knees, and leaned on them.

"No one knows the truth, here we are generations on from that time when she lived in Avalon, and it is almost eighteen years since the death of Rhiannon, and she is still controlling the narrative." Ariel leaned in her.

"It is true, but the word of a queen has great impact, and with luck, once crowned, you will be able to undo what Rhiannon has done." Iona frowned and turned to her.

"How do you mean with luck, Ariel, I intend to do this as queen?" Ariel looked at her, her grey eyes filled with life, and she reached up and took Iona by the hand.

"Iona, there is an issue, we need to talk."

Chapter Nineteen.

Change to a Queen.

Ariel sat on Iona's bed, and talked her through all of what had been happening. Iona was a little upset no one had said anything, but Ariel assured her, she was better off following her quest for truth. It gave them the time to assess everything, and after a lot of discussion with Master Elgin and Gwynfor, they had a plan, and at the moment in Florae there was a lot of preparation going on behind the scenes ready for her arrival. Ariel took a deep breath.

"Iona, you will be queen, have no doubts, this is just political posturing by a man who spent a lot of time as the ambassador of Florae, during Rhiannon's reign."

Ariel took Iona to the house, where Sapphire and Jett had arrived, and a debate was going on, Iona felt nervous, and afraid. In many ways, she had been panicking a little, as it was a huge task, and even though she had spent a great deal of time with Ariel and Sapphire being instructed, the closer it got, the more nervous she became. This was just yet more to add to the weight on her already burdened shoulders.

Rune was explaining what Alder had done and what it all meant to Jett, and how he was justifying his arguments based on the fact she was not a direct descendant of Gwendolyn, and how she was just a pretender. Iona turned around, and looked at Ariel, standing next to her mother.

"But how can he say that? Mum… Tell them, because I have been told all my life that I was destined to be a queen, so either I am, or I am not, which is it?" Jett leaned off the wall.

"What does this Alder want, because if he wants to oust a queen, he has something in mind, and that could be the answer to stopping him?" Ariel shook her head.

"He is drunk on power, he knows that if a queen does not take the seat, he can rule in her stead as a consort of the people. He has enjoyed his position these last twelve years since Master Elgin stepped down, and within the month, he will be replaced as ruler. This is the last act of a desperate man fighting to keep his hold on the throne. That was proven by his attack on Tila, as he also wishes to discredit me, as he knows, I will do everything I can to stop him." Jett nodded and looked around the room.

"Give me an hour, and Blades, and you will have a free house." Iona shook her head, looking panicked.

"No… Aunt Jett, please don't kill him, I do not want to be crowned knowing a man was slaughtered for my throne." Jett shrugged.

"Honestly, it is not a problem, I could use the action." Iona looked mortified.

"I cannot allow you to kill anyone of Fae, please Auntie." Jett smirked, and looked at Rune.

"Told you… Totally freaked out, but sincere, she is your queen alright." Iona frowned, and looked at her mother, who was trying to keep her face straight.

"She was joking, that was what, some sort of twisted test?" Rune tried not to smile, as she walked towards her, and slipped her arms around her.

"It is just your aunt being who she is. She told us, no queen would let her subjects die, so if you agreed Alder was right, and if not, you were the rightful heir to the throne." Iona frowned and looked at Jett.

"Seriously, you said that?" Jett smirked and put her head down.

"I like simple and efficient, and you know, we all know you. Iona, you are without doubt their queen. It worked, didn't it?" Iona sighed, and looked at her mother.

"Aunt Treen and Una have both sat through this, whatever it was, test, interview, questioning, so if he wants me to do that, fine, I will answer his questions, and prove he is wrong." Ariel gave a nod as she stood beside Rune.

"It is the best way, but knowing him, he will stack the deck against you. I will not allow you in there alone, and so we will do this by the book, which hopefully Bade has all laid out for us, and he will be ready when we get there." Iona gave a nod, and looked at everyone.

"Okay, how do we do this?" Ariel smiled, and rubbed her hands together.

"Right, we still have a lot to do, and we will be making a big show of this, after all, the people have been preparing for this for some time, and so we will be making the best entrance possible." Ariel looked around at all of them.

"All of you know your tasks, Gwynfor and Master Elgin are already working behind the scenes with Bade, so we have time, and as we do, Alder will grow more and more confident he is right. Although, at the same time, he will become even more nervous. If we drag this out a little while longer, then that will add to Alder's concerns, and we will be able to make the most of that."

Everybody split, and headed towards their various tasks, and Iona stood alone in the living room of her parents' house, she looked at Ariel, not really sure of what was expected of her.

"What do I need to do?" Ariel gestured to her, and slid open the door, and Iona followed her.

Side by side they walked down the long meadow towards the edge of the large lake, Ariel turned to face her, and smiled.

"Iona, shortly I will be briefing you with Sapphire, so when you walk into the hall to face the Council of Elders, you will know what to do. I do not want you worrying over this, for now, I want you to write down everything you have learned about Morgana and Rhiannon. Iona, do not rush, note every detail you can, so that you have a very accurate record of all this, and I will also add, spare no one. This is to be the complete honest truth." Iona looked at the floor.

"I feel so useless, I can help, I want to help. Ariel, this will be my throne, my place to rule the people of Fae, I feel I should be doing more." Ariel understood and smiled.

"But you already are, this task, your search for truth is the most important aspect of being a queen. Iona, there is nothing more important than this, this is how you understand everything, and in doing so, it will be your greatest guide in the way that the realm thrives. Sit and reflect, then write all of it down. Iona, this will be held in the archives forever, so do it justice, and add everything, even your thoughts and perception." She nodded and gave a sigh.

"Alright, I understand, and I do want to write, I have so much to write down. You know, the person she was when she was a student, I feel I have become close to her, I honestly think had I been in Avalon, we would have been friends. I feel I know her, I care about her, and it is so strange because we have never actually met. I feel she was wronged in the most severe way, and I am not sure how I should write that."

Ariel took her hand, and gave it a squeeze, her grey eyes were so filled with life and love as she smiled, and looked deeply into Iona's violet, her voice was soft and filled with care.

"You will be the queen of your people, and your thoughts and feelings will be important to everything you write, and so, I feel, put those words on paper in your truest form, for that will be the mark of who you will become."

*I*ona and Ariel walked and talked along the edge of the mere, and eventually they turned as Iona told Ariel the story of Morgana, and her perception of what she thought that must have been like for her. The conversation moved back to Ursula, and how she felt talking to her, and how she was concerned that Raven had run off, because of the book. Ariel appeared to be very interested in that part of her tale, and Iona answered her questions.

"Even in crystal, I could feel something, and it felt dark, which is why I asked the Lord Albanlin to take it. I know it sounds strange, but I did not think it was the merle, I felt like it was a person, I felt it was Maud." Ariel shook her head.

"Bran destroyed that page, Maud was destroyed." Iona shook her head.

"I do not think so, the book I gave to the white lord contained some sort of corrupted power. I don't think even he realised that Maud had been within more pages, and I have thought a lot about it, especially in regard to Morgana's more crazed moments. I think it was that book that drove her insane, because I have noticed things, like Ursula's account, she talked of how when she held the other book, she was different. I think whatever this other book was, it contained good, and it in a strange sense protected her, I suppose we will never know, because as far as I can tell, that book has never been found."

Ariel thought about it as they walked onto the path that led to the cabin of Iona, she stopped at the door with Iona, and gave her a hug, she needed to head home, and as Iona went inside to start to write, Ariel headed back to Avalon.

She sat at Bran's desk and lifted the first of her journals, and as preparations got underway in Florae, she read every instalment of Bran's life, especially those that concerned Morgana after the ritual where she had been forced to be tied to the raven Rajani. There was little about which books Morgana used, except one passage, which read.

'I fear for Morgana and her mind, she will not hand back the book written by Maud, and Berengar and myself have found the remains of a creature of an unnatural state dead below Maud's workrooms. I fear Maud was doing things that transform other creatures, especially Fae, it is hard to know without the book, but I think Maud was experimenting on them. I also feel she was trying to tap their essence, so she could enhance her own, and become more powerful. I fear my daughter was trying to make something that would give her the force of her magic to defeat me. I find myself sat here, considering the point, that Morgana's defeat of her, has saved both myself and Ariel.'

Ariel read down more paragraphs that outlined how Morgana created a race of a gentlefolk, which could transform into wild beings, and in an act of revenge, even though Rhiannon had left the realm, she released them into Avalon to destroy it. Rhiannon was forced to return, and destroy them, but acted so quickly, Morgana did not have the chance to attack her and kill her, which had been her goal. Branna wrote a year later.

'I visited Morgana tonight and we shared a meal, Morgana appeared different, and I noticed Maud's book was not there. On her table was the book I gifted her on that first visit to the castle, it was the one she used in Avalon. I could not get close to it, but I am convinced it is her book of white line study, and I think the book helps her fight the darkness. I have copied many parts of it on her early visits to me, and I am sure that within the Whitelines is a cure for the darkness, which I still seek. I am sure Morgana's book can save her, but fear she is too invested in the black book of Maud.'

Ariel sat back in her seat and thought for a moment, as she stared at the hand written book on the desk.

"Is that the answer, learn the white lines, would that work? No one knows what became of the book, and yet we now know Maud's book went to Ursula and has plagued the dreams of Raven Merle. Has it corrupted her, and if it has, will the other book help? I wonder where it is, a book of power does not lose itself, so where is it?"

Out of all that they had learned, it was the one question, that had to be answered, and it now appeared, neither herself, or Iona knew of its whereabouts. How had a book that powerful, simply slipped out of sight?

*I*ona sat in her cabin at her small desk, and began her writing, in her mind she had the story of Morgana planned out, from her birth, right up until her being forced to be tied to the raven. She lifted her white quill feather and dipped it into the ink, and started to write.

'When we talk of truth, which truth are we talking about? Is it the facts of a situation we speak of, or is it how we have read the situation, and formed an opinion based on what surrounds us, and the people we interact with? If a young girl loses her father in battle at just four years of age, is that sad? Well, yes, it is, unless of course her father was standing in the way of people of power, who wanted to seat a man they deemed was the one to rule. If that is the case, the pain of a small child at the death of her father was a price worth paying. They got their king, and he failed, and the young girl who had been left lost and alone, was expected to continue regardless of the pain and suffering she faced. Is it wrong to rob a child of the love of her father, is that a fair price to pay for an ideal? I find as I sit here and write this, her need was greater than the views of the powerful, who wanted to manipulate the lives of others. The loneliness she felt in her isolation shaped the woman she would become, and as I have seen in recent days, the view of her, even to this day, is not shaped by the facts, it has been shaped by the opinion of those of power.

I aim to write her truth, the facts of a life from a child who was forced to give up the father she loved, and face the world alone, as she fended for herself and forged forward with the words of her father inside her, as she fought to become the daughter, he had always wanted her to be. This is the truth of the life of Morgana, Countess of Cornwall, who became later in her life, Morgan le Fey, the countess of darkness.'

*R*une stood by the window and smiled to herself, as she saw her daughter dipping her quill and writing away. She looked lost to the world, and yet wore a faint smile, and Rune understood that this was right for her, and she was right about herself. Iona was to be a queen, and no matter how controversial the words she wrote were, she was writing the truth, as the facts showed it.

Robbie came up at her side and slid his arm around her waist, and she smiled and leaned onto him.

"She has grown up Rob, and I am not sure how I feel about it. Look at her, she is a woman, and no longer a child. Soon she will leave us, and head out into the world alone without us, and if I am honest, I don't want her to." He pulled her tighter, she turned and looked up at him, as he gave a small smile.

"We knew before she was born this day would come, but yes, I am going to miss her, more than even she realises." Rune sighed.

"She was our first Rob, she came at a time of great fear, and she brought us a joy I did not even realise. I will never forget being stuck in Avalon; it was my need to see her that drove me to find a way out to connect with everyone. I know it sounds strange, but Iona and Halbert have always been special to me. I love our children, and I love our life, it is what we fought for, but they were our first Robbie, and it is hard for me to know she will not be here anymore." He leaned down and kissed the top of her head.

"It is no different than Steph, when she gave her consent to let you join me in a search for the heirs. That was her moment Rune, as this is yours. It is time to step back and release her, but we are not letting her go, she will always be our child, nothing will change that."

She looked up into his dark eyes, so filled with love and wisdom, and just as she had when she was only seventeen, she felt her heart flutter and felt safe. She smiled at him.

"I love you, I always have, this is the life I always wanted, even though for most of the start, I was filled with fear, I would never change a moment of it." He gave a soft nod.

"We belong Runestone Sapphire, and just as we do, by the same chalk, Iona does to. I will always be her father and you will always be her mother, nothing can change that, and I think we both know, she will always return home to us. We did good Runestone, we created an amazing woman."

Rune smiled and lifted up on her toes, and softly kissed him. She slid back and her eyes sparkled with the most beautiful sapphire blue.

"Yes, you are right." He gave a giggle.

"Really, I thought you may correct me, because, well, you know stuff?" She smiled and her eyes danced.

"I do, it is a fact… You know, I am sure I proved it to you." The door behind them banged.

"Dad, will you tell that little fungus Fern, that skirt she is wearing is mine, she won't listen!" He gave a sigh, and turned to look at Tegan stood with her hands on her hips, looking annoyed. He started to walk towards her.

"Tegan, does it really matter, the house is filled with rolls of fabric and you are a seamstress, can you just not make another?" She frowned, and looked at him like he was mental.

"NO… Dad, I spent ages making that one." He shrugged.

"Think about it, it is Fern, she is wearing a skirt… She is actually dressing like a female." Tegan gave it some thought, and then looked at him.

"That is a good point Dad, and yes, it does matter, I made it, and only I wear it." Rune came up at his side and looked at her daughter.

"Tegan sweetheart, go back in, look her in the eye, and simply tell her she looks beautiful in it, and tell her it brings out all her feminine charms, and you will have it back within minutes." Tegan nodded, and pointed at her mother as she looked at her father.

"See that, do you see how she understands us?"

Robbie stood stunned, as Tegan turned with a smug smile, and walked back in the house, he turned to Rune, and she giggled.

"Told you… I know stuff."

*I*ona wrote all day, and then made herself a meal in her cabin. The following morning, she packed her bag with her book and her inks, and went through her window into Avalon, and revisited the site of the burned out old cottage. There was a large stump that had over the years, decayed slightly, but it was still solid, and she placed a small cushion she had brought with her on it. It was warm and sunny, and Iona sat feeling her own sense of the place, and felt it helped her remember everything clearly. For most of the day she sat with her feather and wrote, documenting Morgana's childhood, and growing up as a lonely and sad individual.

Slowly the story of her life came together, as she met with Merlin, and he agreed to teach her the Whitelines as a student. The time ticked past and she took a break and stopped, and stood up to stretch her legs, and walked around what was her overgrown garden. It was easy to see where her raised flower beds had been, many had rotted away, and the contents had spilled out, filling what would have been the paths between them. At the apple tree, Iona pulled off a large red apple and bit into it, the apple tasted sweet and juicy and she smiled, understanding for Ursula on her birthday, it must have been a big treat for her. She turned around as she chewed, and over by the fence, stood Amethyst, she smiled.

"It looks tasty." Iona gave a nod as she chewed, and then swallowed.

"It is, it is a known fact that apples from here are best." Amethyst walked in through the gate, and noted the book on the pillow covered stump.

"I see you have decided to write up your discoveries, is there anything I should be prepared for, in regard to my grandmother?"

Iona felt a pang of guilt, she had promised to see Amethyst before releasing what she knew, although to date, she had spoken to no one apart from Ariel about her discovery. She chose her words carefully.

"Your grandmother played her part in Morgana's isolation with her fabrications of the truth about her. She felt threatened by Morgana, partly because she was learning the Whitelines, and partly because she was the daughter of a powerful queen of those celebrating the Fae of Earth."

"Knowing what I know Iona, I am not surprised to hear that. Morgana appeared to be trying to do good here, is it true that she helped to cure and save a lot of lives?"

Iona gave a sigh and walked over to the stump, she picked up her book and sat down, and looked up at Amethyst.

"Everything I have heard about the Morgana who lived here, I would say whilst she was here in Avalon, everything she did was for the benefit of the Fae. In the world of men, she worked very hard in support of the Earth Faith, and her medicines really did help a lot of people. Amethyst, Morgana as a young woman, was true to her oath of the Whitelines, she was kind hearted, and at heart she was a good person."

"I have heard that, and I have looked into my table and seen many things related to her, all of them kind." She looked at Iona, and sighed.

"The woman I fought against with her vile monsters, was not a good person Iona, she is hated for a very good reason. I saw her in action, she was evil, of that there is no doubt in my mind, so I have to ask, do you know what happened to her?" Iona nodded and looked down.

"I do… For now, that is information I do not wish to share…

Not yet, in time as a queen to your people, you will know." Amethyst understood.

"I feel your loyalty, and also the pain you feel over her fate, can you at least answer me one question?" Iona looked up at her, and gave a slight nod.

"If I can do, I will."

"I cannot explain the feelings within you, but I have a sense of them, for here in my realm, my powers are at their strongest. I know you have cried over the pain you have felt, I feel it. Iona, answer me honestly, this fate, whatever you may call it, that turned her against the light, was it the fault of my grandmother? Did she create the monster she became?"

It was a really tough question to answer, and she was not completely sure how to. She considered it for a second, and looked at Amethyst, and she could see in her eyes how she was preparing for dark news, Iona shook her head.

"Not directly, that was a different set of circumstances, although your grandmother was cruel, I take no pleasure in saying that, but she lied about a lot of things. Morgana had nothing to do with the death of Eleanor, or Eve, Morgana was innocent, but she was blamed anyhow. The truth is, Morgana, believed in Eve, she respected and admired her, and stood her ground against Arthur and defended all of the council in the defence of the Earth Faith. What your grandmother did, helped isolate her, and it brought her great pain. Even now many still believe the lies she spun, and they are not easy to stop. Morgana discovered how your grandmother dealt with the Fae that disagreed with her, and how she ordered their deaths in secret." Amethyst took a deep breath in.

"That cannot be right, a queen of Fae would never knowingly kill her own people." Iona shrugged at her.

"The market traders saw Morgana as one of their own, and when your grandmother confronted her on the market, and Morgana stood her ground, all of the traders admired her. When she was banned from the market, the other traders took a stand and refused to serve the elites that pandered to the queen, so she ordered her marshals to remove them. They fled out of the realm, but as was revealed to me, they were met just outside the realm and slaughtered, not by Fae, but by fighters of the realm of men paid for with Avalon gold. I take no pleasure in telling you this, but whole families were slaughtered on her order, I am sure now you know, and because you are a queen of great power, your table will find it and show it you."

Amethyst felt sick to the stomach, it went against every creed of the Fae of Moon, she swallowed hard as the high emotions swirled inside her, and held her stomach. Her voice was just a whisper.

"I find it hard to accept this news, yet I know you do not lie, I will seek these lost souls and recover them to their natural land. This news distresses me, I understand her fight to hang onto power, but I cannot understand the taking of the lives of her people, it sickens me knowing it." It was understandable, it had sickened Iona to learn of it, she stood up and took a step forward and reached out her hand to touch her arm.

"I am sorry, I truly am, but I promised to share the facts that I knew of her with you, and now I have kept my word." Amethyst looked saddened, and her eyes appeared duller with the news, she nodded and tried to smile at her.

"It is right you told me; the truth must be known. Will you tell all you meet this news?" Iona shook her head softly.

"Who would believe me if I did? It matters not what we know, Morgana was hated so much, no one will believe what I have learned."

"So why do it Iona, why do all of this if it serves no purpose?" Iona smiled.

"It does serve a purpose; it serves my purpose. I felt compelled to learn the truth, and now that I have, it will shape the way I make decisions and rule, and within that, I hope to enhance the lives of all of the Fae of Earth. It matters not if they know or not, I do, and that in turn will be to their benefit, as I will always be careful and never judge too quickly." Amethyst smiled at her.

"You have changed a great deal in the last few months, and if you want my thoughts, I feel you will rule well, and your people will prosper Iona Violet. There will be a great friendship between us and our realms, together all the Fae will be united as one. I promise you now, in any hour of need, I will be there at your side always." Iona looked at her and smiled.

"Then our people will thrive, and I too will always be there if you need it."

Amethyst turned, and with a small flash of violet, she was gone, and Iona stood in the centre of the ruins of Morgana's cottage, and turned to her pillow. The sun was shining high in the sky, and she sat down, lifted her book and nib, and continued to write.

What started in that moment, became over a years worth of work, as she focused on Morgana, and through it, her visions showed her more of the life she had lived. Sat alone in Avalon, and then later at Tintagel, Iona isolated herself simply to focus on her writing. There would be several interruptions as she sought out the facts of Branna and Morgana, and also, she had to prepare for her crowning. Her life was changing and the young girl who was raised in Loxley would now have to take all that she had been taught by her parents, Sapphire and Ariel, and adapt to that of the role of a queen.

Chapter Twenty.

Plan to Seat a Queen.

It took five more days for Ariel and Elgin to work out how to allow Iona to sit before Alder, and be judged fit to rule as queen. Ariel sought Iona out, sat on a low wall at Tintagel, where she had taken to sitting alone and writing her book. In the ruins of the old castle, overgrown with weeds, the very nervous, Iona was schooled by Ariel, and Sapphire when she arrived to join them.

Iona was uncertain, when she had been so sure, and was still struggling to come to terms with the fact, that she had been accused of being a fake pretender to the throne. She found it hard to concentrate, and took to making notes, which she would read sat in her bed at night, which did not help her sleep. Most nights she would dream of either Morgana or Alder, and after two days of lessons, she had dark lines under her eyes from lack of sleep.

Rune was worried, she was unsure of the pressure being placed on her daughter, and what she saw as Iona approaching exhaustion, and so on the night before she needed to be ready, she sat at her table and watched as Iona went to bed early, as she lay back in her bed with a sigh, Rune snapped her fingers, and Iona went out flat, and slept deep.

It was early morning, and Alder had suffered yet another restless night, the last five days of taunting had been too much for him. It had gotten so bad, that he shipped in some of the guards from the quarry zones on the Isle of Ada, to replace the soldiers that had spoken to Treen, Una and Gwynfor. The guards were not allowed down the steps into the Royal Circle, to ensure no one could speak to them. To add to his problems, he had noted how other members of the council would stop talking the moment he arrived in a room, and was becoming convinced, they were plotting his downfall.

He sat at his desk in his study and was served breakfast, which was tasted first by the maid with a sigh. He had bags under his dark eyes, his skin was pale, and his hair unkempt. For over a week, he had eaten alone, and never touched any of the food in the council room, which was where the rest of the council met at meal times. There had been little discussion over the past five days, and the rest of the council were nervous, as Princess Iona had not appeared to be questioned by the council, and doubt was setting in. As all through the House of Scribes, the Council of Elders and all their staff sat eating, whilst over on the isle of Sora, preparations were underway, as the day was about to arrive, and Iona was set to appear.

In the farmhouse set off the great wide white road that ran from the sea, all the way up to the Royal Circle, Bade was busy with all the scribes of the house, as they prepared inside the barn, which was the only place big enough to house them all. He looked tired, for the last five days he had sat up late reading the laws to ensure he had missed nothing, and between him and Gwynfor, with extra advice from Elgin, they had planned out every detail of what was to be expected of Iona Violet's interview with the council.

In Loxley, Rune was up and had sorted out the children and got them off to school, Isolde smiled, as Rune walked back in through the doors, and took a breath.

"Relax, she is queen, it will show, I have felt her spirit and power since she was a tiny child." Rune gave a slight nod.

"I know that, and you know that, but sadly that fool who holds her throne hostage does not. I am her mother, and even when she is crowned, not a day will pass that I will not worry about her." They walked slowly towards the kitchen door.

"Lady Runestone, I will never forget the first time I lifted her on the isle of my fathers, and the power of purity that I felt as I held her for the first time. I had dreamed all my life of being the one to care for my queen, and her power flowed to me, and it was pure white circle. I have no understanding of the complex spell my Queen Gwendolyn wove, but I could feel her presence flowing through your daughter. I feel it at times within Lord Loxley, he too has the powers of his line, and I knew as I held your daughter, she was a line of life and truth. I cannot wait until I kneel before her wearing a crown, and name her my Queen of Fae, I spoke often with my sister of it, for us it will be the completion of our greatest desire, we raised our queen." Rune gave a soft smile.

Rune often thought of Filomena, who lost her life in the fire to help save her daughter. She had always felt guilty that she had not been there to protect them. Filomena was so young and had so much to look forward to in her life, and it had come to an abrupt end with the attack of the Houlen. Isolde smiled at her as she handed her a cup.

"My sister knew the risks, it was never your fault, and she would never say such things. My Lady if I may… My sister held a deep love for this family, living here was the happiest time of her life, she felt such huge honour to be a part of your daughter's life, as do I. You took a great darkness from the world, and revealed the truth of many things, and in doing so, this realm and all the realms that were tainted by her hand, now see better times. My sister will see her queen sit in her rightful place, I believe her spirit will live in on in our land, and walk with the queen she helped raise to help guide her." Rune felt the surge of emotion inside her, and simply smiled.

"If I had another chance, I would do things differently, and one of those things would have been to send you and your sister with my daughter to Florae." Isolde shook her head.

"What is meant to be always will be, for that is the journey we all undertake, and at times it may feel wrong, dark, or unjust, but that does not mean it is the wrong road. All roads lead somewhere, and some of them are longer than expected, but they still bring us to the place they are meant to take us. My grandfather told me that shortly before I returned here after the fight, and I feel, he was right. If I may also say so, I feel it is something that our new queen is learning as we speak, for her road may look uncertain, but it is still the right road, and she needs to follow it right until its end." The door opened and Iona walked in yawning.

"Morning."

Rune turned and looked at her, as she stood in the door blinking. Her hair was all over the place, and she was wearing green pants and a loose woodsman's top. She yawned again.

"Is there any food, my place is empty?" Isolde smirked, and Rune fussed.

"Iona, today is your big day and look at you." Iona looked down, and shrugged.

"I needed clothes, I mean, I sleep naked, so felt I should put something on, and these were handy. I am hungry Mum, I have time."

Rune gave a sigh.

"You eat, then you bathe, and then I will be dressing you." Iona sighed and walked to the table and sat down, and gave another yawn, Isolde chuckled and turned to the stove.

"I will make you something, and then young lady, it will be time for you to start to look like a queen to be." Iona shrugged.

"Yeah, but food first."

Rune shook her head, and headed out of the kitchen to prepare the new dress she had made for her daughter, and get everything organised in her room.

As Rune prepared for Iona, Ariel sat on a large rock where the grass faded and dropped onto the white sandy beach, in front of Gwynfor's cabin, her mind lost in thoughts, as she held her mug in front of her. In her mind, she was focused on the day she sat in the forest outside of Branna's castle, and conducted her ritual of farewell to honour her queen. It was so long ago, and yet for her, it felt like just years past, and was another reminder of the vast space of time she had been sealed in the crystal box.

There was movement at her side, and Gwynfor sat down beside her, she blinked out of her thoughts, and turned her head to see his old smiling face, and bright blue eyes sparkling with life.

"I thought she would come to mind today; I too have thought of her." He patted Ariel softly on the knee.

"She will be here, she never really left us." Ariel took a deep breath, and swallowed the emotion within her.

"I miss her, I should have been here with her, I should also have been here for your sister. I did not lose just my queens, I lost a mother figure, and a great friend. Both of them were held in high regard by me, and yet I deserted them both in their times of need." Gwynfor shook his head.

"How can one so wise, also be so wrong? Ariel, you were never meant to be on that road at that time, your road was to be here, when they could not be. Ariel, it was always your task to guide the Violet Stone, and I may add, my sister always understood that." Ariel turned, and watched the waves rolling up the beach.

"How can you be so sure, when even I did not see the outcome of everything?" He looked out at the sea, and smiled.

"She told me… I once sat on this beach with her, and she told me that you would return, and that the queen who came after her would be guided to her seat by you. My sister was a wise woman, I was very proud of her, and I miss her a great deal. I think she saw further than she admitted, I think she knew of these times, and that she would not be a part of it. She once told me, knowing you would return, gave her great hope for the future, and to be honest, I agree with her." Ariel gave a slight laugh.

"I have always admired your faith in your sister Gwynfor, your love for her has always radiated out of you. I cannot help the way I feel, when I suggested to Bran that she put me in that box, I did not realise it would be for so long. Bran was so clever, I was convinced she would find a way to balance her light and dark, and in doing so would release me. I did not want it to be the way it was; I did not wish to wake alone without her, Gwynfor if I had known it would be like this, I would have left and made my way here to you. I feel wretched all the time, there is a part of me that knows I could have saved your sister, and in that I failed her, I failed my queen." He leaned over and pattered her back.

"She never blamed you Ariel, she was happy you found the love you did. Today, you will have the chance to start and undo the pain of the past, this realm has lacked a queen for a long time. It is up to us, we are all that is left of the line of Bridget Violet, and today we will start the process of seating the first queen to this realm for many generations. It is time Ariel, those of that time will fade, and lines of the new will rise to replace us." He patted her shoulder and stood up.

"It is time we got prepared."

Ariel nodded as he turned and walked slowly back towards the cabin, Ariel pulled her knees up to her chin and stared at the water lapping the edge of the beach, and breathed out a long sad sigh.

"I wish you were here today, Bran, I am missing you. If I knew where he had taken you, I would gladly give up my mortal form and come to you. Iona Violet needs to be seated, but after that I feel my tasks here are done, and I shall return here no more. Florae is no longer my home; I feel I shall remain for evermore in Avalon."

She gave a sigh and stood up, and turned back to the cabin, where she saw Sapphire walking in the long grass down near the barn, her eyes flickering blue. She walked slowly down the path avoiding the house and around towards the heavily built barn, in which she knew the horses awaited them all. Sapphire looked up as she approached her, and gave a smile.

"Our young princess is bathing, and young Jessie has just arrived to act as her lady in waiting today. Rune is preparing the gowns as we speak." Ariel nodded.

"How is she feeling?" Sapphire shrugged.

"It's Rune, she loves dressing up, and has made the gown for Iona especially, so she is pretty excited." Ariel gave a little giggle.

"I meant our young princess." She nodded.

"Oh, she is nervous, which is to be expected, but what more can we do, she is as prepared as possible?"

"We have prepared her the best we can, never have I known such goings on, and yet I feel Alder still has tricks to turn. We must be on our toes Sapphire; I still feel he will do everything to undermine her and hold the seat for himself." Sapphire walked over to her and linked her arm with a smile.

"Somehow I am not sure he will pull that off, the people of Florae have already embraced her… Come see." Ariel frowned.

Sapphire walked her slowly towards the large barn doors, set on a heavy iron rail, on which they could be slid back to reveal the entrance. She stopped at the door and pointed inside, and gave a wide smile.

"I think Gwynfor is resolute that she is to be crowned." Ariel turned, and looked inside the doors and gave a gasp of surprise, Sapphire smiled as she watched.

"He is good, and possibly the most accomplished of all the Fae. Now you tell me, is that, or is that not a true queen of Fae?"

Ariel walked in through the doors lost for words, and she walked up and looked up at the fifteen foot statue of Iona, carved out of a mighty piece of wood. It was a stunningly beautiful piece of work, that captured every single detail of her, so much so it was almost life like. Ariel had never seen anything as beautiful in her life, Sapphire stood smiling as she looked up at it.

"It is her in every way, now you tell me, is that not the next queen of Fae?"

Ariel was captivated, she really was struggling to find the right words, and stared at it lost on the beauty and power of it, her voice was soft and low.

"I find it stirs me deeply, and it is remarkable. I have seen his work on many houses, none more so than the House of Scribes, but this… Sapphire, I have never seen anything like it, and it stirs me deeply." Sapphire nodded.

"Ariel, this is Gwendolyn's brother, Bridget Violet's grandson showing all of Florae, that the White Circle, is backing their queen. Now honestly, do you really feel looking at that, there is anything Alder can do to prevent her sitting on the throne?" She shook her head slowly, and her voice was almost a whisper.

"No… No one seeing this would oppose her." Sapphire chuckled.

"No, no one in this or any other realm would speak out against him, Gwynfor has always known far more than he has ever let on. I still say Gwendolyn told him far more than any realise. If you ask me, she saw this time, she knew Iona would come, which in a way is why I think she chose Rune, it protected Iona from Rhiannon. If you ask me, Gwendolyn never feared the darkness, she feared those in the light." Ariel turned to look at her.

"Have you seen something I haven't?" Sapphire smiled.

"I looked at that, and felt I was right, and if there is one thing I have learned looking into my table, it is Gwendolyn White Circle listened far more to her grandmother than any of us have ever realised."

It was something Ariel knew, even as a young princess Gwendolyn had always been quick to pick up on things, and she remembered the day she visited Merlin's cottage in Avalon. Gwendolyn had asked her about the symbol of her mother, the red star in a white circle, and she had to wonder, did Gwendolyn at that time think she may need it? Ariel stared up at the statue of Iona, and her mind focused on that time in her life, was Sapphire right, did Gwendolyn realise far more than she had said? In a strange way, it made sense, maybe Gwendolyn thought she would need it at Branna's house, which is why she gave her one?

It made Ariel think, and yet, she also knew that in her time in the box, Gwendolyn believed a lot of what was said about Branna. She turned and walked quietly out of the barn, lost to her thoughts. Sapphire felt the emotions wash inside her and watched, as Ariel slowly walked away, as the pictures she had witnessed on Rune's table came to mind.

Gwendolyn looked at Branna watching her from the floor, she smiled.

"Ariel is free, it is time you let her go and let her live again, as she once did when you shared her life in Avalon. Let her be that person again, let go of her Branna, if you love or ever truly loved her, let her go." Tears welled in Branna's eyes.

"She was my light, it got so dark, I needed her light to see again." Gwendolyn gave a smile.

"She always will be, if you do the one thing that bird never allowed you to do…Open your heart Branna, and let the love of Ariel back in, it has been empty for too long."

Ariel felt the surge inside her as she remembered watching it with Rune. She stood once again on the beach, her eyes filled with tears as she stared out to sea. Gwendolyn understood, she knew how deep the love went, and encouraged Branna to embrace that love. For almost eighteen years she had believed that Gwendolyn hated Branna, as did everyone else, and yet stood in the barn talking with Sapphire, she realised that Sapphire was right. Gwendolyn must have seen more into the future, like her grandmother, understood the corruption that had happened in the council. Ariel took a deep breath, she had to prepare, as Iona was depending on her, but her heart was once again filled with the truth of the injustice she and Branna had faced, and it felt difficult to suppress.

The sound of the waves rolling onto the beach felt calming, and she felt the soft breeze warm her face, she needed her focus, and needed to clear her mind. Ariel turned, and walked back to the cabin, she needed to change and prepare for Iona's arrival, and all she could think about, was getting this over with, and heading home to Avalon.

*R*une smiled as she saw Jessie and Iona chatting away, they had been close friends all their life, and the bond showed, as Jessie sat and giggled along with her. There was a great deal of Alice in Jessie, and Rune could see how alike to her and Alice they were. She took a breath and prepared, the day was about to get busy, as she leaned on the bedroom door.

"Girl's, you cannot sit around all day in towels, it is time you both got dressed, come on." Rune headed back to her room, where the dresses were laid out, as behind her the two girls came giggling down the hallway, as Iona looked at Jessie and asked.

"He asked you out, oh Hearne, what did you say to him?" Jessie smiled.

"I told him I was a mystic and could see the future, and he was not in mine." Iona sniggered.

"Seriously… How did he take it?" She shrugged, as they reached the bedroom door.

"He looked worried and asked me if I had seen anything he should know of in his future, so I told him avoid Penelope Vale, she would bring him great harm. I felt that would keep him at bay, he is way too besotted with her, everyone knows she humiliates him."

They staggered in giggling, and Rune shook her head as she held up Iona's dress, and both of the girl's gasped in awe. It was clear, as they started to gossip about the dress, that for Rune, it was going to feel like the day was twice as long.

*T*he hour ticked past, and finally after great effort, she stood back and looked at her daughter, as she stood dressed in a long violet dress trimmed with gold. Around her shoulders was the violet cloak, bearing what would become the crest of the Violet Stone. Her hair of brown and gold was pulled back at the sides and held in place at the back of her head with a golden pin, on which was an amethyst cut like a violet flower. Rune smiled as she lifted the final piece in place, a tiara of diamonds and amethysts, she slid it carefully into place, and stepped back.

Iona stood watching, her violet eyes filled with life as they shone, she smiled a shy smile and spoke quietly.

"Well Mum, do I look alright, because I will not deny, I am terrified? Mum, I really want to do this, I want to be a ruler that is fairhanded and good to the people, but this man could stop me, and I am afraid he could succeed." Rune wiped her eyes of the tears, and smiled.

"Iona Violet Loxley, you are my daughter, and your father is the hooded man returned, you will sit on that throne and you will be a queen of truth. Seriously, do you think your father will allow this man to stop you, no man is a match for his arrows? Even though he has renounced violence of any sort, I know him, and his love for you is so pure and deep. Iona, you are possibly the only reason he would lift that sword again, for I know he would fight to the death to protect you, he already did." She took a deep breath and nodded.

"I know that, but I never want him to fight again, even for me. After what he went through, he deserves the peace he has found."

Jessie was wearing a pale lilac dress, and also had a cloak of violet to match, which had Iona's emblem on it. She looked down at it and was thrilled, she looked up at Rune.

"This is mine isn't it, you know, I can keep it can't I?" Rune chuckled, and shook her head, she leaned in and kissed Jessie on the cheek.

"You are so like your mother; she was just the same the day we gave her a Loxley able bowman cloak."

It was almost time, and she needed to get ready, and for today, she was going to do something she had not done before, she was going to wear all red, and show Alder that she was indeed, the heir of Eve. In her closet she had two cloaks, one given her by her grandfather, and one Fagan had found when he visited the garden of Eve in Avalon. He had felt she left it for Runestone, as she had once worn it to travel out of Avalon to the castle at Caerleon. He had handed it her on one of her first visits back to his house, shortly after the battle for Loxley had ended.

Rune lifted it off the hanger and looked at it, for her in many ways, it symbolised all that Eve had been to her, and she had never wanted her to fully leave the realm. It was a bitter sweet reminder of her time alone in the Forest of Time with Eve, and the defining moment of her life, as she understood who she was to become, the Lady of Life. It hung in her hands, deep red and edged with the embroidered golden leaves of every tree from every realm, and was the perfect symbol of Hearne and Eve, the start of her family line. She pulled the cloak over her shoulders and clipped together the acorn clasp, and turned to the mirror, to see herself.

She had aged since her time in the circle of darkness, yet not enough to show her full age, but she noted around her eyes, she had a look of someone more mature, even for her thirty six years, she still looked only in her early twenties, and yet deep inside she felt older, as she had so much knowledge stored within her. Behind her the girls came down the stairs, and stopped as Rune turned, both of them gave a curtsy.

"My Lady of Life." Iona stood up, and walked over with a smile.

"You look amazing, and as the heir to Eve, even a queen should bow or curtsy before you." Rune gave a her a sweet smile.

"I am your mother." Iona smiled a soft smile.

"Which is why before you I will always curtsy, for it is a mark of the woman you are, and the woman you made me. Mum, even with a crown on my head, you will always be a greater power than I, all queens should bow to you, for you are the source of the violet lines, and you are the centre of all of us."

They were almost ready, and Rune took a deep breath, as she prepared to leave, Isolde was watching on and gave a nod, she would have to stay behind, as she had to be home when the children got home. All she needed was Robbie to arrive back with Jett.

On the main isle of Florae, Gwynfor and his party had moved to the farm house on the outskirts of the main city. Master Elgin had made sure the word had been spread that their future queen was to appear before Alder, and those who supported her should show it, and line the road.

Alder watched from his window scowling as it looked like most of the realm had appeared, and were lining the road. He took a breath, and blew it down his nose in frustration, and then turned to his assistant.

"What do they have planned now, have you heard anything at all?" She nodded her head.

"Only what the messengers have brought, and that Princess Iona will appear before the council, but as yet no date has been set. Whatever this is, no one is saying Master Alder." He nodded, and looked back out of the window.

"No doubt we will soon find out."

Rune's archway appeared, and Ariel smiled as she stood at the back of the farm near the side of the river. Rune walked out with Robbie, and Ariel gave a curtsy.

"My Lady of Life." Jade stepped out behind them holding Rowan's hand, with big smiles, as behind her Jett with Rafe walked out, and Ariel bowed to such revered company.

"My Ladies, and Lords, would you please walk this way, the master of the realm is waiting for you."

The party all walked across the short grass, to where Gwynfor stood wearing his usual big smile. Iona came through, and Ariel took a breath, she looked nervous on the arm of her brother Halbert Thorn, followed by Jessica Sapphire. Iona took a huge breath as she faced Ariel.

"Do I look the part… I look alright… don't I?" Ariel gave a nod.

"You look like a true queen of the Fae, and you carry the authority well, Iona, trust in yourself. This was destined for you, and even though your full powers have not come to you yet, they are very strong within you, and they will show." She nodded.

"I feel sick." Thorn smiled.

"Well, that is always a good sign." She slapped his arm.

"Thorn, I am terrified, this man could stop me from fulfilling the destiny set for me." He shrugged.

"I doubt it, he may think he can, but I will never allow that, I feel his days as a council man are numbered. Trust me, mum knows stuff." Jessie giggled behind them, and bent to lift Iona's cloak off the floor.

Chapter Twenty One.

Brought for Judgement.

For the next forty minutes, there was a lot of organising, made difficult by Jett, who was loving seeing Treen and Una, and was distracted as she laughed and joked with them and Jade. There was a long line of horses all being attended to by the farm hands, who had saddled them, and brushed and plaited their manes and tails.

Iona stood with Ariel, waiting for the moment when they prepared to leave and make the short journey towards the House of Scribes. As they stood there watching and waiting, Iona felt an electric surge around her, and she turned to look behind her. Some distance behind them, next to the edge of the river, stood a figure in long black tatty robes, she turned and walked over the grass, and headed towards him, as Ariel watched on with a smile. Iona approached the White Lord and went down into a graceful curtsy before him.

"My Lord Albanlin, I am surprised to see you." His hood moved.

"Violet Stone, this man who opposes you has no understanding of the truth of your line, he may think he will prevail, but he will not. What destiny has written into the stones, cannot be changed, no matter how much he may wish to emulate his mentor." Iona looked up and frowned.

"Mentor, of whom do you speak My Lord?"

"I speak of the last Queen of the Moon, for he was the replacement of the lady of white when she returned to this realm. The lord you face was in service to his queen of this realm, and yet his loyalties were never here, they were in the realm of the white rock and the golden hand."

His arm moved, and a translucent looking hand slipped out of the long baggy sleeve, and within the faint hand, was a small white star shaped stone.

"This Violet Stone, is the white star taken from the table of the white circle, which I replaced with a red one. I created the table of the queen, White Circle, on the instruction of the Queen Bridget Violet. She instructed me to pass this on to you before the ceremony of the crowning. Only the true Queen of Fae can wield this, for it was destined to be hers since the day it was cut free. Take it, and hold it, for I feel the truth that flows within you, will activate the stone and work in your favour." He dropped the cold white star into her hand.

"Long ago this was destined for you, take it and use it, for there is more to being a queen, than this man who wishes to block you knows. Some secrets, should only be known by a true queen, and this is the means, use it to guide you." Iona looked up.

"My Lord I do not know how to."

"Hold it in your hand and speak the truth, and it will work in your favour."

Iona looked down at her hand, and closed her fingers around it, and she felt it pulse in her palm, she looked back up to her lord, and the white lord was gone. She looked from side to side, but there was no sign of him. She stood up, and looked down at her hand, where she could feel the power of the stone star pulsate through her fingers, and she whispered to herself.

"Hold it, and speak the truth."

*A*riel turned and looked to the long white road, as Bade walked out from the farm sensing something, Gwynfor smiled, and gave a happy chuckle.

"I do believe it is starting, shall we get a move on, I do love a good get together?"

Gwynfor sprang up onto his horse, as the staff helped pull his long white and blue edged cloak neatly over the back of the horse. He was surprisingly nimble for a man of his great age, as he sat with his bright blue eyes twinkling in his old lined face.

"This is going to be a most rewarding event; I feel I am quite looking forward to it."

Rune giggled, as she saw the look of puzzlement on Robbie and Rowan's faces, as they frowned at Gwynfor, and then mounted their horses. Jade sat with her eyes shining like emeralds and wearing a big happy smile, her long golden hair flowing down her back. Jett sat mounted in her long red cloak waiting, as Rafe looked around puzzled understanding nothing that was happening.

All of them mounted up in a long line and prepared, Bade stood on the edge of the fence line, looking out at the road and gave the signal by raising his arm, he turned with a solemn face.

"It has begun."

As Alder watched out of his window, he saw Master Elgin walk along the front of the outer deck to the House of Scribes, and his face turned to anger instantly.

"Why is he out, I placed him under house arrest?"

He turned to move when something caught his eye, and he stopped and stared out, and down the valley basin, to the end of the road, where a bright light exploded out of the sky and lit up all of Florae. Alder could do nothing but stare, as the huge white light dimmed, and out of the light rode Luminaria on a white horse, behind her, walked one thousand men dressed in blue tunics, wearing armour breast plates of gold. They marched holding long silver spears, on which hung tassels of deep purple, that swung in rhythm to the crunch of their feet on the road way.

Behind them sat on her horse rode Queen Amethyst Diamond of Fae, and behind her dressed in the uniform of a general, rode Anthony, consort to the queen, with his young daughter Vivian of Avalon. Gwynne and Rayne who was wearing a violet eye patch, smiled as the people of Fae bowed. With her escort of imperial guards of Avalon, Amethyst smiled as she saw the assembled group all waiting to fall in behind her, Jade giggled and lifted her hand and gave a tiny wave, and all assembled nodded as she passed them, heading for the House of Scribes.

Old Master Elgin stood at the top of the wooden steps, as the guards of Fae split and walked to the edges of the huge circle of white stone of the Royal Circle, in which the centre held the round cavern where the water fell into the Whispering Falls. The people of the Fae gathered in droves, and crowded around the outside of the circle to view the spectacle. As Amethyst rode into the circle, all of the Fae bowed, and Elgin smiled as she rode to the bottom of the steps, and was helped from her horse. Elgin stood proud, one hand steadying himself on his stick, and bowed his head low.

"My Queen Amethyst, I am honoured to see you at the steps of our humble house." Amethyst walked onto the steps, as Anthony looked up at the huge impressive building.

"It is hardly humble, I for one, am impressed." Vivian at his side, gave a little giggle. Elgin gave a nod to Anthony, and the young Vivian.

"If you would care to wait with me, I believe we have other guests, and shall enter the house as a party?"

Amethyst turned and looked out, and smiled as she saw the thousands of faces watching her, she watched the road, where two hundred scribes dressed in white with long pale green cloaks walked in a procession. They were led by Bade and Tila, all holding a small tray in front of themselves, containing a long quill, ink bottles, and fresh parchment. They approached the Royal Circle, and divided to stand in front of the guards of the Fae of Moon, and Bade with Tila walked to the base of the steps and bowed to Queen Amethyst.

"Your Royal Majesties, welcome to Florae, and our humble House of Scribes, you have honoured us greatly." Treen with Brandon rode up behind them, and Treen winked at Amethyst. She slid down off her horse and walked onto the steps, her long orange cloak flowing behind her.

"It eez been some time my cousin, I am appy to see you ave joined in with us all." Amethyst hugged Treen, with a smile.

"I am pleased to see you well Cousin, it has been too long, we must gather more." Treen smiled.

"You ave the size of place, no? We ave not been with the seeing of each enough, I shall talk with everyone, and make this possible, yes?" Skip leaned in.

"I am sure we shall all be there for Iona and Hal's birthday; we really must have a regular reunion."

Behind them Una with Wilson, Jett and Rafe, Jade and Rowan, and Sapphire all arrived and dismounted, and came up the steps as a hush fell on the crowd, and Rune rode up with Robbie, her long cloak of red and gold flowing down over the back of her horse. The crowd all lowered to their knees, and bowed their heads, as the Lady of Life rode into the circle, wearing a huge smile, with Robbie looking uncomfortable in his best clothes, and yet looking like a proud father. Una smiled at the side of Sapphire, as both of them watched her enter the circle.

"She has changed little, and yet commands more respect than all of us, look at the dedication and love in the eyes of our people for her." Sapphire in many ways loved seeing it.

"I cannot answer Una, I feel the same way, I would lay my life on the line for both of them, hell, we all have many times. She is my mentor, and always will be, I owe her everything." Una smiled; she understood Sapphire perfectly. Robbie and Rune came up the steps and hugged Amethyst.

*O*nce assembled all of them stood in a line, as Ariel walked dressed in pure white, her long cloak edged with gold, bearing a plain golden crest of a golden tree surrounded by twelve golden stars. Behind her rode Gwynfor, Lord of the White Circle, and behind him, Iona Violet Stone, her tiara sparkling in her hair, shooting beams of soft purple light all around her. Lord Thorn rode to one side in deep woodland green, and on her other side, rode Jessica Sapphire dressed in the same deep violet cloak of Iona.

There was total silence, as Iona Violet slipped from her horse. and came to the bottom of the steps and looked up. She bowed her head, and gave a formal curtsy, and then walked up the steps looking very nervous, Robbie smiled with immense pride next to Rowan, who looked equally as proud. Iona took a deep breath, as the group parted and Ariel walked through the gap and approached the large doors of the House of Scribes. She looked at the two guards either side.

"Do your duty, open the house and welcome our esteemed guests." One of them looked terrified, and leaned forward slightly, and spoke very quietly.

"Mistress Ariel, we want to, but we have been forbidden." Ariel took a deep breath and stepped back and lifted her arms.

"It is probably a good thing I designed this place then."

Ariel looked up above the door, where in Fae runes was written, 'to record the truth, is the noblest of acts.' She lifted her voice, and holding her palms to the sky, she spoke with great authority.

"OPEN TO THE MISTRESS OF THE HOUSE OF SCRIBES!"

The door frame glowed white, and Ariel gave a little chuckle as the two large doors swung silently open. Bade frowned and leaned over to her.

"I did not know they could do that." She gave him a sweet smile.

"I know, I have a few design secrets that I kept to myself."

*S*he walked in, through the large entrance hall, into the massive chamber of the house, to Alder who stood staring at her looking angry.

"This house is sealed by the head of the council; how dare you

force your way in and challenge my authority." Ariel stared at him;
her dislike as obvious as her curt manner.

"You want to question the Violet Stone, she is here, so stand back,
if it is a court you want to judge her worthiness, as Mistress of this
house, I will ensure you get one, now get out of my way, and for the
love of all the lords, we have royal company, tidy yourself up, and
wear a robe of standing." He looked past her shoulder and saw the
line of dignitaries.

"She will be interviewed alone." Ariel shook her head.

"She has nothing to hide, and will be judged publicly, otherwise
I will order the guards of the house to arrest you for the blatant act
of denying the people of this realm a full and proper account of this
session, as is laid out in the creed of all Fae."

Alder sneered and turned quickly, and scurried off down the
hallway to the council meeting room. Bade stood in the doorway as
the royal guests waited in the entrance hall, and marvelled at the
sheer beauty of the old carved building, much of which Malcolm and
Ninian had worked on. Ariel walked slowly back towards the doorway,
and turned to face the massive room.

"PREPARE THE HOUSE FOR A FULL COURT OF SESSION!"

This was one part Bade knew about, as levers were pulled, and
long panels of the floor lifted, to reveal long benches that raised out
of the floor, in a large semi circle to seat the audience. At the front,
a table appeared in front of the twelve seats of the council, and two
assistants walked in and placed two green padded chairs behind it.

The whole room which had been a large expanse of open space,
now took on the look of a court house, and Ariel turned, and offered
her hand, in a motion of welcome.

"My Lords and Ladies, please make your way to the front seats, you
will find them to suit your comfort, the court of the council will begin
soon."

The room filled up slowly, to one side, all the scribes filled in with
their trays, and sat to the further end of the hall on a raised platform,
where they prepared on small desks before them. Rune and all the
members of her circle and family, sat in the booths at the front on
padded seats. Gwynfor and Ariel sat just in front of them at the table,
and across the room, Tila took up her place at a small table, she would
be acting as court clerk, before her sat three large red leather bound
books.

*I*ona stood with her brother and Jessica in a small room, to one side of the entrance hallway, where she had been instructed to wait until called. She paced nervously up and down, her nervousness growing inside her. Halbert Thorn walked over and took her hands in his and looked her in the eyes.

"My sister, who I love dearly, please calm yourself. You are the rightful heir to that throne, and no greedy and manipulative clerk of a council will prevent that. We were born together side by side, and as you walk in there today, we will remain side by side. If for any moment you feel afraid, turn to me, for I will hold all my courage and love for you to use. You are already my queen; you always have been." She breathed in and swallowed hard.

"I love you too Thorn, and yes, I will always be at your side, no matter what, we came into this world side by side, and I would wish that to remain so."

He smiled and his eyes sparkled, he had that calmness of their father within in, and it helped. The door behind them opened, and a slender woman walked in and bowed to Iona.

"Your royal highness, I am Evangeline, and have been appointed to aid your welfare for your duration, I will also head up your staff in the royal apartments when you take the throne." She walked towards her, and Thorn watched her carefully.

Evangeline was slender and elegant, with long deep red hair and intense green eyes, her face was pale and covered with faint dusky freckles. Hallbert lifted his hand.

"I am Lord Thorn, her brother, thank you for your service, I feel we need it." She looked up with bright green eyes, and she smiled a soft smile.

"My Lord, I am aware of your presence."

He grinned and nodded like an idiot, she turned a little pink, and broke her gaze, and looked down. Jessie tittered, and bit her lip as the moment was much longer than expected, and Thorn was clearly enamoured, Iona smirked.

"I am grateful to you Evangeline, I will not deny, I feel more than a little nervous." She looked up, to where Thorn was still fixed upon her and turned to Iona.

"You must not concern yourself, I have spoken at length with Mistress Ariel, and you have nothing to fear, for the truth of your line is obvious to everyone in this realm, and we long to see you as should be and was destined. You are already our queen."

Inside what was now, the court room of the council, the residents of Florae entered and seated themselves on all the remaining seats available and there was a loud hum of voices, as parents, children and elder members of the realm all spoke with hushed voices. Ariel busied herself at her table with her papers, and spoke quietly with Gwynfor. across the room Bade was deep in a quiet conversation with Tila, as he quickly instructed her on points of law from the red books.

The anticipation of the atmosphere was growing, as Rune relaxed. She could feel the presence of Iona, and feel her fear, she closed her eyes, and breathed in.

"Hear me my daughter, we are here, you are not alone."

There was a boom at the end of the corridor leading down to the chambers, Tila jumped up in her seat, and Bade gave her a slight nod, she looked into the room filled with faces.

"Silence, the court of the council is in session."

The place went instantly quiet, as the ten members of the Council of Elders walked into the room, and headed for the seats, and were joined by Elgin and Bade, Alder turned and looked at them.

"What do you think you are doing?" Elgin looked down the line.

"You may think you run this realm Alder, but if you wish to judge a future queen, without twelve, your decision will be seen as unapplicable. If you must continue with this charade to hide your greed, then myself and Lord Bade will sit."

Alder gave a heavy snort of anger and sat down, as the rest of the council seated themselves, and adjusted their positions to that of comfort. Tila walked up and bowed to Lord Alder, he sneered down his nose at her.

"I ordered your arrest, why are you not in bracelets?" She looked up at him.

"Lady Ariel mistress of this house is indisposed as she will be acting for our queen as her counsel, and as her assistant, I am duty bound to this house to fulfil her role."

His eyes moved to Ariel where she sat a few yards in front consulting quietly with Gwynfor, he looked down at Tila, and she smiled and handed him a sheet of parchment, on which was outlined the charges, as written by him and handed to his assistant. He lifted his gavel and banged hard on the wide piece of flat polished wood, at the side of his seat. He looked out at the audience.

"Seal all the doors, the court of the council is now in session. All will remain silent, or they will be removed to suffer penance." He looked at Tila, sat at her desk with hate.

"Have the accused brought forth."

*T*ila lifted a small bell off the desk, and rang it, all eyes turned as the large doors to the hall closed tight. At the side of the large main doors, a side door opened, and Iona accompanied by Thorn and Jessica was escorted into the court to two chairs that sat in the middle of the room. Thorn and Jessica slipped onto the line of seats next to Robbie and Rune, and Iona and Evangeline walked before the two chairs, and stood facing the council.

Iona looked up at Alder stood in the centre of the line, his face as cold and fixed as stone as he looked at her. She stood tall and straight, her eyes of bright violet fixed upon him, her hands held together in front of her, it was clear she was nervous. Alder smirked.

"Name yourself and swear your oath." She swallowed hard and took a slight breath, and then spoke clearly.

"I am Iona Violet Stone, born of the Violet Isle and Fae. I swear before this council that I see before me two honest men only, and yet I will be truthful in all I say and do in this court."

Robbie smirked as the whole room gasped, and Elgin looked down with a titter. Iona stood looking defiant, as Alder rose in his seat.

"You have a nerve to walk into this court of a Council of Elders, and slander the names of those who have served this realm faithfully. How dare you speak such wicked things." Iona held her stance, and Rune noted the pulse in her hand and smiled. Iona looked Alder in the eyes.

"I am Iona Violet, named to be queen, a queen that will serve this realm with great loyalty, and I will serve this realm as a queen of truth. I did not lie; I see before me two men of great loyalty to this realm, who have served it faithfully since the demise of Queen Gwendolyn White Circle." Sapphire gave a little giggle, and leaned into Crystal.

"Wow, she is so like her mum and dad; I feel this is going to be very interesting." Treen and Una gave little titters. Alder stood staring at her, his face twisted, he had noticed the smirks of Ariel, he lifted his eyes to look at her.

"Is this how you train a candidate for the throne of this realm, to insult her superiors?" Ariel rose calmly from her seat.

"No, My Lord Alder. I do not train candidates, I train queens, the ones destined to wear the crown and carry the crest of her realm, as I note, her Royal Highness, does."

Alder sat down and turned to look at Tila as she sat wearing her usual wide smile, he scowled at her.

"Clerk, read the charges." Tila stood up and lifted the parchment, she looked at it and frowned, and looked back up.

"I cannot My Lord." He frowned as he stared at her.

"You are supposed to be a scribe, now read it." Tila looked at Iona.

"I cannot My Lord, for it violates my oath to this house, my realm, and to my queen, who I swore loyalty to as a young child, in whom I kneeled before seventeen years ago. I will not utter these falsehoods, and violate the oath I took."

Iona smiled, and looked down, Gwynfor nodded in his seat, and felt great pride in his people. Alder flopped back in his seat, and snatched up his copy of the charges, and gave a heavy sigh. He looked at Iona.

"Iona Violet of Loxley."

"Objection!" Alder lifted his eyes to Ariel, stood behind her desk.

"What now!?" Ariel stood calmly and looked at him.

"My Lord Alder, she is Princess Iona Violet Stone of Fae, for she was born on the Violet Isle. If you mispronounce her name and title, then any charges you may feel will be applied will be void. Her Royal Highness, is in her realm of rule, and so therefore should only be addressed by her full title of Florae only." He looked at Iona.

"My apologies Lady Violet…"

"Objection!" His eyes moved with his sigh to Ariel, she smiled.

"My Lord, her correct title, is not lady, it is her Royal Highness." He gave another loud and audible sigh, and looked at Iona.

"My apologies, your ROYAL HIGHNESS!" Gwynfor tittered behind his table. Alder lifted his parchment.

"If there are no more objections, may I please read the charges?" Ariel gave a nod and sat down, he turned to Iona.

"Princess Violet Stone of Fae." He glanced at Ariel, she did not move, so his eyes looked back at the sheet.

"You have been called before this council to answer to the following charges. You have knowingly chosen to name yourself heir to the throne of Florae and Fae of Earth. You have provided no proof or information that would corroborate your right as queen. You have misrepresented yourself in order to gain access to the private chambers of this realm's royal apartments, and you have ordered decrees to be made before any proof of your position, has been confirmed. In doing so, you have impersonated a member of the royal line, and brought your council into disrepute. You have staked an unwarranted and unjustifiable claim, that you alleged was made by the past queen of this line, and have in doing so, soiled the name and reputation of Gwendolyn White Circle. Your false claims to be the rightful heir of this realm are in contempt of the creed of this realms peoples, and are as a result considered to be treasonous before this house." He took a deep breath, and looked up at the house filled with silent faces.

"Considering these charges, you have been called here this day to stand trial and prove your innocence, and be judged by this council as to your suitability, and validity to your false claims as queen of this realm."

"Objection!" Alder lowered the paper.

"Lady Ariel, how will we ever progress if you constantly object?" Ariel looked at him with cold eyes.

"If you conducted yourself in the manner expected of a head of the council I would not have to. You make the claim of suitability, My Lord Alder, as you well know, the future heir to the throne is always named by the previous queen, and therefore passes onto the throne by the consent of the queen. Do you have proof that Queen Gwendolyn White Circle did not name her? If you do, present it first before making such outlandish statements." Heads all around the room nodded in agreement

"My Lady Ariel, may I remind you, that ten members of this council voted by a majority that this candidate was not considered to be suitable unless valid and undeniable proof was presented before this council, which to date it has not?" Ariel nodded at him.

"I understand that My Lord Alder, but in matters of such magnitude, a vote of such significance needs to be authorised by the reigning queen, before debate can begin. Can you inform this court as to when this approval was given?" Elgin tittered, and nodded in his seat.

"She is good, but I always knew she would be." Alder glanced down the line at Elgin, and could feel his temper building inside him. He turned back to Ariel.

"Lady Ariel, sadly our queen passed on leaving the guardianship of this realm, in the hands of this house, and this council. It became a necessity that we made the difficult decisions to ensure the survival of this realm, not all of us had the benefit of resting in a glass box for that duration." Ariel's face clouded over.

"Your comments are offensive to me Lord Alder, I demand you withdraw them, this is not about me, it is about the welfare and care of this realm under the rule of a new queen." He gave a small laugh.

"Correct me Lady Ariel, but do I lie, did you or did you not choose to go willingly into your confinement abandoning your people to the mercy of the dark Morgan le Fey? I am sorry your feelings are so easily hurt, but here in this house we seek truth, and the facts remain the same no matter what you may or may not feel, you went willingly into that demon's lair, and was ensnared by her. Now if you do not mind, this house has the task of judging what is right for these people, as we have done for ten generations of your sleep." Ariel felt the hurt, and Iona turned to her, and spoke with a soft voice.

"Ariel, it is fine, we expected this, please, do not listen to the hate I feel in his heart." Ariel sat down and swallowed, as she wiped the tears from her eyes.

"My Queen, I never deserted my people, they have lived in my heart always." Iona smiled and gave a nod.

"I know that, I feel it from here. Dry your eyes, I am fine."

*A*lder gave a cough, and Iona turned around to face him again, she looked up at him, feeling the white soft star in her hand, and feeling stronger and less afraid. Alder looked at her.

"Princess Iona Violet Stone, you have heard the charges that have been levied against you, before we make a judgement, how do you plead?"

Iona looked back to see her family, and then looked back at the council, as all of them watched her carefully, she took a moment of thought, and then looked up at Alder.

"Lord Alder, I will not deny, I have not lived in this realm, but it is a fact that I was born on the Violet Isle, and within the week of my birth, I was presented to all the ancestral history of our people, who named me the rightful heir. I stand here before you as your future queen, embraced by most of your people, and yet I am told that I have to be judged and deemed fit enough. I would ask of you just one thing, who here is fit to judge a queen?" Quiet titters broke out behind her, and Elgin smiled, and whispered quietly.

"Good girl." Alder looked confused.

"You will be judged by us, the Council of Elders." She gave a slight nod.

"So, if I am correct Lord Alder, I am to be judged by ordinary members of the Fae, not of royal descent?"

Ariel suddenly understood what was happening, as she felt the pulse once again from Iona's hand, and she smiled. Alder shook his head.

"There is no royal blood left, who could judge you, we are all you have." Iona frowned.

"Are you sure?" She turned around to see a line of faces.

"My Lord Alder, I see the Lord of the Isles of White Circle, I see a queen of Fae, a Queen of Caerleon, a Queen of Morbihan, and also a direct descendant of the line of Eve." She turned back around to face him.

"I am a direct descendant of Eve, the Lady of Life who was sister to Albanlin the White Lord of Time. I am also a direct descendant of Gwynfor, brother of Queen Gwendolyn White Circle, Granddaughter of Queen Bridget Violet, sister to Rhiannon of Moon, who I may add, were both created by my great, great grandmother Eve, with the help of my great, great grandfather, the Lord Hearne, and the assistance of the White Lord himself. I feel my line is greater than all of your queens, for I am descendant of their creator, and so therefore feel this council is not qualified to judge me." Elgin snorted, and laughed out loud; Alder frowned in disbelief.

"You are a mere farm girl, you have no understanding of the role of a queen, I am more than qualified to judge you, who else could?"

Robbie gritted his teeth and slid his hand towards his belt, but there was no sword there. Rune smiled, and rested her hand on his, and leaned into him.

"I love that you would pick up your sword again in defence of your daughter, but Robbie, I feel she is not alone up there. Sit back and be proud of your daughter, she just truly became a queen." Along the row, Rafe growled at Alder, and Jett giggled. Iona lifted her closed hand, and smiled.

"My Lord Alder, you are not fit to judge me, when you should kneel before me and beg my forgiveness, but I will humour you." Iona opened her hand, and there was the glowing star shaped stone of white.

"My lords and ladies of the council, in my hand, is the stone that was removed by the White Lord himself from the table destined to be Queen Gwendolyn's. He removed this star of the truth, and placed in the space the red star of Enaria." There were gasps as the stone sparkled brightly, and Gwynfor sat back with a radiant smile, and looked at Ariel.

"I am feeling quite excited, this is going to be as much fun as going on holiday." Iona looked at the council.

"If I am to be judged, I demand I am judged in the Court of Queens."

There was a massive burst of bright white light, and all the startled squeals were instantly drowned out, as white light rushed out of the floor, and flooded the whole of the room.

Chapter Twenty Two.

The Court of Queens.

The white light faded, and Iona stood proud as everyone looked around shocked. Iona looked down, and up the edges of her deep purple cloak, small embroidered white stars had appeared. At her feet was a large round red circle. She looked up, and Alder looked afraid, he had no idea where they were. It appeared to be a large flat plateaux of rock, that was above the clouds, and the sky was filled with bright twinkling stars. He looked at Iona and his voice wavered.

"What have you done?" Iona held her palm up with the white star.

"Something only a queen could do, I have summoned the court where only truth can be told, the court of queens, as is my right. I stand on the stone of all that has been written, the red stone of my mother. In this place, no lie can be hidden, here only the truth can be told, and I will be a queen of truth for my people. You accuse me of being a liar and a fake, and so Lord Alder, I will grant you all of your wishes, and prove myself worthy of my people, and call my witnesses to testify."

Alder was visibly shaken, as were many others, Rune was quite calm, but there again, she was on the red stone, it was hers, and Robbie understood that. Jett grinned at Una and lifted her eyebrows, and Una giggled as she remembered her first night alone when Jett came back and she told her of the relationship she had formed with Woody. The rest of the council were uncomfortable, and moved around uneasily in their seats, Iona turned and looked at Ariel.

"Mistress of the House, I wish to call my first witness, I call Enaria, mystic of Fae."

Ariel took a deep breath and stared at the stone, as the faint figure of her mother rose out of the floor, and her eyes filled with tears, as she saw her mother in the flesh for the first time since she was a small child. Enaria smiled at her.

"My daughter, I am so proud of you."

Gwynfor leaned over and put his arm around her shoulder, as Iona turned, and looked at the slightly shimmering figure of Enaria. She bowed to her.

"My lady of sight, please show us your truth."

Enaria turned and pictures rose out of the floor, as she explained her story, and everyone watched as she found the moon realm deserted, and the remains of Tideguyde. They all watched, as a black almost creeping smoke wove around her, and she described what happened.

"I had not realised that the Merle had taken the realm in the absence of our Goddess of the Moon, and before I realised, it was too late. I fought it with all my light, and knew of only one thing that would clear it, a charm that my husband and I had worked on for many years."

All of them watched as Enaria rose up high glowing in the brightest of white to push back the merle, there was an explosive blast, and a huge white circle burned into the moon. She dropped from the sky, and as she struggled, with her hand, she cut a star of white out of the filled circle, and threw it into the darkness. Breathing hard, with her eyes and nose bleeding, she fell into the hole, and the space filled up with her blood and turned a bright red. There were hideous screams, as the merle was torn from the moon and cast back into the darkness, and Enaria arose from the red star and staggered towards the remnant of the Goddess of the moon. Gripping it firm, she exploded in light, and disappeared. Enaria faced the council.

"I did not realise I was so badly infected, I called to my queen, and when she arrived, I told her of what I had seen, and told her to take the last piece of the garment to Eve and protect it. I also asked her to take my husband and daughter away to protect them, and then bring the White Lord to me. I knew I was dying and could not be saved, but I had to get whatever was inside me out of me, and out of the realm. Only he had the power to do this, I had no other choice, and asked my dearest friend to save the most precious thing I had, my daughter, in whom I had already placed all of my gifts. Ariel, I am so sorry, it was a mistake, I had seen things, and I needed to stop them for your sake. I realised that day you left, I did not prevent what was destined for you, I caused it." Ariel wept deep bitter sobs, in her seat, Enaria wiped her own tears away.

"I left a small fragment of the garment on the moon, and when Rhiannon was created, it attracted her. She found it when her realm was built, and she understood the power it held, and in that, she began a journey to study it, that would change the fate of everyone. I never realised that our Moon Goddess had been infected, there was so much inside me, but I no longer had the strength to fight it, and I missed the fragments within the garment, had I known, I would have destroyed them first." Enaria turned to the council.

"My Lords, I created the White Circle, and placed within them a protection to defend all realms, and so began the lines that followed Queen Bridget, every person from that date onwards has protections from the darkness that lives within the merle. I stand before you the creator of a line, that includes Iona Violet Stone, she has the gifts of all queens, you are mistaken in your judgements." She turned, and walked slowly across the floor towards the table of Ariel.

Ariel stood up her face filled with tears as they dripped off her chin, and her mother pulled her close and embraced her. She pushed her head into her daughter's hair as she hugged her tight.

"I am with you, I always have been, I never left you my beautiful and gifted daughter. I live on in your heart, and I am sorry for the pain you endured because of my stupid mistake." Ariel looked up into her mothers' eyes, and Enaria smiled.

"You are without doubt my daughter, and I love you, and I am so incredibly proud of you, for what you have done for our people." Ariel sniffled, and tried to talk.

"I love you Mother, I never got to say goodbye, and I have always regretted it. I miss you so much." Enaria smiled as her eyes sparkled.

"I know that, I feel it all the time, it flows from you through the water towards me constantly. When you walk in water I feel you, for I am there in all that flows through Avalon, and I have rejoiced in the happiness that you found." Enaria kissed her head.

"I must leave now, farewell my child, and live in the light."

"Goodbye Mother, I love you too." Enaria faded from view, and there were many who wiped their eyes, Iona turned to the council.

"There is the source of all the evil that surrounds us, as shown and taught to us by Enaria mystic of Fae, and now, you can hear from your queen. I call Queen Bridget Violet." Alder could not believe what he was hearing or seeing as Bridget rose out of the floor, and faced the council, her eyes were a deep dark violet.

"Shame on you, all of you for betraying the trust of your people." She walked over and stood in front of Alder.

"I remember you when you were a sad and whimpering little boy, as you cried outside your home when your parents were taken ill. I sent you to your aunt Gerbera's home until I could take the fragment of the merle from them, and aid them to recover. I absorbed every speck of the merle in Florae to save all of you, and now you look at my line, and shame her, and call her? How dare you disobey the rule of your queen."

Bridget Violet turned and saw the pictures of Albanlin as he withdrew the merle from her and placed it into the black star of the merle. Bridget smiled as she looked upon Iona and then glanced towards Runestone.

"She has the eyes of your great grandmother, and one of my most trusted friends, my Lady of Life." She smiled at Runestone.

"Know child of the red stone, that I will be forever indebted to your line, for it protected mine, and aided the cause of taking that star of evil to a place where no one will ever touch it again. It gives me great joy to see our lines join, for in life, I felt joined to Eve, and cared very deeply for her. Your daughter holds many of the qualities of both of us, and I place all of my trust in her to guide my people safely."

Bridget Violet turned and looked at Iona Violet Stone, and she smiled a soft smile, she glanced to Ariel sat at her table with red eyes.

"My adopted daughter has taught you well, she is a person of great value to me, which is why I sent her to Avalon, no other could have survived that trial to be here for you. Place great trust in her for she is worthy of it, I see in your hand the White Star of Truth, and it pleases me to see such a queen of high quality wield it with great skill. Your path of truth is not an easy one, but it is the right one for our people. Know this Iona Violet Stone, you were marked with violet long before you were born, for I knew of you." There were gasps all around the space, and Iona was shocked, and gasped out her words.

"But how could you know, how, it was over thousands of years before me?" Bridget smiled, and glanced at Ariel.

"I had the greatest friend I could ever know, such was our deep bond, she entrusted me with the care of her most precious possession, her daughter. It was hard to me to walk away from my dearest of friends knowing her daughter or I, would never see her again. I grew to love her deeply, as if she was my own, and even now as I look upon her, I still see her as one of my children, such is the love I feel for her." Her eyes moved back to Iona.

"When you are done, the court of queens will judge you, not these fools, you are Violet Stone, and that is my line, for I am Bridget Violet, first queen to the Fae of Earth. It is a time for the truth, and so now before you my future queen of Fae, I will reveal what has never been seen." Bridget lifted her hand, and the images of her and Rhiannon rose out of the floor, and everyone watched on stunned.

Bridget turned, and faced the red faced Rhiannon, and stared at her in disbelief.

"This is folly, how can you sit in judgement over half of your race, and persecute them? You are the queen to your people, you do not get to pick and choose, and for what, the lust of a glimpse of power you saw in the darkness? You are a hypocrite, you talk to the darkness to try and fool it into giving up its secrets, for what, do you really feel so powerful you think it can be drained and used? Listen to yourself, it is foolish, you are of the light, no good can come from meddling with the darkness, especially when you have enslaved half your race. Rhiannon my sister, I beg you, turn from this road of folly, before you destroy all of us."

Rhiannon grew angrier as she looked at Bridget as she pleaded with her, and scoffed at her.

"You have no understanding; you do not know what I have learned. Half of our races are tainted, it is already here with us, and I will master it and force it to submit to me. When I rule it, all Fae will be spared, and our races will thrive, and we will hold so much power that none will ever resist us. Bridget my sister can you not see, we will bring peace to the lines of men with but a click of our fingers, all realms will look to us, we could wield such power that…" Bridget shook her head.

"That what, we could rule over the council, is that what you want, Eve, Hearne, and Albanlin as your pets to do your bidding? Rhiannon, please I beg you, see reason, we may feel we have power, but compared to them, we are much lesser, they are the true sources, surely even you can see that? We are powerful, we rule our lines, but we will never harness what they do, and it is right it is that way, for that is where true balance lies. What you suggest is madness, it will tip the scales of power and throw everything into chaos, you may think you can control this, but you are wrong, what we are is what it feeds upon, do you understand that, it ate Enaria away? The purest soul I have ever known was devoured by it in front of my eyes, please my sister I beg you, stop this madness, release your people to live freely, and bring back equality to your realm."

Rhiannon stormed across the room and lifted her wine; she turned and gave a long sigh as she looked at Bridget.

"I have no idea why I even thought you could comprehend what I envision, you have lived in the trees for too long, it is time you walked into the modern age. Changes are coming my sister, and you will be left behind, half your race will turn on you, well, I can assure you, I will never let that happen here. I will crush them before they overrule me, no arrogant dark haired Fae will ever challenge me, I will destroy them first." Bridget walked slowly towards the door of Rhiannon's library, she took the handle, and turned to look back.

"I feel deep sadness my sister, for you will end up hated and despise by all, and the good you have done, will mean little when they see the darkness that lives in your heart, I pity your people."

"GET OUT!" The glass smashed on the door as Bridget pulled it closed behind her, and left.

There was utter silence as Bridget faced her Council of Elders, with a saddened face, and took a pause as the emotion washed over her.

"I fear for all who allow darkness into their hearts, and it saddens me deeply that so many still hold her in such high esteem. The truth of the Moon Queen, is she failed her people in order to advance her own ambitions. I have only one gift I could bestow on the Fae of the Moon, and I did it that day."

Bridget turned, and walked across the red stone to where Amethyst sat looking saddened by what she had seen. She leaned forward and took hold of Amethyst hands, and Amethyst looked up into her eyes, as Bridget smiled.

"As I left the moon that day, I marked both realms of Fae with the gift of violet. Where violet is seen, truth and goodness grow. Shortly after my visit, your father came along and he had the most beautiful violet eyes, and I knew him to be a man of great honour." Amethyst smiled and gave a nod, as Bridget looked to Rayne and smiled.

"He is, he is my rock in every way, and always has been. There is no other man more honourable in my eyes, my Queen Bridget." Bridget gave a lovely warm and loving smile.

"I completely agree with you, and I have a great care of him, for in my hour of need, he came to me, and gave me great comfort." She looked away from Rayne who nodded, and looked down at Amethyst.

"I see you too have his eyes, and you are a great queen to your people Amethyst Diamond."

To hear that from Bridget Violet was a huge compliment for Amethyst, for to her, Rayne was an icon, and man of great honour who had served his people better than his mother had. Bridget walked slowly over to the council.

"What I marked violet, is your duty to obey, remember that always."

*E*lgin smiled and nodded his head, Bridget faded from sight, and there was complete silence as many sat in deep thought, as Iona watched on with bright shining violet eyes. She walked slowly towards the council, and looked at them all one at a time as she walked the length of the line of twelve seats.

"My Lords and Ladies, you have seen with your own eyes, how your queen, confronted Rhiannon and showed the truth of her. This is not new to you, the Mistress of the House asked Scribe Tila to write her translated coded journals and all of you saw the truth, and yet you denied it and condemned Scribe Tila to a sentence. Tila wrote nothing that was untrue, and yet like many sat here in this room, all of you believed the version of the truth that Rhiannon said was the truth. None of you questioned it, not one of you decided to look into it and seek the real truth, you simply followed her lead with blind belief, even Eve fell pray to the cunning of Rhiannon, and it caused her death, and if you do not believe me, watch for yourselves."

*T*he pictures rose out of the floor, as a young girl with a happy face looked into the forest, and spoke to Eve, Rune leaned forward to look at the images, as Eve spoke to Morgana of Cornwall.

"The forest of my husband is indeed a place of great beauty, and I feel you were drawn here out of need, for within this realm, you will find the peace to ease your heart. There is much here that would aide you, and all but this one plant, could be harvested for your garden. This sadly only grows within the boundaries of this forest, and to move it, would bring about its demise." Morgana understood, Branna had told her of the flower.

"I would not do that to something of such great beauty." Eve gave a small chuckle.

"You may take some of the flowers, for I hear you wish to aide those who live within the Moon Realm with tinctures to ease their ills. They are very potent, so use them with great care." Morgana looked down at the flower.

"I am grateful, and yet, I do not wish to spoil this place, for I feel it would lessen the beauty of it." Eve gave a smile, as she walked towards Morgana.

"Then hold out your palm, you show such respect for my husband's forest, and it will be rewarded." Morgana lifted her hand and looked at her palm, her hand trembled slightly.

"I am unsure as to why My Lady." Eve watched with intense eyes, and waved her hand softly, and Morgana gasped, as in the centre of her palm, a small plant appeared, and grew two tiny leaves.

"Treasure it and nurture it, and lay its feet within the boundary of your garden, for it is a plant of high value that will aid your quest to comfort the sick." Morgana could feel her breath lost in her throat as she looked up at Eve.

"I feel at a loss for the words to express my joy, this will do much good for those who come to me." Eve gave a smile.

"You have chosen a hard path to walk, Merlin is not an easy man to be apprentice to, and the queen at times is overruled by her passions. Know this little Morgana, we have addressed your cause with the queen, and your innocence has been proven. Stay resolute in your quest to do good for these people and you will be rewarded greatly, it is a straight path, but one that can be easily strayed from. Stay true to your path, and go forth with my blessing and help those with great need. The life of the earth will always aid you in the cause you have chosen." Morgana looked at the small plant, it had grown a third tiny leaf.

"I will head home with great haste and plant this where it will get the sun and the rain, and yet be protected beneath my large apple tree. I shall tend it with great care."

"If you do, and stay true to your cause, it will flourish to aid you. Be warned, this is one plant a veil of the Fae cannot hide you from, stay true to the values of a healer, and it will thrive." Morgana looked up and gave a huge smile.

"Thank you, My Lady, I am working hard with all Merlin teaches me, and already using it to help others, and I will honour this flower in all my tasks." She nodded.

"May your worries and troubles ease as you walk back, go in peace with my blessing."

The picture faded, and Iona turned to the Council, she looked at them sat trying to understand what they were seeing, she smiled.

"That was Morgana of Cornwall, and young student of the Whitelines, she was given a precious gift indeed, for the White Star of Albanlin, grows in only two other locations, apart from the Forest of Time. One is my home in Loxley, and the other is in the ruined cottage of Morgana of Cornwall in Avalon. I know you are all aware of Branna of Fae, and you are also aware of who this young innocent girl would grow to become, for that was the young Morgan le Fey. Eve showed her great kindness and gave her a very precious thing, one which you heard Eve just say would only thrive if the owner stayed true to the path of truth. I would imagine it would probably surprise you to know that the White Star of Albanlin still to this day thrives in that ruined cottage garden in Avalon, so the flower states that Morgana of Cornwall stayed true to her oath, how do you explain that, you who are fit to judge a queen?" Alder gave a snort.

"What does it matter, she is dead now, she killed Eleanor and Eve, it is just a flower, like any other. Morgan is dead and we all rejoiced at the news, it is not relevant to your proof of innocence." Iona turned and walked back to the centre of the red stone on the floor.

"It matters a great deal, especially when judging a queen. Rhiannon convinced everyone that both Branna and Morgana were evil, she coined the term Dark Fae to label them. As I said earlier, even to this day, the only truth believed is her version. I am accused of passing a false decree, which under the laws and creed of the Fae, is treason against the crown, because I commuted the sentence of Scribe Tila, who was tried and found guilty of a false charge. Lord Alder, you praised Queen Rhiannon highly, and spoke of her purity, wisdom and truth, and yet as I have discovered it was not true, you were misguided in your reasoning." Alder narrowed his eyes as he looked at her with distaste.

"You stand there and call me a liar?" Iona shook her head.

"I believe I said, misguided, let me show with my next witness. I call to the Lady of Life; I call Eve Life." Alder sat back in shock, lost for words as Eve rose out of the floor. Eve looked at the council.

"The Lady Violet Stone does not lie. The Ruling Council made many mistakes, we were far too powerful. We had too much control, we should have left things alone, but our interference brought with it great pain, none more so than to the life of Morgana of Cornwall. In my dying hour, I saw my folly, and felt great guilt for the part I played in her life, for the truth of it was, Morgana was a better person than all of us." The gasps all around were instant, Jett stood up and faced Eve, her hand on the hilt of her sword.

"HOW CAN YOU EVEN SAY THAT, SHE KILLED YOU IN COLD BLOOD?"

Alder should have banged his gavel, but such was his shock, he could hardly move as he stared at the Lady of life. Eve turned and walked slowly towards Jett.

"My brave Red Queen, you are without doubt favoured highly in the house of your lord and master of the green realm, but like myself, you are misguided. Sit my dear Queen, and listen to my words, for it is time that the truth be known, for as I see now, there are two truths, one which was told me by my dear sister and Queen of the Moon, and the facts of the life we all lived, for the real truth was there before us, we just chose to ignore it and listen to the words of someone we respected. I admired Morgana, because she was true to her oath, and true to herself, she wanted nothing more than to be left alone, a simple life, a life dedicated to study. Sadly, she resembled that of Branna, and for that she was wrongly marked by the queen, and blamed for many things not of her doing, but the truth shone out of her, as I saw in my last day. Morgana faced me, and pointed out my faults, and it was a revelation to me."

The pictures rose from the floor as Morgana stood holding her basket of flowers and herbs, and faced Eve on the edge of Avalon, as Eve spoke to her.

"I was not aware you had returned to these lands, I feel the queen of the realm is also unaware, Merlin schooled you well, if you can slip in and out without the queen knowing. I feel you have matured greatly in the short time since we last met, and wonder if the flowers of your garden still grow white."

Morgana did not feel as nervous as she had in the past, maybe she had just gone through the point of no return where she no longer cared, she looked deep into the eyes of Eve, and gave a slight laugh.

"What does it matter, nothing I do will ever be good enough for the Ruling Council? All of you have watched me, tracked me, and found criticism in every aspect of my life. I have to live under a veil just to have what everyone else alive has, privacy to just be me. All I have ever wished for is to be left alone, to live my life making teas and tinctures, and helping those I meet. I am Whitelines, yet when the golden queen has a problem, she points the finger at me, and all of you simply believe her." She gave a slight laugh, as she looked at the Ruling Council member.

"You are a hypocrite Eve, you play the role of purity well, but you and all of the council have blood on your hands, you accuse me, and yet your crimes are far worse. All of you murdered my father because he stood in the way of your so called 'One True King.' It makes me laugh. I lived with Uther, I saw the way he treated my mother and bedded the women of the village. I lived with the stench of his vomit from his excessive drinking all over the floor, I saw the way he taunted and bullied those who were weak, and yet in your eyes, he was perfect, so perfect you armed him with a sword of high honour." She gave a loud laugh.

"What honour, tell me Lady Eve, high ruler of the forests, tell me, where was his honour when Merlin helped him rape my mother? You all sit in judgement of me, and yet it is all of you who should be judged. You destroyed my life, and took away my father who I loved deeply, and never once, has any of you, apart from Merlin, ever shown the slightest bit of sympathy, or regret. None of you, why can you not just leave me in peace to live my life of grief, remembering the only honourable man I have ever known?" The tears filled her eyes.

"My Father." Morgana lifted her basket, and walked off at a fast pace along the path, and left Eve watching filled with sadness. Eve turned to face the Council of Elders, her face filled with sadness, as they watched her, unable to comprehend what they were seeing.

"Morgana was right, it was not mine or anyone else's right to meddle in her life and take her father away. Uther proved in the end to be unsuitable, something a child of only four summers could clearly see as he raped her mother. I was riddled with guilt and felt a need to know what had befallen me, and why the truth had evaded me. I rushed to the top of the summit not able to think, and there I was faced with another, but it was not Morgana." The pictures rose out of the floor.

"Branna!" Branna wasted no time, and plunged the tainted knife into her.

"It is Raven… Lady Raven to be precise, you should have left Morgana alone." Eve looked down and her blood ran red, she looked up at Branna in shock.

"I am Eve, I am life, I have no mortal life, I am life." Branna nodded, and smiled.

"Queen Rhiannon knows that, which is why she created the means to defeat you, and I found it." Eve frowned.

"Rhiannon is my sister." Branna smirked.

"Rhiannon is evil, she is the darkness in all the realms, why could none of you ever see that, didn't Enaria tell you that?"

Eve shook her head and then flinched, as she felt pain for the first time in her long life, the liquid on the blade was working.

"This is not true; she is the Queen of this realm." Branna jerked her hand. and pulled out the knife.

"You should have listened to Bridget Violet, and Ariel, they were the truth, and yet all of you forced them to make peace with the evil they knew her to be. You helped her kill my grandson, imprison my family, and take Ariel from me, and you sided with that golden traitor to her people. It is time you all paid, now is the time of the rising of the raven, your time is over, and you are not as full of life as you think, Rhiannon has assured it."

*T*his was too much, no one in the court could believe their eyes, as Eve slipped to the floor and smoke billowed up as Branna disappeared. Eve turned to face the whole room.

"Branna was right, we have destroyed many lives in our bid to bring what we thought should be the way of man. Morgana spoke truth, Rhiannon lied to us all, she was clear it was Morgana who killed Eleanor and Uther, and it was in that final moment as I faced Branna I saw the full truth. I had lost control of who I was, I was no longer the lady of life, for I had taken far too many to aid my friend's control everything. Morgana was right to speak her truth, we were all guilty and had blood on our hands, and I feel the deep regret of it all, which is why I have never returned to the forest, and now I guard the evil to prevent it from spreading more."

Jett stood up and shook her head, she could not fully understand what was happening, she looked to her left and right at all the others within the line.

"No, she was evil, we all faced her and Branna, they were destroying and killing everything, I cannot accept this. Runestone, speak, you know what we faced, you know of the lives that were lost, and the souls you guided into the other realm." Rune looked at her daughter.

"I believe there is more to learn Jett, and I want to know all the facts. My daughter will rule as a queen of the truth, and I wish to know the truth, so I stand with honour at her side, for at this moment, I feel I am not worthy of her, and I wish to be."

Jett stared lost for words and fell back down onto her seat utterly shocked. Iona took a deep breath, and turned to Eve.

"My Lady of Life, I owe you my thanks." She smiled at Iona.

"I am your great, great grandmother, and I have watched you with great pride. I feel you hold the same power of truth as Morgana did, and that reassures me greatly."

She smiled and faded away, and the council looked on dumbstruck. Elgin sat back relaxed and smiling. Iona held the white stone firmly and it pulsed in her hand.

"My Lords and Ladies, for my next witness, I call Branna of Moon." Ariel looked up and gasped.

"WHAT!?"

Chapter Twenty Three.

White Star of Truth.

Ariel was out of her seat, and hurried over to Iona in the centre of the red stone marked on the floor. She turned her back to the council and faced Iona.

"How can you do this, has she not suffered enough, you have no right Iona, no right to do this, is my life not hell enough for you?"

Iona looked over her shoulder, where Branna hung limp in the air. Her face was pale, her eyes were closed, and from her stomach blood had run down her dress and legs, and dripped onto the floor, everyone looked horrified, as Ariel wept in front of Iona.

"How could you do this to me, I trusted you Iona, I was there for you?" The voice was soft and weak.

"Ariel." She spun around, and her heart broke as she saw Branna hanging, and fell to her knees, as the tears flowed out of her and she wept.

"What have they done to you? Oh Bran, why did you come, you must have known I could not bear to see you this way." Branna opened her eyes, and looked down at her, as she wept on the floor.

"I miss you Ariel. The golden queen is dead, and I cannot be with you, and I wanted to so badly. I waited an age, and I was so close. They came and stole you from me, how could I not see you one more time, I love you?" Ariel took a deep breath, and tried to wipe her eyes.

"I miss you too, I live alone in our home in Avalon, and I think of you every day."

Branna smiled; she looked so white her skin was almost transparent, as she hung limp unable to move, her eyes lifted to Iona, and she gave a slight nod.

"I came because the truth should be known, it is all I ever wanted, for the truth to be told. I also owe you my gratitude Violet Stone, you spoke truthfully about Morgana, she is a daughter to me, and I have suffered watching the wrongs that were done to her, you spoke her truth, and that matters to me." Iona nodded.

"This is hard on Ariel, and I love her deeply, and have no wish to hurt her more than she has already suffered, and she has suffered without you. Branna, I know that you have a story that started before you came to Avalon, and I need you to speak your truth for the sake of all of us here." Branna looked up and saw Runestone, she gave her a nod.

"You were right to act Lady of Life, I was losing all hope, and I induced long sleeps to avoid doing more harm, but I was close, I almost had the balance. The key was always in the Whitelines, I think you knew that, which is why you took Morgana's connection, you were clever. It weakened her, and misshaped her spells, and set her back many years of learning." Rune took a deep breath, and nodded at her in acknowledgement. Branna looked down to her feet where her blood dripped onto the floor.

"Ariel, go to your seat, so I can look at you, my eyes are tired of darkness and while I have them, I want to see your beautiful light."

Ariel stood up and sniffled, as her lip trembled, and tears ran onto her cheeks, she looked at Iona, and then walked past her back to her table, and sat down. Branna watched her with a smile, and her eyes never left Ariel.

"When I was on the moon realm, I was allowed to study one aspect of our world, and I chose the merle. The golden queen demanded I sit a test, and so I agreed. She said it was a hard test, that took a lot of study, and so I was allowed access to her personal library. I wore only a dress, which was tied around the waist with a cord belt. Each day as I left her library, I had to undo the cord, so my dress hung loose, it was to ensure I did not remove papers from her library. With no cord, nothing could be hidden under my dress. I was skinny and not well fed, so the dress was baggy on me, it was her way of controlling us, less food, that was our reward, more food."

Ariel and Branna had their eyes locked on each other as they always had when they spoke. Iona understood what Branna was saying.

"Why is this important Branna, it means little to us?" Branna stared at Ariel.

"It was her private library, and held everything she too had researched, and she was afraid some of her secrets would slip out, for she hid many things in that room." Iona frowned.

"What things?"

"She had a recipe for a mixture that would destroy a creator, by poisoning their garment, so they could never return in human form, and would remain in spirit only." The council gasped out loud, that was treason, Branna gave a little chuckle.

"Listen to them Ariel, they are shocked, they wish to call me and punish me, but I fear nothing now, what else can be done that has not already been done?" It made sense to Iona.

"So, it was Rhiannon who created the thing you used on Eve, why Eve?" Branna smiled at Ariel.

"Why not, the golden queen planned to kill her first, then Hearne, and after that Merlin and Gwendolyn. It was all planned out with her secrets and recipes; she wanted to control everything and rule every realm from the moon where no one could unseat her. She never intended to share her power with any, not even her granddaughter, which is why she kept her father separated from her, she feared he would teach her how to take power from her. That is who she was, and obviously an evil merle riddled ruler, and she called me, I was tame by comparison." Alder stood up, looking angered.

"This is outrageous, and the lies of a dark Fae, known to be tied to a raven of the merle." Branna gave a laugh.

"You are not wrong Master Alder, which if you think about it, makes me the best to judge, I know her better than any of you ever will. Sit down and shut up and let me talk, or I will set my bird on you." Her eyes twinkled and never left Ariel's.

"It can be proven and will be, for I wrote all of it in my journals and left them in the keep of Jarron." She winked at Ariel, and she smiled a soft smile, knowing Jarron had shown her where they were.

"I took a fine silken thread and tied it under my breasts, and tied another around my waist, and then slipped on my dress, and when I was alone in the library, I copied out all her recipes. I also copied out her charm for the binding of the raven, for as I discovered, it was not a Fae charm as she told everyone, it was a charm given her by the merle. I copied that and a few other things that would help me in my own research, and slid the parchments through the thread, which held it close to my skin. When I undid the cord on my dress, nothing fell out, and I was cleared to go back to my quarters." Iona smiled, it was simple, and yet, clever.

"What did you do about the test?"

"That was easy, I did it in a day, but made out like it was really hard and took my time. I ate more on breaks in that room in one day than I did in a week in the bunk cells, and I needed the food, it helped me focus better when my stomach was full. At the end of the week, I handed her the papers filled in with what I knew already about the merle, and what could be a way of communicating with it. She bought it hook line and sinker, and rewarded me with a place down to Avalon, where I could work on the merle after a day of duty in her service. She gave me a thick black book into which to write up all my notes, and I was happy with that as I had little." Iona looked at her.

"So, she was looking into the merle even before she came down to Avalon?"

"She was more than looking, I got the impression she was already trying to communicate with it, and may have been successful, I found out later through Roack, they had spoken."

*I*t was a stunning revelation, and everyone stared at her transfixed unable to fully comprehend what Branna was saying, although Runestone and Amethyst did not appear to be that surprised. Iona watched carefully.

"Branna, tell me of the night when the merle came to you, and how you were infected." Branna sighed.

"I knew it was watching, so I rigged a trap, and used a copper rod as a conductor to draw it down to me, and into a large jar. It was not much, it was no bigger than my ink bottle, and I sealed it in a jar, and hid it away from the light. It fears the light, and it should, for I know that pure love has a light so strong it destroys it." She smiled at Ariel, and she gave a small smile back, both of them fully understood that. Iona thought about it.

"So, it was not inside you, it was in a jar." Branna gave a chuckle.

"The golden queen wanted it to kill me, it was long after I left Avalon I realised. She wanted me to write my findings and then let it kill me, and she would then come and take my findings and burn the house with me in it to remove all proof. The problem was Bridget sent her adopted daughter Ariel to me, and I fell hopelessly in love with her."

Ariel smiled, and Branna gave a wide grin to her, Ariel knew she was loving this, it was perfectly Branna, and she had missed her rebellious spirit. Branna chuckled.

"Ariel, the golden queen sent you to me hoping you would become infected and die like your mother did, but I knew that would never happen, because when we made love, I felt the power of your light, and I knew your mother had protected you in some way I did not understand. I could feel it… I felt a lot that night."

Ariel blurted out a laugh, as Branna giggled, and Ariel bit her lip, and tried to hold it in, she could see Bade's disapproving stare at her. Iona smirked, as she looked at Branna.

"You think she wanted Ariel dead?"

"Yes, she saw Bridget as an enemy, and knew what Ariel was up to. That cute corporal who collected the reports told me he found it strange, that all the other reports were taken to the main offices, but Ariel's were sent with a messenger straight to the queen on the moon realm, before being sent on to Florae. He told me for every ten sent, only eight ever came back, Florae was not getting the full truth, she was hiding the important stuff. I did not really care, I knew she was corrupt, if I had known what I know now, I would have told you Ariel. When they took you back to Florae, I was relieved, and that was why I planned to run, I wanted to find us somewhere safe. I did it, and lived such a glorious life in your caravan with you."

She smiled and Ariel smiled with her, the memories were flowing through her thoughts, and she loved how Branna was even naughty now, hanging in the air in the courts, she had always been drawn to her spirit of adventure. Iona understood the bond between them, and she gave a soft smile as she looked at Branna.

"May I ask, is love so powerful it destroys the darkness?" Branna looked Ariel directly in her eyes.

"It is, and it is glorious, it saved me, I was tied to a raven and yet it could not over power me, for the love in my heart was too powerful. The merle could only ever connect with Roack, it could never really take me, but because of Roack, it could influence my thoughts. It took me a long time to master that, and I fought hard to gain control of my mind. In that time, I did things I was not proud of, but once back in control, and when Ariel came to me, I gained a greater control. Ariel saved me, sadly, my family were consumed by it, because they were not full Fae, and they did things I am ashamed to admit. I was head of the family and to blame, and it was right I bore the shame of my family, for it was an error in my calculations that caused the pain that followed, and I regret that." Iona gave a sad sigh.

"Is there anything else you wish to say before you must return to your white lord?" Branna took a deep breath, and smiled at Ariel.

"I wanted to come, I wanted to put some things right. I wanted to see you one more time, I needed to see you and tell you that I still exist. I have not gone yet, and every day and moment I live in the darkness with your light in my thoughts. I am happy Ariel, I am happy to see you, I really wanted to, I wanted you to know I love you more than ever, and I always will. We never got to say goodbye, and as much as I hate that, I want to. Goodbye my love, live in our house for me."

She smiled as her eyes filled with tears, and Ariel nodded and stood up. She walked slowly towards her and smiled.

"Goodbye my love, I will always love you, my light will be with you."

Ariel leaned in, and kissed her softly, and Branna felt her mind spin, as she breathed her light inside her. She closed her eyes, and felt such warmth flow into her, as Ariel stepped back, she opened her eyes and smiled, Ariel gave her a soft nod.

"My light is with you." Ariel watched as Branna smiled, and then faded away.

"Bye!"

Her last soft words, echoed in Ariel's ears, and she smiled, and wiped her eyes on a small lace piece of cloth. Iona stood at her side.

"I am sorry, I never meant to hurt you, but her side of the truth needed to be spoken." Ariel sniffled, as she turned and looked into the eyes of Iona.

"I am not angry, I am grateful, you gave me something very precious, and I did not realise until she spoke to me in my mind, it gave us a chance to say what really mattered." Iona smiled.

"I had hoped you would talk in private using your Fae skills, I am glad you could, and her story has revealed more truth, and we needed that."

Ariel nodded and tried to smile, but her emotions were overwhelming her. Alder gave a cough.

"I fail to see how this proves you are the rightful queen." Iona gave a smile.

"I understand that Lord Alder, which is why I brought you all here. I aim to prove the truth has been hidden, and in doing so, do the one thing only a true queen can do." He smirked.

"Really, please do tell us what this thing only a queen can do is." Iona smiled a sweet smile, not unsimilar to her mother's.

"I can stand here and confront the full truth, no matter how unsavoury, and not fear being exposed, for a queen who fears being exposed, is not a queen. No Fae who fears exposure, is a true and loyal Fae."

Alder and the other members of the council all looked on unsure of what she was saying, she gave a little giggle as she looked at them, with the white star in her hand, she felt far more confident than she ever had in her life.

"My Lords and Ladies, you will see soon. For my next witness, I call Morgana of Cornwall." There were yet more gasps, and Jett sat still, but bit her lip, as she stared at Iona.

"This is becoming too much; she is making a mockery of all of us." Jade leaned over, and took her hand and gave it a squeeze.

"That is not who she is, and she would never do that, especially of Rowan and her father, she loves them too much, as she does us, and you know that Jett." Jett sat back as a young dark hair girl rose out of the floor, Jett frowned.

"Who the hell is that?" Una gave a titter, and leaned over Rafe.

"Jett, that is Morgana of Cornwall, that is the young girl who grew to become le Fey. That is what she looked like when she lived in Avalon, I knew of her then, and she was nothing like the Morgan we know." Iona looked at Morgana.

"Morgana, do you know me?" She shook her head.

"I am sorry My Lady, but no, I do not." Iona smiled.

"That is fine, you would not know me, although there is one person here you may know." She turned and pointed at Una. Morgana frowned as she leaned forward a little.

"Should I know her, she is sort of familiar, but I cannot say I do, what is this about and where am I?"

"This is the court of queens, and you have been summoned before us, to speak of your time in Avalon." She stiffened and looked at Iona.

"Why must I speak of that, I live alone and do not involve myself with others?" Iona smiled at her, her voice was soft and gentle.

"Morgana, you suffered injustices, and we wish to know about them, nothing more. We know you were targeted by the queen." She stepped back away from Iona.

"What do you want with me, I want no trouble, and the queen means to harm me?"

"Morgana, I want to show you something, will you watch and then tell me of it." She looked unsure.

"That time for me, has patches of lost thoughts, something happened to me, and parts of me were lost." Iona gave a smile.

"I know of what you suffered, but watch, and tell me of your thoughts." She looked unsure.

Behind Iona the cottage rebuilt itself as it did in Avalon, and Morgana saw herself as the door burst open, and Fagan swept in with his scythe, and swept it round, as Morgana looked him in the eyes.

"She is wrong, it was not me Fagan, I would never do that, I believed in Eve, I am innocent." His blade swept around and she disappeared as smoke funnelled up from the floor. Morgana looked distressed.

"I do not want to remember that, why would you show me that?" Everyone watched as Iona took a step forward.

"It is alright Morgana, that was a long time ago, and you are safe now, you have nothing to fear." Morgana shook her head, and laughed.

"You have never met the golden queen then. I have more to fear than you realise, that was Fagan, I thought he was my friend, I thought he of all people would understand, and yet the mighty golden queen clicked her fingers and in he ran to kill me." Iona nodded to her.

"Morgana, when that happened you dropped your veil, it was your only protection, why did you do that?" She shrugged.

"He was a mystic, I was innocent, I hoped he would see that and help me."

"You wanted him to look inside you, and see the truth of who you really were?" She nodded.

"She accused me of killing Eve, and it was not true, no one believed me. She just told everyone, and that was then seen as the truth, but she lied, it was not me, I was with Commander Stenlow. I was scared, the wails in the sky were terrifying. He told me to run home, and he would watch over me, but she appeared and tried to kill me, she told everyone she saw me do it, but I didn't. I tricked her, and jumped inside my cottage, but I was not fast enough, Fagan came in, and I had to take what I could, and leave. They burned my home down." Her voice cracked a little.

"It was my home, I owned it, Merlin gave it me for becoming a fellow of the Whitelines. I was true to my oath, and he knew how happy I was living there alone, so he gave it me, and they burned it down, because she ordered it." The tears filled her eyes, Iona felt her pain, and it was hard not to react.

"Morgana, Rhiannon accused you of the murder of Eleanor, Uther, and Eve." She gave a sob.

"It was not me, Merlin spoke up for me and proved it, as I was with him, it was the night he told me he would train me. I was innocent, but she would not believe me, and she told everyone I killed them, but it was not true." Iona looked at her as the tears rolled onto her cheeks.

"Morgana, we know it was not true, we know you told the truth." Iona lifted her hand, and the pictures changed. Morgana sat with Branna in the seats by the large fireplace of the castle in the Hidden Realm.

"Morgana, how are you, you have all of them out of the way, you have achieved your goal without taking a life, all there is left is the golden queen. Tell me, was it worth it, is your revenge sweet or bitter?" Morgana sat back in her seat, with a sigh. Her eyes lifted to Branna, and her voice was quiet and reflective.

"All I wanted was to stop them acting like gods and meddling in the lives of others, and I have. I listened to Merlin and I used my mind, not powers, simple thinking, and it outsmarted them all. Now I have them, they will never do to another what they did to my life, my parents and me, it matters not how I feel Branna, someone had to do it. It may sound crazy, but I miss my cottage, I know I have this castle, but that tiny little house, was all I had ever dreamed of, and Merlin gave it to me. I hated him for such a long time, but I am glad I did not kill him as I had planned. He was kind to me Branna, he taught me the powers I hold, I am now a fellow of the Whitelines, because of him, with this pendant to prove it. I have thought a great deal of late, I aim to finish his work, I have nothing left now my parents and my son are gone, and I do not want to rule an empire like the golden queen. I will go out into the world and bring help to those who suffer, and for as long as I can do that, I feel my life from now on will have value. It is what I wanted when I was twelve summers old, and I will do that now."

Morgana watched and it was clear, she remembered the moment, Iona gave her a small soft smile.

"You were a fellow of the Whitelines, and yet you trapped all of the Ruling Council, and then told Branna you wanted to continue the work of Merlin, can you explain that to me?"

Morgana looked around and everyone was watching her, her dark eyes scanned the faces, it was clear to her a good number believed what the queen had told them. She looked resolute as she faced Iona.

"The Ruling Council walked all over everyone, they killed my father, and helped that vile brute rape my mother. They supported a king who turned on them, and banned the Earth Faith, in favour of his new god. Can you imagine that, they supported a king who wanted to destroy the very faith that was dedicated to them? They cared for no one other than those they deemed fit to rule, and a lot of people died, because of what, they wanted it their way and no other? What was the point of giving man free will, and then taking it away demanding he did as they wished?" She looked angry, and it was clear it was a deeply held conviction within her.

"My father was a good man, he helped those all around us, our people admired and respected him, but because he did not want to be ruled over by them, and that brute desired my mother, they killed him and let Uther take her in any manner he saw fit. He was a brute and defiled her, she was a queen of a high Celt line, he was not fit to kiss her feet. I stopped them, I did not kill them, but I put them where no one would ever be hurt by them again, and I swore I would never let another council do that again. I do not apologise; the world of men was better without them." Iona looked at the room, they were silent, as Morgana wiped her eyes.

"So, Morgana, you trapped the council, and put them in the Hidden Realm, out of reach of anyone. Did you think about how long?" She nodded.

"Forever, they could not be trusted to do good. They acted moral, but they were not, many died when they did their acts of so called good. Their idea of helping was to dictate and remove those who opposed them, to place who they could have control over on a throne. They were all as bad as Rhiannon, so I sealed them away. I am a white raven, I walked the path Merlin placed me on, and I will continue his work." Iona smiled.

"You used little magic and outsmarted them, is that right?" Morgana nodded.

"Something like that, I did not hurt them, in a way I wanted to

protect them, I did not want them to follow Eve. I admired Eve, and I
believed in her, I was devastated that she died, I really did believe in
her, but even she did not understand how evil the golden queen was.
No one did, they all listened to her, they could not see how she used
everyone she met, and she hurt a lot of her own people." Una stood
up, and her eyes contained fire.

"That is not true. You placed my mother in a tube of glass, and you
syphoned her essence away and killed her, I know, I gave up the life of
a child to restore her. You are evil le Fey, and I can never forgive you."
Morgana looked panicked, and looked at Iona.

"That is not true, why is she saying that, I hurt no one, I only faced
Maud, and I did not want that, I was tired of death, it haunted my
life?" Her eyes filled with tears again.

*I*ona looked back at Una, and pointed at the floor, and the
pictures rose out of it.

"Te, hee, hee, Poor little Morgana lost and alone, a damaged brain,
and a burned out home."

Morgana felt a cold prickle run down her arms, as she scanned
through the dim corners of her room, she knew that voice, but it was
not possible.

"Maud?"

She felt the ice cold grip on her shoulders, lifted into the air, and
was dragged backwards, and slammed spread eagled into the wall,
and winced with the pain. Morgana felt panicked, she was stuck five
feet off the floor. She looked at her arms, nothing was holding them,
but they were pinned, as were her legs. She tried with all her might,
but she could not move, and then movement caught her eye, and she
turned to face forward and saw it.

The candle on the table flickered illuminating the open book,
and black smoke was rising out of it. Morgana pulled with all her
might, as she watched it forming, and it slowly crept off the table, she
knew exactly which form it would take. Maud appeared in a dusty
smoky form, her black elongated form, stretching back to the pages
of the book, like a writhing snake. She smiled that sick smile as she
approached, and Morgana pulled with all her might, and struggled
frantically, but she could not move. Maud advanced with a face filled
with hatred.

"Take my life, take my book, steal my spells and use my magic, little perfect raven, Branna's perfect pet, a half breed bitch who thought she was better than the rest. You pride yourself on your intelligence, well tell me now, who is the smarter one?"

Morgana looked down as Maud lifted her left hand, and Morgana's silver dagger slid off the table and flew into her hand. She gritted her teeth, and fought to free her bonds, and could feel the fear growing inside her, she was caught and could not get free, and she was starting to panic, as Maud came closer.

"So perfect, so pure, so unattached to a raven, Branna's pride and joy. She named you daughter, and replaced me, you owe me half breed, you took my bird."

She smiled another ugly smile, and then her face wrinkled as Morgana watched on helpless unable to move. Maud gazed up at her with utter hate.

"You want my bird, take her, but take her as all of us have."

She leaned back and laughed, as she lifted the knife, and held it up to the roof, and then started to chant. The words were dark and corrupted, and Morgana could not work them out as her mind panicked and struggled to try and get free. Above her in the tower, black clouds appeared and thunder rumbled, Morgana looked up, and suddenly understood what Maud had in mind, and she screamed.

"NO…. BRANNAAAAAAAAAAA!"

The room was silent, as Morgana fell to her knees and wept into her hands.

"Please no more…. I do not want this in my head any more, please I beg you, make it stop, I am tired of darkness, all I want is to be left alone."

Iona knelt down, and pulled her arms around Morgana as the pictures continued and Morgana screamed for her life as Branna tried to save her and failed, and on her knees, Morgana wailed into Iona.

*R*une stood up, and looked across the space, at Iona, she lifted her hand, snapped her fingers, and the pictures fell into the floor as Morgana wailed.

"Daughter, you have proved your point, let her go, send her back, we have seen the truth, it is enough." Iona stood up, and faced her mother.

"Is it Mother?" Behind her, the weeping young Morgana faded away, as Iona faced all of them, and Rune nodded at her.

"It is Iona, it is enough, your point is proven, nothing will be achieved by torturing a young girl more. She paid for what she did, she faced her White Lord as all of us will one day do. I too will be held accountable for my actions, as will everyone present. Your case is proven, and the case of how power corrupts is clear for all to see. You stood up for what you believed, and you faced your own truth, and proved beyond doubt that the Violet Stone will rule with truth, without fear. End this here, for nothing we can see now will add more to aid your cause." Iona nodded.

"Alright Mother, I trust in your wisdom, but I have one more thing I need to show." Iona waved her hand, and the large hall of Rhiannon came up. Rhiannon stood at the top of her steps.

"Well ambassador, what have you to say, has my request been carried out?"

There were gasps in the crowd as Alder walked with a smile down the hall towards her. The other members of the Council all turned and looked at him, as Alder shrank back in his seat. The pictures showed him smile to Rhiannon with pleasure.

"Ariel is under lock and key and bound by bracelets. They all believe that a line of dark Fae exists, and they will not be convinced of her innocence easily. The only problem is Elgin, he will not be swayed easily, even her good friend Lord Bade is only half believing in her innocence, your plan is working perfectly."

No one watching could believe their eyes. Iona lifted the white star, and flicked her wrist, and the pictures changed. Alder stood with Rhiannon in her crystal castle entrance as they looked out across the mirrored waters, Alder took a sip of his drink.

"See my glorious queen, one right word in the right place at the right time, and now everyone believes that Morgana murdered Eleanor, and Uther. We have all of them saying she is evil and she is now completely isolated with no help whatever. Even that bumbling idiot Fagan goes round to her place less, if she makes one wrong move, pounce on her, and then kill her, and everyone will worship you as their saviour." Rhiannon tilted back her head and laughed with a wild happiness.

"My dear Alder, you are wasted to Florae, they have no idea of how useful you can be, they should throw out that useless White Circle and put you in power, you have the right mind to rule." Iona flicked her hand and the pictures fell into the floor and she stared at

Alder.

"I am Violet Stone. I am the legitimate heir to the throne of Florae and the peoples of Fae of Earth. I have proven my abilities, and shown my people that I will rule from truth, tell me Lord Alder, where is your truth? I rest my case, and will not be judged by you, who has shown his disloyalty to my people, I will be judged only in the court of queens."

"NOT GUILTY!"

Iona's head snapped around, and she saw Gwendolyn White Circle. Iona turned to face her, and Gwendolyn gave a nod to her.

"I chose you Violet Stone, and in front of our people, I name you Queen. I did indeed hide my line from Rhiannon, because I knew there was someone in Florae in league with her, and I am disappointed to see it was you Lord Alder, for I knew your family well. They would hang their heads in shame if they were here now. I now know I was right to place my trust in the red stone, for through her, you gained protections and greater powers. All people here this day know I have named you Violet Stone to rule, and I trust in my brother to ensure it happens, for as Lord of the Isle, it is his duty to carry out the last wishes of the previous queen. Leave now and return to Florae, this court of queens is over."

The white light blasted up from the floor, and everything turned white, and moments later, they blinked as the light fell to the ground, Elgin turned and looked across the seats, but Alder was nowhere to be seen.

*A*lder fell to his knees as a figure in black tatty robes walked towards him over the large red stone marked on the floor, with a large black bird on his shoulder. Alder shook as Albanlin approached him, and lifted his hand towards his hood.

"Are you prepared to face your lord, Master Alder, and see the crimes that were created by your greed?" Alder fell to the floor shaking in terror, Albanlin leaned over him and slid back his hood.

"Look at me, and see your true self."

Alder looked up, and screamed at the top of his lungs, wails of terrifying fear, and then suddenly there was silence, and the black tatty robed figure faded away. The large bird pecked at something, swallowed it, and then with a squark, flew after its master.

The House of Scribes was filled with noise as people talked quickly, in hundreds of conversations, many of them not understanding much of what had happened to them. Elgin patted Bade on the shoulder, as he looked for Ariel, and Iona walked towards the large doors as they swung open. She stepped out into the fresh air and breathed in, her window opened, and she stepped through it, and with a faint flash, it closed and disappeared.

Chapter Twenty Four.

Dealing with the Truth.

*T*he House of Scribes was busy, and filled with the conversations of many. The people of Fae dwindled slowly over the hour, and Elgin had the staff prepare the guest meeting room, for all the high profile guests, and the Council of Elders all gathered to speak with each of the dignitaries. Ariel and Iona were nowhere to be seen.

For the group who once went under the name of Specialists, there was joy and some sadness, and a lot of talking and reflecting on the day's events and antics of the past. There were many quiet conversations, and Rune talked to many who gave her lovely compliments about her daughter, but deep inside she felt unsettled. Rune excused herself, and slipped quietly out of the room, and walked up the corridor and into the main hall, which was now back to normal, with just the long row of twelve seats at one end, and two large royal thrones at the other. She slowly crossed the hall lost in thought, and walked out onto the wide deck, turned slightly, and veered off towards the wooden railings.

Out in the air and breathing deeply, she gazed down the wide valley basin towards the sea, Florae was indeed a very beautiful place. She stared down the realm her eyes not really fixed on anything, as many memories flicked through her mind. Movement at her side alerted her, and she blinked and turned to see Una standing beside her, Rune breathed in the clean air.

"Was I wrong?" She turned her head to Una.

"Did I guide all of you wrong, and as a result persecute someone I should not have done? Should I have been more lenient and helped her, because if so, I was the one that led the charge to kill her?" Una took a deep breath.

"Today, really opened my eyes, I will not deny Rune, your daughter has challenged me much of late, and I have spent many nights in deep thought about so much of my life. I need time to think, but as I stand here with the centre of my circle, feeling you have as many doubts as I do, all I can say is this. Much of what happened took place a very long time before you came along, I was there, I am the only one left who was. Iona showed me that Morgan, was two people, Morgana the young isolated and lonely girl I knew, and Morgan, the dark and vicious person we dealt with together. It appears to me; they were complete opposites. Seeing Morgana suffer and be forcefully tied to a raven, deeply disturbed me, I felt her fear and pain, as I know you did. I would not wish that on anyone, it was cruel and vile, of that there is no doubt, and it is in that action we need to understand the truth of all of this." Rune leaned back onto the rail.

"Una, Morgana could have killed all of you, and yet she did not. In many ways when I heard that, I felt chills, because I had the same choice, and yet I killed first without questioning. You heard her Una, she vowed to never allow another council to interfere, and in that she was true to her word, she opposed us every step of the way."

"I do not believe it is that simple Rune, I think there is far more to this than we yet know. That was Morgana, and we faced Morgan, you know, three nights ago I sat lost in thought and I remembered sitting at home, listening to my parents at the table talking. It is strange, because there was so much clarity to my thoughts. My father was speaking of Morgana, and he expressed his concerns about the pressure he was putting on her. My mother believed she had some form of power gained from her mother's line, who were indeed powerful druids, and it appeared clear to both of them, her mind was far stronger than most men. My father was afraid that if he was not careful her mind could break, but she refused to stop, and worked harder to master the Whitelines, he really admired her, I even think he cared for her." Rune gave it a moment of thought.

"So, what are you saying, Morgana injured herself and her mind fractured, and that was what created who we know as Morgan?" Una turned to her, and her eyes sparkled with life.

"Think about it, my father was concerned the Whitelines would harm her, what if the addition of the black was simply too much? Rune, she was half mortal, even Branna admitted it consumed her family because they were not Fae enough to fight and control it." Rune gave a sigh.

"That does not help me Una, if that is true, then Morgana was a victim. We were supposed to be the ones who stand for those who could not fight for themselves. Think about it, that is like Billy being trapped inside Mordred, even Robbie did better than I did. He released Billy and let him go free, what if I could have freed her from the raven, would she have reverted back to Morgana, could I have saved her, wasn't that what Eve understood, which is why she was so upset?" Una gave a sigh.

"Honestly, I do not know, what I do know is that your daughter was destined to find the truth and show it for what it was. Rune, no matter what we may feel, I think she was right. I hate it, but she showed us the truth, and no one is feeling at ease at the moment, and we have to all now figure this out. Rune, she will be a queen, and if you ask me, a bloody powerful one. She stood in that court, and yes, I will not deny, she really angered me, and yet I looked at her, and she stood firm, she did not waver, she was bloody strong, and a tad intimidating. I know that feeling well, I lived with my mother, and she was the bloody same, trust me, I loved her more than anyone realises, but at times, she could be bloody terrifying." Rune nodded, and stared out over Florae.

"None of this sits well with me, I cannot look at Robbie, I could feel the turmoil inside him. Honestly Una, I feel clueless, and I am struggling for direction."

"I say, we finish up here and head back to Loxley, this is their realm and they need to deal with whatever it is they need to do. Their Council of Elders does not feel very wise at the moment, and they need to sort that out. Rune, go home, hug your kids and take some time, all of us need to walk through this with clear heads, none of us are thinking very straight at the moment. Wilson and I will head back with you if that is alright?" Rune smiled.

"You are always welcome, you know that, and to be honest Una, it will help to have you there." She leaned off the rail, and looked back at the House of Scribes.

"Okay Rune, let's gather the troops and head home, we have some goodbyes to make, and then we will head back to the land of sanity." Rune gave a giggle.

"Una, it has our kids in it, there will never be sanity." She smiled.

"I get cuddles, that is fine by me at the moment, I could use all the extras I can get."

With small giggles, they headed inside and rounded everyone up. It took a long time to finally get everyone assembled, Robbie and Rowan were especially interested in the archives, and got the full tour from Tila. Rafe was very interested in the weapons, and spent a great deal of time looking at the weapons with Jett, Amethyst sat quietly with Elgin and discussed much of what had happened.

Elgin requested he recalled Ambassador Sedden from Avalon, as he wanted to replace Alder on the council, and in return, he suggested a scribe named Eloise, who had trained with Ariel and Tila. Amethyst agreed to it, and was grateful to him, as they stood, she smiled.

"If I may say so Master Elgin, as much as I feel you enjoy your retirement, I would think Queen Violet Stone, I feel, would be much more at ease if for now at least, you took back your former role, and returned to lead the council. Stay at least for her initial ceremonies, I do believe that would serve the people of Fae best." He gave a sigh, but agreed.

"It appears that these days, I cannot go fast enough to outrun the position. It will have to be decided by the members, there are time honoured traditions to be upheld, and I feel, it is time that was noted and we returned to the ways of our creed. Any modernisation proposals will be reviewed by the queen when she is seated, of which I have one or two to suggest."

After many interruptions, and tracking a lost Jade who had snuck off to see the work of a Fae smithy, Rune finally gathered everyone together, and opened her window after many long goodbyes. As the group walked into Loxley, Amethyst said her farewells to the council, and headed back to Avalon with her honour guard, and a very happy Vivian, who it appeared had acquired several new dresses, from some of the Fae dress makers. Florae fell silent as the door to the house closed, and the council sat lost in thought in their meeting room.

Peace had returned to the realm of the Fae of Earth, and for now, in the tall A frame houses all over the realm, people sat in quiet reflection, as they talked of the past, and waited for a future that was unwritten. Without really understanding, the power and impact of her findings, Iona had brought a truth into the light that had challenged every leader across many realms. Deep below Avalon, Amethyst looked into her table of power and sought the truth of what had happened, Ariel sat alone in her garden below the ancient tree lost in thought, and occasionally wiping her eyes. Jade sat alone in her workshop, and Robbie walked through the trees, his mind on events from his past.

Sapphire stood high on the cliff tops a short way from her home, as the wind lifted her long hair, streaked with fine grey lines, a mark of a time of great pain that had been unwritten, and Runestone sat alone watching images on her table, and going back through the past as she looked into all she had done. Lord Thorn walked through the woodlands of Florae, at the side of Evangeline, as they quietly talked of the future, and what was to be expected of his sister.

In all that had happened, one person had been absent, for she had not been seen for some time. The white cloak brushed the floor, as it flowed down from her shoulders and underneath her long snow white hair. She stopped at the wide circle of black sand and looked across it, her voice was soft and gentle, and filled with kindness, as she saw what she had been searching for.

"You cannot return to her here my child, she can no longer walk here. You were pushed out by the dark force, and in doing so, your mistress was lost to the darkness. Come, all of her memories of that time, are still locked inside you, and we need to find her, and put you back where you belong."

She smiled, then crouched down as the tiny grey looking figure came slowly out from under the leaves. Her long tatty hair was caught up with leaves and small twigs. Stephanie gave her a beautiful smile, and held out her hand.

"I feel, we shall take our time and get you a little more presentable, I do believe a comb or brush would suffice. I am Stephanie, some call me Mother Whiteline, what name did she give you?"

The shy and nervous little sandling came slowly forward, and took Steph by the hand, and looked up at her with large sad eyes, she blinked twice, and Stephanie smiled.

"Lottie, what a beautiful name, she named you after the first true love of her life, she never did recover from him, even though she hid it so well from others. I shall share with you a secret, Lord Lot loved her deeply until his dying day, and often sat alone remembering his time with her, what a shame, it was such a powerful love, they really were perfectly matched. Well Lottie, I must say, I am very pleased to have finally found you, it has taken a very long time because you have no idea how much your mistress needs you now. You contain much of her love and her courage, and she really needs you back with her, before she can move on. She is with my master, so we shall go to him, and reunite her and you together forever."

The little figure blinked rapidly and shook her head as her legs trembled, and Steph understood, her bright green eyes were filled with love as she smiled.

"That part of her is gone, all that remains is who she was before that time, the true Morgana, not the one clouded by darkness, you have nothing to fear, she is like me, she has some of my powers, and is a fellow of the Whitelines. She needs you Lottie, we must go to her." The little sandling blinked, and Steph smiled.

"Come on then."

Holding her hand, Stephanie walked slowly down the long path, talking quietly to the small sandling, she gave a little smile, as she noticed a little black colour flow into the hair of Lottie.

"I feel a new era is upon us, as the age of dreams ends. We face a new age my little friend, the time of the Violet Stone is upon us, and the new Age of Light, for it will shine the truth over everything." Both of them faded away, and the Chimerical Forest sung to the sounds of birds and insects.

*E*lgin stood in the doorway of the council meeting room, and viewed the scene, at his side stood the round figure with grey hair and glasses of Lord Sedden, he was highly skilled in the affairs of the realms and dealings with other dignitaries. He gave a bow, as Elgin introduced him as a possible candidate for the council's newly vacant seat.

The members viewed him with approval, he had been considered many times in the past, and so it was not like a completely new candidate was being offered, and very quickly the vote was made, and he was welcomed in. Once business was concluded, Elgin turned to leave, and Bade stood up.

"Excuse me Master Elgin, but there is still the matter of who will lead the council." Elgin turned and viewed the room, they appeared to be in no rush to suggestions.

"You know how this works, discuss, and then vote, it really is up to you, I am quite sure Alder has not had that detrimental effect on your abilities to unite behind a leader. I will go with the majority, when you have selected, let me know." Bade fidgeted, and his feet shuffled on the floor a little.

"Master Elgin, the thing is we have done that, and we all have only one candidate in mind, which is you." Elgin gave a sigh.

"My Lords and Ladies, you honour me deeply, but I retired to sit back as an ordinary member. My great age has its limits." Bade nodded in agreement, but looked at Elgin in an almost pleading manner.

"My Lord, we have considered that, please hear us out." Elgin gave a nod.

"Never let it be said I did not give time to my friends and colleagues, state your case Bade."

Bade breathed a sigh of relief, and looked around at the others who all gave a nod of their approval for him to speak up for them, he turned back to his master and mentor.

"If it pleases you My Lord, we ask you serve to ensure the new queen's arrival. What we propose is a small term of office, many of us here have been shaken by the events of recent times. We feel for now, it would be prudent to place the council in steadier hands. We all need some time to adjust, and once our new Queen Violet Stone takes the seat, we will then consult on a replacement for you. We also propose that during this time, Mistress Tila take on the role of Mistress of Scribes, she is indeed highly efficient as trained by yourself and Ariel. To be frank, she has exceeded all expectations of all of us, we feel in time, she too should be considered for a council seat. Just not yet, we need to calm her and the waters first." Elgin gave a little titter.

"Well, I know for a fact, she will feel a great honour to know she is thought of with such high praise, and you are quite right Bade, she is exceptional in her duty, and does remind me very much of a young Ariel. I will also add that you should consider approaching Ariel, she would be an asset to this body as you well know?" Many of the council all nodded in unison, Bade smiled, he knew better than to hope.

"My Lord, as much as I would wish that, for I agree with you wholeheartedly, I think we both know, Ariel will never return to the full service of this house, and if I may add, I do not blame her My Lord. As we all know, there was a time when this house conspired against her, it is a source of great regret to all of us, for we were the ones misguided by the folly of others. We all appreciate her services to the house and her queens, and she will always remain the Mistress of the House to all of us, but we also are aware, she will never take her seat beside us." Elgin gave a slight nod.

"I feel you are right, and you show greater wisdom in this matter. I will take on the role to ensure the smooth transition of a new queen, and then I will finally leave the post and the council for good, but I will do it only on one condition." Bade frowned.

"What would that be My Lord?" Elgin smiled.

"Bade I am getting old, I will fulfil the role, only if you will stand at my side as support, and as my second." He was momentary lost for words, Cullen smiled, and gave a nod.

"I will second that My Lord Elgin, you show great wisdom."

Bade turned to look at Cullen and the others, and they all gave a gentle nod, he turned back to Master Elgin and smiled.

"My Lord Elgin, it would be my greatest honour of this house to serve beside you as second." Elgin gave a cheeky smile.

"It will not be easy, I drive hard, ask Tila, but all things considered, I believe we have a full council and leader, I will message the future queen and let her know."

Telling Tila was not easy, they had to find a quiet place, and then Bade broke the news, and she exploded into tears and wept with joy. She was nowhere as near as exuberant as they had thought, and she went down on one knee, with tears in her eyes and swore her oath with great pride, and restraint. Once done, she ran out of the house whooping and screaming, to go and find Crystal, to tell her the good news, and peace drifted again over Florae.

*T*he days slipped past with no sign of Iona. Jett and Rafe returned to their castle, Una left for Avalon, and the house returned to normal. Well, almost normal, it was far quieter than it had been, Robbie was especially quiet. When Rune went to bed, he was always asleep, and when she woke each morning, he was already gone, and she sat for several days in silence, sat below the house staring at pictures rising from her table of her times with the Specialists.

Even the children were subdued, and nowhere near as loud as they normally were, and she could not remember when Robbie last spoke to her, and it was eating her up inside. It was late, the children were in bed and she was feeling tired and emotional. She lifted her empty cup and walked up the steps, back into the house, the door was open, and she walked over to slide it shut. As she looked at the door, she noticed Robbie stood down by the merc, his hands in his pockets and his hair down, as his shirt flapped open in the breeze. Rune put her cup down, walked out of the door, down the steps, and through the garden and the open gate.

She walked slowly and quietly, she had done this so many times before in her life, and could remember so many occasions from her life with him. She stopped, and took a breath, her voice was almost a whisper.

"Robbie." He turned to see her as she stood feeling insecure and alone in the falling darkness, he looked tired and worn, she took a small step forward, her voice low.

"Was I wrong, have I hurt us, am I to blame for our past mistakes? If I am, please do not ignore me, because it is tearing me apart, I want to fix this, I want us back as we were, and I don't know what to do."

Her tears dripped onto the grass and violets sprung up everywhere, he looked at her with sad eyes, and tried to smile. His voice was soft and loving.

"It is not you, Rune, I just have so much to think about, it weighs heavy on me." He opened his arms, and she lurched into them and wept on his shoulder.

"I thought I had made such big mistakes that it had damaged us, Robbie I can take anything, nothing frightens me, but this, this silence between us is tearing me apart." He pulled her close and held her tight.

"Rune, it is nothing to do with us, this is something I need to think about. That is all, and it is stuck in my mind. I hated what Iona did, but I have to admit, she was right to do it. Rune, I have always stood for what I thought was the truth, I taught her that, hell, I have taught all my kids that, but she showed clearly, I did not know the real truth, and in that I have questioned everything."

Rune gave a sniffle and pulled out of his shoulder, and looked at him, as her eyes glistened with her tears.

"Robbie, I feel the same, were we wrong to do what we did? Morgan was a victim of a cruel twist, should I have saved her instead of killing her. Could I have reached in and tore out her darkness, and brought her back to the side of the light? Robbie if that was possible, I should have done it, but she was hurting all of us, I felt I had to fight her."

He gave a small smile and gently stroked her damp hair from her face, she was so powerful, a force of nature and life, and yet at times, he looked at her and saw that shy quiet girl he fell so deeply in love with. Her eyes were bright and filled with life, this was the Runestone that captured his heart all those years ago, she had not gone away, she had not got lost in the power, she was simply Runestone, and the young girl he loved. He gave a sigh.

"Rune, that is the question I need to answer, not only about le Fey, but also about Billy." She frowned.

"Billy… Robbie, you gave him his life, you let him walk free, how can you even doubt yourself; you did what I should have done with Morgan?" He gave another long sigh.

"Did I? Rune, he has a daughter who has never known him because of me, did I have the right to stop that? I looked at our daughter who came across very much like her mother, and acted like a true queen, she even taught me the meaning of my own words. Rune, she is my daughter, and I love her deeply, you have no idea how much I am going to miss her, shouldn't Billy have the same right as me?"

"Robbie, he could never return here, oh hell, the Specialists would rip him apart. Billy can never come back to Loxley, we all knew that long before you banished him, not one of us would have tolerated him." He lifted his eyebrows.

"Really… Yet the Sage would be welcomed with open arms? I am no fool Runestone Sapphire, I worked it out, a man of Loxley stands out, even when he hides behind a mask. I know of his deeds; I know what he did in our cause to repay his wrong doings." She leaned back looking surprised.

"You do?" He smirked.

"You are not quite as clever as you thought, soldiers talk. Sapphire is good, so is Louisa, but neither of them could bluff me that well, just Tila's explanation of the masked man told me straight away. Rune, his behaviour, the things he said, the way he organised his men, those are things we learned side by side, they were the things he could never hide from a lord of Loxley." She smiled at him.

"Wow, I am actually really impressed, and to be honest, I find it a bit of a turn on, your clever side is very attractive." She giggled, as she slipped out of his arms.

"If you two are going to take off your clothes and do weird things with each other, just so you know, I am stood right here, and I really do not want to see that." Rune gave a sigh, and turned to see Tegan.

"What now?" She shrugged.

"Lania is upset, and she has been crying, she says she had bad dreams again." Rune smiled at Robbie, and turned.

"Okay, I am coming." Tegan nodded, and pointed at her dad.

"Sorry… You know how she gets; they really scare her?" He nodded, and walked up to her and slipped his arm around her shoulder.

"I know, it is a violet line thing, all of you have been through it." Tegan nodded.

"Yeah, I feel sorry for the little weed, it is pretty scary." He pulled her close, and she slid her arm around him.

"You two are alright aren't you, I saw the violets, she does not cry often?" He smiled.

"We are fine, something came up from something your sister did, it has ruffled a few feathers, and we are sorting it out."

"Yeah, I get that, big sisters can be like that. You know Dad, if you think about it, her cabin will go to waste if someone is not in there keeping it heated?" Robbie gave a chuckle, as he looked at her and she smiled.

"You are good, there is no doubt, but alas my dear daughter, you are of an age that I will not allow out of the house, until I know you can cope properly." She appeared pleased.

"So, what you are saying is, if I look the part and do all my chores, and act more responsible, you will build me one too?" Robbie frowned.

"No, that is not what I said at all." She grinned.

"No, but admit it, just for a second you considered it?"

Robbie laughed for the first time in days, as he walked up the grass with Tegan, and headed back to the house to sit with his youngest, who he knew at some point would need him.

*T*wo hours later with Gailania settled and once again asleep, Robbie slipped into bed beside Rune, and closed his eyes with a sigh of relief. The bed moved and he opened one eye, and saw her facing him, her eyes twinkling in the dark.

"What?" She smiled and slid up close.

"I was thinking."

"Oh dear!"

Rune slid over him, sat on his waist and looked down at him, he smiled and looked at her toned body. She had hardly changed, even after having their children, she looked the same as she did when they first got together. She smiled at him.

"Why don't you talk with Alice, she will be here soon. Robbie, you and her knew him better than anyone else, and you know what she is like, she talks sense in a way that always helps you?"

He understood and she was right, Alice did have a way of talking to him that felt like plain speak. He had to admit, he had not seen her in a while, it would be nice to spend some time with her. He looked at her and she was still watching him.

"What?" She gave a sigh.

"What do we do Robbie, were we wrong?" He shook his head.

"No… I have thought about what you said as I sat with Lania, and no Rune. The way I see it, she was probably a decent person, and then that awful thing happened to her. I think from that moment onwards, she was a different person, I am not sure, let us say for arguments sake, one Morgan was light, and the other was dark." Rune nodded.

"The dark was evil and had to be stopped, I can understand that. The problem is Robbie, she did not start off that way, Morgana of Cornwall appeared to be a good person, I mean, come on Rob, if we had been alive then, we would have stood with her." He nodded.

"Yes, we would, and that is the point Rune, we were not, it was long before we got dragged into all this. The darkness took her, no matter how sad what happened was, and I hated seeing that, it changes nothing, she was no longer that person. If you ask me, maybe the darkness unhinged her mind, I am not sure, all I know is, she and her son wanted us dead, and we stood up to stop that." Rune gave a sigh and nodded softly.

"Do you think I could have saved her, because if I could have I would?" He shook his head.

"Why do you ask, you already know the answer to that?" She frowned as she looked at him.

"How, I have been sat for days trying to answer it?" He slid his hands up the side of her waist, feeling her warm skin.

"Rune, she was tied to a raven, you could cut the connection, but you could not destroy the raven, without releasing the merle into this realm, it is why you asked the White Lord to help. No matter how much you think you could have saved her, the truth is, you couldn't, not without risking everyone else. The only person who could have saved her was Branna, and she was not fast enough, after that, Morgan was doomed to her fate. You removed her the only way you could, you stepped back, and let the White Lord deal with her. Rune, you keep saying you killed her, but you didn't, he took her, and we have no idea what happened to her. If we can be blamed by any for what we did, all they can do, is call us for stopping her, after that, it was out of our hands."

It made sense, and she knew that he was right. There was no way they could have prevented her from going dark, and they had to deal with her as she was. He was right, even then all they did was face her and stop her, it was to a degree the white lords call, and he made it for them. She gave a sigh of relief, and looked down at him and he smiled.

"Feel better?" She nodded and smiled.

"Yeah, you make a lot of sense, I got lost in things for a while, but you really made a lot of sense." He smiled and slid his hands up her front, and she shuddered and then giggled.

"Rune?"

"Hmmm!"

"The kids are asleep." She gave a little giggle and reached back for the covers.

"Hmm, I was thinking the same thing… Oh, Robbie."

She pulled at the covers, and they came over them both and she giggled, quietly and breathed in sharply, then gave a little happy moan.

Chapter Twenty Five.

Starting Over.

*A*cross the cliff tops from Tintagel Castle, next to the old collapsed church, stood an old green heavy canvass tent, that flapped in the wind. Inside were a pile of messed up blankets, a thick book, some quills and bottles of ink. Around the other side of the church on the seaward side, Iona stood and looked at her work, as her hair blew around her shoulders, and flapped round into her face.

She was dressed in woodman's clothing, of tight heavy canvass pants, with the thick padded long waistcoat, and an old green shirt of her dad's. She stood back and admired her work, she felt it was enough, now she had laid the last stone. For four days, she had laboured hard, and had cut away all of the brambles, and pulled out all of the weeds. After erecting two large stones from the ruin of the church, she had then paved all of the site, and built low dry stonewalls to protect three sides of the space she had created.

Before her, stood four stones, one which was already there and she had cleaned up, which belonged to Victor of Cornwall, and a new one, on which was inscribed, 'Igraine, Queen, Wife, and loving Mother.' To the left side of them was Medraut's grave, and next to that was another stone, on which was inscribed, 'Morgana of Cornwall, Loved Daughter and Mother, Saviour of her people.' The whole of the area between the walls, had been paved and was clear of all plant life, apart from a small bunch of wild flowers, Iona had placed in front of Morgana's marker. Iona had charmed the flowers as Albanlin had done at Igraine's tomb in Avalon. Iona looked down, and spoke quietly.

"It is all I can do as the future line of those who wrong you. It is little in way of amends for your suffering, and I have no idea where your remains are. Morgana, here you are remembered as a family, and I feel that would matter to you. Few live in these parts, yet from this day on, if anyone walks by, they will know your name and that you were important in these parts. I hope it is enough."

Iona lowered her head, and closed her eyes for a moment, and she could see her vision of Morgana stood in this very same place crying, many years ago. She tried to clear her thoughts and spoke from her heart.

"My Lord Hearne, hear me, just a simple woodsman. I know Morgana is not laid to rest here, but I ask you look out for her, and when you find her, protect her. She was not always the evil we all grew to know, and in her heart, I believe there was kindness, for she protected and looked after the young child Ursula, and spared her from the darkness. I realise I am not yet anointed, but I would consider this a great personal favour to a queen of Fae, of which, I will repay you at some future point. Hearne protect her." Iona opened her eyes, and bowed to the graves.

"Fare thee well, Victor, and your family, may you all find better days to reunite in." Iona turned, to see the white cloaked figure stood silently watching her, she smiled.

"Your words held great honour, I found it touching… How are you granddaughter, I believe you have made quite a stir?" Iona smiled.

"I could use a family member who is not angry with me at the moment." Steph smiled.

"Then you have found one." Steph walked up, pulled her close, and gave her a hug.

"This is a nice tribute Iona, I feel having spoken with my high lord, she would be happy to know someone did this for her." Iona looked back at the small space within the stone walls.

"All she ever wanted was to be left alone with her family, and when that was taken from her, she simply wanted to live in her cottage. I am not sure anyone really understood that about her. I mean, yes, she was the daughter of a queen, but she did not care about the title, that was always their preoccupation, not hers. The cottage was her world, like my cabin has been to me, it literally was her greatest possession. She valued the life she had there above everything, being independent, and self reliant was the life she cared about. I understand that Grandmother, I feel the same way, the life I have lived is the reason I can stand on my own two feet as a queen."

Steph stood as Iona took a breath, and then Iona took Steph by the hand, and walked her slowly around to the tent. Steph recognised the tent; Robbie had used it a few times in the early days on the moors of

York to get out of the wind.

"I feel your life and Morgana's have a few parallels. I can understand why you felt you must do this. Maybe others do not see it, but I can, and in a strange way, I am glad that you have." Iona crouched down, and threw more wood on the fire so she could boil a pan of water, to brew a tea.

"I think we do have many similarities, all except one, I have the life she wanted. I have my family around me, so in my times of deep sadness or loneliness, I have a place I can go for comfort. No matter which way you look at her story, the Ruling Council took that away from her, and in that one aspect of Morgana's life, I agree with her." Iona stood up, and looked at Steph.

"They were wrong Grandmother, and it should never be allowed to happen again. The heirs of all long past, should never have been allowed to choose the right course for man. I agree with the White Lord, I understand why he stood back and allowed Morgana to take the council and seal them away. Like me, he agreed with her, he saw what they didn't, he saw their lack of compassion." Steph smiled at her, and nodded her head.

"I do believe you are right, I know my father suffered, because in the end he realised what had been done, and he felt great guilt." Iona knelt down, and swung her pan over the fire to boil.

"That is why he lived, he tried to undo some of what he did. He made her his assistant, defended her with Rhiannon, and most importantly, he gave her the cottage. I am not certain he ever really understood the importance of that one act, for her it must have been like giving her Camelot. She suffered so much with Rhiannon, and her biggest insecurity was the cottage belonged to Merlin, that must have been so frightening for her." Steph frowned at her.

"I am not sure I follow, in what way was that frightening, she was protected?" Iona stood up, and gave a small smirk.

"Grandmother, they convinced your father that it was alright to help Uther rape her mother. Can you imagine how terrifying it must have been to think at any moment, Rhiannon could convince Merlin to throw her out of the only place she felt safe? Think about it, every trip home to the castle, she risked getting caught on route and murdered by Rhiannon's men, the cottage was the only place she was safe. Your father will never understand what a huge act of kindness he did in that one moment, he literally handed Morgana her greatest freedom."

Suddenly, Steph understood, and marvelled at how Iona had worked out everything. She was completely blown away, she had thought of this often, and yet even with her white powers, she had never spotted what was the most obvious aspect of all of her story, she gave a smile, and nodded slowly at Iona.

"You are really gifted, and truly a queen Iona Violet, for no other would spot that so easily, and yet, it makes perfect sense." Iona watched as the pan started to bubble.

"It was no huge feat to see it, Rhiannon certainly did, which is why when she had her chance, she took it and ordered the cottage burned down. I think out of everything she did, that was by far the cruellest, she knew Morgana was innocent, and yet she did it anyway."

Iona poured the water onto the two cups with fine cloth bags of tea inside them, and lifted one up and handed it to Steph. Steph stood swirling her cup to mix the tea as she thought about it.

"You say she knew Morgana was innocent, Iona, how could she?" Iona sipped her tea.

"I have thought about it a lot, and two things appear obvious to me. The first was the distance Morgana was from the place Eve died, Rhiannon arrived as Eve was down on the floor and still alive. Think about it, you have been there, Morgana was so panicked, she ran on her legs, when she could have jumped, and she was almost home. That was a great distance, there is no way she could have done it as quickly as Rhiannon implied, she chose to point the finger, for no other reason than she looked like Branna. The second thing was the manner in which Eve died, that was very advanced Fae magic, even with her mastery of the Whitelines, Morgana was no way near advanced enough to make that potion. Rhiannon knew it must have been a pure Fae, and because it was her invention, a Fae she let into her library. I would imagine it was a short list, and we all know, Morgana was never on it. Rhiannon knew Branna was back, and she was the shadow Sequana talked of, because she had other spells there known only to her, and one, was the shadow being. Ariel from what she told me showed Branna how to jump great distances, but to become the shadow being, that is not Fae of Earth, it was Rhiannon's invention."

Steph sat on the grass with her cup, and was amazed at what she was hearing. Iona had it all worked out, and she was right, the truth was revealed in a way that was shocking to know, because with hardly trying, she saw what Gwendolyn never had. It was right there in front of her, and yet the White Circle, known for her vast skills, had completely missed what was glaringly obvious.

"I have to admit Iona, you have figured something out all of us should have seen, and yet we have not." Iona smiled, and nodded.

"My dad is the real genius, he was the one that taught me, the simplest of things to do, was hide in plain sight. When you understand that and apply it to Rhiannon, you see her truly for what she is, I think my dad is pretty amazing." Steph giggled.

"I think you are right." She chuckled as she sipped her tea.

"So, what is next?" Iona leaned back on the grass in front of her tent.

"I am going to pack up here now I have done what I came here to do, and then I want to go back to Florae. They have had time, so I want to talk to Master Elgin, I do like him, I feel I can trust him. I want to get to know Florae better before I am crowned, and then I want to head home and finish writing her story. I am still seeing images from her life, and more of the puzzle fits with them, so I will continue until I am done." It made perfect sense to Steph, Iona smiled.

"How come you are here, were you checking up on me for mum?" Steph looked at her and smirked.

"No, I think you are old enough now to make your own way, and anyhow, your mother has many other means, you may not feel it, but trust me, she knows you are safe. No, I was here dropping something off for my lord, something he needed, and I felt your presence, and yes, I am very nosey like my father."

Iona nodded, and understood how the Whitelines worked, she knew Steph would never give her the full story. They sat for a time and talked, and once Steph finished her drink, she hugged Iona and walked away, and faded into the distance. Iona turned and threw what was left of her drink on the fire, and then began packing up her camp.

*T*wo hours later she arrived in Florae and walked up to the house, and at the bottom of the steps she was challenged by the guards. She looked up the steps with mud on her face, and smiled.

"Am I to be challenged every time I walk in the realm I will rule?"

The guard was mortified as he looked closer, and realised who the mud covered woodsman was. He apologised continuously as he led her to the Royal Apartments. Iona thought it was quite funny and giggled as she walked in, and was greeted by Evangeline.

Iona bathed, which she needed, and dressed in clothing more akin to a queen, and then sat with Master Elgin, and her day continued with talk of her realm, and the results of her revelations, and the changes to the council. She decided to spend the night, and had a meal as a guest of the council, and for her first time in Florae, she got a small glimpse of what her life would be like as a queen. By the end of the night, she knew all of her council by name, and relaxed in a large soft bed of the guest room, and was asleep in minutes. Elgin sent word with Sapphire to Runestone, so she was aware of her daughters' location.

*T*he following morning, Iona woke earlier to find all of her woodsman clothing washed, dried, and pressed neatly in a pile. It made her laugh as she walked through into her main room, and found the table laid and two staff ready to serve her. After her meal, she spent the day with Sapphire, who gave her the tour, much to the excitement of those she met. Sapphire found it amusing as Iona stopped and asked people questions about their lives, and way of life. Most of them were lost for words, this had never really happened before, and they were delighted to show her their gardens, and talk about their animals.

It created quite a stir, so much so, that long after she had left the realm, polished purple stones would appear, stuck to the posts of the steps to the house, with pine resin. It was a token to show the queen had visited their residence, of which Tila had the largest, as Iona had eaten a meal with her. Iona stayed for an extra day, and visited Sora, to see Gwynfor, and personally thank him for all he had done. Like all visitors, she got to walk alone on his beach, and it reminded her greatly of Ariel's story of when she stayed here with Gwendolyn.

The next day, Iona returned home, she opened her window in her bedroom and stepped out, and put down her bag. After changing her clothes, she made a coffee, and sat at her table and drank it, as she tried to find the words she needed to talk to her parents. It could not be put off, and she unlocked her door, and stepped out to see the house twenty yards away, and her father stood down near the mere in the distance.

*I*t was time to face the music, and so she took a deep breath, and walked down the side of the house, and onto the wide expanse of grass that led down to the waterline, and her father. Iona walked closer than she thought would and stopped, up at the house Rune leaned on the side of the door and watched, as Iona took a nervous step forward.

"Dad… Can we talk?"

Robbie turned, and she saw the dark lines under his eyes and felt guilty. He looked at her and tried to smile.

"You are home then, are you going to drop another bomb on me and leave again?" She gave a sigh, and shook her head.

"I would like to explain, you always taught me I should let someone explain themselves." He nodded at her; his dark eyes fixed on her.

"You know, I have never once had to discipline you, I have thought a great deal about that over the last few days." Iona shrugged.

"I have never wanted to disappoint you, and yet now I feel that I have, and I would like to make amends… Dad, I will be leaving soon, I don't want to leave with bad air between us." He nodded gently.

"I understand that Iona, I will not deny, what you did to defend yourself shocked me, it has resonated deeply within me, and brought back a lot of memories."

Iona swallowed hard, trying to hold back her tears, and she took another step forward as she shook her head slowly.

"I never wanted to hurt you, Dad you must know that? You and mum are my world, I love you both so very deeply."

Her tears ran down her cheeks and dripped onto the grass, and tiny white daisies edged with pale purple, sprang up out of the ground where they landed, he saw them and gave a sigh, she was so like her mother, he looked up at her tear filled violet eyes.

"Iona, I am not angry, I know what you did was right, the truth should always be told. Hell, I have taught you and brother and sisters that all your life." She swallowed hard as she looked at him.

"Then why do I feel you are disappointed in me, because I do Dad, I feel it?" He smiled at her.

"What you feel is my disappointment in myself, not in you." She gave a sniffle and frowned.

"That makes no sense to me Dad, no daughter could wish for a better father." He gave a sigh, this was not easy for him, he took a deep breath.

"Iona, a long time ago, I had a choice to kill an enemy, or let him live." He frowned as he tried to think of the right way to tell his daughter, she nodded.

"Yeah, Billy, I know Dad, I saw it all."

"What, that is not possible, you were not born?" She smiled.

"Not at the time, but I was inside mum, and she was connected to her table and her sisters. I was connected to her, and I saw everything she did." He frowned at her.

"Is that even possible, can you even remember that far back to inside the womb?" She nodded.

"Apparently I can, I have no idea how it works, I just see stuff and remember it." He gave a sigh, and shook his head.

"Oh hell, one knows stuff, and now the other one sees stuff, no wonder I am so bloody confused all the time." Iona smiled at him; he could be so funny at times.

"Dad, for what it is worth, I think you did the right thing." He looked up at her, and she could see he was struggling with it all.

"Did I though? Iona he is Jessie's father, and I took him away from her, and banned him from Loxley. I did exactly what they did to Morgan, it matters to me, was it the right thing to do?"

"Jessie is a mystic, and a good one at that, do you not think whenever you hugged her, she did not see the truth of you? Jessie sees by touch; she knows the truth of her real father. She was hardly alone like Morgana, she had Uncle Jacques, and he has been an excellent father to her." Robbie understood that.

"Iona, she had a right to know, and a right to see him." Iona agreed.

"You are right, but she is old enough Dad. If she wants to, she knows how to find him, and where he will be. He is also a mystic, and there are places only they can go."

"The Hidden Realm?" She gave a slight nod.

"That and other places. Dad it is not for you to decide, it never was, that was for her to choose. If you want to see him, well, that is a different matter, and if you do, I will find him for you, as long as it is not to kill him?" Robbie shook his head.

"I let him live, and that will never change. I have no wish to see him, although, I am also aware he now lives as Master Sage, and did things that helped Loxley." She nodded at him.

"He is a man of Loxley, he had to lose it to understand its value, which I feel he now does." Robbie smiled.

"You are so like her, you know?"

"That's funny because mum thinks I am more like you." He gave her a wide grin, and nodded his head at her.

"You have qualities I suppose." She agreed with him.

"I can be stubborn, I know that, Sapphire often reminds me." He gave a chuckle; he had noted it at times.

"Iona, I did not like what I saw, and yes it has caused ripples for a lot of us. The truth does that, but again, it may hurt, but we recover quicker from it than we would a lie. I admired what you did, you presented the facts, and they were irrefutable, and difficult to accept, but you cannot argue with cold facts."

"Dad, cold facts mean nothing to me if it means losing you. I would rather live a lie with you, than live a truth without you. Never question my loyalty, I will be a queen of Fae, but this… Here, you, mum, and my family, this is where my roots are, and always will be. I aim to rule with truth, but I am not excused from that, I too will be accountable to all of Fae, and all of Loxley, for I am Violet Line, and Violet Stone, and the two cannot be separated."

Rune smiled as she watched him pull her into his arms and hug her, she had always known he would be an ideal father for her children, and he was. A soft warm hand slipped into hers and she looked down, and saw little Gailania looking up at her with bright sapphire blue eyes.

"Hi Sweet pea."

She bent down and lifted her daughter into her arms, and held her close. Gailania snuggled into her.

"I am glad they made up, dad needs Nona, and she needs him." Rune smiled, and squeezed her daughter tight, and turned from the door.

"We all need him Sweet pea." Gailana pulled back, and gave her a strange look.

"What, even you, because you know Mum, you are pretty powerful? Even Pan is nervous when you point, she told me you can be really scary, her mum said you terrified everyone, and the cutter men." Rune giggled.

"Oh, Sweet pea, you have no idea, I remember one time, when your dad stood on top of a roof, and lifted his bow in the air, and the cutter men trembled in their boots." Her eyes opened wide with surprise.

"REALLY!?" Rune gave a serious nod.

"He once faced an evil dark woman, who was sucking the life out of everything. Honestly, she was really scary and I was afraid, and even though he was losing all his hope, he pulled out his sword, and with one massive swipe, he cut off two of her fingers." Gailania blinked, and her mouth fell open.

"NO WAY?" Rune looked really serious, and nodded at her.

"Your dad is pretty brave, and I must say, I loved him more than I ever had loved anything in my life, and then he did something so remarkable, and so magic, and I knew I would never stop loving him for as long as I lived."

"Wow, what was that?" Rune smiled a beautiful smile.

"He helped me make you." Gailania broke out into a big smile.

"Okay, yeah, that is pretty cool." Rune giggled.

"I think so too… Come on, I need to cook, and you can help me, and we will make something for your big strong dad." Gailania nodded.

"Not carrots, we have eaten thousands with Iona cooking, she never cooks anything different." Rune frowned.

"Okay, no carrots, we have some kale." Gailania giggled.

"Will it be like wet lettuce?"

Rune gave a mighty laugh, as she walked through the door into the kitchen, carrying her youngest daughter, and for no real reason, she felt incredibly happy.

Chapter Twenty Six.

Life Left Behind.

*I*ona worked late writing, and fell asleep with her quill in her hand. She woke with a start as yet another dream startled her awake, she sat up and rubbed her eyes, she felt exhausted. She had dreamt of Bridget's tomb, and felt she should head there, so dressed and ate, and then jumped to the high pass, and entered the tunnel that led to where the whole of the family lay.

She lit an incense stick, and placed it into the holder, and spoke her words of hope for peace quietly, for her two predecessors, and hoped she could emulate their wisdom and guidance for their people. On her knees she looked at the tomb of Bridget, surrounded by a wide ring of flowers, as was the one for Gwendolyn.

"Such love and such loyalty, even after all these years your legacy endures and they bring you fresh flowers. I hope in time I will earn the love and respect you both have. I want to, I want the people of Fae to live only in the light, to know happiness and prosperity. There has been too much darkness in all the realms, it is time for the light to illuminate everything."

Iona stood, and bowed to each tomb, then turned and headed for the tunnel to leave. She walked out and stood in the sunlight, and noticed the track, that forked. One led down, and the other led upwards. She turned and walked slowly, her thoughts lost as they flowed through her mind, she took the left fork, and headed onto the path that rose up towards the top of the mountain.

*I*ona walked up towards the top of the high pass, and turned to look out over Florae, she gave a sigh and breathed in, as she looked down on the valley basin below with its long white road, that cut through the heart of the realm. The sun was high in the sky, and below her the land was lush and green, scattered with the small A frame houses of what would become her people, her responsibility. The last few weeks had felt hard, and she felt weary as she turned slowly, and could just make out all of the nine islands that surrounded the mainland. Their peaks touched the clouds, across the sea, and it looked idyllic and peaceful. She breathed in feeling calm wash through her, her words reflective, and almost whispered as she spoke to herself.

"I find it strange, that I have never lived here, and yet I feel such a bond with these people, and yet I also feel scared. What will the judgement of me be when I finally leave the seat to go to another, will I be seen as fair, I wonder?"

She looked down the mountain, and below was the road that led to the cave of Bridget and Gwendolyn, and further down below that, was the Royal House and the House of Scribes.

"Two queens have ruled here, both of them loved, and both of them wise, did they struggle as I have in the days before the crown? All my life I watched my mother, and she has always appeared so natural in her ability to choose the right path, will that part of her walk at my side, for I feel strongly I need it?"

There was an electric atmosphere this high up, and her window opened up in front of her, and she frowned.

"Did I do that?" Somewhere on the other side of her window she heard a voice, and she recognised it.

"Queen of Fae come to me." It was the Lord Albanlin.

*I*ona stepped through, and walked out on to a place she recognised immediately, it was the top of the cliff on which the old ruins of Tintagel sat. She breathed deeply as she walked to the cliff edge, and stared out at the sea. The light of the day was starting to slip, and the breeze lifted her hair. She felt a presence behind her and turned, and then caught her breath with surprise.

Morgana of Cornwall stood looking at her, her hair moving on her shoulders, she had aged a little, and her hair had long streaks of white through it, but she still looked younger than her age. She nodded her head, and smiled.

"I was given one request, and I asked to meet you." Iona gave a slight nod, lost for words.

"Why, I am nothing in the sands of time?" Morgana gave a little smile.

"A very important part of me was missing, and it was returned to me partly through your efforts. The lady of the Whitelines had it within her pocket, and it saw what you have done for my family. I am grateful to you for that Queen of Fae. When the missing part of me was given back to me, and I became whole again, the memory of your efforts and words were given to me, and I wanted to thank you." Iona gave a nod.

"It probably sounds weird, but are you real, or are you another illusion, because I have had many of you?" She smiled, and gave a little giggle.

"I am quite real… I have so many words I wish to share, but my time is limited here. I wanted to face you and thank you; I wanted you to know that what you did mattered deeply to me. For much of the time I remember, I fought to survive and I struggled, and in the end, it all felt like it was for nothing. I see now, that it would take a long time before what I did made a difference, and I owe that to you." Iona was unsure, she had not really done a great deal.

"I am not sure that I have done that much, most of what I have learned others still do not know. You are the one that should be honoured, for you stood up for your people, and made a stand against those who would hurt them. I feel you were brave to stand alone against such odds, and I have admired you for it. I just stated the facts, you were not wrong Morgana, and they needed to see that. Can I ask, you say what time you remembered, do you not recall all of it?"

Morgana walked towards her, and stopped close to her, and Iona could see she was still very young looking, although she felt she looked a little older than her mother. Her eyes were dark and sparkled brightly, she was pale skinned, which looked whiter set against her black hair. She wore a simple hand made black dress, that looked stitched by her own hand. She had a kindness to her, and Iona could feel it, a gentleness, almost as though she had a deep capacity to love. Morgana smiled, and looked down a little, almost as if ashamed, her voice was soft and reflective.

"I lost a great deal of who I was, I did try to fight, but it consumed me, and who I had become was taken from me. I did things that I am ashamed of, especially to Gwendolyn, who I never meant to harm, your people have suffered because of that, and I feel deeply shamed of what I became. I did not want the darkness, I wanted to be a white raven, not a dark one, and Branna understood that." Morgana looked up, and there was a slight sadness to her eyes.

"Branna was seen as a bad person, but she was never as evil as the golden queen. To me, she was only ever kind and gentle with me, I came to see her as a mother figure, I loved her as deeply as I did my parents. When the darkness came, I lost the person I am, the person you see here, and all of those memories as I fought to try and claw my way back to the light. I never wanted to be that other one, and it hurts to know that I was." She looked at Iona, and it was clear she felt the pain of knowing, Iona could feel it.

"The Ruling Council hurt a lot of people in my time, they valued some more highly than others, and my people suffered a great deal, especially my family. All I wanted was for them to live by the same rules they placed on us, and yet they refused to. They walked all over those who they deemed of less value, and their lives had little meaning to them, as they trampled over them. I wanted to stop them, and I did, I did not take their lives, I put them where they could never harm another again. I paid a high price for it, I understand that now, but I would do it again to protect those who looked to me for help. You are to be the new Queen, Gwendolyn's heir, she was not a bad person, she was kind to me and meant well. She was a good queen to her people, but she also allowed the golden queen to lead her with lies, instead of learning from her grandmother. I hope you have learned from all of this, and if you have, my fight is finally over?" Iona smiled.

"I have, your story has inspired me, and I will always try to rule in a way that all get a voice. You suffered for the truth, and that has had a big impact on me. I came to admire you greatly Morgana of Cornwall, you taught me much, and it will guide me. I am writing your story to be added to the House for all to read, I feel strongly the truth should be read." Morgana smiled a beautiful smile.

"That was all I ever wanted, my cottage that I love so dearly, the solitude to work and read, and to simply be heard and understood. Thank You, My Queen, just knowing one person knows the real truth, matters deeply, as then I know I am not alone." Iona took a deep breath, as she felt a deep sadness rise inside her.

"What will become of you now?" She shrugged.

"I lived my life, there can be no return for me, for the evil acts I committed as a dark raven. I did the best I could before the darkness came upon me, and seeing you here, I feel it was enough." She turned slightly and smiled, as she looked over the ruins of Tintagel.

"This is where my heart will always lie now, in the stones my father and mother lifted into place, and where I held his hand and he told me stories of his homeland. My time here is over, and it will end in the place I started and loved the most, the home of my father. For this was once a beautiful place, filled with the love of my parents, and that will remain always with me, as will this place in my heart." Iona smiled.

"I am happy that you finally saw that what you did had great meaning, I am grateful for what you did for your people Morgana, I owe you my thanks." She nodded, and looked behind her as a white window opened.

"I have to go, I wanted so much to walk here once more and speak with you, and I am glad that I did. Farewell Iona Violet, Queen Violet Stone of Fae. Live well, rule long, and care for your people."

Iona felt sadness that she had to leave, as Morgana turned, her heart felt heavy, as she watched her walk towards the light. Iona took a slight step forward.

"Before you go, can I ask you one question, for it is something I must know?" She turned, and looked back, and gave a nod, Iona hesitated for a second.

"One day, I too will be judged for the rule I held, and I cannot help but wonder… What did you see that scared you so much that last day on the castle wall, before your White Lord?" Morgana looked at her, and her eyes appeared to sadden, her voice was soft, almost reflective, and yet Iona felt the pain in her words.

"I looked into the face of the White Lord, and I saw who I was, what I could have been, and what I had become. It was everything I hated and fought against, for I was no different than the golden queen, and that terrified me to my core." Iona nodded.

"Thank you, I understand it all now." She smiled.

"I only ever wanted to be a white raven, never dark, you be one for me."

Iona smiled with tears in her eyes, as Morgana turned, and walked into the light, it snapped closed, and was gone. She breathed out, her emotions swirling, and yet funnily, she also felt happy.

"Good luck my White Raven, fly free from now on, you earned it the hardest way of all."

Iona wiped her eyes, and turned back to the sea, as more tears filled her eyes, and stood watching the sun begin to set. She lifted her hand and wiped her eyes again, and nodded to herself.

"It took many generations, but I did it, I told her truth, and it does matter, no matter what anyone else ever thinks, it matters deeply to me."

She took a huge breath inward, and gave a sob, and stood alone watching the sky darken, as her tears rolled down her cheeks. She breathed in with a sigh.

"I will be a raven for white, I will be your raven Morgana, and I will be the whitest of the white, that will be my tribute to you."

She sobbed, and stood alone weeping until the sun slid down below the horizon. Iona Violet, Queen of Fae was the only one apart from Branna, to weep for the loss of Morgana of Cornwall. No one saw the tears that fell from her eyes, but in the morning when the sun rose, the cliff was empty and silent, and all of the edge of the cliff, was filled with thousands of small bright white daisies, edged with a slight tint of violet.

*F*or the weekend before the eighteenth birthday, of Halbert Thorn, and Iona Violet of Loxley a large gathering of friends and family was planned. The following day, the Mere was a hive of activity, as the area was prepared for the party of the year. Iona was not there, she stood once again by the fence of the cottage in Avalon, and looked to the old worn brick chimney, onto which she placed a bunch of wild flowers.

Una had sensed her and came walking down the road towards her, Iona blinked out of her thoughts and turned to see her as she walked up. Una gave her a nod, Iona took a deep breath, and decided to take the initiative.

"Aunt Una, I know the truth of all of it now, and yes to a degree you were right, Morgan le Fey did indeed try to kill your mother by draining her essence. I would not deny that she was an evil, and vile person. I wanted to know the truth of who she was before that, and try to understand how she became what you fought, I know many will not forgive me, and I will never ask it, not even from you. Morgana of Cornwall, you knew of, she lived here, but she was nothing to do with Morgan le Fey. Morgana tried to protect your mother from Rhiannon, she tried to warn her, in hope that she would listen to her grandmother and not believe the lies of Rhiannon. I know that Aunt

Una, I saw it." Una frowned.

"I do not understand, how did Morgana try to protect her?" Iona breathed in.

"Morgana did know the truth, she was the one who took all of you with Branna, but she did not want you dead. She wanted you away from her people, because the council no matter what you may think, did not care for who they slaughtered on their road to a perfect realm of men and king. Morgana placed all of you in safety, because just like her potion to kill Eve, Rhiannon would have slain all of you and ruled supreme. Look at Amethyst, she was the rightful heir, and yet Rhiannon would not give up the moon realm, she allowed Amethyst to rule here, but not both realms." Una looked at her, and Iona could see there was some understanding of what she had seen. Iona lifted her arms.

"Morgana tried to warn your mother, see for yourself."

Iona touched Una's forehead, and her mind flashed and she closed her eyes, as the pictures of a solemn funeral appeared in her thoughts. Una understood it was at Tintagel, and then she gasped as she saw Morgana, and her own mother, Gwendolyn appeared behind Morgana's back. Morgana smirked.

"Come to kill me have you, well my back is turned to you, so take a shot, that is the usual way the council act?" Gwendolyn stood still; her bright blue eyes focused on her.

"I did not come to fight you Morgana, your mother has died, and I believe that is a time of truce. You are not easy to find, and yet I knew you would be here, and I want to talk." Morgana turned and faced her.

"I would not tell your sister the golden queen, she will curse you for not killing me the moment you saw me." Gwendolyn looked her in the eyes.

"All I want is the truth, every lead I have, crosses the path of you. I know that you know something, and I need to know how to find my family members, my daughter's need their children back."

Morgana gave a small laugh, as she looked at Gwendolyn in her long thick white robes, her blue cloak, and her long golden hair flowing behind her in the wind.

"You talk of truth, which truth, the facts as they are, or the words of the great golden queen, for it appears to me, only her words matter, and my voice is silenced?"

"Morgana, all I seek is the full truth, your words do not have to be silenced, tell me."

"Then what, you will go to the golden queen and set things right?" Morgana laughed.

"You look at me and see evil, would you truly believe anything I say? The golden queen has smeared my name, and accused me of every wrong in the kingdom. Just because it is the great and glorious golden queen, everyone bows down and agrees with her. Are you honestly telling me anything I say will be believed, for if you are, then you know you speak lies?" Gwendolyn stared at her with hope in her eyes, she took a step forward.

"I know you know something, and what you know can help me, Morgana, please talk to me, and I will listen." Morgana shook her head.

"Gwendolyn, I know you to be a reasonable person, but have you any idea of what my truth will do? She will destroy your kingdom, and tear down everything to hide what the truth of her is. If I told you what I know, you would not live long enough to listen, do you not think she is watching you now, and is ready to pounce the moment you leave? I already sense her guards approaching." Gwendolyn looked round, as Morgana smiled.

"Her hand is long, and even you are not safe. I am not guilty of the sins she has given me, but that matters not to her." The smoke swirled up from her feet, and Gwendolyn reached out to grab her.

"Please Morgana no, I need to know what you know!"

It was too late she was gone, and Gwendolyn gave a frustrated sigh, as marshals popped out of the air and surrounded her, she spun round her eyes blazing with blue light.

"WHY ARE YOU HERE, HAVE YOU ANY IDEA OF THE DAMAGE YOU HAVE DONE?"

There was a massive burst of bright blue, and all of the guards were blown over, and Gwendolyn was gone, as the marshals of Rhiannon lay on the floor stunned and bewildered.

*U*na swooned and opened her eyes, and saw Iona standing with her eyes filled with purple light, and Una nodded, as she understood the vision. Iona gave a small sigh, and her eyes came back to normal.

"Morgana knew the truth of Rhiannon; she was the only one who stood up to her and faced her out. She thought your mother was a good person, but she knew, if she ever revealed the truth to Gwendolyn, Rhiannon would kill all of you and your mother. You showed outrage at Morgana, when it should have been aimed at the golden queen. Aunt Una, even now almost eighteen years after her death, her lies still control the thoughts of everyone. Not mine, I know the truth, the actual facts, and I will not change my mind ever, Morgana of Cornwall was the real saviour of her people, but she suffered a terrible fate and was dragged into the darkness, but even so, that does not dim her life that was light." Una felt the power of Iona and leaned on the fence.

"I understand now, I never realised, I feel the guilt Iona, I knew her, she lived here not minutes from our home, and yet I never once made the effort to talk to her. I have thought about nothing but what you said and what you showed us in the court, and I have asked many things of myself." She moved her head to look at the young future queen.

"Had I befriended her, would it have been different?" Iona shrugged.

"Maybe, I do not know, and it is too late to change things now, but it is not too late to learn the facts, and understand the truth of those times." Iona took a deep breath as she thought of all she had learned.

"Your mother was a great queen Una, and I realised she suffered, but it is important you understand that the woman who tortured her, was not Morgana of Cornwall. She did fight from within, she tried to control that darkness that engulfed her, but she was only half Fae, and could not win against the force of darkness. It was the darkness that drove her to drain her essence, the evil that consumed her to create the monster she became. Morgana of Cornwall tried to protect the council, in a strange way she admired them, just disagreed with their actions towards the people." Una gave a slight nod.

"I understand that now Iona. My mother suffered, when we finally got her free, she was almost dead, I gave a life to save her, but she never really recovered. She was taken to Morbihan, and never returned to Florae to finish her rule as queen, she was not strong enough. It bought her the time to work with Hearne and Opal, and allowed her mind to advise them on how to recover and win against le Fey and her vile son, and through her spirit and mind, she taught us all in our isolation, hidden from the world, as we tried to adapt to the way in which the world had changed, I was not there when she died, and always have regretted it."

"We need to learn from the story of your mother and Morgana, so that the same mistakes are never made again. In a strange way Morgana's story holds many lessons for all of us, which we can use to guide us away from the darkness and into the light."

Una leaned on the fence, and turned to look into what was once the cottage, and she gave a sigh of sadness.

"It is such a waste, my father admired her mind, he told me often how disappointed he was that someone so bright could be seduced by the darkness. He always spoke of how he never understood how she could fall for such madness, he honestly believed she would become a great power for white. I think it haunted him right up until the day he left."

"She still is a great power for the white." Una turned.

"How, she is gone, taken by the White Lord?" Iona smiled.

"She may not be here as a person, but her words and her actions still live on for the good of all. I am writing her story, and documenting the facts of her short life as Morgana of Cornwall. Others will read it eventually, and when they do, her words will inspire them to keep the path of white. In that, she will teach us to see the truth more clearly as she did." Una gave a chuckle.

"Considering your powers have not yet come fully, you have gained some great wisdom Iona." She gave a soft smile, and looked at the flowers on the old chimney.

"I did not gain it, Morgana taught it me, it is her wisdom learned from the hardest life, and the deepest pain aged four summers old. My only regret, is her personal book of what your father taught has never been found, for I believe that is a true book of truth, and I would like to read it."

"Me too… I would like to read a story of my own lifetime. I am many generations from the time I knew as a girl, I am probably the last who actually saw her and knew of her, apart from Fagan. I came back here, so I did not have to live in your world, for even now I struggle with it, I never really did become as accustomed to it as my sisters. I miss it Iona, I miss the times of my youth, and the life we lived, it was simple and basic, but I liked it. That time was really my home and real life. This time has not been good, I lost my mother, father, son, and my sisters. In a strange way, I feel I understand Morgana better than I do others." It made a lot of sense to Iona.

"I think I shall walk in your realm Aunt Una, I have to head home for the party, but before that, I will walk the same paths as she did, and try for a while to walk in her shoes."

*U*na gave a nod, but Iona could see she was already lost to her thoughts staring at the old ruins. Iona turned and quietly walked away to walk up the road, past the point where Stenlow stopped Morgana, and past Merlin's ancient cottage, and into the wild lands of Avalon, where Morgana would gather her herbs and talk to Eve.

It was so strange that she could walk in all the same places and understand Morgana's life, and see the similarities that they shared. Morgana was the daughter of a powerful queen, and she was the daughter of Runestone life. At age four Morgana lost her father, and if she had not had Opal and Gwendolyn, she too would have lost her father. Morgana loved her cottage dearly, as much as she loved her cabin. Morgana chopped her own wood and grew her own food, and cooked her own meals, which was how she was raised in Loxley. Most importantly, her father was the most important person in her life, and Robbie was to her, for she saw him as a man of truth, just as Morgana saw hers. Her thoughts focused for a moment, and she smiled as she walked.

"You did learn from her Gwendolyn, in a strange way you did understand her, you came to me when I was four with Opal, and you showed me how to save my father, so I would never suffer the same fate as Morgana."

She stopped and looked down at the wild camomile, growing next to an old stump, and walked over and sat down on it to be closer to the plant and smell the aroma. She was not even aware this was the very same stump as Morgana had sat on, it was older and white, and the underside had decayed slightly, so it was probably not as high. She sat lost in thought as she stroked the softness of the plants, and smiled.

"It must have been such a different life, and yet in many ways, it has not changed that much. We live off the land, tend our plants, although I have never dried my own tea, old Hilda makes such good mixes I have never thought of blending my own. I wonder what your teas tasted like Morgana, they say many loved them, and you sold a lot? I would have liked to drink tea with you, sat in your cottage next to your window as we talked of blends and flavours. Yes, I think I would have enjoyed that, a simple life, and the peace to read and learn my skills, I could also live that life."

*I*ona sat and drifted for a while; her eyes closed as she remembered those moments she had seen. To many it would appear like a hard life, and yet for her that was quite normal, it was how she had grown up, she drifted with a smile as she heard her father in her mind.

"You may think because you will be a queen one day you are free of this. You are wrong, this is our life, your life, and here we live by the rules of the land, and we stand for the code of a woodsman. Iona Violet of Loxley, if you ever want to be a queen, then you must become a woodsman first." She gave a little giggle.

"Yes Daddy." He handed her the axe, and she took it with both hands, and felt it drag her down.

"Daddy it is too heavy." He smiled.

"I know, the day you lift that and swing at the wood, you will know the meaning of Loxley life." She looked at him and frowned.

"Daddy, I am only nine summers you know?" He smirked, and flicked back his long hair.

"Good point… Go over to your mother, you can plant seeds." She gave a grin, and he winked.

"Thanks Daddy."

Iona opened her eyes, and smiled to herself as she stood up. She looked around the wild grasses, and thick woodland in the distance, which she knew rolled down into the huge Lake of Passing, and spoke quietly to herself as her window opened.

"Half Violet Line, and half Violet Stone, but there is no doubt, I am a Lox through and through."

She gave a little giggle, and stepped through into Loxley and the Mere in front of her parents' house. She stood still and took a good long look at the house, the woods, and the long wide Mere.

"This is my Tintagel, this is my father's home, and it will always be the centre of my heart."

She turned with a smile, and hurried towards the house. She moved quickly through the gate, and up the path lined with small violet flowers, and up the wooden steps of the deck. Iona gripped the glass door handle and slid it open and looked inside.

"NONA!" Thump… Thump… Thump! Robbie sighed at his desk next to Rowan.

"Does that child ever do anything quietly?" Rowan gave a chuckle and looked up.

"Stuff rags in your ears when she comes round, that is what I do, it is bliss." Robbie frowned.

"Does that work?" Rowan nodded.

"It does for me." Robbie smiled. Suddenly his thoughts were filled with the bliss of a child free, peaceful house.

Chapter Twenty Seven.

Shadows of the Past.

*I*ona moaned, and rolled around in her bed, as the sweat glowed on her face, and in her mind, images flashed at speed, and she gave out a startled cry.

"No… End him." She felt a jolt in her stomach, as she looked at Roack.

"What… No… I cannot do that; I have never killed anything; I am Fae we do not do that."

"You must, now end him, we are but a small creature, we cannot do it, he cannot live as others will come looking, he must be silenced, now end him." Branna panicked slightly.

"You cannot be serious, I am unharmed, he was never a match for a member of the Fae. Roack you ask too much."

"You want freedom, don't you?"

Her hands were shaking, and she stepped back a little away from Halbrand, who was still rolling around in agony. He screamed out at her.

"You friggin witch, I am blind, I should have known when I saw them three yesterday morn, I should have known it would be you, only a witch could do such things that defile all the gods of the land. Just you wait… Just you friggin wait you whore, I will find you and I will rip out your black evil heart and burn it."

Panic flooded into her, he rolled around and kicked out all around him, what should she do? Roack appeared right, and she did not know what to do, but Roack knew.

"End him, take the rock and smash his head in, he will talk, and he will tell everyone about you, not only will the marshals look for you, his people will hunt you, now end this now… Take the Rock!"

Branna felt the sweat on her face; she had no idea how to do this. He was shouting at her and calling her names she did not understand, his foot caught the fire and the flames erupted into the air, and she jumped back as Roack flew into the air to get away from the red light. Her heart was pounding in her chest and she was finding it hard to breathe, she could see the large rock on the floor a few feet away, but she really did not want to use it, Roack was getting louder in her head and sounded angry.

"DO IT, KILL HIM!"

She knew Roack was right, she just wanted to be free, but this was not what she wanted, but she knew that he would come after her. Roack continued to talk, filling her head with her croaky voice, and clouding her thoughts even more.

"You must, you must kill him and take the things he has, you need to leave this land and his furs will fetch a good trade. Kill him and take what is his and use it to escape, now do it, end him, take the rock and end him."

She had not even realised that she had moved round the fire closer to the rock. The rock was just a foot away, it was round and rugged, and she knew that it would be enough. Roack continued to shout in her head, and Halbrand screamed all sorts of words she did not understand at the top of his voice, as he kicked and lashed out on the floor. It was all becoming too much for her to handle, and she felt her own panicked temper rising within her, without even thinking she screamed out at the top of her lungs, and then snatched the rock off the floor and lifted it up into the air above her head, she screamed from the depths of her being at both of them.

"FOR THE LOVE OF THE GODS, BE QUIET!" Crunch!

She shuddered and lurched under her covers, her breath coming in short bursts as she shook below the sheets. More images flashed into her mind, and she settled, and then moaned in a different way, bucking her hips up and sliding her hands down there as she moaned softly, the pictures in her mind guiding her, and she breathed in and held it, before letting it slip back out in a long low seductive moan.

Lost in her dreams as she moaned and writhed, Iona held up a long black feather dipped in blood, and then lowered it cutting the runes into his skin on his chest, he gasped and pushed at his hips, and Iona moaned in her sleep, matching his hips to her rhythm. Her own hips lifted, and then dropped, as she kept up his ever quickening pace, as she saw herself, naked, writhing and covered in sweat as she ground down on him even harder.

She plunged the feather down into his chest and he wailed and thrust up hard, Iona wailed with delight. The lightening shot down from the sky, exploding before her as it hit him square on the forehead, and she saw herself arch back as he thrust up his hips and held them there, as his whole body shuddered. Iona wailed in her sleep, and then another voice spoke, it was a woman's.

"It is done." Iona turned and looked straight into the dark eyes of Branna.

Iona screamed at the top of her lungs, and shot out of bed dragging the covers off the bed with her, and there was a bright white, followed by a bright violet flash, and Iona stood naked, covered in sweat and shaking violently, as she saw her bed, covered in blood. She looked down, and saw the blood running down her legs, and gave an almighty scream of terror.

Ariel's arms came around her, and pulled her shaking into her arms, and she held her tight.

"Shush My Queen, it is fine, all is well, you are home and we are here."

Iona's eyes were wide as she slowly looked around and saw her mother, her eyes filled with tears.

"Mum, I think I killed someone." Rune stepped closer, as Ariel released her.

"No my darling, it was a dream, a very bad one."

Iona leaned into her and shook, she was so frightened, and she wept. Ariel looked at the sheets, and then Iona's legs. She lifted her eyes to Runestone, and took a deep breath.

"Well, there is no doubt now, she is perfectly aligned to the moon. She is a queen of Fae, there is no doubt." Rune nodded not really understanding.

"So, this is normal?" Ariel smiled.

"Quite normal, this happens a week before a queen takes her crown. Her body will purge and clean itself so she is pure for the ceremony." Iona was settling, but still trembled, Rune looked at the bed.

"Is it normal to lose that much blood?" Ariel glanced at it; the bed was covered.

"Yes Runestone, this is very normal, her cycles are now matched perfectly to the moon. Her powers can feel the moment coming, and they are preparing to come fourth. Her visions will be far more vivid than they have been, and she will feel a great many things as she comes closer. This is her time of senses, and over the coming week, she will start to feel the life of all things." Rune gave a nod of understanding.

"Yeah, I remember that time, it was not my most pleasant, it really freaked me out, but my whites of my eyes went lilac first." Ariel turned and pulled at the sheets as Iona came back round to her senses, and pulled out of her mother's shoulder. Ariel looked at her and smiled.

"This is quite normal, your mother was unaware of this, all lines differ in the signals the body gives off. The worst of it is over My Queen, I am sorry, I thought you would have at least another two days. A good wash, and some boiled in salt sheets, and all will go right back to normal." Iona gave a nod, her face still shone with what was a cold sweat, and she was still trembling.

"So, no one is dead, I did not kill someone?" Ariel gave a titter.

"No, I saw your dream, I know what you saw, I have seen it too. It is a part of her life that does bother me so, that was the moment she made her biggest mistake, and she spent the rest of her life trying to undo it. I wish you had not seen that, I truly do, for it is a terrible thing to witness." Iona nodded; her breathing was much better.

"It terrified me, but I also felt something more, I felt fear, but not hers or his." Ariel stopped and looked at her.

"You felt the fear… Did you hear the cries?" Iona nodded, she looked pale, and her voice croaked a little.

"Who was she?" Ariel gave a long sigh, and stood holding the blooded sheet.

"I always thought she did, but I have never felt it. Iona, what you felt was Bridget Violet's pain, and the fear she felt. I knew it at the time, but could never prove it. Bridget had taken the merle of her people into her to save them, she was connected to it, she felt the ritual, she felt Branna and Berengar… She also felt Roack." Rune looked at her not sure of how to react.

"Ariel, how was that possible?" Ariel shrugged.

"She was a great and powerful queen, I always said she was more powerful than Rhiannon, but most people scoffed at the idea, but I was right. She was connected and fought it every day of her life so it never consumed her. Bridget managed to do what Bran failed to, she found the balance and controlled it." Ariel rolled up the sheet as Iona looked at her mother.

"Was it that terrifying for you?" Rune looked at her, and gave a soft smile.

"No, my darling, it wasn't, I saw some things that frightened me, but nothing as scary as you did. Iona, you have the power of Gwendolyn, and also my line, we always knew one day you would do amazing things. Think about it, your powers have not come yet, but you could summon a court of queens, and look at the way you can manifest your visions in front of you. I have never seen that in my life before, all of that has been done before your powers are released." Iona understood.

"Mum, I am scared, I do not want to harm anyone, and I am not sure I can control such things." Rune gave her a smile and shook her head slowly.

"Iona, that is not how the powers work, they are part of you, and they are driven by the love in your heart. You have chosen the path of truth and light, and your truth and light will always protect your people, never fear them." Iona swallowed hard, and took a breath, Ariel gave a smile.

"A bath and a good cup of tea, you will be fine. Come on, we will take you to your mum's house, she has a good deep bath, you will feel much better once you are clean."

Rune took Iona's hand, and with Ariel, they left the cabin and ran through the rain over to the house. Rune took towels out of the hallway cupboard and looked at Ariel naked, apart from a long black shawl, Ariel smirked, and looked down.

"Like you, I sleep naked too, I always have, and I felt her fear, and just jumped." Rune looked down at her wet legs from the rain, and gave a chuckle.

"Yeah, me too… Parenting, it has its drawbacks, we could have been in the village." They both giggled.

As Rune stocked up the wood stove, and went up to run a bath for Iona, as the copper pipe wrapped around the tall black pipe of the stove to heat the water, heated up, Ariel wrapped Iona in a towel, and then went into the kitchen to make her a strong cup of tea, and spoke quietly with her. Unknown to all of them, just over a week away by foot, out in the rain, someone else had felt Iona's dream.

*I*n an old barn on the moors of northern Yorkshire, a small figure had slipped inside to get out of the rain. She climbed up into the hay loft, and sat out of sight in the corner, surrounded by soft warm hay. She closed her eyes and pulled the cloak around her tighter, and in her mind was a quiet whispering.

"Te Hee Hee, she hides in the trees, there she sleeps in their keep, but not for long, because she is the key, and with it the book unlocks, and we are free. Fly my little raven, fly to wood where the old man roamed, and with this locked unpicked, you will take her throne."

Her eyes snapped open, under her fringe of her jet black hair, and even in the darkness, they shone with a tinge of malice. From below the thick pile of hay behind which she hid, there was a faint and sinister chuckle.

Iona stood in the kitchen and felt the goosebumps rise on her arms and she shuddered, Ariel saw them and looked at her.

"What do you feel?" Iona shook her head.

"There is something, I can sort of feel it, but not quite if that makes sense." Ariel nodded.

As Iona sipped her drink, Ariel's mind moved, to a place in the far northern eastern coast, and in her mind, she spoke to herself.

"It must be, she is not returning with him, our little raven has a guide. Sapphire, can you see her, is she close?"

"I am not sure, she is so vague, she is hard to pinpoint, but she is out there somewhere, and I am convinced she has a guide."

"Yes, that is what worries me, if she gets out, we will have more on our plate than we realised."

"Ariel, I am watching, do not fear, Iona is safe."

*R*une came down and took Iona upstairs to bathe, ten minutes later Rune came down in a robe, and handed one to Ariel who was stood next to the woodstove keeping warm. She handed Ariel the robe and she slipped it on over her shawl, Rune frowned and Ariel gave a chuckle.

"It is one of very few things I have that belonged to Bran. I made her this when we lived in Avalon together. I know no one understands it, I wear it around me in bed, it helps me sleep, and makes me feel close to her." Rune smiled.

"I think that is nice. Ariel, I understand the power of love you feel,

I have that too with Robbie. It is hard for me to talk to you about her, because I understand, and I am the one who got her taken from you. I have no understanding of how you cope, because without Robbie, I would not survive. I feel your pain, and your loss, I have all this time, and I feel the responsibility of that." Ariel bit her lip and smiled.

"I know, I feel it in you. Rune, let it go, it is my burden to carry, not yours. We all made mistakes, she did, it was her biggest, and she regretted it. What is done is done, we cannot go back, for that time is over." Rune felt the pull at her heart and breathed in.

"As long as you know… Well, you know?" Ariel gave a nod and took a deep breath.

"Alright… Back to business, whilst she bathes, tell me what you know about the shard that was struck from the Star of the Merle." Rune frowned.

"The star is gone; Eve took it where no one will ever be able to touch it again." Ariel sat down on the chair, and Rune took the one at its side, and sat down as Ariel gave it a moment of thought and then looked at her.

"I know you fought her, and a small piece was chipped off, and I think that is what Morgan wanted Ursula to stab the Lord Hearne with. That was the last it was seen; do you know where that place was?" Rune sat back and thought about it.

"I will not deny I have looked, but apart from a black stain on the soil, because nothing grows there, I have never been able to feel it. I spoke a long time ago with Sapphire, and we think Ursula must have picked it back up and took it with her when she failed." Ariel shook her head.

"She does not have it." Rune frowned.

"Do you know where she is?" Ariel gave a sigh.

"Rune you cannot let Ena know. I know where she is, and she is living a quiet life of good, there is no dark in her. Rune she is my grandchild." Rune narrowed her eyes.

"She has Raven Merle, doesn't she?" Ariel sighed.

"I am supposed to be the mystic here. Ursula was told to seek out Raven with Dana. She found them, and Dana took her and Tom in, and like any Knox, she treated her like a servant. Tom worked the land, and Ursula took care of the baby. You know how Sapphire watched Dana be murdered? Well, when she went back, Ursula and Tom had fled, and they took the child. Ursula has raised Raven, and everything was fine, until a little while back, when Raven started with dark dreams, Ursula tried, but was not skilled enough." Rune understood.

"Her time of power is coming; she is a little older than Iona so it cannot be much longer." Ariel agreed.

"I was watching and had hoped to catch the moment, but Raven ran away, and both Sapphire and I have been looking for her. We think, she is looking for the shard, we cannot be sure, but we think something is connecting to her, and helping her." Rune sat forward.

"Helping, you mean the Merle is reaching out to her?" Ariel looked worried.

"Sapphire does not know, but I think it's Maud." Rune gave a frown, as she looked at her.

"Maud, Branna's daughter, the one Morgan killed?" Ariel sat forward in her seat, and lowered her voice.

"We know Maud was in the book, we know it was her who tied Morgana to the raven against her will, and I cannot say I am convinced, but what if Runestone, what if she is still in the book and calling to Raven Merle?" Rune looked at her, and shook her head.

"Branna burned the page she was in."

"Runestone, Ursula has said, when she was alone in the castle, she heard the book whisper. I know once again I sound mad, but I think, that Maud put more of herself in that book than even Bran realised. Think of her grandson William, and how she poured Mordred into him, and how he was stuck. What if when Morgana was tied to the raven, Maud added a little of herself? Think about Morgana's character change completely, almost like she was another person, you saw William when Mordred was in there, he too acted like a completely different person." Rune shuddered, and rubbed her arms.

"Hearne, you mystics can be bloody creepy. I do not understand Fae magic much, but if what you are saying is right, you are implying Maud intends to rise up as another dark raven."

"It is only a theory, but I cannot deny, she wanted Bran's seat, and this is her best shot now Bran has gone, it makes sense. What if Maud wants to use Raven as a vessel, the way she did Morgana?"

"No one wants that Ariel, especially me, my daughter is going to be a queen, and no more dark bitches are creeping up out of the ground to ruin that. Well, not on my watch they are not, wherever that shard is, we need to find it and fast." Ariel smiled.

"So, you will help us then?" Rune gave yet another frown.

"She is my daughter, of course I am helping."

"Good… It's a pity we don't have any blood of her line, that would really help." Rune shuddered.

"You know Ariel, at times, you worry me, are you sure all those years with Branna, you did not pick something up, because tonight, you are getting creepier by the minute?"

Ariel started to giggle, and Rune smiled, and both of them sat giggling together, as Iona came to the top of the stairs, and smiled. She was wrapped in a towel, and she looked a lot better. Ariel left Rune with Iona, and went to her cabin and made up her bed with clean sheets, and once Iona was calm and felt better, Iona came back to her cabin to sleep. Ariel made sure she was fine, and once Iona was sleeping, she headed back to her home. Rune sat in the chair by Iona's bed and dozed, her mind filled with thoughts of the past, and her encounters with Ursula.

*T*here was a party on the horizon, and the mere was loud, and noisy. Iona slept late, and took her time getting ready. She wanted quiet, and so slipped her book into a canvas shoulder bag, and jumped to Tintagel, where she sat on a low wall, opened her book and started to write. Further up the western coast close to the old edges of Whitehaven, Tom had arrived back in the night, during a rain storm.

It was late, dark, and the weather was howling, as it blew in off the sea, when he staggered back into the house, much to the relief of Ursula. It soon went from joy to heart break, as he sat by the fire shivering, and told her of how he had found her, but she had run off in the storm. He sat as the fire flickered, his eyes dark underneath, his usually tanned skin looking white, and his dark hair lined with streaks of grey. Ursula watched him, and could feel his sadness which was clear in his dull eyes, as he tried to find something to hold on to that would give her hope.

They talked for most of the night, as he explained how she was different, not herself, and she kept rambling on about she could help her family. Ursula talked of the new queen, and told him she now had the book, and he was relieved to hear that. Tom was convinced the book and the ring were connected, and it was that which was growing a hold on her. He gave a long, tired sigh, and rubbed the dark bristles on his chin.

"I am tired, so tired love, I cannot think straight. I need rest, and then maybe the answer will come, because all I can say, is she feels there is something she must get, and I cannot for the life of me work out what. Nothing of that time is left."

He was tired and soon slept, as Ursula sat in the bed at his side, and drifted in her thoughts. What had he meant, there really was nothing left to go back to, everything had gone?

With the start of the morning, he was back up and about, and stocked up the stove. The rain had stopped, so Ursula cooked him a good meal, he had not eaten a great deal and he was weakened. Ursula put down his plate of food, and looked at him with worried eyes.

"You can say it Tom, I know what you are thinking, but you are wrong." He gave a long sigh.

"I told you; ever since we gave her that ring of her family, she is different, she is not herself. Rae has been driven to know more, and she wants to know the truth, and I don't want her knowing. I am sorry, what else should I say, I raised her with you, and she was such a happy girl, but not anymore, she has changed. Rae has something more, and I do not know what, it is like a dark shadow over her, hiding her truth, smothering who she really is." Ursula shook her head.

"You're wrong, she is a good girl, she is kind and filled with joy."

Tom looked up at her and saw the tears, he gave another sigh and put down his fork. Tom stood up, and held out his arm, and she came to him, and he pulled her close, so she could rest her head on his shoulder.

"Look, don't go upsetting yourself, she is a good natured girl at heart, but we have always known what her bloodline was. Love, no matter which way we look at it, it is their blood, and there is a history there, we always knew as she grew, she would ask or go looking."

"I am afraid for her, no good can come of that family, look at what has happened to them all? Tom, we got away from all that, we made it to freedom, I want Rae to be free of them. Rae is a good girl, it was that book and whatever evil was living in it, but it is gone now, she can come home and be free of it." Tom was not sure.

"I want her home love, but for that, we need to find her first."

Deep in the back of his mind, Tom was really worried, he had no idea what was happening with Rae. She had always been happy and filled with life, but the last few months, he had felt she had become moody and brooding. Both of them blamed the book, but what bothered him the most, was neither of them really understood what it could do.

The one thing he did know after many years of talking, is that Branna had once told Ursula that Morgana had never wanted the darkness she had, but Maud who hated her, found a way to overcome her from somewhere inside the pages. Tom knew of Morgana and how strong she was, and that was his biggest fear, if the book could overcome Morgana, what chance did young and inexperienced Rae have?

At the far end of North Yorkshire, having spent the night in the barn, Rae slipped out, and walked quietly away. As she walked under the cloudy sky, she pulled out of her bag, a chunk of bread, and a thick wedge of cheese. As she walked towards the south, she chewed and smiled, happy to know she had slipped away from her father, and was now free to fulfil her destiny.

Chapter Twenty Eight.

Long Awaited Reunion.

For three days, Robbie and Halbert had overseen the building of a large covered area, under which tables were to be set up, for the forthcoming celebrations. Rune walked up to the side of the house, where Robbie and Halbert were both sanding the wooden legs of tables. Robbie looked up as she approached.

"Look at these, how can any carpenter call this finished, my dad would have thrown them out of the shed?" Rune gave a chuckle, as she approached.

"Robbie, I doubt there are any in Loxley who could work to the standards set by your father." Halbert grinned as he saw his dad frown.

"This is Loxley, we have standards." Rune chuckled, and slipped up close and pulled him close to her.

"Hmm, I love it when you smell of wood."

"Really?" Her eyes danced as she smiled at him.

"I do, the smell of a carpenter is very alluring Lord Loxley."

"Oh Mum, that is gross, Mum, please, not in front of us." She giggled as she slipped back to see Fern, Galaina, Pan and Tegan. Robbie smirked, and she leaned in closer.

"You are not bathing until very late tonight." She smiled, and turned to Tegan, who gave a sigh, and rolled her eyes.

"Isolde said we had to see you for jobs." Rune walked towards them with a smile.

"Yes, my children, at the front of the house there is a stack of chairs, and you my little flowers, can place them down both sides of the tables." Tegan pulled her face.

"Mum, there is loads of them." Rune smiled.

"I know, which is why I need all of you, if you start now, with four of you, it will not take long." Gailania looked up worried, and spoke quietly.

"Mum, they are big, how will I carry them?" Rune smiled at her.

"You have Pan, she is a strong fighting woman, she will help you lift them." Pan nodded.

"Yeah, Lania, this for us is easy as cake, we will move three times what they do." Tegan snorted.

"Yeah weeds, that won't happen, I will leave all of you behind." Rune looked at the girls.

"Well then, if that is true, it looks like Tegan will win the big treat for who moved the most." Fern frowned.

"Hang on, there is a treat for the one who moves the most?" Rune nodded.

"There is, and it is worth the effort." Fern looked back at Tegan.

"Yeah, you ain't winning, I will beat all of you, and I am getting my start now."

Fern turned, and ran for her life, suddenly realising, the others screamed and flew after her. Rune turned to Robbie, who was watching with a smile, and she smiled a sweet smile.

"They are so easy; all you have to do is appeal to their stomachs."

Robbie gave a giggle as Rune turned at the door, and went into the house. He lifted his sanding block, and carried on working.

While the children raced, Jessie, Alice, who had arrived home much to the delight of Rune, joined in with Jade and Sapphire, preparing the coverings. Tomorrow would be the party of the year at the Mere, as everyone arrived in Loxley and were shared out all around the village, to house them. Yvee worked in Jade's workshop, with Willow, to create large flower arrangements for the tables.

*I*ona was nowhere to be seen, she was yet again sat at Tintagel, with a small picnic basket, and her thick cloak, lost in thought as she wrote the truth of Morgana in her book. She loved Loxley life, but it was always noisy and busy, and in the last few weeks, she had felt a strong sense of peace inside herself. Tintagel had simply been about looking back, looking for truth, understanding the life others had lived, and yet since the first time she visited the place to find clues to the life of Morgana, it had become significant to her.

The silence was broken only by the sound of the sea, crashing on the rocks below, which lulled her into a sense of calm. It was almost like the rhythm of a heartbeat, rolling across the water below, and the regularity of the beat brought her a powerful sense of connection and peace. She took a break, and looked up, noting the far side of the island where her father and his team once blew away one side completely. It felt strange knowing at one time, Morgana would have walked right across to the headland.

Most of what Morgana had built, had crumbled away with her death, and Iona felt like that was a good thing, because it crumbled to dust, and in doing so, the old ruins of what had been built by Victor had re-emerged. Iona felt like this place of ancient life, felt familiar to her, and in a way, maybe it was, after all, she did inherit some of Gwendolyn's powers. Was there a part of her that was from that time, was some part of Gwendolyn that was inside her identifying with it?

She really did not know, she just felt a strong sense of ease and comfort, and that helped her focus her mind to write the words she wanted to say, as Loxley felt too intense for her to write with clarity. She walked along the edge of the big crater created by the explosion, it felt strange that all traces of Morgana were gone, and yet the sign of her mother and father and their fight was still here. That part of their life, which was also here still existed, and yet the force they struggled against was gone forever, leaving no trace. She stopped as she walked and thought about it, and it appeared to her, that it felt like they faced some form of invisible enemy, and that felt like a revelation. She looked down into the depth, where the water crashed against the wall of rock.

"Is that what it was like for you Morgana? You knew Rhiannon had it in for you, and yet you never really knew who was aligned with her. The village you visited to see Seth, and the way they turned on you, that must have felt so terrible, because you really did not expect that to ever happen? How hard was it to never really know who to trust, because you trusted Fagan, and yet he did not see what you wanted to show him, that must have been so hard? You came to Stenlow in his final hour, was that your way of showing him, that in a strange sort of way you trusted him? He was the only one, who did not let you down, he protected you, he was the least likely, and yet he did it, that must have been such a relief for you?" She turned and hurried over to her book, sat down, and started to write with a renewed energy. Alone with the sea crashing in the background, Iona wrote away with a strong sense of purpose, and the day slipped away until dusk, and she returned home, tired and yet her mind filled with the story of the life of Morgana.

*T*he following morning, started asleep, when Halbert sat on her bed, and gave her a small shake. She opened her eyes to his smile, and a coffee. He leaned over and kissed her cheek.

"Happy early birthday, I know we still have a week to go, but next week you will be busy, and so I wanted to do this, and also, they wanted to, as well."

Iona turned, and saw three small smiling faces peeping around the side of the door frame, she smiled. Gailania moved forward with a huge smiling face, with big bright blue eyes. She gave a cheeky giggle, and then ran in and jumped on the bed, and suddenly, she was surrounded with noise, hugs and gifts. It was special, a precious moment of her life, as she understood the joy of the family that surrounded her.

For over two hours, Halbert and Iona were surrounded by family, and received gifts from Jett and Rafe, Una and Wilson, Tod and Katie, and Jade with Rowan. It all felt overwhelming, and Iona slipped out of the house back to her cabin, with her arms filled with her gifts. She stood in her small room, and suddenly the emotion hit her. She looked around the small room, it had been home, her shelter, and a place that had become so sacred to her. This is where growing up, her mother sat with her as she struggled with the dreams, or her father sat with her and talked of family. The walls had pictures from Tegan, Fern and Gailania pinned everywhere, and the wave of emotion crashed into her, as she realised, within a week, she would have to leave.

She stood with her back to the door, and wiped her eyes, and tried to compose herself, she needed to get back to the house, and took a deep breath. In the doorway Robbie stood watching her.

"It is good that you feel such a great power of love for this place, but listen to me. Iona, this is not the centre of your world, it is the centre of mine, for your mother is here. It is time you took that step, and walked into the world as I once did, to make your mark, and experience what will be a good life. Iona, I am content here, because I left, travelled and then came back, and for you, it should be the same. It is good to weep, but this is just the start, no one else will ever take this cabin while you live, I built it for you, and only you." Her eyes filled with tears.

"That is why it is going to be hard to leave here, this is your work, in the heart of your realm. Dad this is my centre also, how can I leave it?" Her tears ran down her cheeks, as she gave a sob, and he walked in and came to her, and pulled her into an embrace.

"I am going to miss you so much." He held her tight as she wept, and he softly stroked her back.

"Iona, I have told you, I will be a regular visitor. Your mother has been informed we have guest rooms in the royal building, so we will spend time there as well as here. Iona, you will not be a prisoner, you can come and see us anytime you need to." She gave a sniffle and pulled back.

"I am teaching Lania maths, who is going to do her lessons? Dad she is going to miss so much time with me." He smiled.

"We will bring her, and you can always give her an extra lesson, Jade is going to help her, she teaches Willow, so she will join those lessons." Iona nodded, and wiped her eyes.

"I know I am being silly, but it really feels painful to me." He understood her.

"In a way, the fact it feels so painful helps me." She frowned at him.

"How… Dad this really feels hard for me?"

"If it hurts so much, that means I did a good job, and I made a home you grew up happy in, which is all we have ever wanted." She slid back onto his shoulder and slid her arms around him.

"I have loved my life here, no parent could have been better than both of you, I have had the most amazing time growing up here, it has been perfect." He squeezed her hard.

"Then you can leave safe in the knowledge that you always have here."

Robbie held her tight for a long time, and softly spoke of his pride and his love for her, and she shared her thoughts and memories with him. It took longer than expected, and when he had done, he left her to wash her face, and prepare, for the day was moving and the cooks had arrived, and the mere was getting very busy.

*T*he afternoon became a huge celebration of Iona and Halbert. Guests poured in from all over, and in amongst them most of the Specialist's were present. Out on the wide expanse of grass, a minstrel band played music, and many of the guests danced and laughed. There were many happy reunions, Rafe was especially pleased to see

Hawk had made it, and dragged him into a crushing hug, and after meeting his wife, they sat and laughed with Big John, and his wife, as they sat with Fish, and talked tales of old. Doc and Louisa hugged Woody and Una, and it was so lovely to see everyone mingling and having such a wonderful time. Sapphire stood back with Rune and watched on.

"We should have done this a long time ago. I have to say Rune, they have clearly missed each other, and it is nice to see this." Rune watched on.

"They were a close group, we lived, and fought side by side for a long time. All of us shed many tears together as we endured some desperate moments, it is nice to see those bonds have not lessened in times of peace."

Treen arrived with Brandon, and Robbie hugged them both, Brandon smiled, it had been a long time since they had seen each other.

"Robert… It has been too long; the life of a woodsman appears to have favoured you highly." Robbie smiled.

"It has, although, I believe the life of a sailor is equally as good for the soul." Brandon looked around at all the happy faces, and groups of people stood around laughing and joking.

"This is nice to see, such good friends, I am sure Simmonds would have loved this." Robbie nodded his head slowly.

"Yes, it would bring great joy to his heart to see this, I am quite sure without him, this may not have been possible."

"I visited his plot on arrival, I wanted to see him, and say a few words."

Robbie understood that, Fuse was a vital part of the operation, but more than that, he was a father figure to Brandon at a time when he was at his most vulnerable. Rags laughed and joked, John and Jess arrived and made a huge fuss of Iona and Hal, and after drinks and conversation, everyone was led to their seats. The tables were laid out under the huge wooden structure that had been built, and covered with a large canvass roof, providing shade, and shelter should it rain.

*T*here were two hundred guests, and each with a label for their allotted seat. For the chairs of the Specialists, each one had a new green Loxley cloak hung over the back of it. As the guests all were seated, Robbie stood, and waited for silence, and slowly the noise died down. He took a deep breath.

"Would the Specialists of Loxley please stand."

They looked at each other and stood up, Robbie gave a soft nod, and looked to the far end of the table, where there was a lone table draped in black cloths, but laid, each with a glass in front of their plates.

"My Specialists, we are twenty two faces short today, but in my heart, I know all of us are here in spirit. Without you, my daughter and son would not be here, so this day is made even more special with your presence. Gaynor, Will, Judith, Magg's and Bear have sent their apologies and messages of celebration to my children. It saddens my heart that Fuse is no longer with us to see this, I know it would give him great joy to be amongst us this day. I still grieve the loss of my Uncle Harry, but if he was here, he would no doubt offer us all his love and good vibes. That still leaves us fifteen of the most significant faces missing, and as is tradition, they still have the right, to a place at my table."

All the Specialist's turned, and looked to the table draped with black cloth, Robbie took another huge breath, and lifted his glass, his Specialist's followed his lead, as he lifted it up in salute.

"Eric, Anthony, Martin, Scarlet, Ruby, Alley, Lee, Rose, Forbes, Leenard, Melanie, David, Madeline, Beth and my father, Robert. Without them, we would not be here, for their bravery assured that we lived, they paid by making the greatest sacrifice, and gave up everything to bring us through that awful war. We salute them with sadness in our hearts, but offer our thanks that through them, all of us can stand here free and at peace, so we can be here together in safety at this time. We will always remember them with sadness, but also with great pride that they served at our side. Raise your glasses… To friends, brothers, and sisters in arms."

All the Specialist's turned, raised their glasses, and saluted their friends. They took a sip, as all the others watched with sad faces. Robbie sat down and the helpers moved in to serve food. Iona smiled a sad smile and reached over and took her father's hand in hers and gave it a squeeze. She knew the pain that still haunted him from their loss. He smiled, and breathed in, and she nodded at him. Rune leaned on his shoulder; she knew there were no words that could be said.

The meal was loud, as everyone talked, and leaned on each other as they laughed and joked, which for Ariel who had been used to living a quiet solitary life, she was not really used to, although Tila, was loving being back with the Specialist's. Halbert was happy as he sat with Evangeline, who would be spending the week with Iona, as she helped Ariel and Isolde prepare. Halbert was all smiles, and it had not gone unnoticed how much the two had been spending time with each other.

*T*he evening moved on, and the large paraffin lamps were lit, as the meal came towards the end. Robbie and Rune both stood up and looked at their friends, neighbours and families, and the table felt silent. Robbie took the lead.

"Friends, on this day almost eighteen years ago, I stood surrounded by many of you, some Specialists, and some of you enlisted, as we faced a dark enemy, and fought hard to hold the land of the Violet Isle, on which, my wife had just given birth to our children. It was one of many brutal days of fighting at that time, and some of you here, stayed back to protect the home we loved so much from being destroyed." Rune smiled as she looked down at her children. Robbie looked at everyone.

"As parents, Rune and myself owe you all such a huge debt of gratitude, for on that dreadful day, you all worked to ensure our children lived, and came home to Loxley. Through you, our lives have been blessed with two wonderful children, who today, we mark with a celebration, as they both reach their eighteenth year. We are proud of who they have grown to become, and within the week, our daughter, Iona, will leave to take up the role destined for her in the realm of Florae. Our son will remain for now in Loxley, but we know that he too may one day walk out into the wider world, as we did." Rune smiled as Iona put down her head, and Halbert slipped his arm around her, she took a deep breath.

"My children, we are so proud of you both. You have both grown into people of great quality, and carry the principles of true Loxley spirit within you. As you reach this time of your coming of age, we wish you to know, that all here love you, and no matter where your paths lie, there will always be a path back to here, where you will be greeted with joy and the love in our hearts. Ladies and gentlemen, would you raise a glass to Iona and Halbert Thorn."

Everyone stood and raised their glasses, and Iona blushed, as Halbert laughed, and nudged her, so she giggled. Tegan yelled.

"CAKE!"

Everyone laughed, as a huge cake was carried slowly to another table in full view, and Robbie took a taper and lit the candles, as everyone burst into song, which was loud, raucous and completely out of tune, which was how it should be, as Iona and Halbert joked side by side, looking at the flickering flames. The song ended, and holding hands, they both leaned forward and blew through their giggles, and the candles went out to huge applause and cheers. Halbert turned and pulled Iona into his arms.

"Happy birthday big sis." She pulled him close, and hugged him hard.

"It is only five minutes; it does not count that much. Happy birthday little brother, I love you so much, and I am going to miss you." He held her tight.

"We are twins, and a part of each other, I will be there with you always, because we are the same but different, like two peas in a pod. I will be in Florae often, possibly more than you realise, and I love you too." She leaned back, and looked at him with a soft smile.

"She is a really nice person, Hal; I wish you so much love, you have been my rock living here." He winked.

"You have been a pain, but you know, I put up with you because you were better at maths, and I needed the help."

He leaned forward and kissed her cheek, and she smiled, as she saw her mother watching them, knowing that for her, it was going to be hard to see them leave. The band struck up more merry tunes, and everyone rose from the table, as cake was served on small plates, and they all mingled. Iona and Halbert got a lot of attention, and both were hugged by Steph, Smokes, Rayne and Gwynne. Rags and Lucy handed over small gifts with Katie and Jay at their side, as Iona carried her gifts to the table, Sapphire gave her a big smile.

"You have done well, and learned a great deal, and I must say, you have been a model student. You will make a great queen." Iona felt emotional.

"I owe you so much, I honestly do not have the words to say how much I wish to thank you." Sapphire gave a smile.

"Honestly, when I was told I would become your teacher, I was terrified. Iona, like you, I felt I had no connection with Florae, I had been raised in solitude around the Stones. Callanish was my home, but through you, I too have felt a sense of belonging to that beautiful realm that you will rule. I know you are nervous, that is to be expected, but I think you will find that the warmth and love of the people, will make all the difference, it has for me."

*T*he party raged on, and it started to get late, and with great protests, the children with Isolde and Rune were taken to get ready for bed. Iona took her moment after dancing with her father to slip slowly away, she gathered up her gifts, and walked away quietly to her cabin. Ariel sat outside on her little seat, and when she saw Iona coming, she got up, and opened the door. Iona walked in, and put her things down on the table, as Ariel closed the door behind her, she turned to see Ariel holding two boxes. Ariel smiled.

"I wanted to see you alone, I have these for you."

She held out the boxes, and Iona took them and looked down, one box was thin and long, the other deeper and square. Iona looked up at her.

"You did not need to get me a gift, I should be thanking you for all the guidance you have given me."

"Open them."

Iona placed the square box on her table and opened the long box, where she saw a long feather of pure white, and on its tip, was a sleeve with a golden nib. Ariel took a step forward.

"It belonged to Bran, she had two, they came from a bird named Jarron, who was a raven of the purest white. Bran gave him to Morgana, and used the bird to carry the messages from Morgana to her, in a sense, it was Morgana's life line in her sadness at Avalon. Jarron got injured protecting Morgana from Maud, and lost his ability to fly, so Bran took care of him in her workroom. Iona, Jarron was a precious part of Morgana's life, and became the symbol of everything Morgana saw as good. It is why she wanted to become a raven of white, and I think it would be fitting for a queen to finish her story with a feather of her messenger."

Iona lifted it out of the box and held it up, it was a great age, and yet had not decayed, she looked at Ariel.

"If this was Bran's, you should keep it." Ariel shook her head.

"Iona, Bran charmed it to protect it, and there is no darkness in the charm she used, for she did it with love, and you will feel that as you write with it. The other box contains something Bran made, it is a piece of black cloth, onto which is an embroidered white raven. She made it for Morgana and started it the night she swore to me in my crystal box, that Morgana would never be tied to a raven. After you finish writing the story of Morgana, take it out and hold it. I have told few of my full life with Bran, for I find it hard to talk of even now, and I know you want to know the truth of her. Bran made it, she pricked her fingers a few times, and the cloth does contain some of her blood. In the hands of a queen, the truth will be revealed to you, and that is why I give it to you. learn her story from her, not me, for there were many years of loneliness in her life, and you should see all of them."

Iona looked down at the square box, she felt that Ariel should keep it, but she also knew from the few conversations that they had, it was hard for Ariel to talk of, and so she accepted it in the spirit given. Ariel smiled at her.

"You will be a great queen, and also, the whitest of ravens." Iona understood.

"You saw that?" Ariel nodded, and turned to the door.

"I did, and you should honour Morgana, and be a white raven for her. Enjoy this day and I will see you soon." Ariel closed the door behind her, and disappeared in a flash of white.

*I*ona sat for a while lost in thought holding the feather, the last few weeks had taken its toll and she felt drained. Even though she had learned the truth of the young life of Morgana of Cornwall, she felt a tinge of sadness. Outside there was still laughter as the Specialist's sat at the long tables talking and reminiscing over old times. It was a reunion that had been long anticipated, and finally they gathered and spoke of their life, and their adventures and struggles. There was a great deal of mirth, and some tears shed, as they honoured their fallen friends.

*I*ona made her way to her bedroom, slipped off her things and climbed into bed. She lay back in the dark drifting in her thoughts, when she heard a creak. She turned to see little Gailania stood in the doorway rubbing her eyes.

"I cannot sleep, they are noisy."

Iona smirked, there was an irony to that, considering the thousands of nights she had been kept awake by her sister talking. She lifted the blankets, and Gailania smiled, and ran to the bed and climbed in with her. Iona pulled her small warm body close to her.

"It is quiet here, sleep with me." Gailania snuggled back into her with a happy sigh, and Iona held her close.

"If you are going to be a queen, does that mean I will be a princess, because Grandad Pete always calls mum a princess?" Iona settled back and smiled.

"You can be anything you want to be Lania, because you have two of the greatest parents ever."

"Nona, I am going to miss you, I have to have lessons with Willow." Iona gave a sigh; she had no idea how much she would miss her too.

"You will be able to come and spend time with me, and live in my apartments, and I will be checking on your maths, so do not think you can slack off with me gone." Gailania gave a little wiggle back into her.

"I won't, because I will be seeing you, and so I know I will work hard so I am not a disappointment. Tegan is an idiot, and really bad at maths, I don't want to be like that, I want to be like you and mum."

Iona blew out the candle, and smiled in the dark. Gailania had no idea how like their mother she was, but Iona did, she could already feel the power growing inside her. Gailania would be a big force within the violet circle, of that there was no doubt at all. Soft breathing came up from the pillow at her side, and it felt calm and peaceful, and so she closed her eyes feeling content, and drifted into a deep calm sleep, it had been such a hectic day, and yet it had been special, the most special of all her years in Loxley.

*O*utside on the mere, old friends calmed down and talked softly to each other, Robbie sat beside Rowan listening to all of them talk, and watching Rune with all the girls talking. He patted Rowan on the leg.

"We did good Rowan; we saved the life we wanted." Rowan looked at all their friends, as they talked wearing smiles, and softly nodded.

"We did, it was a high price to pay Robbie, there are many left behind us who should have been here with us this day." Robbie leaned back, and looked up at the stars.

"They are here, they never left us, I feel them every day as they walk beside us."

Chapter Twenty Nine.

The Day Before Destiny.

*T*here was something about the white feather quill Ariel had given her. The morning after her birthday, Iona woke to find Gailania still curled in front of her, sleeping peacefully. For quite some time, she lay still, listening to the sound of her breathing softly, not wanting to move and wake her. Once her youngest sister had awoken, and they shared a breakfast of hot buttered toast, with blackberry jam, Gailania left, and Iona felt like she wanted to write.

She lifted the white feather, dipped it in the ink, and began to write, and the words flowed. It felt strange, but images flashed through her mind, as she recorded the progress of Morgana during her life in Avalon. She wrote all day, and then slept, only to rise to begin again, and that was her pattern of her life for four days, apart from the moments she spent with Sapphire and Evangeline, as they instructed her on her royal duties.

*O*n the fifth day Ariel arrived, and marked out the mere with sticks, where she placed a large box, which would act as the throne. For hours, joined by Sapphire and her mother, they rehearsed the whole crowning ceremony, and went through all of the process, until she understood what would happen. That night all of them had a meal at the house with Robbie, Rune, and the children, and for Iona it felt somehow, more precious than ever before. Rune walked her over to her cabin as she got ready for bed and sleep.

Rune sat on her bed next to her, and handed her a small box, Iona looked down at it, unsure as to why she had done this. Rune smiled at her as she turned to look at her, and her voice was soft and tender.

"The day you were born, I had known for some time you would be named after the isle of your birth. I wrote an equation of power to mark the moment, which was Life, Circle, Line, and I created a new runic symbol, so it could be written. I did not realise, that what I did was reverse the symbol of the power of the Whiteline joined with the green circle, and in doing so, I created a new line of power, that has since become known as the Violet Line. At that time, I had this made, knowing one day I would sit at your side and hand it to you. Iona, you are the reason for everything that has grown around me, the love that I felt and the joy in my heart to know I was with child, brought forth a great power. In many ways, I have never seen it as mine, it has always felt like this was a power you created, and so now, on this day, I want to give you what I made at that time for you."

Iona understood and opened the box, to see the runic symbol necklace of her birth carefully cut from a piece of very high quality amethyst, and it was beautiful. She had no idea what to say as she lifted it from the box, Rune leaned into her.

"Wear it always, for it really is a stone of violet, and carries within it such purity of love, for this represents the union of your father and myself."

Iona had no idea what to say, she turned to her mother, feeling choked for words, and whispered.

"My love for you and dad is equally as pure, I owe you both so much, I have no idea what words to use." Rune smiled.

"You have no need, I remember when I was your age, and my mother guided me. I was so scared back then of what would or could happen, and she told me simply to trust. I will give you the same advice, trust in you, listen to your instincts, and let them guide you, that is all your father and I have ever done." Iona smiled, and nodded.

Rune lifted out the gold chain, and Iona leaned forward as Rune placed it around her neck, and fastened the clasp. Iona looked down and could see it set against her white skin, where it appeared to radiate with light, Rune got up off the bed.

"Wear it always my precious daughter, and I will be forever with you."

Rune left her to settle into her bed, and Iona took a deep breath, her nerves and sadness washed together, and yet when she touched the pendant, she felt a warmth within her that calmed her. She closed her eyes, and slipped into sleep, tomorrow she would leave for Sora, and prepare for her day of the crowning.

As she slept, her mind wandered through her whole life, as the memories of a life lived within a woodland, rose up and filled her dreams of happy moments of great joy, and through all of it, she felt the presence of her mother and father.

*T*he morning brought tears, the day had finally arrived, and she would be leaving for Sora, and then the Royal Apartments, of Florae. A team of Fae arrived, and the things she had boxed up were prepared, and would travel to her new room in the large complex that was the home of the royal line of Fae. Her stomach was in knots as the time approached, the emotion flowed up inside as she hugged her sisters. Jade tried to look brave, as did Rowan, as they wished her well, and told them they would see her tomorrow. Jade's eyes flowed with tears as they hugged, and Rowan's voice cracked, as he told her of the love and pride, they felt for her.

Alice like her mother Beth, wept buckets and dragged her into a crushing hug, and wailed more. Rune was stood in a wide patch of violets, as she tried to be brave, but it was the hardest thing in her life to do, and she wept as she pulled her daughter close, with a squeaky voice.

"I love you my daughter, and I am so proud of the woman you have become, I know you will be a queen of great value, for you already are to me."

It was so hard for Iona, as she stepped back from her mother, she turned to her father and broke down, as he pulled her tight, and whispered in her ear.

"No man could be prouder than I, and no man could love his child more than I do."

"I love you, Dad; I love you so much."

He released her, and she turned to Isolde, who to her, was a member of the family. Isolde gave a curtsy, and smiled.

"I cannot leave your sisters; I have grown as fond of them as I am you. It has been the greatest honour of my life to serve you for your life to this date, as it was for my sister. I picked Evangeline especially, and you will find she has all of the knowledge she needs to aid you. If you need me, I will come to you, for you are like a daughter to me, as well as my queen." Iona pulled her into a hug, and held her so tight, it surprised her, and she put her arms round her and held her for a moment.

"I love you Isolde, all those nights you sat with me, and talked of Florae and the duties of a queen, and all those others where you were like a big sister to me, they meant everything to me. I have learned so much from you, I see you as kin.”

For Isolde, who could be starchy at times, it took her quite by surprise, and her eyes welled up with tears.

“Go and prepare, and be the queen I know you to be.” Iona wiped her eyes and looked back, Gailania had eyes filled with tears, as did Fern and Tegan, and it felt so hard to leave. She smiled at them.

“See you tomorrow.” They all nodded with tears in their eyes.

Sapphire took her hand, and with Ariel, they walked through the light and onto Sora, where Evangeline and Jessica Sapphire, stood waiting with Halbert Thorn to meet her, and Gwynfor stood on the steps of his cabin with his usual big smile. Iona was no longer Iona Violet of Loxley, and over the rest of the day, the transformation would begin, and she would emerge, Violet Stone, Queen of Fae.

*R*une sat quietly, her heart filled with sadness, as she leaned back on the bench and watched the mere, Gailania curled on her lap, having cried herself to sleep. She watched as Robbie stood staring out into the water, and felt the pain in his heart. Alice walked from the trees, and came up at his side and took his hand in hers, and he turned to look at her, she gave a sad smile.

“You have not lost her Rob; she will always be a huge part of you.” He understood that, but it did not feel any easier.

“We have lost too many, and seeing her leave feels harder than any of the others. They should be here Alice; I should have done things differently.” Alice shook her head softly.

“Rob, you could never have seen any of that coming, there was no way you could have changed anything, you are not to blame for their deaths.” He took a deep breath.

“What about Billy? I was the one who banned him, and in doing so, deprived a daughter of a father. Be honest, he had a right to have known who she was, as I do Iona. Was it right for me to do that to both of them?” Alice felt the surprise hit her, and shook her head.

“You let him live where others would have killed him, you had no choice. If you had pardoned him, many would have deserted you, and we all would have lost the war. Billy had choices, and he chose the wrong path, that was not you Rob, it was him. You gave him life, and freed him from that monster trapped inside him, that was the act of a great man, and I admired and respected you for it.” He watched the water, which was like glass reflecting the trees.

"But was it right?" She gave a nod.

"Yes… Yes, it was Rob." Robbie turned to her, and looked down at her.

"I have never seen you as a cousin, to me you have always been my sister. Look me in the eye and tell me honestly you no longer loved him, because I remember that day stood in this very place, when you asked me if he lived, and I saw the look in your eye. When I banished him, it broke your heart, because if the truth be told, had things been different, you would still be with him now, having raised your daughter together?" Just seeing her face, he knew he was right, as he could see it in her pale blue eyes. His voice softened.

"I knew Alice, I knew if I pardoned him, he would return here and take you away in secret, and I knew you would go with him." Alice looked down at the floor.

"It matters not Rob, I married Jacques, and I have known such happiness, for I love him deeply, and have borne him a son. Jessie is a woman I raised, and I am proud of the woman she has become, I have never hidden the truth of her father Rob, she is free to find him if she so chooses." Rob took a deep breath.

"Answer me just one thing, and do not lie to me Alice, for I will know." She looked up at him nervously.

"What is it you want to know?" Robbie's dark eyes locked on hers.

"Do you love Jacques more than you loved Billy?" She gasped, and her eyes opened wide.

"You cannot ask me that Rob."

"Why not, I am as a brother to you, if I cannot ask, who can?" She looked even more nervous and unsettled, and took a deep breath.

"I loved Billy with all my heart, it was not a game to me, I meant everything I said at the time. Rob, I married Jacques, he is my husband and a good man, and I love him deeply." Robbie gave a nod and smiled.

"Deeply is good, but it is not with all of your heart. I am sorry Alice, you were the last person at that time I would have knowingly hurt, and yet as I knew then, I know now for certain. I took someone away from you that you loved deeply, and for that I am sorry, I truly am." She gave his hand a squeeze, and moved closer to his side and looked out across the mere.

"He lived, and that mattered to me, and I have always been

grateful to you for that. Mad as it sounds Rob, it was enough, it made a difference to me." He slipped his hand out of hers, and lifted his arm to her shoulder, and pulled her close. She snuggled into his side as she had always done, and he took a deep breath.

"Being a lord is not easy Alice, I have struggled with it at times." She smiled.

"And there was me thinking you had it whipped." He smiled and gave a chuckle.

"I miss you Alice, you need to come home more." She squeezed him hard.

"I know, and I miss Loxley too, I love being here with you like old times."

He nodded, in a strange way, even though he hated the war, it had always saddened him to see them all leave, and go their separate ways. There was a part of him that had always hoped they would all stay closer.

*I*ona walked slowly along the beach, where up in front of her, ten yards away, Ariel stared into space. She walked up quietly, and seeing a space on the bank she sat down at her side, and Ariel came out of her thoughts, and turned to her. Iona smiled at her.

"I did not want to disturb you, I could feel the intensity of your thoughts, and assumed you were thinking of Branna." Ariel gave a sigh.

"Almost, I was thinking of the time I came here with Gwendolyn, but at that time, I was missing Bran, we had been separated for some time, and I was worried about her. Sat here, it all came back, so few are left from that time." Iona understood that.

"Can I ask you something?" Ariel turned to look at her.

"What about?" Iona looked out across the sand.

"I went to the tomb of Igraine, and whilst I was there the White Lord came to me, and he showed me a moment from Morgana's past. I questioned as to why he had not stopped it all, because he knew all of it, and did nothing about it. He told me it was the free will that had been given to man, and it was not his place to prevent it all." Iona took a deep breath and looked to her side, where Ariel watched her.

"Ariel, Morgana challenged him, and asked why he had not prevented it all, and she rebuked him, telling him he should have acted. Ariel, he could have prevented Eve's death, and yet he didn't, he told me that the Ruling Council were wrong and Morgana was right to call them out for their crimes. I want to understand it all, but I am finding it hard, why let his sister die, why allow Maud to do that awful thing to Morgana? I do not understand why he did not prevent it all." Ariel rolled her eyes.

"Oh Iona, you have no idea how much he infuriates me at times. I remember one time, when my father took me down to the river near our home. He sat me in the boat and told me we were going for a short trip to allow my mother to cool down, as the White Lord had enraged her. I remember him chuckling as he rowed, telling me she called him fool hardy and illogical. I have seen him capable of great acts of wisdom, and yet, he allowed Merlin to help Uther, and did not stop Rhiannon when he knew she was wrong. Were the council right to do what they did? I would say no, and it ruined the life of Morgana, and yes, she was right to point out their wrong doings, and he still did nothing to resolve it. He could have done so much Iona, and things would have been very different." Iona nodded; her eyes filled with life as they sparkled violet.

"You see, it makes no sense, he told me they had to go, and their error would be corrected, but how? Morgana could have been a force for good, but his lack of interference left her dark and brooding. Ariel, he could have stopped Rhiannon, and allowed you to live happily with Branna. I understand I do not know her whole story, but it appears to me that while she was with you in Avalon, she was protected. Leaving is what ultimately destroyed her, on that I am sure I am right."

"I will not deny, I have thought of it often, and I am sure you are right, she was protected when I was close to her. I know the power of my mother helped her to overcome it." Iona gave a long sigh, Iona's mind puzzled over it.

"I am struggling with it all, why cure all of the Fae of Moon and not cure Branna, because it would have been so easy, she deserved better from him?" Ariel shook her head.

"You cannot ask me that, although, in my long life, you are the first to actually see and understand that, no one else ever will. I suppose it does not really matter, the council are gone now, and the past is as it was, maybe our lesson is to learn from it and move forward in a way that is an improvement on them. Maybe it is our task to do better than them?" Iona flicked a small stone with her toe, and it bounced across the sand.

"I really am trying to understand all this, but somehow, I do not see what he had in mind. All the council apart from the green lord are gone, whether I know the truth or not does not really matter now, it mattered then. That was when something should have been done, that was when things could have been changed for the better, knowing the truth does little these days, it helps no one."

Ariel watched the waves rolling over each other, as her mind drifted and she remembered a moment alone in her caravan with Branna, she smiled to herself, and breathed out.

"Bran used to tell me, it matters not Ariel, if it takes me a thousand years to undo her evil, I will do, not because I care what others think, but because I care what I think. In a way I understand that now, I was never sure at the time, but thinking back, she had been so badly wronged, Rhiannon gave her that duty so she would die, and not one of her precious golden haired wonders. In many ways, I feel it is why I was sent to her by Rhiannon, because if I died like my mother, Rhiannon would have been able to blame Bran for it, and prove to Bridget she was right. I think Bran knew that back then, it took me a while to work it all out, if I had sooner, things would have been different." Iona agreed.

"That is my point, you could have acted, Eve would not have had to die, and Morgana and Branna would not have suffered as they did, neither would have you. He could have stopped all of it, he could have ended years of pain and devastation." Ariel gave a slight nod and spoke quietly.

"Possibly, but how then would we have learned Iona? Maybe that is his point, both of us have hindsight, like Opal once predicted, we have looked to the past and we have learned from it. Think about it, your mother has done a great deal to help the natural world recover, your father has a hatred of war and helps keep the peace. Young William has been a good king and united the country, there is trade and recovery for those who survived the red death. All of the Specialists have been prominent in helping the recovery of everyone, all of them encourage life and resist war, they solve conflict, not add to it. The realms are more stable, because of the lessons all of them learned, would that have happened if it had not been for Bran and Morgana?" It was a strange moment of understanding between them, Iona thought about it, and started to see what Ariel said had merit.

"You are right, but what about Branna and Morgana, was it their part to be exploited, victimised and destroyed, because that feels wrong, both of them could have been saved?" Ariel smiled.

"Maybe that is your real task, to correct the narrative as a queen of truth, maybe writing the story is the way to record the injustice and change the way things are seen, after all, that has been my whole life, writing down the events, and to us Scribes, it makes a huge difference. History should always be recorded, for others in future to learn from."

That actually made a lot of sense, she had been influenced all her life by books, maybe when she became queen, and had access to the archive, she would learn far more than she realised, after all hadn't Gwendolyn been a prolific writer?

*R*une gave a sigh as Fern stood at the top of the stairs looking glum, in a beautiful long rose coloured dress. She looked down at her mother stood next to her Aunt Jade, and gave an exasperated sigh.

"Okay, I put it on, but I am telling you now, I am not wearing those stupid shoes, I am a woodswoman, and I stay in boots." She lifted her dress, and Rune sighed, and turned as Jade gave a giggle.

"She is my daughter; she is not supposed to be like you." Jade gave a laugh, and her green eyes sparkled.

"I think she looks lovely." Rune glanced at her, and she smiled a big smile as her eyes danced. Rune shook her head and looked up at Fern.

"Okay come here and let me double check the fit, I want everything perfect." Fern gave a snort, and thumped onto the stairs, as Rune turned and picked up a brush. Fern stopped and stared at her.

"What is that for?" Rune turned holding the brush, she looked down at it, and then back up to Fern.

"It's a brush, I want to do your hair." Fern shook her head, and took a step backwards, she lifted her hand, and pointed at the brush.

"Oh no, you are not touching me with that thing, isn't wearing this ridiculous thing, torture enough?" Rune glared at her.

"Fern Bluebell, get down here now, no daughter of mine is going to her sister's crowning, looking like she lives in a tree." Fern looked terrified, and shook her head.

"Please Mum, don't, let me do it, the last time you did it you raked out half of my hair, and technically I do live in a woodland, so I do sort of live in trees." Jade smirked, as Rune's eyes glared purple.

"I will not tell you another time, now get down those stairs." Fern swallowed and looked back to her room, undecided, she looked back down at her mother and her eyes filled with tears.

"Please Mum, let me do it." Rune pointed at the floor.

"NOW!" Jade stepped away from Rune, and looked up the stairs.

"Don't piss her off Fern, I like you, and I want you to live."

Fern put her head down, and walked down the stairs, and Jade could see her tears drip onto the carpet, as Rune returned to normal.

"Right young lady, we will do our best to make the world believe you are not the feral beast that lives in our trees, and you are actually female."

She lifted the brush, and raked it through Fern's hair, and she squealed loudly, as her head yanked sideways. Jade cringed and screwed up her eyes.

"Hearne Rune, that is eviller than you were with me." Rune gave an evil smile.

"I aim to have my family on show and looking respectable, and nothing, not even this little wood louse is going to stop me."

Fern squealed even louder, as Rune smiled a smug smile. She was the lady of the house, and it was an important lesson for Fern to learn, Jade watched on cringing with each squeal from Fern.

*O*n Sora, a meal was being prepared as Gwynfor cooked outside, working on his special recipe of marinaded beef. Inside, Jessica and Sapphire set up the table, with a meal for a queen, or at least queen to be. The table was laid out with crystal glasses and a very high quality red wine, and awaited the arrival of Bade and Master Elgin and his wife. In the heart of Florae massive preparations were underway, as carpenters toiled to finish building the stands and seats for all the people to view the event, and all the railings were decorated by the women of Florae with wide garlands of fresh flowers and foliage.

There was a buzz all over the realm, as the Fae excitedly talked of the following day, which had been a long time in coming. Through the crowd, various scribes sat documenting the events of the day as they saw them, and as Ariel walked alone along the beach, her thoughts were cast back to Avalon, and the rehearsals of the coming of Rhiannon, and all of the ceremony of that day.

Everything was in place, and one of Rhiannon's closest advisors dressed as Rhiannon, so all could see what would be the spectacle of the era.

Ariel had stood on the Citadel Mount with Branna at her side, as they watched the huge stairway open, and lower to touch the base of the long white Queen's Road. Branna gave a snort of a laugh.

"Wow, just look at her, all smug and full of herself, as she walks down to her golden carriage, surrounded by her golden haired lackies. You have to admit, she is pretty good at impersonating our glorious golden queen, it shows clearly, she works closely with her? So smug and filled with her own myth, yet everything she will ever touch has been made and crafted by us, the undesirables held back up here out of view. She makes me sick, they all do, we are supposed to be honoured as we finish off the last bits, before she ships us all off up there, what a joke."

"Bran, you should lower your voice, you know what they are like." Branna turned to her, and looked deeply into her eyes, with those dark beautiful eyes, as her tatty hair blew around on her shoulders.

"Tell me Ariel, do I lie?" She gave a sigh.

"Well, no, but Bran, you know what it is like here, please be careful, I don't want you taking away from me. Please Bran, I get scared when you talk so openly in public, I could not take you being shipped up there without me." Branna smiled, leaned in a kissed her softly, and lowered her voice.

"Alright, for you Ariel, I will keep it down, I want to stay here too, it is all I want, a life alone in peace in our cottage, just us, no one interfering." Ariel smiled.

"It is all I want too, but we must not be as vocal, Bran, I am so happy right now, please, do not do anything to spoil it."

Branna gave a nod and held her hand tightly, as they turned back to the ceremony, where the Rhiannon impersonator, had arrived, and was stepping up into her golden coach. Ariel watched the road lined with thousands of Fae, all with golden hair and wearing the very best clothes Fae could produce. In the back of her mind, she knew Branna was right, and yet she was also aware that her adopted mother had told her to keep a low profile. Bridget Violet knew the truth, and yet her comments had divided the Fae, and as she saw the power of Rhiannon, played out before her for the first time in her life, she could see, that she was a queen of immense power, and not to be trifled with.

Chapter Thirty.

Arrival of a Queen to be.

In Loxley at the wooden house on the mere, Runestone was running around trying to get all her children ready. Gailania was dancing around shouting she was a princess, because Nona told her so, whilst Rune tried to plait her hair. Fern was grumpy and dragging out dressing, and Tegan was sat sulking, because Rune would not let her borrow her makeup. Jade arrived with a perfectly groomed Willow, and Yvee, and Grover stood with an immaculately groomed Frayne. Somewhere upstairs, Jett instructed Pan, who had caused a stir as she wore black satin pants, to which, Fern and Tegan had both been outraged, and immediately objected to the fact Rune made them wear dresses. Isolde looked on, trying her best to assist Rune, as both of them were dragged by the happy and jovial Gailania, as they hung onto her hair trying their best to both do a plait each.

Rune gave an exasperated sigh, as she looked up at Robbie and Rowan, both dressed in their best clothes. He came down towards her, and looked puzzled.

"Why are you not dressed yet?" Rune looked at him in absolute shock.

"Why do you think…. Robbie, it is like trying to dress wild hogs, not one of them will stand still, especially this one?" Gailania ran to him, dragging Rune and Isolde behind her. Robbie smiled, and lifted her into his arms, where her bright blue eyes sparkled with happiness.

"Dad, look, I am a princess just like Nona."

Rune breathed out, finally, she had her still in one spot, and her and Isolde did her hair quickly, adding large pale lilac bows to match her dress. Robbie held her close and kissed her cheek, and then looked at Rune.

"You better hurry, or we will be late."

Her eyes opened wide, and she went to speak, then shut her

mouth as she realised, then ran at full speed up the stairs. Robbie looked at Gailania.

"You will always be a princess to me." She smiled a beautiful wide smile, there was no doubt, she was cute, she was just like her mother.

*I*ona woke up as Sapphire sat on the bed and handed her a plate, and a steaming cup of coffee.

"Enjoy that, the Fae do not drink coffee, you will find it hard to find around here, although, as queen, you could maybe bring some in to be grown." Iona smiled, as she sipped her coffee.

"I have been trying to wean myself off it for a while, I have developed quite a taste for chamomile tea of late."

Iona finished her meal, and then threw an old shirt of her dad's on, and walked down stairs, where an army of assistants were waiting. Her big day had arrived after eighteen years of being prepared, and she was very nervous.

Over the next two hours, her hair was done, and pinned up at the sides, and she was finally helped into her robes, and taking a deep breath, she felt the cords up the back tighten. Her long deep violet cloak was lifted carefully onto her shoulders, and the transformation was complete, as Evangeline added just the right, small amount of makeup, to finish her off. Iona stood in front of the mirror, and before her stood the new Queen of Fae, and it all felt terrifying and intimidating.

She had one last coffee stood with Ariel and Sapphire, who both looked stunning in their own ceremonial robes. The time drew closer, as she prepared to be taken to a specially fitted out boat, for the short journey to the bottom of the long road, which ran from the sea to the centre of what was the central city of Florae. Ariel stood at the door and smiled.

"It is time my Queen." She gave a polite curtsy.

*R*une gathered everyone together on the mere, holding on to Tegan and Fern, as Robbie held the hand of Gailania, who was still giddy. Jade and Rowan stood ready with Jett, Rafe, and Pandora, and Yvee, Frayne, Grover and Willow all stood in a line with Isolde. Rune lifted her hand, and her window opened, and she stepped through to be met by Gwynfor, who stood by a row of carriages.

"Welcome to Florae, oh and aren't you all looking delightful?

Alright, follow me, Queen of Caerleon, you are here, My Lady of the Woods and party, this will be you, and at the rear, our star of the show, My Lady of Life and Hooded Man." Gailania smiled up at him.

"I am a princess." The old Celt smiled a lovely smile.

"You are indeed, and I may add, a very beautiful one." She tugged on her father's hand.

"I like him."

Robbie giggled, as he lifted her up into the carriage, where Rune was organising the other two girls. Gwynfor turned.

"We will not be long, I believe Lady Una, White Circle, will be arriving shortly, with The Queen of Morbihan and Carnac."

The whole of the road from the sea, right up to the royal apartments was packed with onlookers, many who had left Florae in the past, had returned for the crowning of their queen. All around the Royal Circle, large ornate stands had been built with ten levels, so the people of Florae could watch the day's events, and all of them were heaving with excited faces, and a lot of fast conversations.

*E*lgin sat in a chair in his royal robes, with Bade at his side, and waited, and to one side, all seated and waiting, sat the Council of Elders. They had not forgotten their encounter with Iona Violet, and what had been an impossible feat. They all now held a very different opinion, and deeply regretted siding with Alder, who had not been seen since. A runner appeared, and bowed as he panted to Lord Elgin.

"Master Elgin, the Royal boat has arrived at the dock."

Elgin gave a nod, and Bade leaned down to assist him in standing. He walked to the edge of the rail at the top of the steps, and banged hard on the floor with his staff, and suddenly the place was as silent as a grave. Elgin turned around, and looked back to where all of the council stood waiting, his voice was deep, and echoed in the quiet royal court circle.

"Prepare for the coming of a new queen."

*G*wynfor gave the nod from his own carriage, and they all rolled slowly in a line towards the lines of waiting scribes, who once again dressed in all white, stepped onto the white road, and the line of open carriages followed. Behind them on the long jetty, Iona Violet was met by her brother, who bowed to her, and then aided her into the carriage. Halbert Thorn would be travelling with her to the ceremony as her official escort for the day. Evangeline with Jessie, arranged her dress and cloak, to ensure she was comfortable, and smiled when she saw Iona grip Halbert's hand, she was clearly very nervous. Evangeline gave a nod and smiled.

"You look beautiful, do not be nervous, this is just a formality, the people of Fae already have embraced you as queen." Iona nodded; she was as white as a sheet.

"I know that, but I am still terrified, I want to be a good queen, but at the moment, I am engulfed by fear." Halbert smiled at her.

"You will be fine, this is your destiny, and have no fear, I will be with you." She looked at him and took a deep breath.

"My legs are shaking." He smiled, at her terrified look.

"That is a good thing." She frowned at him.

"Why, I am scared to death?" He shrugged.

"You should be scared; one wrong decision, and you could destroy a whole race." She blinked.

"WHAT?" Halbert burst into laughter, as she looked utterly petrified, and then gave a gasp and smiled.

"I hate you at times." He simply smiled.

"And I love you my sweet sister, and I know you. Iona, you will make a wonderful ruler for your people, it is all there inside you, I see it." She took a deep breath and then smiled, he had always been there for her, and she was really glad he was here now.

*A*t the front of the long lines of Scribes, a lone drummer stood with a large Bodhran like drum. He held a long stick, with a soft round leather covered end, as he waited for the order to move. The signal came, and he struck the drum, and it echoed around the whole of the inner basin of Florae. Slowly the procession began, and every fifteen seconds, the drum gave off another loud beat, as they walked in procession up the long white road towards the House of Scribes.

The first carriage contained Treen and Skip, then came Una and Wilson, followed by Jett and Rafe. Behind them marched a company of Marshals of Avalon, behind which came Amethyst and James, and then there was a troop of Loxley Bowmen, followed by Jade and Rowan, then Robbie and Runestone. Behind them a few yards back rode Gwynfor, and behind him Ariel and Sapphire with Jessica Sapphire, followed by Stephanie and Pete, and then came Iona Violet with her brother. The line stretched all the way down the road, as Iona moved slowly, and could not help but gasp, as she saw lines of people at least thirty deep on each side of the road.

As she passed, all of them placed their right hands on their chests, and raised their left, which was the traditional greeting of old, towards friends of Fae. She found it moving and felt emotional, and although not conventional, she smiled, and bowed her head in thanks. Evangeline who was sat opposite her smiled, she could see the joy in the eyes of the people to be recognised with such respect, and somehow, she felt, Iona would test the court rules, and establish her own unique way of ruling.

As the procession appeared a short way down the roadway and Elgin saw them, he turned to the guards, who stood in a long line in front of the Royal House.

"Open the house for a new queen of Fae, and her guests."

Each soldier turned, and as they faced the wall of the Royal House, inside large bolts were withdrawn, and the wall moved and folded, as the large thirty foot high panels of the outer wall hinged, and began to fold as the whole of the wall to the huge Royal Hall opened to allow all outside to see the golden throne of the queen to be.

There was a wide isle down the centre at least twenty feet across, and then either side were long rows of padded seats for the guests and dignitaries. Everyone outside in the stands would have a full view of the new queen as she was crowned, and high above the throne, on a balcony, an orchestra of musicians prepared and lifted their flutes, and pulled close their harps, and prepared to play for the guests as they arrived. The Scribes came first, as the drummer stepped aside, and stood at the base of the steps.

The scribes came up the steps in rows of four, and on the top step, they all bowed to Master Elgin, and entered the Royal House to take up their seats. Invited members of fae entered next, as the carriages arrived ready for the next waves of guests. Next came Treen, and Elgin bowed and greeted her, a royal guard stepped up, and escorted her dressed in deep burgundy into the house to her seat, and so each member of the family followed, Jade giggled, she was really enjoying this, Rowan stood proud with his children and was taken inside.

Rune waved to the crowd with huge smiles, as she stepped down to tremendous applause, and looked back, Iona was not yet in sight, but saw her mother smiling and nodding her head to the people. Rune came up the steps holding Gailania by the hand, at the side of Robbie, behind them Fern and Tegan looked around in awe, they had never been to Florae, and it was mind blowing for them. Master Elgin smiled as he bowed.

"My lady of Life, we are honoured to have you here this day. Lord Loxley, it is a great privilege to host you as our guest." He smiled, as he looked round at the huge house.

"Master Elgin, and Lord Bade I believe, we are grateful for your warm hospitality."

Both the men bowed again, and they were taken through to be seated, just a few yards away from the throne. Ariel smiled as she walked up the steps, and took Master Elgin's hands in hers.

"Master Elgin, you have no idea how thrilled I am to see you here today, I feared for a while you would not be available. You see the entrance to the third queen of this house, and I feel that bodes well for the people of this land." He smiled a faint smile.

"Spoken like a true scribe of the house, it pleases me that she will be guided by your light, as our queen, Bridget Violet was by your mother's. This is a good day for our people Ariel, it is needed." She smiled.

"Indeed, it is, there has been too much darkness in these houses, it is time for the light to flow into them as it should be." Ariel was escorted in, as Sapphire and Jessie were welcomed, and then came the old Celt, he walked up the steps, and gave a huge smile.

"Well Elgin my old friend, it appears my sister did the impossible again, I feel this is our last ceremony for us two old goats, we are too long in the tooth for all this." Elgin gave a nod as he smiled.

"I fear my old friend you may be right, my time of service draws near to its completion, as I see in a third queen of Fae." Gwynfor nodded, and looked at Bade.

"It is time you took the leash off this one, I feel he has learned all he can from you, and it is time for younger men with stronger legs." Elgin agreed.

"He will stand in my stead when I leave, but I still have a trick or two to show him before I am done."

Gwynfor gave off a mighty laugh, and walked into the hall, and waved at everyone, although, he did wink at Gailania as he passed, which made her giggle.

Iona approached the large Royal Circle, and then noticed the door to the house of scribes was closed, she looked around, and then saw the packed stands and the huge front doors of the Royal House open, as the carriage drew slowly into the massive square before it.

"Are we not doing this in the house?" Evangeline smiled at her.

"Your Highness, this is the crowning of a queen, that is the purpose of the Royal House, it is far larger than the space in the House of Scribes."

She was really surprised, she had never seen anything as large as the house, and yet as she came up before the steps and she saw the size of the Royal House, she caught her breath, for it was stunning, and huge. The whole place had fallen silent, as all the Fae stood in salute, and suddenly, everything felt very real, as Halbert and Evangeline stepped down from the carriage and waited for her to stand.

Iona stood up, and for a moment she stood in full view of all the people who would become her subjects. She stood and looked around at what appeared to be thousands of people, and then to their utter surprise, she gave a curtsy to them, and then stood up, and turned, as she saw the smiles of thousands of people. Bade gave a gasp.

"Why did she do that, a queen does not go down on her knee to her people?" Master Elgin gave a hearty smile.

"Not until now they didn't, I feel Iona Violet Stone will set many new features to this seat, and I feel, letting her be raised in Loxley by Runestone Life, was possibly the best move we ever made." Bade was not sure.

"It is not tradition Master." Elgin gave another smile.

"And that my dear Bade, is why I like her so much."

*I*ona took deep breaths, as Evangeline helped sort out her gown and cloak, and when she was ready, she took her first step up, and walked slowly up the steps, until she reached the top, where Bade and Elgin bowed low to her. Iona nodded back to them, and then met the eyes of Master Elgin.

"My Lord Elgin, Master of the House, I seek your consent to enter the house as your queen." He smiled a big smile and stepped back, and bowed, and then lifted his head, and bellowed.

"OPEN THE HOUSE, MAKE WAY FOR PRINCESS VIOLET STONE, FUTURE QUEEN OF FAE!"

He gestured with his hand, and all the guards snapped to attention,

and the horn players played a fanfare, as the gathered people of
Fae roared with approval, and cheered. Iona took her first step, and
walked into the house, followed by Elgin and Bade, and behind them
came Evangeline and Lord Thorn.

With a packed house of dignitaries and guests, Iona Violet of
Loxley, walked down the centre of what was the biggest place she had
ever seen, and she was nervous, and afraid, and yet she also felt a huge
happiness building inside her. This was what she had been told about
all her life, this was her destiny, and this was the new life that she
would start from this day. She reached her mother, and she smiled, as
she saw the love and devotion in the eyes of her mother, and also the
great pride in her father. Gailania lifted her hand and gave a tiny little
wave, and Iona could not help but give a little giggle, and quick wave
back.

She came face to face with the large golden throne, and as
instructed she turned around, and outside she could see all of the
people of Fae as they watched. Evangeline and her brother moved
to their seats, and Ariel came forward with Sapphire. Sapphire knelt
down, and placed a thick padded cushion on the floor, and then
stepped to one side, as Ariel moved to her other, and Master Elgin, in
his ceremonial robes bowed to her.

"Your Royal Highness, would you kneel, and receive the blessings
and the oath of your people?"

Iona lowered to her knees, and felt the soft padding of the cushion.
Breathing in hard, she prepared herself, for her moment of truth was
here. Master Elgin smiled at her, and she felt a great comfort to know
it was him, and not Alder who would crown her. Lord Elgin held up
his arms, and outside there was instant silence.

"The white circle is no more, I open this realm for a new line, take
her into your hearts, and prepare for the new line of the Violet Stone."
Outside there were great cheers.

Ariel lit the herbs in a dish, and handed them to Sapphire, and
she walked slowly around Iona. Wafting the sweet scent of the herbs
onto her with a small fan of woven grasses, Ariel spoke, and due to the
design of the house, her voice was amplified, and boomed out towards
the crowd.

"Take this blessing from all of your people into your heart, and
know in the hearts of all who dwell here, that you are loved and

respected by all of us. Breathe in the joy of this land, to guide you through the rule of your reign, and speak your oath to those you will serve."

Sapphire stepped back, and bowed to her, Bade stepped up, bowed, and handed her a scroll he had prepared in advance with her. One of the scribes came forth with a small table, Iona looked under the hood and saw the bright happy face of Tila. She placed it down in front of her, Tila winked, and moved back and then bowed, and moved off. Elgin came forward.

"Your Royal Highness, if you would care to speak your vow."

Iona took a deep breath, and unrolled the parchment, and looked at the words she had learned off by heart, and yet now she was here, she was so nervous, she was glad to have them written in front of her. Her hands shook slightly, as she held the parchment, and saw the first few lines, and remembered what Bade had taught her.

"I kneel before the people of Fae, your humble servant, Iona Violet of Loxley and the Violet Isle." She took a quick glance up, and could see the people outside watching intently, she lifted her head and looked right at them, and spoke, with a voice that showed her nerves.

"I swear to be faithful and loyal in all of my duty, and to protect and defend the realm of Florae, and the Fae and the rights of all Fae of Earth in every realm. I swear here my devotion to duty, and before all here present, that I will serve as queen, and serve to bring truth and fairness to all who carry at heart their loyalty to Fae. I swear that I shall dedicate my life in service and rule as queen, and as I kneel before all of you, I humbly ask all of you, take me in your hearts as queen, and if you do, I shall arise your queen, and be named Violet Stone."

There was a massive explosion of cheers outside, and Iona took a deep breath of relief, her heart was pounding inside her chest, Elgin gave a nod, and stepped forward and handed her a quill dipped in ink.

"I feel, your Royal Highness, the people approve highly of you. Please sign the oath you swore to be taken to the archives of the House of Scribes."

Iona took the feather with a golden tip, and looked down at the parchment. She placed the tip on the parchment, and for the first time in her life she wrote what would become her new identity, and wrote in neat fluid writing, 'Violet Stone.'

Elgin gave an approving nod as Bade lifted the parchment, and Tila swept in to remove the small table. Bade held up the parchment for all to see, and Elgin cleared his throat, and turned to face the people.

"Let it be known, the oath is taken and signed, to be placed in the royal archives in the House of Scribes. All be warned, this document is agreed upon, and witnessed by all, let no one cast doubt on this act and this oath, from this day forth."

Two members of the royal guards walked up with a tray covered in black cloth, and came to a halt at the side of Ariel. She lifted her white hood up slowly, and then took the tray, and turned to the kneeling Iona. Holding the tray above her head, Sapphire, with her hood up, stepped forward and took hold of the other side of the tray, and gave a nod. Both of them stood there holding the tray, as Elgin came forth, he reached out, and took hold of the object and the cloth, and Ariel and Sapphire moved the tray back, so Elgin stood holding the object high above the head of Iona, it was utterly silent.

Elgin carefully lowered down what was the crown of Fae, covered in black cloth, and placed it carefully onto Iona's head.

"You kneel before your people, Iona Violet of Loxley and the Violet Isle."

He pulled slowly and the black cloth slipped back revealing a crown of gold and deep purple gems that sparkled casting violet beams all around the hall, and he smiled as he saw it, and heard the gasps from everyone around him. He lifted his voice and it boomed out of the hall.

"ARISE, VIOLET STONE, QUEEN OF FAE AND TRUTH!"

Iona rose slowly, terrified it would slip, and the whole realm exploded with deafening cheers. She breathed slowly, feeling the pressure of the heavy crown, but it did not move, as inside and outside people cheered, and Master Elgin stood before her and gave a regal bow.

"My Queen, Accept me as your loyal servant." She felt a huge surge of emotion rush up inside her, as he stood up with a smile.

"My Lord Elgin, my thanks, for without your support, I would not be here, and I am grateful you will be at my side for the start of my reign." He offered his hand.

"Your Majesty, I believe your people await."

*T*he new queen, Violet Stone, walked slowly back up the centre of the hall, and as she did, all bowed or curtsied to her. She came out of the open doors to cheers and the population of Florae all bowed in unison, and she felt the emotion and the tears in her eyes, as she saw such devotion, and it touched her deeply. Iona stood at the top of the steps as the people cheered, and Rune stood behind her with tears in her eyes smiling, she reached out, and took hold of Robbie's arm, and gently pulled him back a little.

As the new queen stood before her people, out of the sky, twelve golden stars came hurtling down and slammed into the floor, and then up from the centre exploded the purest of white light, and it shot up into the heavens, as Iona was completely engulfed.

All the people cheered and screamed with joy, and from the centre of the light, a deep thick strand of violet curled and twisted skyward, and then the whole column of white went a deep and vivid purple. She was marked as queen as her powers of Fae came forth, and Rune felt the strength that was unleased within her daughter, and she knew she was indeed a true power of the Fae. The light suddenly fell to the earth, and Queen Violet Stone stood as her people cheered, and she smiled. She stood for a few minutes breathing deeply, then turned, and was face to face with her mother, Rune smiled, and gave a small curtsy, and Iona gasped.

"Mother, please, you are life, you are a higher power than I." Rune rose up with a smile.

"My daughter is a queen, and I would never disrespect her in public." She held up her arm.

"Your majesty, I believe your throne awaits you?"

*A*s the new queen of Fae walked into the Royal House, all over the nine islands of Florae, on every official building, deep violet flags were raised up the poles, bearing the crest of a golden tree, surrounded by twelve blue stars, and all set within a circle of gold, the reign of the Violet Stone had begun.

Iona sat on her seat, and one by one, starting with the Council of Elders, each one came up, bowed and swore their allegiance to the crown. As she sat, Isolde walked up with a stance of great pride, she stopped, and stood tall in front of the new queen, and went down on one knee, she raised her face and there were tears in her eyes.

"My Queen, I am honoured to be your servant, and I swear now, as I did on the day of your birth, my loyalty to you always. It has been the greatest honour of my life to have been in service to you, as it was my sisters, who spoke daily of the pride she felt to be with you. Today is the happiest day of my life, as I look upon you sat where you rightfully belong." Iona took a deep breath, and leaned forward slightly.

"I am the one who should feel the honour, for I had two of the most dedicated members of my race to educate me as a small girl. Filomena will never be forgotten, and I hold such love in my heart for her, as I do you for the endless care you have shown me. Here in this room, I thank you, and honour you above all."

Lord Elgin stood filled with immense pride, as he heard the gasps, and the Queen Violet Stone honoured his granddaughter highly.

*T*he other guests followed, and bowed, which felt strange for her, as her father and mother bowed, and swore friendship between their realms. Jett pulled out her golden sword, and saluted the new queen, before going down on one knee, and swearing a deep bond between their two realms. It all felt weird and surreal, and as the guests gathered, and walked down the long deck towards the House of Scribes where a banquet was prepared, Rune slid her arm into Robbie's.

"I am not sure how I feel." He looked at her.

"I know, she is our little girl, and now she is a queen, I am not sure I will ever get used to it. Rune, she is my daughter, that little girl who rode on my shoulders and learned to chop wood, because she wanted to be self reliant. It will feel strange not having her lying all over the place reading books." Rune smiled; she understood him perfectly.

"She will be home soon, and back in pants, being tatty and smelly like her dad, just you watch." Rune giggled, and then looked up at the mountain behind the trees, and smiled.

High above Florae, the White Lord Albanlin stood and watched below, and his hood twitched.

"It is nearly done, just a few more pieces to slip into place, and all will have been corrected. This time is the start of renewal, the Age of Dreams has ended, and now I welcome the new Age of Light, for now is the time of peace, and the spreading of truth."

Chapter Thirty One.

The Life of the Queen.

For over an hour all the guests mingled with Fae officials, including the ambassadors to all the realms, and talked and sipped wine. Isolde stood with her parents, and waited for her grandfather. Halbert stood talking with Evangeline and her family and friends, and Robbie and Rowan stood at the back and watched on. Outside, Florae was in full swing with street parties, as the whole realm was alive with the celebrations.

Iona finally arrived, free of her cloak, in her long violet dress, and her crown replaced with a dazzling tiara of amethysts and diamonds, and all of the guests were escorted to the table, to eat and celebrate. Officials gave many speeches, the shortest of which was Master Elgin, who praised the new queen, and thanked the guests, and finally the wine was all that was left, of which Iona had not drunken any, as she was trying to remain clear headed.

The moment she had been most nervous of approached, and as the guests spilled out onto the deck in the late afternoon sunshine to join in with more celebrations. Ariel took Iona by the hand, and led her to the stairway below the house, and down to the tunnels below. Ariel turned at the end of the tunnel and pointed down it.

"There is nothing to fear, this is the heart of the realm, and everything added to the archive can be accessed by the queen with a simple question. Iona, only you may enter that chamber, the Whispering Falls will only obey your command. Walk in and seat yourself, and then introduce yourself, and the falls will embrace you as the new queen." Iona nodded feeling really nervous.

"Okay… I can do this, after all it is just water." Ariel smirked.

"It is a little more than water, there is a lot of power in that room." Iona glanced at it, and then looked back at Ariel.

"I really do wish you had not said that." Ariel gave a giggle, and gave her a small push.

"Go on, this is the last big task, and then you can relax and enjoy what is left of the day."

Taking a huge breath, she turned, and walked slowly down the tunnel. As she approached, the bridge slid silently under the water. Iona could see inside the room, and saw the seat of stone, on which was a violet cushion. She stepped onto the bridge, and walked across it, not knowing what to expect, and then walked off the bridge, and onto the round table of stone, that appeared to glow like daylight.

Iona gave a slight gasp as she turned to see the bridge had slipped away, and she stood completely enclosed in a room that had walls of fast flowing water. Her words were spoken a little nervously, but also contained her awe at the beauty of the room.

"This truly is amazing, and so beautiful."

"It is yours to use, and here to serve you, Queen Violet Stone."

She gave a startled gasp, and spun around, and as she did, a figure made entirely of liquid stepped out from the falls, and bowed to her.

"My Queen… Welcome to the Whispering Falls, I am the voice of the falls, and here to answer any question from any document stored in the house, for I am the memory of the House of Scribes. Please take a seat, and we shall talk."

This was all a little out of her comfort zone, she was speaking to a completely transparent woman, who looked vaguely familiar to her, although she rippled when she moved which was weird. Iona sat down, and looked at the watery figure.

"This is all a little new, and honestly, I never expected this, and I have no idea what to do." The figure appeared pleased.

"This is only an introduction, I usually stay in the water, although if it pleases, I can appear before you, to put you at ease?" Iona gave a nod.

"Yes, if you don't mind, I like to see who is talking." The figure came closer.

"In time we will build a rapport as we both adjust. Today, all I need you to do is to listen, and then when we are done, you will need to connect to your table, and then if I have need of you, I can use your table to let you know." She lifted her arm and swept it across her front.

"You will need these." Iona looked down as she felt pressure on her legs, and saw a long white box.

"What is this?"

"The box contains the twelve stars of life and death, in order to complete your table of power, you will need them. Sadly, my daughter was so angry with me, she forgot them on her last visit." Iona frowned.

"Your daughter, I thought only a queen could enter here, who is your daughter, because I know Gwendolyn was Bridget's granddaughter?" The figure tilted its head.

"Indeed, you are very astute. Here I am the voice of the falls, and in the life I had before, I was Enaria, mystic to the Fae, and…"

"Ariel's mother?" The figure gave another nod, and rippled.

"Indeed, she got so annoyed that she forgot that box, which is very important, as she will need to place them into your table, for within you, will be the means of light to illuminate the truth of everything." It made a strange sort of sense to her.

"So, I will need Ariel's help with my table, that is good, I mean, I know how they work, my mother has one, I am not so certain how it all works though?"

The figure turned, and walked back towards the water where Iona had entered.

"Once you connect, the table will communicate through your mind. Ariel and I would say your mother will help you, for she is powerful within the Violet Circle, which is now joined to Fae. Go now, and when your table is joined with you, I feel we will speak often." Iona stood up and looked at her.

"Thank you, I appreciate you taking time for me, I will get better, I promise." The water all around her gave a little ripple, and the voice that was Enaria chuckled.

"You are the Queen; we all are at your command." Iona knew that.

"I understand, but my father taught me I should always be truthful and polite, and even as Queen, I feel that is the right way to be." The figure bowed.

"Go in peace My Queen, and soon we shall discuss all the realms in which our people thrive."

She slipped back into the water and the bridge moved silently through. Iona felt some relief, that was easier than she had expected, although, she was a little panicked as she realised the bridge went right through where she had walked into the water, and did hope it had not separated her.

She came back up the tunnel greatly relieved, and Ariel gave her a smile as they turned to the spiral stairwell that led back up to the house above. Rune was stood with the children, most of the guests had apartments, and Iona's family would be guests in the Royal Apartments. Evangeline walked over with Isolde.

"Come, I will show you your new quarters, they adjoin your royal meeting rooms."

Rune linked her arm, the children chatted away behind her with her father and Isolde, as Evangeline guided them through the royal meeting rooms into a long corridor. The corridor stepped out into a large spacious garden, which had three walls that surrounded her, two of which had doors with glass panels, Evangeline pointed to a white door.

"That is Ariel's apartment for when she stays here, which is not very often. Apart from that, these are your own private gardens, to rest, entertain, or take private meetings in a calm environment."

Iona looked around at the green lawn, flower filled raised wooden beds and a few tall elegant trees which she did not recognise, and smiled, it was a very restful place. They walked along the small pathway, and in through a royal blue door, and Evangeline pointed everything out.

"Parlour, private library, additional relaxing room. Your sleeping quarters are above to the right, and your guest accommodations are above to the left, you may use those stairs there and there. All rooms have a bell, and should you require anything, if no one is present, just ring. There are plenty of staff on hand for anything you may require. The room at the end will be my living quarters, and I will always be there if you need me."

*P*utting the children to bed was not easy, the room was very luxurious. When they arrived at the room, they were tired, but once they saw the room, they became alive and excited. Having finally wrestled Gailania into bed, and pulled up the covers, Rune sat on the bed, and leaned over to kiss her on the forehead.

"Night Sweetpea, if you need us in the night, we will be in the room next door." She nodded.

"Night Mum… Where will Nona sleep?" Rune smiled.

"Like the cabin, she has her own quarters on the other side, which is where she will live when she is not at home." Gailania understood that.

"She is a queen now, do you think she will let me try her crown on, because I am a princess now?" Rune gave a little chuckle.

"I am not sure she wears it all the time, I think it is just for big occasions."

She understood and snuggled into her bed, and Rune got up off the bed, kissed the other two good night, and pulled the door closed. She returned downstairs where Robbie was sat with Iona outside in the garden. She walked out as a door on the other side opened and Ariel came out of it with Sapphire, and they walked towards her.

Iona was holding the long box, and Ariel understood what her instructions had been, she looked at Iona and gave her a soft nod.

"It is best done tonight, as soon as you connect, that marks the full seal of you as rightful heir, and it will allow you to use your powers with maximum effect to rule, for your table will be a source of great knowledge to you."

*T*he decision was made, and Robbie hung back and stayed just in case the children needed anything. Iona slid her arm into her mother's and they walked back into the corridor, and through the second door, and there was the large stone table. Iona approached it with Rune and Ariel at her side.

Iona walked up to the table and looked down at it, she could see it was not as large as the one her mother used, but to her it looked big, Ariel came up at her side, and looked upon it.

"I remember seeing Bridget Violet use this, sadly, I never saw Gwendolyn use it. Hold your hand about six inches above the table." Iona glanced at her.

"Do I not put my hand on it?" Ariel shook her head.

"Not yet, this is still a table of the White Circle, it needs to be commanded by a new queen."

Iona slowly pushed her hand out to hover just above the table, and it gave a soft pulse of light, and she blinked and breathed in, as she felt a power run up her arm. The table turned a brilliant white, and then a large red star rose up to the surface, Ariel smiled as she saw it.

"I should have known; she was the White Circle of protection. Iona, close your eyes and focus, feel the power of the table, and then inform it Gwendolyn has passed and has been replaced."

Iona breathed in slowly as her eyes closed, and she could feel the surge as it came from the table, and connected with her, as she breathed slowly, in her mind she told the table that Gwendolyn was no more, and she felt the power flow back from her arm and into the table, Ariel spoke softly.

"Open your eyes."

Iona opened her eyes, and looked down to see the red star on the table was fading to a soft pink, and she felt saddened by it. The red star sunk into the table, and all that remained was a white disk, Rune understood as did Sapphire, as they both watched on. Ariel looked at Iona.

"Open the box, and walk slowly around the table, with your hand above it as you have been doing, the table will tell you where to place each star."

Iona followed her instructions, and held her hand over the table, Ariel held the box open and followed her, and suddenly the table sparked, and flashed white. Iona jumped and took a quick breath in, and Sapphire giggled. Iona took out the first star of gold, and placed it carefully onto the hard white surface, and then moved on to place all the twelve stars. In the place where she started there was a wider space than between the other stars, and Iona did not fully understand why. She looked at the golden stars glinting in the candle lights of the room, Ariel understood.

"You will see… Stand in the gap, and place your right hand onto the table firmly in the centre of the gap, and then tell the table who you are. Then tell it your Fae name under which you will rule, and ask the table to bond with you as the new queen."

Rune was interested and moved closer to watch, as Iona placed her hand firmly on the cool white surface, and the table gave a slight pulse and flashed white.

"I am Iona Violet, of Loxley and the Violet Isle, raised by my mother of life, and my father the Hooded Man. I ask you to bond with me, so I may rule, as was destined to me by Gwendolyn White Circle, and become the next queen of Fae. I will rule as Queen Violet Stone of Fae." Her hand stuck, and she flinched, but it would not come free.

They all stood and watched in awe, as the gold drained from the twelve stars, and swirled around the edge of the table creating a band of gold, which then flowed under her hand, and Rune smiled as her tree of life, the symbol of her grandfather grew out of the table in a bright gold. Iona gasped as she saw the golden tree and her eyes began to flicker as in her mind, she felt she could hear words being whispered. Her eyes exploded with light and the rest of the table dragged the light down into it, and all of the white was flooded with a deep intense violet.

Sapphire leaned forward, it was beautiful to see it, a deep violet disk, surrounded by a golden band, and in the centre of the table growing from Iona's hand was a golden tree. Around the edges, the twelve stars had been stripped of their gold, and were the pale blue of the sash that Gwendolyn had worn, it truly was stunning to look at. Iona breathed in, and her hand came free. As she pulled it away, little flashes of violet shot up from the table to her hand. She looked at her mother and smiled.

"That is it, I am truly the queen, Mother." Rune gave a little chuckle, and looked down on her table.

"There is no doubt now, we shall often speak to each other, you from here, and me from home. I feel the power of your table Iona, it truly is a table of truth, and a table of life." Ariel smiled.

"In days to come, Sapphire and myself, will instruct you in the many uses of your table. It is late and has been a long day, I think that is enough for tonight, rest your mind My Queen, you will need it."

*O*ne hour later, having seen Evangeline's door open, and leaned in and informed her she intended to sleep, she arrived at her room to find her things from the cabin had been neatly stacked, and her bed cover her mother hand made her for her sixteenth birthday had been placed over her bed, Iona slid into bed and lay back.

All of this was so different for her, the room was larger than her whole cabin, and her bed was carved wood of high quality. She had far more pillows than she was used to, but quite liked that, so she closed her eyes and relaxed, as her tiredness washed over her.

There was a soft creak, and she opened her eyes, and in the doorway was the small figure of Gailania, wrapped in a shawl and rubbing her eyes.

"My room is strange, and I cannot sleep."

Iona gave a smile, and lifted the blankets, and Gailania scampered in, and climbed into bed at her side. She was also feeling a little insecure, and having her younger sister with her helped. She snuggled down, and pulled her small warm body close.

"Nona?"

"Hmm!"

"Where do you put your crown?" Iona frowned for a moment.

"I think Lord Elgin packed it away in a box, I am not really sure."

"So, you won't wear it at home?" Iona gave a little giggle.

"No… I will wear woodsman's clothes in Loxley, and be all smelly and dirty like Dad." Gailania gave a little giggle.

"Mum will hate that." Iona smiled to herself.

"What can she say, I am a queen now." Gailania gave a little giggle, and snuggled back into her, and soon, both of them were fast asleep.

The following morning, Iona was delighted to find Robbie had bought a bag of coffee beans with him, and had gone down to the kitchen to instruct the staff. It caused quite a stir as they all had a taste, and cook wrote down his step by step guide for making the drink for the queen's breakfast.

For Iona it was to be another busy day, and her first day of royal duties, of which her first task was to hold a meeting with her Council of Elders so she could become more acquainted with them. After her long meeting, she toured the House of Scribes with Ariel and Tila, and was given an understanding of the archive.

Rune and Robbie were staying for the day, so Crystal who was free, as Tila was busy, gave them the tour of the realm, and Rowan and Jade tagged on, which was fun. It was made even funnier when Jade remarked on how happy the trees were to see the Lady of Life under them, and Tegan gave her a strange look. Her discovery that Jade could talk to trees freaked her out, especially when she commented.

"How do you think I keep track of Yvee?"

There were sniggers as Yvee looked shocked, and a little panicked, she had taken some long romantic walks with Kale in the woodland, and Rowan's ears perked up. By the time they returned and sat in the royal garden, Iona was busy again with another meeting of her ambassadors to all the realms. The day finally ended with a family meal, and Iona talked of her day, and then afterwards, Rune with her sisters helped her sort out her possessions and organise her room, before crashing into bed.

The following day, Iona was to leave and do a five day tour of the nine Islands with Bade and Master Elgin, and so Robbie and Rune returned home and settled back into their life, and prepared all of the things for the children for school. Life slid slowly back to normal, Iona visited and spent a long weekend, where she wore green pants and hunted with her father, and was the girl they had always known, as she cooked, and even got up early to take care of her sisters.

It was very noticeable to Runestone how much more grown up she was, and how she carried herself with an air of authority and confidence. She admitted to her mother she was enjoying her life and happy, Una had visited her often, as did Sapphire, and she was busy writing the rest of her book on Morgana's life. Rune asked about Ariel, and Iona gave a sigh.

"This time is significant for her, and she has been in Avalon for the last two weeks alone, Mum, it is August, and this is the month she first went to Branna, and it is also the month when Branna was taken by the White Lord, she feels it most at this time." Rune understood and felt the pangs of guilt again.

"Have you learned more of her story?" Iona smiled.

"You have read the books I know; I have a little more insight, but not all of it, Ariel has given me the means, and when I have finished Morgana's story, I will use it." Rune understood, and looked at her daughter with bright blue eyes.

"Do you have news of Ursula?" Iona smiled; she knew how her mother watched everything.

"You already know. Rae has not surfaced yet; I believe the book has taught her how to use a veil." Rune nodded, and agreed with her.

"I think that too, my table has noted a shadow wandering around, I have presumed it is her but I cannot get a fix on her. Iona be careful, she is the daughter of Mason, I know what you think of Morgana, but he was mainly human, and he was vile, if she has his life force, she will be dangerous."

"I know Mum, and I am always cautious." Rune turned back to the baking bowl.

"It worries me that she is undetected and able to move around without us seeing her. I do think she is in the area, call it my gut, but I feel she is close." Iona took note.

"Mum relax, there are two of us watching." Rune nodded.

"When I find her and learn what her mind is, then I will relax, until then, queen or not, you are my daughter, and I will worry about you."

*T*he following day, which was her last day home, Iona woke

early, which was odd as she had been writing until late into the night. She packed a bag with some food and her book, and white quill with ink, she used her window to jump to the old church in Tintagel. The moment she arrived she smelt the air, and smiled as the breeze lifted her hair, her small cleared space was still in good order, and she stood and looked at the stones, bearing the names of Igraine, Victor, Medraut, and Morgana.

"Even now I know little of your relationship with Branna, except you were close to her, and she was good to you. I am writing your story and will soon finish, and then your truth will be told."

She turned and followed the path she knew Morgana had walked a thousand times in her life, as she made her way back towards the weed covered ruins of the old castle. She stopped where the bridge once stood and looked out across to the high cliff, and spotted a hooded white figure. Iona opened her window and walked out on the other side of the gap as she felt the power of the person, and came smiling up the hill.

"I am surprised to see you here." Ariel turned, and looked at her.

"Why, we are both truth seekers?" It made sense.

"If you do not mind, what truth do you seek?" Ariel turned, and looked down at the floor.

"Do you feel the power within all of the stones?" Iona nodded.

"Yes, I have wondered about that, I have speculated that it was done by Morgana, but I am not sure why."

Ariel walked along the edge of one of the walls, and Iona could see how her finger extended to feel the power. Ariel turned.

"It is a charm of protection, focus your mind, and feel it." Iona crouched down and held her hand above the low wall, and she could feel the power, and understood. Ariel walked back towards her.

"I felt the same power at Castle Berengar. It is a charm of Bran's making, and it is also Bran who cast it." Iona looked up at her.

"Branna has gone, how could her powers last after she was taken, surely they would have ended when she did?" Ariel looked around the castle ruins.

"I am not sure, but if you ask me, Bran understood how precious this place was to Morgana, and so after she was taken by the darkness she came here. I am not sure when she did it, but it was her, I really am not certain of when or how. Bran was wounded by Rhiannon, but I think she found a way, possibly in spirit, and she visited here. I think she placed this charm on the castle to make sure it never truly disappeared. Bran wanted this place to stay, and I think, it was because in her mind, Morgana was a true saviour to her people." Iona nodded at her.

"I think similar, I do think this place should not be a symbol of Arthur, it was never his, it should be the symbol of her struggles to protect what was rightfully hers." Ariel smiled.

"You have come a long way in a short space of time. When Morgan built her new fortresses here, she must have felt the power of Bran, and in doing so, knew her place of birth would never fall completely, which is probably why she built another castle on this land. This was her home, her centre, even in her darkness I think the white part of Morgana fought to keep this place preserved. When everything built by the entity that became Morgan le Fey fell, she may have thought Bran's protections would help protect her fortress." Iona stood up and looked to the large crater blown out of the cliff.

"Then along came my mum and dad, and blew a huge hole in it." Ariel looked across at the edge where the rocks had been blown away.

"I think that was the outer walls of the courtyards, this part here, I feel this was where Morgana lived and grew up. This part was her home, that over there, was just the surrounding buildings and defences. Bran protected her home, I would imagine somewhere above where we are standing, was where Morgana came into the world. You were clever Bran, although, you always were."

Iona looked up above her, it felt strange knowing that long ago, a small child came into the world, and yet, had such a huge impact on everything. She was seen as plain and ordinary, and at times a little boring, and yet through her life, she had influenced so many different things. Ariel smiled at her.

"Come on, I have found out what I needed, let's head to your cabin and have tea, so we can talk."

Chapter Thirty Two.

Undoing the Ills of the Past.

In the tall trees around a lost and quiet space, deep within Loxley woodland, the breeze softly stroked the mists, close to the ragged grass and sorrel of the leafy floor. As the birds sang high in the branches to mark the coming to an end of the summer season, somewhere out of sight came the new sound of soft leather boots on the damp floor.

The mist separated between two mighty Oaks, and swirled around the slender figure wrapped in a long cloak of black. The figured moved slowly, as if in search of something on the woodland floor. Leaves fluttered down, as three squirrels above in the branches, were startled, and ran along the long branches, and jumped to other trees. The cloaked figure stopped for a second, frozen by the sudden disturbance, before moving on into the clearing in front of them.

In the centre of the clearing the figure stopped, the cloaked folded on the ground, as the figure softly sunk to their knees, before a small patch of dark bare earth. The patch of bare earth was just a few inches across in a perfectly formed circle, and was nothing that would look normally out of place, except in this particular part of the woodland, all the growth was lush, and covered every square inch, but this one.

The cloak parted, and a soft almost bleached white, elegant hand slipped out, bearing a golden ring set with an onyx black stone. Inlaid in the stone was the shape of a hovering bird of gold. The hand rested a few inches above the exposed circle of soil, and a soft yet cold titter came from below the hood of the cloak.

"Tee he he."

The ground gave a pulse, and began to vibrate, causing the soil to shake and rise in the centre, almost reaching the hand above, before it shook sideways and tumbled back to the floor at the edge of the circle. The tiny particles shook, until up through the centre of what looked like a cone of softly shaking soil, came a long shard of a black glass like material. The hand lifted and the soil fell still, as it rose to meet the other white hand that had appeared from below the folds of the black cloak. The figure that was clearly a woman, gave another soft titter, as she flung back the hood, and long strands of sleek black hair tinted with hues of a deep blue-black fell to the soft green of the woodland floor.

There was a sparkle in the jet black eyes, set within a whiter than white face, with a smile of bright red lips. The figure reached back down, and lifted the shard of black glass up towards her face to examine it. Raven Merle held it before her face, as the pale sun beat down upon it, and yet it did not sparkle, or glint as any normal glass would, the figure gave a long exhale of breath.

"Found you. The rest of you may be buried deep under the water of that wretched moon fairy, but you are all I need for now. Long have I waited for this moment, for you my little piece of precious darkness, are the key to unlocking the past and the truth of my line. You are the key to the rising again of the new raven of greater darkness."

*F*ar away in the realm of Florae, Iona stood next to her stone table baring the crest of a golden tree, set on a background of violet, and circled by twelve pale blue stars. The Queen of Fae of Earth stood alone with her eyes closed, as she focused on the new feeling growing within her. Her thoughts pondered the moment, and then she focused her mind.

"Hear me mother… She has finally revealed herself."

*R*aven Merle turned around and gave a surprised squeal, as she felt a pulse of breeze flow over her, removing her veil of darkness. In front of her was stood a woman who looked about forty years of age. She had long dark hair, streaked with some grey, a pale face, and very dark eyes. She was dressed similar in a thick long black cloak and a plain black dress, and was similar in looks to herself. The woman stared at her.

She reached out her hand and snatched at her wrist, and Raven flinched it was so tight, she tried to lock her arm, and bit down on her lip, and she fought, but the other woman was much stronger. Her arm came up revealing the shard of the Star of the Merle, and she felt fear. The woman looked at it, and gave a long sigh, and with her other hand, as Raven tried her hardest to resist her, she pulled at the shard, and took it out of her hand, Raven screwed up her face.

"You have no right to that, it is mine."

The woman held up her hand with the shard in her palm, and a white light grew out of her hand. The shard crumbled and burned away on her palm. Raven gasped with surprise, and anger, as she watched, not understanding how she could even do that, and she stared at her, as the dark eyes of the woman watched her closely, her voice was soft, yet stern.

"The dreams you have had, and the things you have been shown, are a distortion, they are not the real truth." Raven Merle did not understand.

"Who are you, what do you want with me?" The woman looked at her, unmoved.

"You know who I am, and that was never yours, it was mine. Your dreams lie to you, it is done, it is over, that time has passed, and should never return."

She reached into her cloak, and pulled out an old black ancient book, and handed it to her. Raven did not understand, and looked down at it, as the stranger placed it into her hands.

"What is this?"

"All my work, you want to know of me, well there is everything the wizard taught me, and all I added to complete his work. Learn it, use it, and be who I was meant to be." Raven looked up from the book.

"I do not understand?" She understood that, and smirked.

"You call yourself Rae, but you are Raven Merle, and you are of my line, but you were never meant to be dark. You have powers from my line, a line of a queen dedicated to the earth, take it, learn from this book. Practice and work hard, and when you finish and have mastered everything, be a full raven, but be a white one. Stay off my path, it was the wrong one, walk the one in this book, and never stray from it, do you understand? Never deviate, for that is a road of pain, misery, and horrors like nothing you can ever imagine. Become Rae, healer and friend to all, and protect life, never take it. Seek out the Queen of the Violet Stone, and she will help you."

The figure turned, and walked away into the trees, leaving Raven stood holding the thick black book, she looked down at the cover, and opened it up, to read the first sheet, and gasped as she read the name out loud.

"Morgana of Cornwall!"

She looked up, but the woodland was empty, she had disappeared completely, and it was then that she noticed her ring, which was now white, with the golden raven on it. Raven gave a shudder, closed the book, and slipped it into her cloak. Iona stood at her table with her eyes closed, and smiled, as her eyes flickered with violet under her lids.

"Thank you, my Raven of White."

*R*une sat back in her seat as she looked at her table, and the image of Iona as she stood at her table in Florae.

"How Iona, she died, how could she do that, is she really gone?" Iona shrugged.

"The white lord did say that this was the age when finally, all would be put right, and all the wrongs of the council would be set right. Mum, she destroyed the shard with only her palm, Morgana could never do that, only the white lord could do it." Rune nodded.

"I know, I felt his hand in this. Iona, she may come to you, what do you plan?" Iona looked at her mother's worried face.

"I will talk to Grandma Steph, and help her, Merlin chose Morgana, and he believed in her, and so I will trust in Rae and help her, and hope Grandma will muck in. Mum, if she stays in the light, we can watch over her so no darkness ever touches her, she can live the life Morgana longed for. I would like to help her do that." Rune understood and nodded.

"Alright my darling, if that is what you wish, I will help you."

*T*he white lord smiled, and in a flash of white he appeared on the edge of the vast hole that had once been filled with a tall white pillar of rock. From inside his robes, he slipped out a worn and tattered black book, and looked down at it.

"Even in death you defied the Queen of the Raven's, you were always a hateful fool, well you should have listened."

Roack looked down off his shoulder and croaked, as the white lord held out the black book, and it ignited in his hand. The book screamed out in pain, and within the flames a tormented and tortured face, screamed within the flickering. The hood of the white lord twitched.

"Your time is done, the hate you brought will be wiped away, there are no more Berengar's, they have gone from this world, and the queen of light will never allow them to return. All that remains, is Rae of Fae, and you shall not haunt her as you did my fellow of white. Go back to the darkness and return here no more."

The book screamed as the pages burned, until all that was left, were the ashes that floated down into the void, the white lord straightened, and his hood twitched.

"I am happy you made it; we have much to discuss."

In the trees behind the white lord, stood a slender figure. He was tall, very pale, with short dark black hair, that was tatty and unkempt, his face was drawn and looked undernourished, and yet his eyes which were dark, were very bright. He looked afraid.

"Was that her, was that my sister?" The white lord turned.

"No, that was her daughter, the one who caused most of the pain, your sister was never that evil, and she fought the darkness, whereas her daughter Maud, was vile and corrupted." He gave a nod, he was nervous it was clear, he swallowed as if summoning the courage to speak.

"That is her bird though, isn't it." The hood twitched.

"It is, the bird was always the conduit, your sister never allowed the Merle to enter her, and she fought its influence on her for everyday that she lived." He nodded.

"Yet you took her and healed all of her line?"

"I did." He looked even more afraid as he challenged the white lord.

"Why, why cure us and not her, why let that vile creature on your shoulder live, why could you not have saved her?" The White Lord Albanlin stood tall before the weakened and frightened Mondale of Fae, brother to Branna, and chuckled.

"I see you are like her, and not afraid to challenge those you disagree with. I will tell you Mondale of Fae, I wanted to save her, and yet I was prevented. There are many acts within this world I disagree with, and have worked to undo many of them, as you have seen, what occurred here was one of them. If you wish to see change, then be a reason to aid those in need, and prevent others from following the path of your sister." Mondale frowned.

"How… I am but one worn and weary Fae, released from the prisons of the golden queen, what use am I to any?" The hood tipped, and shook slightly.

"In this world, there walks a living member of your family. She is five generations from your sister, born as granddaughter to Morgana of Cornwall. She has strayed from home, and those who raised her fear for her life. Go to her, tell her your truth, tell her she and you are kin, and help her. Two miles from their home, is a house with good people, and between them lies a cottage, take it, and live there, and allow your kin to come to you, and instruct her as your parents instructed you and your sister. Be to her, as your sister would have been, and guide her in the light." He looked puzzled.

"Where is she, what is she called, and how will I find her?"

"Her name is Rae, and if you wish to find her, simply think of her, for she has the look of your sister." He had no idea how to do that, the white lord turned.

"When she is ready, take her to Violet Stone, Queen of the Fae." The white lord walked slowly away with Roack on his shoulder, leaving Mondale alone to puzzle things out. He gave a sigh.

"He is as confusing as my father, what did he mean, think of her, think of Rae?"

There was a bright flash of white, and he lifted his hand to cover his face, and closed his eyes. A moment later, he opened his eyes and blinked, and then lowered his arm, and there in front of him holding up a branch, was a young woman, with the darkest bright eyes, and she looked angry, she stared at him.

"Well… I won't ask again, where did you come from, and how do you know my name?"

It took a moment to really understand what was happening, and he felt shocked as he looked at her, and he could not believe how like her she was. The eyes, the shape of her face, and certainly the temper, the only real difference was her hair, it was not tatty, it was well cared for. He smiled.

"I know your name because we are kin, I am Mondale, and I am the brother of Branna, grandmother to Morgana of Cornwall. I know who you are Rae, I was sent here to help you, and they wish me to guide you home, and tell you of your true line, the line that is Fae." She looked unsure.

"How do I know you are not trying to fool me, and take me against my will?" He smirked.

"You have no idea how like her you are, and if you had known her, you would know not to ask that, there was no man who could outwit or overpower my sister." She lowered the branch.

"So, you are not lying, you really are Branna's brother, because to be honest, you look sort of pale and unwell?" He nodded at her.

"I am, I was one of many imprisoned for the colour of my hair, Bran was only allowed freedom because she was more intelligent than most of them, which is how she ended up in Avalon." Rae dropped the branch.

"I sense you speak true, alright Mondale, what do we do now?" He looked up at the sky.

"It is going to rain, I have a little money, so I suggest, first thing we do, is find somewhere dry with rooms and a hot meal, and then, we sit, talk, and work things out." She looked up and then nodded.

"Alright… What does that make you, are you like my greatest uncle?" He gave a slight titter, and shrugged.

"I suppose I am your uncle times five, I think for now, uncle will work."

She smiled, and he felt his heart lurch, she was so like her, it was unbelievable, and he had missed her so much. His sister Bran had always taken care of him, and yet now, it felt like it was his turn to take care of her.

"Pull your hood up and stay warm, I feel with the rain you will get cold."

She nodded, and grabbed her hood, and he offered her his hand. Together they walked down the track and away from Loxley woods towards the towns and villages that had grown up nearby. In the trees, the pale violet figure of Runestone watched, and she smiled and closed her eyes.

"He is with her My Lord, she is safe."

*A*s Rune walked slowly back through the woodlands of Loxley, Iona stood at her table watching two pictures, she smiled as she saw the joy her mother took from being alone in the trees, and then turned her eyes to the other picture, where Jessica stood just behind Robbie in the trees, a voice spoke somewhere in front of them.

"Greetings woodsman, would you have business with me, or are you passing by this way, there is hot coffee if you would care to be warmed on this chilly morning?"

Jessica watched as Robbie lifted his arm, and pulled down his hood, and faced the man in the trees.

"It's been a long time Master Sage, or should I say Billy? Like all men trained in Loxley, you have not been easy to find."

"Not you… I always knew if you wanted to, then you would find me, I cannot hide from you. So, is this it, is this where I end?" Robbie lifted his hand as if gesturing to her to wait, and he walked forward towards the other man.

"I will not bandy words with you, after all, you know me better. I banned you from Loxley and that has not changed, but I have heard tales of the Sage and his efforts to aid me, and in a way, I think I always knew. Billy, you have a daughter you have never known, and I am man enough to admit I was wrong, she deserved better of both of us."

Jessica Sapphire moved forward quietly, and found a space to look through, and she could see Robbie with his back to her, standing in front of another man. Robbie lifted his hands, and placed them on Billy's cheeks, and then spread his thumbs to his forehead.

"Knox is dead, that line is gone forever."

Robbie pushed his thumbs across Billy's face, and as he did, the markings of a birch tree came away from his face, and Robbie slid back his palms, and looked down, he saw the patterns of the birch in his hands. He looked back up at Billy's clear, but older skin. Billy was lost for words and unable to speak, and his eyes filled with tears, Robbie nodded at him.

"No child should see her father so." He turned, and walked back towards the trees, and Billy swallowed hard and took a breath.

"What would you have me do, My Lord?" Robbie turned, and looked back.

"Live… Be kind to her."

Robbie held out his hand, and through the trees came a young woman, she was slender and had long slightly wavy blonde hair, and eyes as blue as topaz, she looked nervous as she saw him, and her voice was soft.

"Hello Father."

Billy felt the use of his legs leave him, and dropped to his knees, and he wept, Robbie continued into the trees, and a window of white light opened, he through it, and then walked out, and she pulled him close and woman waiting hugged him.

"Fear not Dad, I will watch over her. Dad, you amaze me, you have filled two holes in the lives of those two, and Jessie will thrive because of it, I love you." She leaned back, and he smiled at her.

"It was the right thing to do, thank you, I know your mother would have done this, but I felt this is your age now, and it is your time. It is right, after all the friendship Jessie has given you that it was you who gave her what she needed the most." She leaned in and kissed his cheek.

"I wish you would stay for a while." He smiled.

"I will return soon with your mother, and your little sister is driving us nuts." Iona gave a happy giggle, and opened her window again.

"Hug both of them for me, and hurry back, I miss you." Robbie pulled his daughter close again and kissed her head.

"We will, see you soon."

He stepped through the window and it closed behind him, and Iona turned back to her table, where Billy held his daughter, and Jessica Sapphire wept in his arms.

*R*une stood waiting as the window opened, and Robbie came through, he walked through the trees and smiled at her. She leaned on the door frame and her bright blue eyes shone with love, as she smiled. He came up close and he knew straight away, there was no hiding anything from her. Robbie held out his arm, and there on his wrist were the faint lines she knew so well, he looked at her and shrugged.

"It was the right thing to do Rune, it was right for me." She looked at his arm, and then slid forward and pulled him close, and leaned back to look at him.

"It is the reason I married you, and why I love you so deeply, you are a true man of Loxley and a man of high honour." He grinned.

"I thought it was my unnatural talent with a bow?" She shook her head.

"No, although the tight trousers did help." She giggled, and he pulled her close and kissed her, and her eyes flickered with violet flashes.

"Oh wow!"

"Erg, Mum, Dad, go do that somewhere dark." Robbie pulled back and turned, and saw Tegan dripping wet, and he frowned.

"What the hell happened to you?" She smirked.

"Uncle Rowan is getting much wiser than we thought, Willow and Grover are much wetter, and he ran after Fern with another large bucket." She lifted her arm.

"She is over there screaming and running for her life, you know, Uncle Rowan can run fast for his age, he surprised us now his leg is better. You are probably better off getting the towels ready, I think Fern is going to get soaked."

Life was back to normal, as the kids ran wild, and Robbie took Rune by the hand and walked her inside, as a wild terrified scream echoed through the trees, it looked like Rowan had not lost his skills, and had got his intended target.

*F*rom that day on, Rune felt Robbie carried a little less weight on his shoulders, he never spoke of it, not even to Alice, who knew, as Jessie told her. Rune could see it had been on his mind for a long time, and in a way, she was happy, although in a strange twist, it surprised her how much her grandfather of the woods understood. The marking on his skin did not change, although she knew, it was not yet time.

*T*hat night, stood by her table, Iona opened the box given her by Ariel, and as she lifted the small piece of fabric, which had an embroidered white raven on it, her eyes flashed violet, and she leant on her table as all of Branna's life flashed through her mind.

For twenty long minutes she swooned, as every moment from her birth to her death entered into the queen of the Fae. Iona fell to her knees and wept as she held her table edge, and saw the reality of the life of Branna, and it was nothing like what she had been led to believe. The following day, when she was recovered, because the experience exhausted her and she went straight to bed, Iona sat down and began to write the full truth of Branna of Moon. It took her four years to get down every detail, and it has become the most accurate version of the life of Branna to date, matched only by her version of the life of Morgana. Both books, now reside in the Queens private archive.

Chapter Thirty Three.

The Final Loose Ends.

Several years passed by, Rae made it home, much to the relief of Ursula and Tom. Mondale true to his word, took on the cottage just up the coast, and established a friendship not just with Ursula and Tom, but also the other couple who lived half a mile south of him, and the seeds for a new community were sown.

He taught Rae all his parents taught him, and he often talked of his sister with great fondness. Four years after he moved to Whitehaven, he took Rae to Florae with the help of Ariel, and there she was introduced to Queen Violet Stone. Rae spent a year living in Florae, where she was visited frequently by Stephanie, who took a great interest in her, and would take her off for weekends to learn in private. Ena only ever asked once about Ursula, and Ariel was quick to respond, with a raised voice.

"You have the life you wanted, and she has hers, and it is free of darkness and living in the light. Leave her alone Ena, all of us have paid the price of our failings. You have a daughter, and the only reason she lives, whether you like it or not, is because Morgana saved her and protected her, no darkness ever touched her. Like you, she thought you were dead, she had no choice. If you hurt her, you will destroy our bond, the one you fought for, and so I ask you as a mother who loves you dearly, walk back to your life and live happily, and let her do the same." Ena took a deep breath and nodded.

"If she is truly free of darkness, and means to live in the light, I will honour the request of the mother I love." Ariel smiled, and breathed a sigh of relief.

"There has been too much darkness in this family, I want no more." Ena hugged her mother.

"I agree, and I love you, and thank you for watching over her." Ariel lifted her arms, and pulled her tight.

Three years later, almost as a miracle, Ursula became pregnant. She had a difficult birth, but bore Tom a son, who she named Vito. It was a name she first heard in a conversation, where Morgana had told her, if she ever had another child, that would be his name, because it meant, "Alive, Life."

Avalon and Florae flourished, and the people of both realms grew close, Halbert Thorn married Evangeline and moved to Florae, where they had a son and two daughters. After the death of Robbie's mother Jess, they moved back to Loxley, where he helped managed the Loxley estate with his aging father. Tegan grew up, and was also married to a soldier in the barracks, and Fern finally married having lived a pretty wild life. She married a forester and had a daughter, and as for Gailania, she lived at home, and grew up identical in every way to her mother.

Master Elgin finally retired and was replaced by Bade, but only after teaching Iona Violet everything she would ever need to know, and one year after leaving his post, he passed away quietly in his sleep. He was a great age, and had seen much in his time, as he served three queens, all of which was documented with precision in the House archives. It hit Ariel and Iona hard, but it hit Bade much harder, for in a strange way, he had seen Elgin as a father figure to him, and he grieved deeply the loss of his mentor and Master.

Once again, Ariel refused her seat on the council, and suggested Tila, who accepted it with far more vigour than any other member ever had. The scribes of Florae continued to write, as they documented the details of all of the realms, creating a complete record of all events, of which Ariel ensured they were all logged and filed correctly.

Life for Ariel did not change much, she spent some time in Florae, and more time in Avalon, keeping her promise and living in the cottage she shared with Branna, and writing about her own life, and experiences. There were good days, and then there were the bad ones, where she struggled with her grief, which she never appeared to get over, and it took its toll as she aged.

It was late morning when Ariel rose, and walked out into the sunlight. She sat on her bench, wrapped in her black shawl, below the kitchen window, and looked across the garden of flowers and herbs, as she lifted her tea and sipped. She had slept little last night, again, her dreams had been vivid, as she relived the moments of her past as an ambassador in Avalon, and her life in the small house with Branna.

After all these years, her love was so strong and she still missed her, as if it had only been days. With her recurring dreams, she found herself thinking of her more and more as her days of isolation wore on. She looked down to her lap and smiled, she opened the cover on what was a large hand made book, to reveal her album of every picture she had ever drawn of her, and she touched the pictures softly with her finger, as she ran it across the drawing of her face.

"I miss you a lot today, Bran, I have the life we planned together, but you are not here to share it as we once promised."

She closed her eyes and leaned back to mask the tears, and to try to stop them from running onto her cheeks, as an overwhelming emotion bubbled up inside her. A voice echoed in her head from a precious moment so very long ago.

"I never wanted this Ariel, I wanted to keep my promise, I wanted to be at your side, it was important to me you understood that."

Ariel gave a sad sigh, and leaned forward, and lifted her hands to her face.

"Why do I do this to myself, why do I torture my insides after such a long span of time?" She gave a sniffle, and breathed into her hands, as she waited for the power of her emotion to fade.

"The purity of love is a wonderful thing Seer of the light; it is not torture. Your time together was short compared to the span of time since, and yet see how the power of your love endures, is that not a precious thing?"

Ariel pulled down her hands, and looked at the tall hooded figure stood on her path, his hood twitched as he spoke.

"I would say, that the love you hold for the dark little raven of your past, is part of your strength. To all she was a corrupted and sinister figure, and yet you saw into her heart, and saw the injustice of her life and the wrongs that were done to her. Is that not a thing of great beauty, to see the truth of a soul, and not stand in judgement as others did?" Ariel gave a sniffle, and lifted her cloth to her eyes to wipe them.

"Bran was never truly evil, if she had been I could never have loved her My Lord Albanlin. No matter what has been said and been written about her, I always knew she was a victim of the corruption that surrounded her. Rhiannon was the corrupt one in Avalon, as my queen proved. That foul bird that sits on your shoulder, knows how it took advantage of her, and bent her anger towards hatred with darkness." Ariel took a breath as the emotion within her welled up.

"Bran had a right to be angry, her treatment in Avalon was wrong, her queen was to blame. Bran endured years of isolation, she was supposed to be an equal to all the other Fae Ofmoon, and yet she was a prisoner up there and here. That so called wise queen imprisoned her family, and used Bran to discover the secrets of the merle. Rhiannon knew it would risk her life, which is why she chose her, because to her it did not matter if she sacrificed a dark haired member of her race. To the great golden queen, it was a meaningless act, but Bran's life was of huge importance, especially to me." Her eyes filled with tears.

"Yes, Bran was seduced by the Merle, but in my time with her at that castle, she was nothing but loving and caring, and she fought hard to keep the darkness down. She was scapegoated for the crimes of her family, and yes, she played her role, but I am sure after all of these years, your bird will tell you that it was driven by the darkness that wretched creature put inside her. Bran was a pawn, nothing more, and she paid for it by being robbed of her only solace, and left to live in lonely misery. She paid her debt to all the realms through the pain she suffered, which was her life with me sealed in a box, that was her punishment."

Roack bobbed on his shoulder, and then stretched out her wings and flew to the low wall, where she pecked at a snail, Ariel eyed her with hate. Albanlin stood motionless before her, Ariel felt her emotions were becoming too much, and she wiped her eyes.

"No one faults the others My Lord Albanlin, no one thinks it was wrong for Merlin to aid a king to rape the wife of his enemy, Merlin was not punished, Morgana was. I have read the text of Bran, and how she tried to prevent Morgana being corrupted, but after all that was done to her, and after what Maud did, do you blame her for fighting back? Was Rhiannon punished for the vile way she treated her people? All of you sided with her, it was Bran that faced her and held her to account, and even in that, she was branded evil because she took the life of her queen. It makes me sick, look how Alder in the house at Florae defended Rhiannon, as Tila transcribed my words of truth, and branded her a liar, because she wrote the truth of Rhiannon. You know as well as I do, from the books recovered, it was Bran who freed Ena, and she took the word of Rhiannon's evil into the world and uncovered the truth, when I was freed. Was Bran given credit and praised, no, she was branded a villain. She suffered alone for years robbed of the love that was saving her, look at poor Tila, all she did was transcribe the books of Branna, and those idiots imprisoned her, thank the lords Iona had the sense to free her. Bran suffered terribly, and here I am, the only one who cares."

"I would agree with you seer of light." Ariel scoffed.

"And yet you still took her into the darkness to die in the one place she never wanted to be. You cleansed the whole realm of the moon, even her brother, and let them live again, could you not have done the same for Bran, and given her back what Rhiannon and Roack robbed her of?" He gave a slight chuckle, and she frowned at him.

"Do I amuse you, is that why you are here with that wretched bird, to take joy in the living misery of my life alone without her?" His black tattered hood shook.

"Forgive me, I see much of your mother in you, she too would berate me for some of my actions, I admired her for that, as I do you also. I had a need to talk with you, and seek out your counsel, for there is a matter of great importance to me, and I knew that you would possibly be the only person in this realm I could debate it with." It surprised her.

"Queen Iona has great wisdom, would she not be more fitting for such a problem, she has grown in great stature since taking the throne?"

He lifted his arm, and from within the cuff came a translucent hand, on which was a black star shaped stone, Ariel stiffened when she saw it, and felt a great fear rise within her.

"I thought my mother's star of death was held tightly in the keep of your sister Eve. My Lord, that stone should not be in this realm, it has powers that could destroy everything."

"You are correct, the stone they name Star of the Merle is still safe within the keep of my sister, she sleeps surrounding it to protect it with a force of life none can penetrate. This is the red star, taken from the table when your queen came to power." Ariel stood up, and took a step back, and felt fear course through her body, her tone was one of great fear, her voice trembled with the shock to her system.

"How has the star of life become so blackened? My Lord, you must take it from here, the protection of our people is solely dependent on the purity of the red star. My Lord, take it into the darkness and cleanse it, for the sake of every race that uses it as protection."

Her eyes were wide, and her long hair that was now as grey as her eyes, hung loose and swayed in the breeze. Ariel felt her fears increase; the White Lord slid the star back within the folds of his sleeve.

"Fear not, the star is unharmed and doing its job. The table of Gwendolyn is no more, for it now wields a tree of gold and the twelve stars of life and death. I removed the red star, and what it contains is but a slight part of the Merle. It is why I am here, for this star contains the fragment of the Merle that lived inside your love from birth, this is the reason the Merle came to her, I wanted you to see it."

Ariel swallowed hard, and shook her head, she felt the jolt in her stomach as he revealed its source, and yet she did not understand why he had come here to show her. Her mind felt confused, why would he taunt her, and show her the merle that had infected Bran?

"My Lord, what is this cruel game you play with me? If that is the core of the darkness that seduced Bran, I have no wish to see it, for that is the reason my whole life has been lonely, since I was pulled from my box." His hood gave a twitch.

"It is why I am here, for you needed to see it. My Lady Ariel, you have no idea of what you did, and so I will show you a moment from your own dreams yet again, for I have sent you many, in hope you would work it out." Ariel did not understand, she felt her body tremble.

"You sent the dreams so I would suffer my heart break over and over, how cruel do you wish to be, is this the price I pay for my part, am I now to suffer the same fate as Bran?"

"In answer to your question, yes... Close your eyes and see the moment."

Ariel did not understand and felt a sudden calm wash into her, and she closed her eyes. As soon as she did, she felt the presence of Branna all around her, and she breathed in deeply, and felt her love flow up within her. In her mind pictures from long ago came to her thoughts, as she walked side by side with Branna through the brightly lit woodlands of Sachsen in the dappled shade.

Branna glanced at her as they walked, her dark eyes shining brightly, her long black tatty hair flowing behind her, she spoke quietly in a soft tone.

"That still does not explain why me?" Ariel gave a chuckle, stopped, leaned in, and kissed her softly on the lips.

"Simply put Bran, I feel deeply in love with you. That day after the storm, when I helped you home, you struggled at the door as if you did not want to enter, but you were weak and I pushed you through it. Once you were inside you could not remember anything, the light within you was still strong enough to resist the Merle. Alone in Florae, I knew if I left you alone then you would be consumed, and I would lose you to the darkness. Bran, I had to come back; I was the only thing that would save you. I have my mothers' gifts of light, as long as we are together, no darkness can harm you, I love you, and want to protect you. Do you see, I had to come back in order to save you, and I really wanted to save you, so I am here." Branna smiled, and then looked at her, and frowned.

"It makes sense to me, but I thought the light destroyed the darkness, how do you explain that?" Ariel simply stared at her, and then smiled.

"I met him."

"Huh… Who?" Ariel giggled.

"A man of extreme kindness, a man who was created by equal parts light and dark. As I sat in my room on Florae, I simply thought of Merlin, and when I did, I knew that your love would fade without me, and when it did, you would be in danger. I waited for you to contact me, knowing that as soon as we made love, all those feelings would grow again, and you would be saved. Merlin's full name is Merleline in the old language of runes, in the modern tongue it would be Darkline. If Merlin can live with both within, and be kind, so could you, because your Fae powers are strong, it made complete sense to me."

"You really do amaze me, you always have, your mind is so deep and filled with such ability. It has always drawn me to you. I love how you think and puzzle things out, I saw it every day in Avalon. I always thought I was the only one to use my mind to work everything out, but then I met you and it left me speechless, so much so, I wanted to get as close to you as I could."

Ariel took her hand, and they started to walk again, she smiled as she looked up at the trees and took in their beauty, as the birds and bees flew all over the canopy of sweet nectar filled flowers.

"I am only a simple Scribe, Bran, Florae is filled with many like me, we read the runes and write down their meanings, and we record everything we see and hear. If I ever return to Florae, I will spend my time there writing about you, just as you have written your life in your black book, I shall write ours in the runes of blood, so only my line will ever truly be able to understand their full meaning."

The picture in her mind faded, but she kept her eyes closed, as all the feelings of that moment swirled within her. It felt so strong, so real, and it had been so long since she had felt her like this, and tears slipped out from under her closed eyelids.

"You showed great wisdom that day Lady Ariel, and I may add the day of your queen's trial in the court of queens, for you saw something even the queens of Fae never saw. Merline was indeed the perfect balance, and without realising, you set in motion a series of events that changed everything for the lines of Fae." She opened her eyes, and saw the old black tattered cloak of her White Lord.

"I did, how?"

"Those moments lived on inside the mind of Branna the Raven, and after you parted, she dedicated her life to unlocking the secrets of the Merle, and on that last fateful day, when you held her for the very last time and kissed her, you gave her the power of the purest light, and that gave her the strength and the power to fight it. You need to finish her story and complete your book, for within those pages is the real truth of that time, and it should be read by your queen." Ariel gave a sigh.

"The book is finished, but it is written in blood runes, only Ena and her children will ever be able to read it. My Lord, no one wants to know the truth of who she really was, but it was important to me that my family understood why I lay in her box for many years. The simple truth was, I was close to her, and she had me close to her also, and in a strange way, I felt my powers protected her. I believed in her My Lord, I never wanted her to lose her fight with the darkness, and I felt having me close would allow her to continue." His hood moved slightly.

"It showed great wisdom, which I may add could only have come from your mother, you were right to do it, for it was that day which motivated her, and ultimately it saved her." Ariel shrugged.

"If she was saved, I am happy, but it still cost me the only soul I could ever love, and because of that, my life has been one of loneliness, for I will never love another as I did her."

"I admire your dedication Ariel, not only to Branna, but also to your people, for you have sacrificed everything, even your happiness for them. Finish her story, Ariel of the Fae, and then allow your queen to read it." He turned, and began to walk down the long path bordered with lush herbs, and green short grass. Ariel felt confused and called out to him.

"My Lord, I just told you, I have finished the book, the story is written." He stopped and turned back to her.

"How, when her story is not over?" Roack lifted up in the air, and flew to his shoulder, his hood twitched.

"Branna the Raven is no longer connected to this bird; this is now my connection as I seek the answers to many things." Ariel shook her head.

"My Lord you make little sense, without the connection to Roack, Branna died in the vast darkness." He began to fade away and gave a small chuckle.

"Are you so sure?"

Ariel stood watching lost and confused, as he faded to nothing with the bird, it was a scene she had watched so many times in her life, but this time it was different. The space that was always left empty was not, for there was a ball of bright shimmering light, it was so bright she screwed up her eyes, and in her head the voice of her white lord echoed.

"There is still much to write Ariel of the Fae, as today, you began another volume, for this is the age of light."

As the bright light began to lessen, Ariel stood watching, feeling a presence around her she had not felt for many long years. As her eyes became used to the light, inside the light there was a figure, it was a woman, and she was dressed in pure white. Her hair was tatty and unkempt, and it was as white and pure as the snow, but those eyes, the bright sparkling dark eyes sent a huge ripple through her that engulfed her, as tears streamed into her eyes, she twitched, and then screamed.

"BRANNA!"

She ran with all her might, and the figure of white smiled that wonderful smile, Ariel ran into her arms and pulled her tight, feeling her warmth as Branna pulled her close. Ariel wept on her shoulder.

"Is this real, is it really you?" Branna's arms tightened around her.

"You saved me, I did it, I worked out the balance, and I am free of it all. Ariel, I am back my love, and against the odds, I have kept my promise to you. I will never leave you alone again, I am home my love, and we are finally free."

Ariel pulled back, and wiped her eyes, as she looked into her dark bright eyes, she had aged slightly, but she did not care, her hair was so white, and yet it suited her. She lifted her hand to her cheek, and smiled through her tears.

"Oh Bran, I have been so lonely without you, I have missed you so much, I never stopped loving you, not for a moment."

Branna smiled that familiar smile, and took her hand, and then leaned in and softly kissed her, and suddenly, it felt like they had not been parted for a day.

*I*n many ways, Ariel was right, it was through the injustice and arrogance of Rhiannon in her own selfish pursuit of power, which had been the cause of the Merle entering into the world. When Rhiannon had died, the White Lord had corrected many of her injustices, and cleansed the realm of the moon. Ariel had always felt bitter that he took Branna, in her mind she felt she should have been cleansed first. Albanlin knew of Branna's struggle to undo the wrongs she had done, and after she refused to be cleansed, he allowed her to fight her way through, and defeat the Merle within her alone, at which point he took the fragment that remained. He understood how important it was for Branna to keep her word to Ariel, although, he had at times prompted her to help.

It was the last act of undoing the wrongs of a queen who lost her way, and once done, he enhanced her powers of white, and returned her to the life she deserved. It was a simple life, of daily ritual around the woman whose love had saved her, and in his eyes, finally, all the wrongs had been set right again. Branna was finally free, to live the only life she had ever wanted, a life of simple free living, with Ariel beside her.

*F*rom the moment that Rhiannon had set Branna a test to break a code, her wrong doings had started to build. She released Branna into Avalon, knowing that her studies would deliberately destroy the dark haired member of the Fae. Her desire for more power, even though she was a mighty queen in her own realm, allowed her to put Branna at risk, and as she had rightfully calculated Branna was infected, and expected to die.

It was always Rhiannon's plan to wait until Branna was dead, and then move in and collect up her papers and notes, so that without fear of contamination, she would learn the secrets of the Merle, and control them. What in her arrogance she never understood, was the high intelligence of Branna, she just naturally assumed, Branna, like all Fae of dark hair was of a lower class, therefore not worthy enough to work things out. It was Rhiannon's greatest mistake, and it backfired.

Bridget Violet was a very clever queen, she worked out Rhiannon's plans, and to try and thwart them, she did not send an ordinary member of the Fae of Earth to act as an ambassador in Avalon. She sent the daughter of the most powerful mystic born from the Fae lines; Ariel was immune to the Merle. It was a massive miscalculation on Rhiannon's part, and that, coupled with the fact that Branna fell in love with Ariel, meant that Branna could not host the Merle within her body as Rhiannon had thought would happen.

The Merle entered into the raven of Roack instead, which Rhiannon never expected, and Branna survived, taking the bird with her out of Avalon, when she realised, Rhiannon intended to imprison Ariel. Leaving Avalon was the only way Branna could protect her love Ariel, and as she ran, Bridget made sure Ariel remained in Florae out of the grip of the Queen of Fae of the Moon. As events began, and they unravelled, they created the birth of Morgana, the exit of Merlin, the imprisonment of Opal, the death of Eve, and the early death of both Bridget Violet and Gwendolyn. It started the chain of events that left the council in tatters, and ultimately led to the search of the true heirs, and the bringing of the last words of the one true king back, in the form of his blood line, and Arthur returned in the form of young William Pendragon.

It was thought that Gwendolyn worked it all out, and kept it secret towards the end of her life, and in realising that her adopted aunt was right, she worked in a fashion Rhiannon would never expect. She passed over Sapphire as a future queen, and wove the magic in a way in which to protect her future line from Rhiannon, who she did not trust. Her future line was in danger from a queen who wanted to rule both lines of Fae, so she placed her heir inside Runestone Sapphire, the one to rule with the full and supreme powers of Eve. When Robbie met Runestone, and knowing he was of the line of her brother, and had her family's blood within him, she knew, if he and Runestone joined together, a new line of Fae could be forged, that would be so powerful, Rhiannon would not dare to try and take control of all the realms of Fae.

Gwendolyn's one hope lay in the trust she carried for her aunt. She trusted the words of Ariel, and hoped that after her death, Branna would return and face Rhiannon and destroy her. She was almost perfectly correct. Gwendolyn's only miscalculation, was she had not realised Morgana was Fae, she assumed it was her mystical powers inherited from the Druids, and she had not realised that the Merle was brought down and entered Roack. Gwendolyn had always suspected that her grandmother knew the full story, and in that, she felt it was Rhiannon's lust for power that was evil, not Branna. When the time came, knowing Gwendolyn suspected that Rhiannon would move against her own granddaughter Amethyst, to keep the throne, Albanlin allowed Gwendolyn a second chance to work with her own granddaughter Sapphire, and aid Runestone to find the circle of darkness and destroy all of the Berengar line.

She played her part well always one step ahead of Rhiannon, and through her hints and suggestions to Sapphire, Runestone was directed towards where Ariel lay in her sealed box. Gwendolyn knew that releasing Ariel, was the key to driving the rage of Branna, she knew if Branna felt she could have Ariel forever and be free, she would attack and remove Rhiannon, clearing a space for Amethyst to rule. Then with time, and with Ariel's help, Iona Violet Stone would be the final piece of the puzzle, that would bring days renewed and a new age of power, which was exactly what Opal had predicted when she saw Arthur lose his life.

It was a political game of power moves, which brought many clashes over the ages, and within that, there were some who became the victims as a result, of which Branna and Morgana were the two greatest. Rayne walked away after the loss of his sister, and left Avalon, which in turn saw others suffer, because he had always spoken out for his people. Would Morgana have been persecuted as badly as she was had Rayne been around? It is difficult to say, but there is no doubt he would have spoken out to protect her. Rhiannon would have been prevented from killing her own people had Rayne not walked away, of that there was no doubt.

In a strange sort of way, others gained much from the actions of Morgana, Merlin and Opal found each other, and when believing Gwendolyn had died, they had three children, in Scarlet, Gwynne and Stephanie, who ultimately was responsible for Runestone and then Iona Violet. It was a benefit that brought about the Age of Light, and the revealing of all truth to reset the balance, and clear all of the darkness from the lines of Fae. The truth brought understanding, followed by healing much of the damage created in the earlier days was repaired. Few of that time lived long enough to see it, but for those who did, it brought them peace.

Ursula lived happily with Tom, and Vito and raised Rae, Rayne returned to his wife and children, Fagan after years of torment, found inner peace in his solitude. Una moved back to Avalon, and lived with Wilson where she found peace away from what she saw as a strange a new world, and Ariel finally got the life she yearned for with a recovered Branna, who was finally able to keep her promise. To most, it felt like it was all finally over and they could all focus on their lives of peace, but there were still some who felt the pain in their heart, and could not forget.

It was quiet as the sun began its way down towards the horizon, and all across Avalon there was peace. It had been a long hot day, and as the sun started to set, a soft breeze blew down from the hot rocks of the mount. The old burned out cottage was silent, the charred remains of a bygone age, one that most who passed by paid little attention to, as most of the past history of the cottage had faded from memory. There was a swirl on the dusty road of white smoke near the trees, and as the smoke cleared a lone figure stood, in a long black cloak with the hood over her head and face. It stood still for a moment, almost as if taking in the scene, and then the figure moved, lifted an arm, and slipped back the hood, and a long tatty mane of snow white hair fell down over the cloak.

Branna stood silently staring at what was the old blackened and burned chimney breast. She took a deep breath, and then walk forward, through the gap, that had once held a bright white gate. Quietly, she walked down what had once been a path of stepping stones, which were now lost below the thick roots of the grass, and through what had once been where the door had stood, and she stepped into the cottage.

Branna stopped in front of the chimney with its worn bricks, all blackened by the fire that had ravaged the whole cottage, and looked down, and there by her feet was the cracked stone, that lay over the gap, that had once contained all of Morgana's precious books. Branna slowly knelt down, and lifted the broken stones to reveal the hole dug out by Morgana, and as she stared down into the empty void, she gave a sob. Her voice was soft and hardly heard, as her tears dropped into the empty hole.

"I am sorry, I failed you, and I miss you. You were a daughter to me in every way, and the one I wanted to spare the hate and pain, and I failed you, and lost you, my beautiful white raven." Branna gave a sniffle and breathed in hard, and swallowed the pain in her throat. She sat back on her haunches and lifted her sleeve to wipe her eyes, and took another deep breath.

"The truth may be out, but it matters not, you have already been forgotten, and wiped from the minds of everyone, and the good that you did has been erased from the memory of everyone. All that lives is the memory of Morgan le Fey, but that was never you, that was Maud in control of you, even now, they do not see it, and have remembered only the hate. You deserve better my raven, you deserve to be known for your life of toil, as you fought for everyone, not just your people, but the people of Fae."

"I agree with you Lady Raven, she did deserve better, but you are mistaken, she will not be forgotten, for I will remember always her contribution to the bringing of truth to this realm."

Branna turned and stood up, and looked back to the road, where stood by the fence was Amethyst Queen of Fae. Branna stared at her as she stood silently watching. She gave a snort.

"Do the people of the realm even understand who lived here? You may remember, but who else will, and tell me honestly, who grieves for her, for I know of only one other than myself, and she is the Queen in Florae?" Amethyst took a pace forward.

"Queen Violet Stone has recorded her truth, and it is there for many to read. Morgana's story will be heard, as others read it and talk of her life, and the truth of what happened here." Branna gave a shrug.

"Be honest, who will read it? Here stands her home, her property as gifted to her by Merlin, a property she still owns as this is not Avalon. Look at it, burned and decayed, and given not so much of a glance as the people of your realm pass by. No one knows of her bravery, and the pain she endured, I do, I held her as she wept, and spent hours listening to her talk of her worries and fears, and yet, my name is as black as hers to the people of your realm. To them, we are exactly as your grandmother named us, Dark Fae, and evil."

"You may not have been recognised, but you were a queen of your realm, and I am the queen of this one. Tell me Lady Raven, I have an interest in undoing the wrong deeds of my grandmother, and you seek remembrance of a lost daughter. Can not two queens find something that restores the good of the work Morgana did?"

Branna watched as Amethyst came down the path towards her, and she gave a soft nod, and withdrew a small black figure from inside her robes. It was all she had left of Morgana, and luckily Ariel had saved it when she rescued her box of precious things.

"I watched Morgana make this; I taught her the skill of our line. It was one of her most treasured possessions, and I came here to remember her, and place it here below the floor, so that something of meaning to her resided here forever. She handled it many times, and through holding it, has given me an insight into her life, for I feel and can read much of her that is contained within it. I wanted only to protect her and I failed her, and I want to do something to show her she is not forgotten." Amethyst smiled at her.

"Then that shall be done. Lady Raven, we are Fae Ofmoon, and we have gifts, and with your consent, I would like to hold it for a moment, for if this contains the true essence of her, then in the hands of a queen, it is a mighty thing." Branna frowned.

"I do not understand." Amethyst held out her hand.

"Some secrets of Fae queens, are yet to be revealed. Let me hold it, and I will show you."

Branna looked down at the statue carved from the black stone of her home, and not really understanding why, she gave a nod, and handed it over to her. Amethyst took the small statue of Branna, that was carved by Morgana, and closed her eyes. Branna stepped back as she felt the huge power contained within Amethyst, and watched.

Amethyst stood still, her hand closed around the figure, and Branna could see the small flashes of violet below her eye lids, as all the memories of when Morgana held the statue raced through her mind. It was several long drawn out minutes before she opened her eyes, and looked to the floor, and drew in a long breath. Branna understood the emotion, as Amethyst saw first hand Morgana's life. Amethyst lifted her face, and there were tears on her cheeks, and looked at Branna.

"I have a clear picture of everything, as seen through the eyes of Morgana." She took a deep breath, and then stretched out her arms, and her eyes began to glow with violet light. Her voice was soft, and yet contained a lot of power.

"Right the wrongs, return what was stolen."

Branna looked up, as above them a dome of violet appeared, and it covered all of the space within the fence line. It gave a huge pulse of deep violet, and then Branna jumped, as out of the floor all of the decayed and burned particles of Morgana's cottage lifted up into the air and swirled like a cloud of thick flies.

Branna could do nothing but stand speechless, as the house of the past rose up and renewed itself, and to Branna's amazement the house repaired and rebuilt itself recreating the cottage of Morgana exactly as it had been the night of the fire. Glass jars repaired, shelves appeared, even the clothing she left hung on the nails on the wall rose up out of the floor. Everything shuddered to a halt, and Branna felt her breath caught in her throat, and the emotion rose up within her. She looked around at the jars, the table and chairs with their legs fixed, the blanket on the door to her bedroom which was carefully tied back, and her bed made neatly, and it brought back so many memories as her eyes filled with tears. Amethyst stood in the small cottage, and smiled at Branna.

"I do think passersby will notice it now, all is restored, and it will never age or decay, it will stand here for all time as a tribute to the white raven, and healer of Avalon. Branna gave a soft nod, and sobbed.

"Thank you." Amethyst smiled.

"I will leave you to your remembrance of your great granddaughter."

She handed back the small figure, and with a flash she was gone, and Branna stood in the small room and wept. She turned and looked at the small figure of herself, and then gently placed it back on the top above the hearth.

*B*ranna sat on Morgana's bed for a long time, her mind filled with precious memories, as she remembered the good natured and happy girl she had known. To her, Morgana was bright and intelligent, kind and caring, but most importantly, a daughter who had filled a very important place in her life of loneliness without Ariel.

The night grew dark long before Branna stood up, and looked at the large bag filled with her stock of teas for the market, she smiled and slipped her hand inside, and lifted out four neatly made bags. She gave them a sniff and their fragrance filled her nose, as she remembered the handfuls Morgana had often brought her at the castle. She slipped them into her pocket, and headed for the door.

Outside on the fence was a plaque, which read, 'Morgana of Cornwall, healer of Avalon, and White Raven to all.' Branna stood and gave a soft smile, as she looked upon the cottage, perfectly restored, with the garden as well tended as it had always been. It was exactly as she remembered it, and she knew deep inside, that Amethyst had returned the one thing, that had given Morgana the most heartache. Even in her darkness and possessed by Maud, she had returned and found comfort here long after it had been destroyed. She took a deep breath, her emotions still swirling, and turned.

"Should you ever find your way back, you will have the home that was robbed from you. Goodbye my Countess in the Shadows, fare well, wherever you may be."

The white smoke swirled up, and she was gone, back to her cottage, to await the return of Ariel from Florae. Amethyst was right, it was noticed, Una stood often outside and looked at the cottage, as did Fagan, who would pull up on his cart and sit for long periods smiling, as he remembered his times talking with Morgana. It was a fitting tribute that remembered Morgana as she had wanted to be, the Fellow of the Whitelines, and a White Raven for good.

High above the White Mountain, above the mists that shrouded the lake below, Gwendolyn watched as she had for generations across all of the realms. Behind her the figure dressed in tatty robes with a large black bird on his shoulder walked towards her. She smiled as she felt his presence.

"Is the final piece in place?"

"It is… You could say in a way, everything has now come around in a full white circle." She gave a smile; his humour had always cheered her up.

"I am glad it is finally done; every heir has been replaced, and the world is born anew. In many ways, it is sad, and it hangs heavy in my heart, for it took the lives of many good people, and all for what, a queen who desired a power she could never hold?"

"Her mistakes, I feel matched her ambition, and were on a grand scale, but finally, after an age, they have all been undone, and there has been a lot of wisdom gained from all that has happened." Gwendolyn gave a soft nod.

"Wisdom is expensive, the price paid was in blood, pain and tears." His hood twitched.

"It always is White Circle; it is why we have always warned that it is prudent to look to the past. The history of these people teaches much, all they have to do now, is to look back and learn, for in that lies a brighter and more rewarding future. I feel the lines that stand now, will gain much, and do things of great wonder to the benefit of all of their lines, better times will come now."

"I hope so My Lord, the lines of the heirs to the kingdom are complete, if they fail, there is nothing left to replace them." He gave a small titter.

"You worry too much, you always have." He turned and started to walk away.

"Have faith White Circle, a white raven has returned to Ariel, and the power that she will gain from the union, will hold eyes that see everything and keep all of them protected. If I learned anything sparring with Enaria, it is that her daughter like her, will never take no for an answer, and she will ensure that all will stay guarded and protected." Gwendolyn gave a smile.

"Such optimism, I wish I could say the same, history has taught me, that Rhiannon was but one spark in her moment of weakness, and yet it started a fire that has burned through many ages, and caused many injustices and deaths. It saddens my heart, for Rhiannon was an inspiration to me as a young Fae girl, she had such great ability, and yet now all I will remember her for, is the hatred she brought to the world created by my makers, Eve and Hearne."

She turned and walked back towards the steps that led to the place she resided, her mind filled with thousands of thoughts of the ages she had lived through, and those moments of great joy in her life. As she reached the bottom of the steps, she stopped with a smile.

"Dear Opal, we sparred so much, and yet your ability to interfere and right the wrongs, made such a difference. I wonder if you still run naked through the woods as you did as a child, I would imagine you do, it is nice to know some things will never change."

Chapter Thirty Four.

The Final Twist of Everything.

It was many years later, when one morning, Rune rose early feeling a strange feeling within her. She rolled over and noticed how the patch around Robbie's wrist had darkened, and she knew the time was close. Over the months that followed, preparations were made, and they announced that they would be leaving the Mere, and moving to a place to retire in peace.

Gailania was engaged, finally, and Rune was happy to know that she would be leaving the house behind for all her children, to have a safe place of happiness. The day after Gailania was married, Robbie and Runestone left Loxley forever, saying their goodbyes and shedding many tears. They moved to a new cabin created on the edge of Eve's Garden, deep within the Forest of Time.

Two days later they stood on the Isle of Tears in Avalon, and faced her grandfather. Hearne stood tall, and smiled at her, his clothing was brown, he had reached his time. He still had eyes that sparkled like fresh berries, and his beard, which was much longer, was dull and lifeless like dead grass. He smiled at her, as she stood fighting back the tears.

"You wear the likeness of her cloak, and have the likeness of her face, she was clever, she lost her garment, and yet she cleverly recreated it through our daughter and you, and now I see your youngest, for she too has the life of Eve within her."

The tears formed in Rune's eyes, and ran onto her cheeks, and dripped onto the white floor where violets sprang up from the ground.

"I wish you did not have to go; I wish you could stay." He smiled at her, and he held such love in his dark eyes.

"I miss her Runestone Life, and it has been far too long. It is time, I am weary, and my strong tree here has what is needed. I wish this, we made so many mistakes and they have all been put to rights, and so it is time. As the last of that time, it is right I too move away and make room for the next line." She breathed in and nodded, as Hearne turned to Robbie, who had grey hair, and was showing his age.

"Grow stronger, and be the guide you have always been, it is time for the tallest tree to protect the smallest, and you have become the tallest in my woodland."

Hearne moved closer, and joined their hands as he had the day they were married, and he smiled.

"Become one with this land, and all the realms."

As Rune looked down, she saw the patch on Robbie's arm, was much larger and darker, and as she looked back up, she saw the old man fade, the leaves of his cloak and the grass of his beard blew, and lifted into the air and swirled around them as they would in the autumn gales, and a bright green light shone before them.

On the floor, in the centre of the large white star, a small star shape piece of stone lifted up into the air, and Robbie and Rune stood holding hands, as the green light swirled, and then shot down under the small raised star, where deep below the ground, Eve waited in her slumber. The small star of stone dropped, and the line sealed, and they both stood watching as the leaves of brown were scattered, her grandfather was no more. Rune took a deep breath.

"It is finally done, the world is reborn anew, all that was, has now gone. Your dream won, it came true Rob, and the age of dreams has now been and gone, all the wrongs have been righted, and now is a new age of light, and truth. The heirs were the new seeds, and they have scattered to create new lines and new ways for all. We have done, what we meant to do, so what do we do now?" Robbie smiled and turned to her, his eyes were dark and sparkled like fresh berries.

"Now Runestone, we live." She smiled, wiped her eyes and nodded to him.

"It is all I have ever wanted, Robbie, to live with you."

Somehow, and not understanding why, he looked only twenty again, and she was the same, it was like their youth had been completely restored, the only difference was, on his right arm, was a dark patch that looked like bark.

Hearne had passed on his gift for Robbie to Billy, and in doing so, assured Robbie did not make the same mistakes as the council had done. Robbie's act to repair some of the pain he caused, ultimately saved him, for the gift of Hearne was to ensure that Robbie never left her side. In doing so, Hearne assured Rune would never suffer his pains of loneliness for his folly. Billy had been the means of repairing everything, and as Robbie removed the bark like skin, so his daughter could see his true face, the gift of Hearne was passed on to him.

*T*he passing of Hearne was felt on the Isle of Sora, as Gwynfor breathed in and smiled, sat in his chair, and gave a nod to himself.

"It was time, and I feel he needs to be back with Eve, he missed her so deeply."

Gwynfor lifted himself from his seat, and gave a little chuckle, as the white orb appeared in front of him on the grass. He stood on his front deck, with a wide smile.

"I thought you would arrive on time as always; you never did let me down. Well, I suppose it is time for yet another happy holiday, I must say, I am feeling very excited about all this." Gwendolyn reached out from the light, and took a hold of his hand.

"Welcome home my precious brother." Gwynfor looked back, where his old body sat sleeping, and turned back to look into the light, and his sisters' bright blue eyes.

"That was much easier than I thought it would be, but there again, you always did say it would be." Gwendolyn smiled at him from the light.

"Come home to me, I have missed you so much." He walked into the light, and she pulled him close and hugged him, and the light disappeared, and Gwynfor was no more.

*T*he passing of Gwynfor Lord of the Isle was felt by everyone, and it marked the final end of the line of the White Circle of Fae. He had never really been involved that much with the lines of men, for most of his life he had worked for the cause of his family, and he was also a little bit of a maverick, who chose his own path, and did things his way.

In Florae, a tearful Queen Violet Stone, gave a beautiful and stirring address to her people, as everyone turned out to mourn the loss of one of the most loved members of Fae. His funeral was one of high honour, as he was taken from Sora, and carried with great honour and respect up to the sacred cave, and placed between his mother and sister. No son or brother had ever shown such respect and loyalty to his family and to his people as Gwynfor had, but in many ways, his loss was felt deeply in every realm. Runestone expressed this perfectly, when she stood in tears, beside her daughter at the top of the steps to the House of Scribes.

"Gwynfor, was a man with a heart for everyone. He saw each person he met as a friend, and treated them with love and respect, and he gave all he met a chance to speak, and he always had an ear to listen. His kindness knew no bounds, and he touched the lives of everyone he met, I feel there will never be another like him in the future." She was not wrong.

Gwynfor was the last, of a long age, and the world was reset, and as Opal had once predicted, was the start of a world renewed. All was now righted in the world, and the sins of the past Ruling Council, in an age of truth, had been rectified, never to be repeated. High above them the High White Lord of Time, breathed a sigh of relief, as he looked down.

"All is done, all loose ends are tied, and everything is as it should be once again, after many ages of man." Roack croaked on his shoulder, and he looked at the large black bird, and sighed.

"I know, she did deserve better, but had you been more alert, you would have seen it too, and maybe then, things would have been different."

He looked down at all the realms floating, they had created so much more than they ever thought possible, and he pointed, and then looked at the bird.

"What about that one?" Roack gave an approving squark, and the White Lord waved his hand.

*S*ome time, somewhere later:

"

There are many realms, too many to count, some connected, and some just floating around, copies of what should be, or should have been. The Ruling Council were not idle in their earlier days, they did many great things, and such works of wonder. At times, I pause, and I wonder, did they become complacent, and lose track of their dreams? There is a balance, and whether you know it or not, it is corrected to repay the work of those who stood for our values. That is my role, it is my undertaking to place what appears to be, next to what should have been, it is the purpose I serve as the White Lord of Time."

She ran up the sand path panting, to the large board, that contained the coloured overhead plan of the island and the bridge, and the many parts of the site that had been discovered. Her eyes wide and dark, as they covered the map taking note of every single detail, as her father came slowly up behind her, red in the face with the heat. She looked back with excited eyes and smiled.

"Dad, look at it, it is awesome, come on."

Victor Bern looked at the large plan on the huge board, as his daughter excitedly pointed things out. His wife slipped her arm around his waist, and smiled to see her daughter so happy. He took a deep breath in, that was not the easiest of walks on a day this hot. She looked back with dark excited eyes, as she pointed at the map.

"Look, there he is, 'Gallos.' Oh god, I am so excited."

Ingrid gave a chuckle, as Victor sighed, and prepared to start walking again, wiping the sweat off his brow. The sky was the brightest of blue, with not a cloud to be seen, the heat from the sun beat down on the dusty track, and yet she appeared unaffected as he watched her. His wife slid her arm from his waist, and took his hand.

"Oh, come on Vic, this will be fun, she has wanted to see this place for years, you know how she loves castles?"

He nodded, and turned to the path, as his wife chuckled, holding his hot hand. He looked up the path as she hurried, bouncing along with excitement, where two ancient walls rose into the air either side of the path. She spun around, looking back to him, and she stood between them with a huge beaming smile. Victor lifted his camera and focused, as she stood in her thin black jeans, and tight black top, with her long black hair blowing around her, and smiled. His camera clicked, and it was a beautiful picture of her utter joy and happiness.

She spun excitedly around, and entered the large ruin, and his wife chuckled as they walked, he glanced at her.

"Is it weird that our daughter is mad on dark ages, and old crumbling buildings?" Ingrid giggled.

"If I am honest, I love this side of her, all her friends are into phones and games, and yet she has little interest in them, she really is into history. You know, last night we were talking about today, God, she was so excited, and I asked her why here? She told me, this place felt special, almost sacred to her and she did not know why, she just knew she had to come here and be present in this place." He frowned at her.

"Really… Do you not think that is odd?" Ingrid shrugged.

"Not really, this is me you know? My grandmother always talked of links to the mountains in Saxony, and how she was born of a line of fairies. I suppose a thirteen year old daughter obsessed with one castle, is not that weird compared to her."

He had to agree. He looked ahead, where she stood up on the wall, and looked over the battlements, and down to the water and caves below, he lifted his hand.

"Morgan, be careful, it is a long drop, stand back a little sweetheart." She turned, waved, and then came down the steps and ran to him.

"This place is magic dad, I love it, thanks for bringing me." He smiled at her.

"No problem, do not cross the bridge without us." She nodded.

"I won't, I want to stand and look out across the cliffs, it is something I have seen in my dreams, and I want to know if they are right."

He did not know quite what to say, and just smiled, as he watched her, as she walked briskly ahead. He gave a slight chuckle, as he saw her taking note of everything, he looked at his wife.

"Is it me, or does she know this place better than the tour guide?" Ingrid smiled.

"She has read everything on this place, she probably knows it as well as the family who built it."

Morgan Bern, stood by the low wall, and looked out across the cliffs. In her dream she was several floors up, and yet as she looked out, she knew this was the same scene. Deep inside she felt a stirring, as if something within her was connected to the past, and she had no idea why, but she felt she belonged here. It made little sense to her, but she knew in her being, this was the right place for her.

For a second, she breathed in, and her mind clouded, as her eyes fixed on the headland in front of her, and images flowed into her mind. As she watched through the haze of her thoughts, she thought she was almost over there, walking towards a figure of a woman dressed in black, and she was smiling at her. It was a strange sensation, and yet she felt no fear, if anything, she felt with this woman, she was safer than she would ever be. The woman held up her hand, on which sat a white bird.

Across the high cliffs on the path, marked by four grave stones carved with ancient runic symbols, surrounded by the long swaying grass, a man stood wearing an old tatty hooded robe. The wind moved his hood slightly, as he looked out towards the bridge that spanned the gap of the two ruins, and the young woman with black hair as she looked out towards him. He bowed his head, in a gesture of greeting and recognition.

"You faltered on the path Little Morgana, as did greater queens than you, but what you started, ultimately saw a correction of our errors. You made the right choice, but were robbed at the last second. Yet, even in the darkness, you protected a line of white. You were Ursula's saving grace, and the protection of a very important line of light. You impressed me young student, few have battled as you did with such integrity, and you have earned your way back into the light of the truth you fought so hard for. All now is restored, the mistakes of the past, have finally been rectified, and we have a balance once again. This is a different time, and a different story, for we have many realms, but here in this one, you will have the life you desired with your parents. Welcome home my Little White Raven."

Albanlin faded, and Morgan took a deep breath and blinked, then felt the goosebumps run up her arms, as her parents caught up, her mother smiled at her.

"Well… Does it match your dreams?" She nodded with a big smile.

"It is exactly as I remember it… Come on Dad, we will walk the bridge together, and I will show you the great hall, and where the traders had all their shops. Do you know the bridge does not meet, and if you look at the rails, they are made up of swords?"

Ingrid watched, as he took her hand, and walked onto the long bridge over the wide span, as below the waves crashed on the rocks. Ingrid stood in thought for a second unsure of what she just heard, and looked out across to the headland where her daughter had been looking.

"Remember… Didn't she mean, dreamt it?"

*T*here are two truths in life, the facts as they are, and the version of the facts that will be presented by someone perceived to be right. We must always be wary of who it is who speaks the truth, for there are those who would weave it to their advantage. One truth is the facts as they happened, and one, is a person's version of the events.

This applies to the two tales of facts I have written after many years of study. Branna of Moon, was nothing but a sacrificial pawn in the game of a queen who warped the truth for unlimited power. Branna was seen as inferior, and yet her struggle to overcome the darkness that infected her, proved her to be of greater standing than a queen who deemed her unworthy, due to the colour of her hair.

Morgana of Cornwall was scapegoated for no other reason than her likeness to Branna, and in doing so, a queen's lies were carried into each generation from that day forth. Even in this day of my reign, many generations since the time when Morgana lived a solitary peaceful life in her cottage at Avalon, Rhiannon's version of the truth, still dominates the opinion of many.

When I started out on this journey to seek only the truthful facts, I was young, inexperienced, and slightly afraid of the task that was before me. I was to be crowned a queen, and felt I lacked the wisdom of my predecessors to rule. Through the story of the lives of two souls marked as the darkest and most evil, I found a truth that has challenged me to my core, and yet, so irrefutable was their truth, it gave me the confidence and wisdom to rule in a manner that I hope will one day be seen as fair and honourable.

I faced many obstacles in the journey I undertook, to reach this point in my life and the rule of my people, and with the knowledge of Branna and Morgana, I overcame them. I owe them a great debt of gratitude, and will never forget the impact they have had on my life, and on myself. As I have seen, it is easy to point the finger and condemn others, it is harder, and yet right, to look someone in the eye, and ask them for their truth. My High Lord Albanlin sat back through all of it, and I questioned as to why? Today, I understand fully, the Ruling Council gave man free will to live as he chose, and yet they interfered, and meddled in their affairs, and through their actions, brought the downfall of man. Lord Albanlin understood that, and over a great expanse of time, he corrected the mistakes of his council, and restored the balance of everything. My work in this task is over, and now I shall spend my life writing my truth, my story, the story of a frightened and nervous girl, who on the day she was born on an isle of violet, was proclaimed future queen of the Fae of Earth.

I will chronicle my journey, of how through two of the darkest times in our history, one woman who stood for light, made a prediction. Through that, she set in motion the long painful journey of corrections that would build a world anew, and bring forth a new age, with new queens, and new lords to rule, for that has been what the age of light has done, it has shone on the truth. It has been documented by me, a simple woman of a woodland realm, who was born with the Fae name of Violet Stone. It has taught me much, for not all of the ravens of Berengar were created dark, the truth now shows, two of them were in fact, created white.

Queen Iona Violet of Fae... Violet Stone

More Author's
From
Violet Circle Publishing

Mike Beale. (Children's Book)
Crumble's Adventures.
ISBN: 978-1-910299-06-7
Digital ISBN: 978-1-910299-08-1

Colin Smith (Play)
Heaven knows I'm Miserable Now
ISBN: 978-1-910299-16-6
Digital ISBN: 978-1-910299-23-4

Ted Morgan. (Poetry and verse)
Wordsmith's Wanderings.
ISBN: 978-1-910299-04-3
Digital ISBN: 978-1-910299-09-8
Peregrinations of the Wordsmith
ISBN: 978-1-910299-18-0
Digital ISBN: 978-1-910299-21-0
Silhouette Soldiers
ISBN: 978-1-910299-19-7
Digital ISBN: 978-1-910299-22-7
A Menu of Memories
Digital ISBN: 978-1-910299-32-6
Digital ISBN: 978-1-910299-33-3

Robin John Morgan. (Fiction/Fantasy/Slice of Life)
Heirs to the Kingdom.
Book One, The Bowman of Loxley.
ISBN: 978-1-910299-00-5
Digital ISBN: 978-1-910299-10-4

Book Two, The Lost Sword of Carnac.
ISBN: 978-1-910299-01-2
Digital ISBN: 978-1-910299-11-1
Book Three, The Darkness of Dunnottar.
ISBN: 978-1-910299-02-9
Digital ISBN: 978-1-910299-12-8
Book Four, Queen of the Violet Isle.
ISBN: 978-1-910299-03-6
Digital ISBN: 978-1-910299-13-5
Book Five, Crystals of the Mirrored Waters.
ISBN: 978-1-910299-05-0
Digital ISBN: 978-1-910299-14-2
Book Six, Last Arrow of the Woodland Realm.
ISBN: 978-1-910299-07-4
Digital ISBN: 978-1-910299-15-9
Book Seven, Bridge Of Sequana.
ISBN: 978-1-910299-17-3
Digital ISBN: 978-1-910299-20-3
Book Eight, The Circle of Darkness.
ISBN: 978-1-910299-26-5
Digital ISBN: 978-1-910299-29-6

The Curio Chronicles.
Part One, Abigail's Summer.
ISBN: 978-1-910299-27-2
Digital ISBN: 978-1-910299-28-9
Part Two, Curio's Summer.
ISBN: 978-1-910299-34-0
Digital ISBN: 978-1-910299-35-7
Part Three, Curio's Christmas.
ISBN: 978-1-910299-38-8
Digital ISBN: 978-1-910299-39-5
Part Four, Abigail's Wedding
ISBN: 978-1-910299-42-5
Digital ISBN: 978-1-910299-43-2

Of The Ravens of Berengar Trilogy.
Rise Of The Raven
ISBN: 978-1-910299-30-2
Digital ISBN: 978-1-910299-31-9
The Countess Of Darkness
ISBN: 978-1-910299-40-1
Digital ISBN: 978-1-910299-41-8

Violet Stone
ISBN: 978-1-910299-44-9
Digital ISBN: 978-1-910299-45-6

Other Works.

Han's Cottage.
ISBN: 978-1-910299-36-4
Digital ISBN: 978-1-910299-37-1

Find out more about our authors and their books at
www.violetcirclepublishing.co.uk

Violet Circle Publishing Manchester UK